See / Saw

A Novel
by Terence Kuch

Ink Smith Publishing
www.ink-smith.com

See/Saw

Printed in the USA

The final approval for this literary material is
granted by the author.
All characters appearing in this work are fictitious.
Any resemblance to real persons, living or dead, is
purely coincidental.

Second Edition 2015

ISBN 9781939156020
Ink Smith Publishing
710 S. Myrtle Ave Suite 209
Monrovia,CA, 91016
www.ink-smith.com

Terence Kuch

See / Saw

The god Odin tamed two ravens, named them Huginn ("thought") and Muninn ("memory"), and taught them to speak. Each day he sent them around the world to look, listen, remember. Each day they returned and cawed softly to him of all they had seen and heard, what people had thought and said. In this way, Odin came to know the designs of rulers, the desires of those who scheme against them, and the dreams of those who only whisper to themselves in the deepening night.

from the Norse Eddas

Terence Kuch

Chapter 1

One of the many things Odin's busy birds might have learned in the year 2030, if the Norse gods had not been extinguished by order of King Olaf the Fat some thousand years before, was that one Robert Morgan, Ph.D., had been fired. Morgan had taught physics at a university that had very recently been a mere "college." Thoughts of the institution's sudden grandeur still sent Deans and Senior Faculty into tizzies of prideful delight. Many were the barely restrained Web postings and carefully modest emails.

An urgent command to upgrade the faculty had cascaded from Board of Trustees to the Chancellor, then to the Provost, and thence as a mighty stream to lesser officials. Who should be retained, promoted, given tenure, or let go? Firing Robert Morgan had been one of the easier choices.

***

Robert Morgan's wristcom waved an inch above the screen. Again. PgDn. Click. PgUp. Click click. "Tired of all that simulated sex? Comp-gen garbage? And those annoying pop-ups, right at the height of your pleasure! Now, MemLabs Global can..."

Morgan mulled bitterly as he browsed the local sexwebs. As he paged and googled and clicked, Morgan rehashed his failures like a child poking at a loose tooth with a dirty finger. He was searching for a turn-on, something that could make him forget the university's decision that someone younger, more diverse, and with more publications should sit in Morgan's office and stare at his walls and mumble his lectures and eat his lunch.

"Are you tired of *you*?" one ad shouted to him. "Now you can Change Your Mind"™. He flipped a page, still bothered by the loss of a job he'd hated. If only it had been his choice, not theirs.

"No more teacher's dirty looks," he thought, since he'd been the teacher, and dirty looks were better than some of his freshman physics students had deserved. But all that was over now.

"No Body Does It Better" ™ "Change Your Mind!" ™ PgUp, PgDn.

***

At that exact moment, Department Chair James Whistler O'Neill was sitting back in his chair, satisfied. Yes, he'd managed to upgrade the Physics Department almost painlessly. He'd never respected Morgan, anyway. Should have eased him out long ago. No grants, few students, no colleagues asking to be *et al*s on his next paper. No citations in the literature except a few *see also*s, which everyone knew meant "don't bother to see also." And he'd always looked so – unlikely.

***

Morgan clicked again. More ads, more salacious photos drifted upward from his screen, moved rhythmically, turned slowly in the air, gradually dissolved. Click your pick: twosome, threesome, foursome, moresome. MMF, FFM, CFNM. He had no idea what kind of bod/bed-bouncing "CFNM" embraced. Morgan timeshared his mind between sexhunt and worries about his future. Could he find some really good simulated sex today? Could he get another teaching job, ever?

His last reputable publication, and the last year of happiness with his now ex-wife Helen, had been back in 2012, the year the Mayans had foreseen for a global disaster. That hadn't happened. Instead, Morgan had been the disaster. Now approaching middle age, he knew that now or never had become never. He'd made his major contribution to science, would probably never make another. And even the little he'd accomplished would be forgotten. His hairline was rapidly going the way of his career: backwards. And Helen, not his wife anymore, not even sure where she was. She'd taken her old name back, he'd heard; the final separation.

Morgan was jerked back to the present. His internet skills, finely honed through years of wasted time, had retrieved an intriguing ad, posted just that morning: "Sex with Truda Vallon? Lookalike mem, very hot. Com Alex at (415) 869-90632."

Truda Vallon, Morgan thought, wetting his lips, the blue-eyed Queen of Pop, the hottest song and dance show on TV. A million imitators, a thousand brands, America's sex symbol. "Tru," as everyone called her, had inspired many lookalikes and wannabes, all affecting her long straight black hair, her swinging, half-dancing stride, pale complexion, dark voice, her rumored promiscuous ways and constant state of alert for the latest illegal drug. "Her Highness," the webloids called her.

At times it seemed like every third woman in town, at least those between fifteen and thirty-five, was another lookalike Tru. Morgan had seen plenty of them on the street and in bars, but had never worked up the nerve to proposition one, especially with all the SoCalls in the city waiting to expose, embarrass, entrap people like him. He hadn't had much sex since Helen had left him that final time, and was desperate for it now. Come to think of it, there hadn't been much sex before she left, either. Not for him, anyway; he was never quite sure about her. But now here was a safe way to have his daydream and wet-night fantasy idol, Truda Vallon, or as near as he was ever likely to get to her overhyped, televised flesh.

Morgan raised his wristcom toward the computer screen. A second later, "Yeah?"

"Alex? Hi. Your ad about the mem?"

"Truda Vallon?"

"That's right."

"Lookalike, y'know, but pretty good; half hour at least."

"Not the real Tru."

"Sorry, fella. Way beyond me; just some hooker."

"OK, your ad said that."

The visual on Alex's com was turned off. Morgan found it disconcerting to have a conversation with a blank screen, had to concentrate. "How much?" he asked.

"You pay the memlab fees, yours and mine both. That's all."

"Nothing for you?"

"Don't need the money."

But if Alex wasn't making money, why bother advertising the mem? Maybe there was a catch. "Refund if she's not hot?" he asked.

"Only if I lied. She's hot, all right."

"OK, you're on. Can we do it tomorrow?"

"How about now?"

"Now? Ah, OK, I guess. Why the rush?"

"Not really a rush, just..." Alex mumbled something Morgan didn't catch.

"OK," Morgan repeated.

"O'Farrell Street memlab?" Alex said.

"I'll be there."

Morgan put on a sweater against the afternoon chill and left his narrow house on Washington Street. Anything for sex. Anything safe, that is. Anything that wouldn't infect him.

Chapter 2

THREE MEN as yet unknown to each other, that bright San Francisco morning, would soon meet. Each of the three was desperate in his own way: one to experience sex, real or not; one to forget a particular sex act that had been only too real; and the third who, with his storefront machines, would smilingly accommodate the other two. One of these three would become, briefly, famous.

***

MORGAN was not unusual in his fear of disease: AIDS had been conquered; a hollow victory, since three even more contagious, debilitating STDs had found their way to America from some dark place. Blame STDs for the enormous popularity of sexmems: feely without touchy. But a catch: the seller didn't get to keep the mem. Even the most athletic, sweaty, heavily breathed sexmem could possess only one mind at a time. Some sexmems had become legendary, had been sold ten, twenty times, reviewed in *Rolling Stone*, sold from person to person like precious gems. Hoarded, resold, treasured, hocked. As the old song asked, I wonder who's kissing her now?

One of our three men, ALEX, wasn't afraid of disease. Given his taste in sex (in person, please) and drugs, he could have had half the diseases circulating in California, and probably did. Alex was scrawny, disheveled, and twenty-four. The inside of his arms, and the veins along his legs, bore the scars of many mis-aimed spikes. No, he didn't look prematurely old. He looked exactly like a twenty-four year old who would never make it to twenty-five.

ED CLARTY, whom we will meet shortly, was very different: tall, a little overweight, ruddy complexion, square jaw, lips upturned at the sides in a perpetual smile. Red-blond hair he

5

was quite proud of. He looked like a TV star, complete to the gleaming teeth. Well, Clarty thought he looked like a TV star, even if no one else did. Undiscovered, that's all. Amazing how one begins to look the part when one's discovered. But now Ed Clarty was whiling away in a dead-end job, just temporary. One break! Just one Goddamn break! Thirty-two years old, fourteen years past his glorious high school days. Fourteen years running the O'Farrell Street memlab. Just temporary.

***

Morgan walked eagerly down Polk Street, inhaling the smells of the city: coffee, incense, people, pot. Not much traffic since private cars had been restricted, almost outlawed. With the price of gas and electricity at record highs and still climbing, laws weren't really needed, but a populist gesture had to be made. Cabs and car rentals were scarce, and pricey when you could find them. Mopeds, bikes, and buses had taken over the streets. Once in a while, suits in company or government cars came by, permit flags waving in the breeze. It had become the custom to wave one's finger as these vehicles passed. Morgan did that three times on his walk downhill to O'Farrell Street, although Morgan's waves were more genteel, less vigorous, than most. Hidden from the cars, actually, just in case a driver...

He wondered why Alex was in such a hurry to dump his mem. And most important, what would Alex think of someone like him? That was it, wasn't it? Morgan had never met a man or woman without immediately worrying about the impression he was making. He was well aware that this was an ultimately self-defeating habit, but he didn't know how to stop.

***

At that moment, Alex was indeed thinking about Morgan, and about how lucky he'd be to dump his new mem on Morgan that very day, assuming that the man he'd spoken with actually showed up. Sounded jittery over the com, unsteady; a newbie, or just horny? And he'd probably give a made-up name at the lab. Who would be dumb enough to give his own name to a memplant partner? Memory transplants were legal, sure, but if that radical SoCalls group ever took over, who knows? All the records of those who'd bought other peoples' mems, lotta damage those guys could do. Alex, dependent on chemicals and shooting up and huffing, and selling sexmems for cash, knew that citizens like him would be the first group the SoCalls would "disappear" if they ever gained power.

Alex resolved to get a look at the other man's ID, catch his name and address. Maybe in the recovery room, before the man woke up. Gotta wake up first, then. Gotta snoop and get that name, he smiled grimly, and where he lived. Wouldn't it be just his luck if the guy was named John Smith, or if he'd used a stolen e-bank account number? Oh well, no choice. It was what it was. That's what his father used to say with a shake of his thin shoulders, before the old man killed himself by snorting coke and shooting shit. The old man was, Alex contemplated with great feeling, what he was, what fate made of him. *Qué sera*, y'know.

***

So was Alex, of course; so are we all. But Alex's talent for introspection couldn't, quite, reach that far. He allowed himself to blame everyone else for his troubles, which mostly consisted of being ripped off by sellers of adulterated coke, or being promised ass that never showed up. In rare moments of calm he thought to make something better of himself.

But then he'd remember his father. *Qué será*.

***

Half an hour later, Morgan approached the memlab. He looked around casually but cautiously, didn't see anyone picketing the place or threatening the customers. One large, bored-looking cop stood by the front door. The cop had a dual purpose, he knew: to keep order and allow U.S. citizens to exercise their right to buy and sell memories, and to intimidate them with icy stares so that, perhaps, they'd think better of it.

Memlabs were tolerated under the laughable fiction that they met a legitimate psychotherapeutic need, and perhaps at first a few did. Realists in the city government reasoned that it was better to have them in the open, where they could be watched, regulated, and of course taxed. Courtesy of the same reasoning, the pot-and-acid shop on the next corner also had its open hours, its customers, and its cop, as did the cluster of pussy parlors a few blocks south, catering to those who, like Alex, needed mems to sell to people like Morgan.

The O'Farrell Street franchise was one of the more reputable memlabs in town; seedy and run down, of course, but its blacked-out windows had that recently washed sheen. Morgan walked in. An indifferently motivated assistant directed him to take a seat in the waiting room. He waited amid ill-assorted chairs whose plastic cushions showed the occasional stab wound. A few minutes later the front door opened and a thin, young, dissolute-looking man walked in, glanced from side to side. That must be Alex, Morgan thought, as he introduced himself, and he was right. Hats off to the hooker who'd sold herself to that wild-haired walking pincushion. But what would Alex make of *him*?

***

Alex was relieved. This "Morgan," and that was probably even his real name, a little run down, but a citizen. He'd be easy to find. Not that Alex ever wanted to see Morgan again, far from it. He'd let someone else know where to find him.

After a few minutes, a white-garbed "clinical advisor" appeared, introduced himself as Ed Clarty, and escorted Morgan and Alex to a small office. Alex's mind was idling in neutral. Out of habit, Morgan's mind was wondering what Clarty thought of him.

***

Ed Clarty was not the type to ponder the psyches of his clients. In this business, they were just brain-meat. Clarty assured himself, for the record and in case of subpoena, that Morgan and Alex had come to the memlab only for psychotherapeutically necessary purposes. He read them the required cautions from a plastic-coated card. "Side effects can include nausea, vomiting, delusions, forgetfulness."

He glanced at his two customers of the moment. They weren't listening. Could probably recite this crap in their sleep. He continued the litany of horrors. "Identity confusion, gender confusion, dizziness, inability to have an erection ever ever ever again." Clarty smiled; that last item was his own invention. It proved to him, once more, that no ever listened to him. To hell with these losers. It was all about sex, ninety percent of it, anyway: fake memories of real sex, replacing real memories of fake sex. "Re-virginize yourself," one of his web ads said. "Wash that man right out of your mind." In your dreams, asshole. But you could dump your dreams, too, he supposed, if they weren't exciting enough, or if they kept waking you up in a damp sweat night after night.

He shouldn't be wasting his time here, running a memlab. He was meant for greater things. He had talent, a voice everybody had loved back in high school, everybody had said so; everybody. He could be a big name entertainer, even now, if someone would give him a chance. He could be a crooner. A rocker. A rapper. He could be the male version of Truda Vallon. He could be loved, no, worshipped, by millions, millions! and rich beyond his... He snapped out of his reverie, cleared his throat, and had the two sign several "if you sue us your ass is grass" forms.

Chapter 3

Morgan and Alex changed into lab gowns and were directed to lie down on adjacent cots. Morgan stole another look at Alex. He had that drugged-out face that meant he'd either shape up pretty soon, or die of un-natural causes before viruses and bacteria could kill him. Clarty stuck a needle into Morgan's arm and began a drip, then did the same to Alex, greased their heads and stuck probes on their temples, behind their ears, and at the back of their heads. He asked Alex to concentrate on the memory to be transplanted, especially where it began and where it ended. Morgan was still bothered by why Alex would be selling a hot mem for zero profit.

"Alex?"

"Yeah?"

"If you didn't want to keep the mem, why didn't you just come here and dump it? Why give it to me?"

"Can't afford the lab fee. You pay this jerk, I'm out of here for nothing."

So much for "Don't need the money," Morgan thought.

"But then why not just keep..." Morgan drifted off under the eyes of a grimacing Ed Clarty, Clinical Advisor. Clarty had just been called a jerk, and not for the first time.

***

The procedure required twenty-two minutes flat. That was by the book. Clarty could do it in seventeen, or even less if there were customers waiting who might become impatient and leave. But there was no one else in the shop, and Clarty let the full twenty-two minutes elapse while he indulged his favorite fantasy of fame, and how his father had stood sternly in the way.

"You'll always be able to make a living, son." Clarty remembered his father telling him years before. "You'll always have a living," he'd said, "in the memplant business. Your voice might be pretty good, what do I know? Your high school friends seem to like it. But," and here came the customary clincher, "do you know how many people who can sing, or play a tune, actually make a career out of it, a paying career?" A smile of triumph had spread across his father's face, the only times Clarty had ever seen him smile. "Very damn few," his father continued, "it's all simmed these days." Clarty knew the script by heart; he mouthed it to himself while it played in his head. "Better get a good solid job, son. I can pay your way to memplant school, even help you get a start in business. Help you franchise one of those memlabs from Global MemLab Corp. But not singing. I'm not paying for that. Now don't you agree that's best for you?"

Clarty's father had died five years before. His last memories were of how successful his son had become, a real small businessman, how Ed had faithfully followed his father's advice, hadn't gone off on some damn fool quest for fame and riches as a singer. Those fatherly memories had not been captured in a memlab. They had been allowed to expire along with thoughts of happy occasions, sad ones, a few excellent meals, one trip to Nashville, and somberly infrequent sex.

***

Alex remembered his own sex scene as it rolled out of his mind and into Morgan's. Odd. Exciting. Different. Good sex, but not in the grand old retro tradition. As the mem reached its mid-point, Alex couldn't remember how it had begun. And as it ended, he no longer had any idea what kind of mem he'd transferred to Morgan. Sex; must have been sex. Nobody had ever paid him for anything else. But he did remember that he wasn't getting paid for the mem. That other guy, Morgan, was it? wasn't paying him. Why the hell had he ever agreed to that? That was how he made his precarious living, for Christ's sake! Alex became agitated. There was a slight flicker of eyelids.

***

Gradually, a memory of having sex with "Truda Vallon" streamed into Morgan's mind. Blurred, choppy, no apparent sequence. Morgan had bought sexmems twice before, knew to expect this kind of vagueness. Patience: in a few hours or days all would be clear, all senses engaged. Artificial? Yes, but how different was that, really, from buying a hooker by the hour? Once it was over, wasn't that just a memory, too?

Morgan's father had always supported him: agreed, encouraged, paid. A decent college, grad school. He remembered an ideal father; never a correction or a stern speech. It took years for Morgan to realize that his father was, by nature, an avoider. Domestic tranquility had never such a faithful custodian. And Morgan had followed his father's good counsel. So far.

***

As Ed Clarty disconnected the probes from Morgan and Alex, he recalled the first and only time he'd received a memplant, as required in the final semester of Memlab School. Each student had been assigned to select a mem and memplant it into another student. Most picked inconsequential mems they didn't mind losing. Clarty's partner Don, however, picked a mem he wanted to forget: Don's father coming home drunk, smashing in a window after his mother had locked him out, crawling through the opening, cutting himself on jagged pieces of glass, bleeding on the carpet, blaming Don and his mother, calling Don a whoreson bastard and his mother a faithless bitch, reaching out, hitting and biting and hurling both of them to the floor time after time until his mother confessed.

That was Clarty's reference point; one more reason for hating his job.

***

Morgan woke in the recovery room beginning, hazily, to remember fucking Truda Vallon, or a near likeness. The mem was indistinct, but he knew it would sharpen, add detail as his mind adjusted to its new contents.

Alex had already left, innocent of the memory. As the labs carefully explained, mem readout was destructive: memories weren't neatly contained in contiguous parts of the brain, but scattered like records in computer storage. And just as database records were associated into files through indexing and pointers, human memories were reconstructed by mapping patterns of brain activity called coherence potentials, with the hippocampus area of the brain as the roadmap. Pull up the patterns intrusively, no records could be accessed later, even though they were still there, scattered around the neocortex. No memory map → no neural decoding → no memories. Alex remembered coming to the memlab and dumping a mem of a Truda Vallon lookalike, but he didn't have the mem itself, the actual experience, anymore.

Morgan waved his com at the lab's computer eye. The eye calculated the fee and displayed his new, alarmingly lower bank balance along with the time, the temperature, the relative humidity, and three subliminal ads. One final payday deposit would be coming from the university; it would have to last. That mem he'd just bought had better be worth it!

Chapter 4

Morgan had just exited the memlab's front door when he heard shouting, saw a bottle hit the lab's blacked-out window with a thump and shatter on the pavement, heard the cop outside yelling "Hey, you, stop that!" Morgan saw that a group of SoCalls had formed a semi-circle around the entrance. They were waving placards, shouting, and throwing street trash at the memlab. Their signs bore some of the group's well-known mottoes:

"Don't Support So-called Mental Health!"

"Don't Sell Your Mems!"

"Don't Have Someone Else's Sex!"

"Memplants Are Mind-Socialism!"

"Down with the Mind-Socialists!"

Then they segued into call and response, the SoCalls' "Three Words":

"Mental Health is a Fraud!"

"Don't Shrink Your Mind!"

"Empathy is Complicity!"

"Insight is Blind!"

"Your Mind is Your Fortress!"

"Defend Your Self!"

Morgan ducked back into the doorway. He'd certainly heard enough about the SoCalls in the past three or four years. They'd even disrupted a few university classes. Fortunately for him, they'd concentrated on the Psychology Department, not Physics where he'd taught. They'd even been accused of bombing one or two buildings in town, including the Noe Valley memlab last year. But their leader, William Linn "Buck" Baker, "Father Buck" as his followers called him, had denied responsibility.

Clarty appeared behind Morgan. "There's a rear exit."

"Don't the SoCalls know about it?"

Clarty gave Morgan a slightly contemptuous stare. "Of course they do." With those enigmatic words he led Morgan out the back door and into an alley that connected to the next street. With relief, Morgan noted that no one was in sight.

Two blocks north, near one of the omnipresent Truda Vallon mini-boutiques, he ran into a different group of SoCalls, about two hundred people protesting "so-called liberals" in the city government who were willing to tolerate memlabs. No wonder the Action Committee for Mental Self-Defense had acquired the nickname "SoCalls."

A slim, white-maned old man stood on a bench in the middle of the group, surrounded by tough-looking toughs with shaved heads. He punched a fist into the air and held forth, bull horn to mouth. "No more memlabs!" he shouted. "Can you imagine? Desecrating the physical act of love by letting a stranger remember it!" He peered into the crowd dramatically. "No tax money for so-called mental health! No more intrusive, insulting psychiatry where no one takes you seriously, because whatever you say, well, it's just a symptom! All that therapy's worth no more'n a hill of beans!"

"No more! No more!" the crowd shouted back to the old man. "No memlabs! No shrinks! No more!"

He smiled at his audience, recharged by their enthusiasm. "And where does it all end? The government, my friends; our government will tell us what to think, how to think, ruining our precious independence, even telling us what to remember and what to forget! And our so-called entertainment industry," and here he pointed to a TruVal boutique nearby where two young Truda Vallon lookalikes cowered in the doorway, "is in deep collusion with them."

He lowered his voice, but it was still audible. "And I'm sure you know, my friends, what goes on right here in San Francisco, the hell-hole of America!" The crowd cheered. "And its ass-hole as well," he winked. Now the crowd was truly agitated. "Two weeks from today!" He shouted. "We're going to have the biggest demonstration this city has ever seen, right here in the heart of the beast! At the TruPlex." He paused. His voice changed to a conspiratorial stage whisper. "My friends, I've heard rumors of what those – those *degenerates* are plotting in their dark tower. Not only more memlabs with their memplants, like we have now, but worse. Can you imagine? Neither could I, until I heard from someone in a position to know." He paused dramatically and almost whispered. "The conspiracy is a highly organized, highly disciplined movement dedicated to subverting our individual and national independence. And this corrupt complicity has a code name: 'Odin.' Remember that name, my friends! The next time you hear it, it may be too late!"

He straightened, and his voice once again rang out like a shot. "Mental Health is a Fraud! Empathy is Complicity! Your Mind is Your Fortress! Now let them hear us all the way to City Hall!"

He smiled again, as his followers began yelling in a deep rumble that reminded Morgan of large hungry animals. The speaker spread his hands. Shouts and cries erupted from the crowd. That was their cue for the grand finale as they took up a chant of "Don't lose your mind! Don't lose your mind!" The old man stepped down from his bench. Morgan noted that the man was shorter than anyone near him. Where would he be without that bench? The group straggled away, presumably to a new protest site.

A shop-keeper had come out of a nearby dry-cleaning business during the speech and had stood silently nearby. Now he turned to Morgan. "I am very worried about them." He sounded foreign, but Morgan couldn't place the accent. "Nazis," he said. "These people are like the Nazis."

Morgan intended to ignore the man, but found himself responding. "Oh, I think they're harmless enough. And they don't seem to hate minorities. They're misguided, for sure, but they're just trying to protect our privacy, our minds." They would, he reflected, ban memlabs if they ever came to power. Oh well, there were other ways he could get his thrills, even though he had never been adept at finding them.

The shop-keeper turned away. "You know, don't you?" he said as he disappeared through the door of his business, "that man on the bench was Buck Baker himself."

Chapter 5

Morgan was astonished. The head of the SoCalls, live and in the flesh! Baker was based in Idaho. He seldom went anywhere in person, seldom let himself be seen or photo'd. But here he was in San Francisco, and Morgan had seen him in person. A thrill ran through Morgan's body. He tried to remember what he knew about the man.

Occasionally the supermarket scandal sites would run an expose of the early life of Buck Baker, but Baker had been smart enough to let his past sins hang out, in public, when he first gained general attention. Yea, brothers, he said numerous times, with colorful variations, I did that, and this, and that, and worse. Stealin', cheatin', smokin', beat up the little woman and the kids, even spent a time or two in jail. A miserable sinner, the worst in the world, but he'd atoned. Reformed. Hallelu', brother! Been saved from sin, redeemed "like a pawnshop pistol" as he put it. Found the true path. Now the scandals couldn't touch him. In fact, they made him stronger, one page click at a time. He had all the trappings of religion but God.

Concentrating on Buck Baker, Morgan found himself, without really intending to be there, inside the TruVal boutique. He surveyed the place. It was barely a storefront, the walls covered with posters, aisles crammed with souvenirs. He picked up a Truda Vallon snow globe, turned it upside down. Tru danced on her head in the snow, legs flailing, skirt falling around her shoulders, a hint of pubic hair. "Hi!" said the Trudite behind the counter, "We've got lots of cute stuff for your grandkids!" Morgan glanced up. Grandkids? He looked old enough to be a grandfather?

***

The shop clerk hesitated, thinking she might have made a gaffe. But no one that old could be a Truda Vallon fan, could he? Maybe it should have been "kids," not "grandkids." Well, the worst that could happen is that he'd walk out. No, the worst would be if he'd report her to her boss for being insensitive, saying something that could mean – old. *Old* wasn't to be spoken of anymore, in any way. Her new-employee training course had emphasized that. No one was "old." Not even "senior." "Senior" used to be OK, but no more. The shop clerk's mom still used "senior" once in a while, not realizing how offensive the word had become in the last few years. Well, this customer looked old to her, a "senior," in fact, but that was no defense.

Or maybe, she reflected, he's some kind of creep who gets off on lots-younger women. While Morgan wandered around the shop, picking up things and putting them down, the shop clerk wavered off into her favorite fantasy of marrying a rich older man. Yes, she'd long ago made peace with the thought of being a trophy wife so she could tell her boss to cram this stupid sales job right up his butt. Yes, she'd love a big house and a real permit-flagged gasoline-burner car of her own, and ritzy parties and real friends and romantic lovers and lots of new clothes all the time!

She noticed Morgan glancing at her. But no way this one's rich, she thought. He's not The One. More the bookish type. "How about a book?" she asked him. That was a pretty neutral subject. Old people read books, didn't they? "We just got in the new edition of *Truisms*! And one or two copies on real paper, of all things! Those cost extra, of course. For..." She was not going to say "For old-timers like you," not ever would she say or even think anything like that! But cripes, he looked at least forty!

"For special readers like you," she finished lamely. "Special readers."

***

Morgan contemplated the shifting meanings of the word "special," how they balanced delicately between compliment and slur. He put down another snow globe and left the shop. His attention, no longer distracted by protestors or forgettable keepsakes, returned to his new mem. Alex's memplant was beginning to jell in his mind, the images less blurry, the sequence of events clearer. He licked his lips, anticipating his evening. He picked up the pace, climbed the hill toward home.

Twenty minutes later Morgan turned the corner onto Washington Street, unlocked his front door, poured himself a double shot of Glenlivet single malt, got casual. He settled down in his living room and worked through the mem slowly, in delicious detail, idly fondling it in his mind. Disorientation: A man was there in a strange room, fucking a woman made up to look like Truda Vallon the TV star. The man was Alex. The man was Morgan. Alex / Morgan. In Plato's cave, not only seeing the shadows but touching them, too, savoring, breathing them in. Intimately.

BEGIN MEM

A soft knock at the door. Alex / Morgan reaches out a hand, unlocks, opens. A woman enters, wearing the Truda Vallon "uniform." She glances up, gives him / him an uneasy smile, hands him a songchip, asks him to put it in his player. She walks past him toward the couch.

Alex / Morgan and the Truda lookalike are in what must be Alex's apt, facing a couch backing up to a floor-to-ceiling window. Morgan recognizes the corner of Turk and Hyde four floors below. Across the street, he / he sees a rooftop marred by juts and protrusions of A/C fans and elevator winch boxes. It is late afternoon, sunlight coming straight in over the shoulder of Buena Vista Heights. "Tru" kneels on the couch, facing the large window, her arms on the couch back. She glances behind her, encourages him / him with a smile. He / he thinks it odd that she doesn't ask what kind of action he wants. Oh, well, he thinks, I'm not paying, so it's her call. He undresses, approaches her, and they begin a jerky dance of sex, "Tru" in front and Alex / Morgan laboring behind her.

It's Morgan now who has the vivid memory of fucking "Truda," all the feels and feelings and touches and tingles and sights and odors and sounds; and all the movements, fast or slow. But he also remembers that he's paid for another man's mem. A strange mind mashup, but he's been through it before and knows what to expect.

Morgan is bothered by the overwhelming sensation of being very drugged and very muddled, a taste he's indulged a few times but doesn't really like. And the hooker's choice in fucking-music, the part that is Morgan thinks, is too loud for him, too fast, and so closely miked the words pour out in a blaring blur.

Sounds like it could be a Truda Vallon song. Oh well, he should have expected a Tru song from a Tru lookalike. The song annoys Morgan. He's always favored massed violins for sex, adagio. He tries to overlay the song in his mind with a less frantic tempo, but fails. The part of him that is Alex thinks, idly, that he's never heard that song before, but it really fits the moment!

Alex / Morgan isn't quite sure what is anatomically going on down below, his mind drugfuddled as it is, but he / he can tell that fucking, of one kind or the other kind, is happening.

Morgan / Alex remembers the heat, the sounds of street noise and colliding flesh, the humming of a disordered electric heater, the "pop" of – what was that? Alex / Morgan raises his head from the neck he's nuzzling, stares out over the woman's shoulder, through the window, to the roof of the building across the street, where – what was that?

Just as Alex / Morgan climaxes, he / he notices something amiss on that rooftop. Sunlight glares into his eyes. He / he squints. A figure dressed as a Trudite, barely seen, is falling, someone pointing at her. Pointing with something. The woman is falling slowly onto her back on the rooftop. The man, he thinks it is a man, is facing her. And a gun. The man has a gun. A puffy cloud is gathering around its muzzle.

The man with the gun turns to his right and then his left, stops, looks again, straight into Alex / Morgan's sunset-lighted face, raises the gun again.

Alex / Morgan dodges left and downward onto the cushions, pulling "Tru" with him / him. A sound of shattering, a spray of glass, "Tru" screaming, the beginning of panic.

END OF MEM

Chapter 6

"Oh, shit!" Morgan jumped up, spilling his scotch. Now he knew why Alex had been so eager to dump that mem on someone else. The gunman could figure out where Alex lived, would want to silence a witness to murder. But how would the killer know that Alex no longer had the mem, could no longer finger him? Morgan had a queasy feeling that he knew the answer. He dressed quickly and caught a cab to Turk and Hyde.

He observed the receding streets, got his bearings. Half a block east on Turk Street was a four-story building, a hotel, and across the street a shabby apartment house. That seemed likely. From a fifth-floor apartment, the hotel's rooftop would be directly across the street.

Morgan entered the apartment house and, out of caution, took the stairs. He'd been concerned that it might not be easy to identify Alex's apt from an inside hallway, but he needn't have worried. The door of 504 was ajar, and on it was taped a hurriedly scrawled note:

"TO WHO IT MAY CONCERN: MEM SOLD TO A ROBERT MORGAN, 1536 WASHINGTON ST. – ROBERT MORGAN – NOT ME!"

Time for another "Oh, shit!" Morgan ripped the note off the door, but it was probably too late, and Alex could come back and tape up another one any time. He knocked on the door, but as he expected, there was no answer. He glanced up and down the corridor, didn't see anyone watching, slipped into the apt. Yes, this was the one: couch in front of the window, the edge of a small round hole in half the window, the other half on the floor, all shards and jagged points. The place smelled of booze, pot, and semen.

He examined the couch more closely. There were various stains, but nothing that appeared to be blood. "Tru," therefore, hadn't been shot; and he knew from his mem that Alex hadn't been, either. Resisting the urge to leave, Morgan decided to explore the apt further. What if Alex were to return? Well, so what? He'd pulled a nasty trick on Morgan; he could hardly object if Morgan had come to complain, or worse.

The apt had a living room with a kitchen alcove, tiny bathroom, and tiny bedroom, all filthy with spoons, candles, matches, pads of cigarette paper, and other signs of long-standing drug use. Empty shelves in the bedroom could have held shirts and pants. If there had been any suitcases or bags, they were gone. It appeared to Morgan that Alex wasn't planning to come back any time soon.

After another look around the apt, Morgan decided that there was nothing more to be seen. He opened the door, but heard voices and footsteps. He jumped back into the room and closed the door quietly. The footsteps moved down the hall and stopped, but the voices didn't.

"Oh, come on, Hazel!" he heard. "Is there something wrong with me?"

"No, Harold. There is nothing wrong with you. Absolutely nothing."

"And you're attracted to me. I know."

"You're attractive enough, Harold. Physically, that is."

"Well, then! And seeing that you're certainly not a virgin, not after I caught you with that guy last week, what was his name, Dave?"

"We weren't doing..."

"And after you telling me over and over that you 'weren't quite ready yet' to have sex with me? Well, why not? Why not with me, right now?"

"Well..."

"I want to hear a reason!"

"Reason has nothing to do with it, Harold."

"Then let's do it!"

"Not now, Harold. Not today." There were brief sounds of struggle. The corridor wall shook slightly after an impact of bodies. "Let go of me!"

"Then when?" the man's voice said.

"I don't know when. Stop. You're hurting my arm!"

"Can't you tell me why?" There was annoyed breathing from both Harold and Hazel.

***

Morgan would encounter Hazel and Harold twice more, in the same corridor, having much the same argument. Sometime in the future, looking back, Morgan would realize what their argument had really been about, and how it reflected the phase of his life that, at the time he first heard the two speak, he was about to enter.

***

Morgan itched to get out of the apt, but certainly didn't want to show his face to anyone in the building who might remember him later, who might give his description to a man with a gun.

While he was waiting for a chance to slip out, he wondered if the lookalike had left the songchip she'd brought. He opened Alex's chip player. Nothing. So, having almost been killed, she'd had the presence of mind to take the songchip with her when she left? Well, it could have been a tool of the sex trade, her trademark. He'd heard that hookers did things like that. Less traceable than downloading. Or Alex could have taken it when he left. Maybe it was a collectible, a song surreptitiously recorded at a live concert. If so, it could be worth a few hundred dollars, or more. Much more if it were really a Truda Vallon, and if it were ebayed to the millions of Tru fans world-wide.

Morgan stopped listening for what might come next between Hazel and Harold. He just wanted them to go to bed or go to hell, whichever could happen first. After a short time that seemed to Morgan like a long time, a door slammed and heavy footsteps jolted angrily down the corridor, accompanied by mutterings of "Goddamn bitch" and "no point reasoning with them" and "shoulda done it to her anyway!" Morgan tiptoed to the door, opened it a crack. No one was in the hall. He scurried out.

On the street, Morgan faced the problem of what to do next. If the killer had read Alex's door-note, home wouldn't be safe. Morgan checked his bank balance on his com, walked to a hotel three blocks away.

After a short discussion with the desk clerk, supplemented with a few bills of middling denomination, Morgan was allowed to register as "Joseph Johnson." He locked himself in his room, closed the blinds, huddled in a corner, shivered with fear. Hearing no suspicious sounds after a time, he began to feel safe in the hotel. If he'd been followed, he'd probably be dead by then.

To take his mind off what had happened, he waved his com at the 3D wallscreen. A brief flicker, and then Truda Vallon's live weekly TV show appeared, complete with her audience of screaming, obsessive, lookalike fans.

Announcer-hype intro'd the show, then five minutes of commercials, the warm-up telling mild jokes to mild applause, five more minutes of commercials, then Truda Vallon came onstage to whoops and shouts. Cameras split-screened the studio audience. Morgan was sure they had been hand-picked, but they seemed genuinely excited, worshipful. They stood, shouted, clapped as Tru went into her first musical number, "Slumber Don't Slumber Just Not With Me," a concoction that seemed written to show off her astonishing singing and dancing ability, the dancing frantic, athletic, but tightly controlled. Her voice must have been synched; no one could go through all those gyrations and not be out of breath. In any case, the voice was firm, high when it needed to be high, low and soft at times.

The realtime ViewerTron banner hovered in holographic midair in Morgan's room. It showed an audience rating fluctuating between 72 and 76. Seven-plus out of ten television viewers were watching "The Truda Vallon Show." That was an unheard-of number before Tru burst onto the scene five years before; but now she averaged above 70 almost every week, once as high as 88.

Then she sang a slow number, "You're My High and Mighty Fine," mimed with gigantic fake syringes danced around the stage by people in white smocks and stethoscopes. (ViewerTron 75) After two more musical pieces, Tru came to the mike, told the audience how much she loved them etc. etc., shared a few "insights," as she called them, into her daily life as a busy (and very rich and very naughty) superstar-slash-executive, uttered a few new Truisms, smiled again and blew kisses to the cameras.

She briefly introduced a guest musical act that Morgan thought wasn't very good (67), interviewed a large-mouthed baggy-eyed bulbous-lipped comic "celeb" Morgan had never heard of (34), paused for another seven commercials (56), sang two final numbers (71), gave a brief talk about how we should all love each other and share each other's triumphs and troubles and empathize and try just try to understand. She bowed and blew kisses in several directions. Show over.

Morgan turned off the wallscreen and sat back on the bed. He had a long time to wonder what he should do. Go to the police, certainly. To report a murder? But Alex's mem didn't exactly show a murder, only what Alex / Morgan thought might be one. What if it had all been a ghastly hoax? He'd be laughed at by every cop in the precinct. And by all his ex-colleagues at the university too, if they heard about his buying a sexmem. He could hear the rattle of shaking heads from here. He'd have to find out, for sure, if something bad had happened on that rooftop, if there were a body. He'd have to go there, himself. He'd have to look.

***

Early the next morning, Morgan went to the building across the street from Alex's apt, a hotel considerably cheaper than the one where he'd just spent the night. He walked in and put on a casual air as if he were a steady customer. There were three people in the shabby lobby, plus the desk clerk. One was a man of perhaps thirty five, trim, short hair beginning to gray, well-dressed, rather out of place here. The other two appeared to be together, a tall shapely woman and a slouchy middle-aged male, both facing the other way. What did she see in him? Morgan was relieved that all four seemed intent on their own business. He didn't want anyone recalling that he'd been there.

Not wanting to risk being seen on an elevator, Morgan took the stairs to the top floor, pausing several times to catch his breath. He found the door to the roof intending to force it, but the lock had already been broken. By the victim? By the assailant?

Slowly and quietly, Morgan opened the door. He jumped at the sudden flight of disturbed pigeons. Recovering a few shards of composure, he peered around the door frame, didn't see anyone. A little more confidently but keeping low, he crept forward on the rooftop, thinking that in the old police movies there were always shell casings that would invariably, immediately, identify the caliber of the weapon and provide infallible clues to the murderer. And a dropped glove. Or a drop of snot to be DNA'd. Or whatnot. Morgan didn't find any casings, or gloves, or whatnots. But he did find a pool of blood behind a heat-exchanger. And a dead woman who looked for all the world like Truda Vallon.

Chapter 7

Morgan swayed unsteadily. This had to be a dream. Stuff like this didn't happen in the real world. Not his real world, at least. Fighting back the urge to run, he studied the scene more closely. This was the woman he'd seen in Alex's mem. And she couldn't be the real Tru, because he'd watched Tru's live TV show the night before. This had to be another lookalike, one of thousands of wannabes; and a really unlucky one.

Morgan bent over her. The woman wore a lanyard around her neck, but whatever had been dangling from it was gone, ripped away. Down the length of the lanyard were the repeated repeated words "TruVal, Inc. TruVal, Inc.," Truda Vallon's production company and the heart of her megabilliondollar entertainment megathing.

There was a sharp noise from nearby, not very loud. Morgan jumped, glanced left and right. Nothing. But the sound had given him the jitters, and he decided to leave immediately. He left the roof and took the stairs again. The well-dressed thirty-something man, and the tall woman and the short man, were nowhere to be seen.

Cautiously, Morgan left the cheap hotel, deep in thought about what he'd seen. He'd have to go to the police for sure now, and explain everything. But it wasn't Morgan who'd witnessed the murder, it was Alex. He knew that, but that's not what his memories told him. Just a few feet from the hotel entrance he barely avoided a collision with an older woman walking a dog, both sweatered in the human + doggy couture of two decades before. He'd stepped sideways at the last moment as both woman and dog gave him a derisive stare.

As he was executing the sideways movement, Morgan heard a "pop" and a "ping" at almost the same time: the "pop" from above him, the "ping" from a dark van parked on the street.

He'd been directly in front of the van when he'd had to dodge the dogged woman. He was sure he hadn't seen that bullet hole in the van's side panel a moment ago. Someone was shooting at him! He spun around intending to warn the woman and dog, but they were several feet away, had apparently not heard the sounds. Morgan fell to the ground, crawled to a hedge and curled up behind it.

The van took off, weaving down the street. Ten minutes passed; Morgan didn't dare move. A crowd gathered, wondering why the strange man – "O look, Mommy!" – was crouching behind a bush. "Takes all kinds," several remarked, sagely nodding heads. "Ought to be a law," others opined wisely, in slow and conservative tones. Using the crowd as cover, Morgan slipped away and went back to his hotel room, frequently glancing behind him and dodging a few more woman + dog combos.

He closed the blinds and used his com to find the address of the new San Francisco police HQ. A palace down in the Mission Rock that had cost twice as much as it should have and got a mayor thrown out of office and three contracting officials put in jail where they could piss in their thousand-dollar toilets and stare hopelessly out through their type-440 stainless steel bars. There really was justice, once in a while. He left the hotel, careful as always, and hailed a cab.

The ride took about fifteen minutes. Morgan observed the changing street scene of SOMA. It was very different from when he was a child, when he hadn't dared go there alone on foot. The area had first become trendy and high-priced, a better-dressed North Beach, complete with clubs and venues and arty galleries and coffee bars. But then the builders and their dollars had moved in and re-created Canary Wharf. "Canary Wharf in California!", all huzzahed, but the official name was Condor Wharf, in honor of the noble bird Californians had extinguished from the planet. The Wharf had ended SOMA's charm, sadly enough even though the charm had always been a little fake.

They arrived at police headquarters. Morgan paid the cabbie, passed through security, and found the place where supplicants assembled to beg audience of the lawmen. He explained, largely incoherently, what had happened. The desk sergeant regarded him coldly, stared at him, pawed accusingly at his ID. Morgan was well-dressed, but he realized that he must be rumpled and unshaven. Finally the sergeant motioned Morgan to a chair where he sat for a long time watching arriving derelicts being given the bum's rush.

After being quizzed, and ignored, and asked to say that again, sir? several times, and how do you spell that, sir? and made to wait and sit and sit and wait, he finally gained an audience with a man who introduced himself as Detective Lieutenant Dennis DeLuca. Morgan observed DeLuca carefully. Not quite like most of the cops on TV: not as chunky or as tall; well-pressed suit but in a final-clearance-sale color; hair long on top but short on the sides, a fashion Morgan hadn't seen in years. DeLuca seemed to Morgan to be a little younger than himself, but close enough to have similar mental idioms, Generation which? X had been the first, then Y, then – what letter were we up to now? Or had the whole silly "generation" thing been dropped?

The detective seemed preoccupied. What does he think of me? Morgan wondered. Now he's staring. Why doesn't he say something?

***

Dennis DeLuca leaned back in his chair. He'd long since learned that silence, coupled with a stern and knowing stare, could un-nerve almost anyone. Thirty seconds of stare could cut the following interview by minutes, sometimes hours. It could even lead, upon occasion, to blurted confessions. His captain had observed DeLuca's technique several times, copied it himself without bothering to give DeLuca praise or credit. The lieutenant, after all, was his subordinate: no credit required.

DeLuca studied the figure opposite him casually, but thoroughly. Decent suit, more expensive than his own, but worn and rumpled. Hair combed over the bald spot. A negative image popped into his mind. He banished it. Not supposed to make snap judgments of citizens, tax-payers. Not unless they're criminals. His last performance review had said so, had documented several instances of his making snap judgments of citizens, with embarrassing results. In one case, much worse than embarrassing. But he couldn't be expected to know every damn City Council member and his or her main squeeze by sight, could he? Especially one from Russian Hill. DeLuca knew his own Councilman well – Councilwoman, really. Good citizens lived in the Sunset, not those damned... OK, I've stared at him enough, put him on the defensive.

The detective asked for and examined Morgan's ID. Another Russian Hill phony, but the address placed him toward Polk. Wrong side of the right hill. DeLuca, who shared an apt on the wrong side of Twin Peaks, warmed toward the man.

"What can I do for you, sir?" The detective put on a patently insincere smile.

Morgan nervously related all that had happened.

DeLuca listened, although not very intently. He made a few notes on a small pad. He tried to count the number of times he'd been through this routine, another mind-witness to a crime the witness never actually saw. Drugs? Bad trip? Bad dream? How many times had he sent out a unit and wasted their time this month already? His captain was down on him for that. Everything had to be followed up, though. Cover your ass before it gets screwed, you know. Wisdom of the Goddamn ages. Eleventh commandment.

"Do you want my mem?" Morgan added plaintively to the end of his recital, "as evidence?"

"Sorry, Mr. Morgan, As you admitted, you didn't have a good view of the suspect, not quite half his face. Now if you had seen the suspect's whole face, or witnessed the crime yourself, not this Alex, we might've been able to work with you. But your mem wouldn't be worth shit in court; just hearsay, or 'see/saw' as we say: somebody sees it, sells it, you buy it, you saw it. I know the media make a big deal out of ID-ing criminals this way, but it never sticks in court, not with a halfway good defense counsel, anyway. And in any case, your mind has already begun modding the mem, because you're you and your mind isn't the same as Alex's.

"And how do you know that your mem wasn't a pass-along?" he continued. "A mem sold to someone else, and then that person sold it to someone else and then maybe someone else again? Any third-rate lawyer could impeach testimony based on transplanted memories, memplants; and as for Alex, he doesn't remember it anymore."

"But the woman with Alex?"

"Hookers aren't likely to volunteer information. And on the witness stand, 'How many arrests was that, miss? Oh? What kinds of drugs?' Well, you can imagine that scene. No, she's no better a witness than you are, sir." He said "sir," now, with a hint of irony, Morgan thought, as in Sir Speedy or Sir Loin.

"So, what should I...?"

"Go home."

"But he'll be after me!"

"The killer, if there is one? If he's smart, he'll know your mem isn't worth shit for evidence, like I said."

"But what if he's not that smart? He took a shot at me, didn't he? Why is he still after me?"

DeLuca gave Morgan a look that could mean that taking a shot at Morgan might have been understandable, one felony count notwithstanding.

"I suppose, if that's really what happened, he could be after you." DeLuca's expression changed to suspicion. "The shooter wouldn't want to be ID'd," he continued, "even if it's inadmissible. Maybe we'd be able to find a way to get at him. Circumstantial, I mean."

Morgan explained, again, that the sun was coming from behind the shooter, and that Morgan had seen only half the man's face, or less.

"The shooter might not have thought of that."

Both Morgan and the detective were silent for a moment. Morgan realized that he'd been in one of those arguments where A made the point that B made before, but by that time B had moved over to A's opinion. He'd had many of those infuriating wrangles with Helen and had never known quite when to wave the white flag and just shut up and leave the house. And slam the door before she could find something to throw, to break.

DeLuca shrugged. What the hell. He'd have to promise some action to rid himself of this distraught citizen without his filing some kind of complaint. Whether or not the action would ever take place, well, that was different. "OK, sir, I'll send a unit out to that rooftop, and park a car outside your house as well."

"How long?"

"How long what?"

"How long will the car be there?"

"Hard to say. Not long."

"'Not long'? That's all?"

"That's all we're going to do, *sir*. There's a lot of crime in this city. Crises. Emergencies. And the Goddamn City Council and their Goddamn cheap-ass budget and their Goddamn holier than thou attitude if you so much as look at..."

And that Goddamn Councilman Brownstein, DeLuca thought with a wince. DeLuca had thought that the short man he was following was a felon named Lawton with three outstanding warrants. But it was Brownstein. He'd roughed him up a little, and that woman with him, too, who'd turned out to be his wife, even though he was sure she was the woman he'd seen in a bar on Ellis Street a few hours before. Wasn't she the one he'd tried to pick up but she'd turned him down? Roughed both of them up a little, just a little.

"OK. OK." Morgan said, taking the detective's absent stare for dismissal. "Thank you."

Morgan went home, kept away from the windows, tiptoed and stayed close to the floor, an uncomfortable combination of positions. He selected the most obscure closet in the house, counted the number of steps to his final redoubt, practiced hiding behind a raincoat. But this was silly. Here he was skulking about in his own home, the proverbial sitting duck. He couldn't stand it anymore, this waiting for a door to be forced, a window to break. Waiting to be killed.

After a few hours, a police cruiser appeared on his block, parked. After one hour more it peeled out, siren wailing. The cruiser might come back, but Morgan knew his protection wouldn't last long in any case. Police have other things to do, emergency calls that might pay off in statistics or headlines. But Morgan needed to figure out what he was going to do for money, get back to his life. Later, maybe. He sat down in the living room, as far as possible from windows and doors. Serious game was afoot, and the game animal of choice seemed to be himself. He was tired, and it was catching up with him. He ate a candy bar. He tried to stay awake and alert, but dozed off.

And woke in the dark. He didn't want to show a light to see what time it was, so he sat still until a sickly purple sunrise rose unsteadily from the general direction of Oakland.

Morgan expected to hear from the police about the body, but no one called. Finally, about noon, he com'd Detective DeLuca. Wait. Wait. Wait. Then

"Mr. Morgan. Everything OK?"

"The cruiser's gone."

"Yeah, we had some calls."

"Will it be back?"

"Will what be back?"

"The patrol car."

"Maybe."

"Maybe what?"

"Just maybe."

"Well, did you send a unit up to that rooftop?"

"That's police business, Mr. Morgan."

"But it was my business that almost got shot off!"

"Well OK, yeah, we were able to find a little blood, a trace. It's at the lab now for a DNA in case this victim – perhaps victim – has his or her DNA on file. But there wasn't a body. Someone had tried very hard to chemically obliterate traces of blood, but we found a few samples we might be able to make."

"No body?"

"No body."

"Doesn't that strike you as...?"

"There might not have been a body at all."

"What?"

"There's no evidence of a crime, Mr. Morgan. Just a little blood. We don't even know, yet, if it's human blood."

"But I told you..."

"We'll see."

Morgan boiled in impotent fury but contained it, more or less. "What are you going to do?"

"Can't comment, Mr. Morgan, Police business. Rest assured."

DeLuca hung up.

"Shit on you, asshole son of a whore!" Morgan yelled futilely into the dial tone. "Fuzz! Pig!" he added for good measure, remembering words his father used to use in referring to the city's badged elite. That's showing the authorities who's who!

Chapter 8

With a level of introspection unusual for him, Morgan realized that he was rapidly becoming unhinged. Had to get calm now, slow everything down. He stayed home the rest of the day, and the next several days. He let the mail pile up inside the mail slot. He found a few unpaid bills and added them to the pile, incrementing his presumed absence by a week in case anyone gained entrance and pawed through the mail. He rummaged in his emergency food supply and ate soup out of cans. And a carton of power bars. And felt thoroughly sick.

The next day dawned to a major stomach ache. I can't go on like this, he thought, then brightened: the murderer hadn't tried to break in. Then gloomed: he could be waiting outside, loitering barely out of sight, where he couldn't see him. Then an inspiration: Dump the mem. Go to the O'Farrell Street Memlab and donate it to an anonymous needy sex-starved hard-up. Put a sign on my door TO WHOM IT MAY CONCERN (Morgan would be sure to write WHOM, not WHO.) He found an old flipchart pad and a marker and scrawled on the back of one sheet TO WHOM. And realized how silly that was: why would the murderer believe him? And the sign would signal that he was still really at home. And... And...

Morgan sat down and took stock. Here he was, being hunted, quite possibly, for a memory that wasn't even his. Possible to dump the mem but impossible to prove that he'd done that in time to avoid becoming the second victim. The police were apparently not interested enough to take action. What could he do, wait to be shot? Who else was there who could help? Or would help? The world, he mused, had given up on helping, probably long before anyone had noticed.

Morgan pondered his customary passivity. Act and you could be blamed; be acted upon, you could shift the blame elsewhere: a third-grade lesson he'd learned very well. It had been successful for him, he'd always assumed on no real evidence. But not now. Not with death possible at any second. How would death feel? A bullet in the head, probably wouldn't feel a thing. Here, and then not here. Forever. He tried to imagine such a state, failed. He noticed that his hands were sweating.

He stood up. "Have to do something," he muttered. He'd have to act. How? He had no idea. But it was that or die.

Morgan was not brave by nature, never had been. But he could be stubborn and ornery. Those traits were almost, as it turned out, enough.

***

Morgan remembered the lanyard. "TruVal, Inc. TruVal, Inc." It was possible that the murdered woman was a TruVal employee, or at least might be known to the organization. Might be missing. Might have been missed.

He tried truval.com. Nothing but a place-holder. truval.biz, same. Then truval.tv. Of course: the TV motif pervaded Tru's television-based empire. He found a "contact us" phone number, listened to a long list of "If you want to ... press or say...," and then touched zero on his com. Three press-or-say choices later, he was speaking to a real live human being at TruVal, Inc.

"TruVal, Incorporated. How may I direct your call?"

Morgan had carefully planned what he could say in the five seconds of grace he expected to have before hang-up.

"Are you missing one of your employees? I witnessed her murder!"

"Ah..."

"The police are working on it, but they don't know about the TruVal connection. I do."

That seemed to be worth a few more seconds of Ah-ing.

"Ah... Ah..."

"Do you have a security department?"

With relief, the voice said "Yes, sir. I'll connect you with our Serve and Protect Department right away."

"Thank you."

Six buzzes and clicks later, "Yes?"

Morgan repeated the approach that had worked for him so far, adding "Are you missing one of your employees? I witnessed her murder!"

A few moments of dead air, then "Ah, sir, we wouldn't know if anyone's missing until the end of the pay period. We do follow up on employees who haven't reported their hours to their supervisors. If you'll call back then, we..."

Morgan interrupted, played his ace. "The police are working on it, but they don't know about the TruVal connection. I do!"

Less dead air.

Then a different voice, guardedly: "And what would that be, sir."

Morgan thought that the lanyard-clue was a little thin, so he made something up.

"Dying words, she said to me 'Tell Tru.' Then, poor thing, she died in my arms."

A bit overdramatic, but it worked. "She? Who was it?"

"I wish I knew! She didn't have any ID on her, or maybe the murderer took it away. But she was on a rooftop in the Tender..."

Whatever it was that did it, that did it.

"Don't hang up! I'll get Ms. Taylor on the line right away!"

Only three and a half finger-drummings later, "Yes? This is Athena Taylor."

"Are you missing one of your employees? I witnessed her murder!"

"Who is this?"

"My name is Dr. Robert Morgan. I'm a professor at San Francisco State." He didn't say that he'd just been fired, and that the most he'd ever been, anywhere, was assistant professor.

"And?"

"And I saw a woman being shot."

"And where and when was this?"

"On a rooftop near Turk and Hyde. Saturday." Morgan was guessing which day Alex had had his vision, but Saturday would have to do. In any case, Saturday seemed to satisfy Athena Taylor.

"All right, Doctor..."

"Morgan."

"Right. Are you available to come down to the TruPlex right away?"

"Right now?"

"Right now." Taylor had that firm kind of voice that reminded Morgan, not entirely unpleasantly, of whips and chains.

"I'll be there."

"I'm sure you will; I'm sending a car."

"There's no need to..."

"1536 Washington Street, right?"

"Uh, yes. How did...?"

He heard Taylor saying "Did you catch that address? Send Melody and Serena over there right away." Click. Silence.

Morgan was not inclined to get into a strange car, not now. Not after being shot at. Not knowing how they knew his home address without asking. Once inside the TruPlex, signed in and his entrance a matter of record and saved on security cams and all that, he'd be safe. Maybe. But a car? Probably long and black, with tinted windows and a black permit flag flying from the antenna. Suits with guns who got by on one-syllable words. His fantasies soared. Don't ask questions, get in. We're here to protect you, wink wink. Why are you going this way? This is not the way to the office / airport / police station / FBI. Yes, he said to himself, I'm being paranoid, but that's me. I trust me. I guess.

Morgan opened his front door very slowly, just a crack. He peeked out with one eye, peered left / right, up / down. No one was in sight who looked like a murderer, whatever a murderer looked like. Morgan waited until a cable car approached, laboriously pulled uphill by its clanking cable. He burst from his door, ran across the sidewalk, between two parked mopeds, and leapt onto the moving car. A few tourists applauded. The conductor took his money, admonished him sir please be more careful sir, you should know that the city can't be liable for injuries if you fall, sir, etc., etc. Did you know that only the other week we had an incident like that, poor fellow, head right on the tracks, went right under the wheels, never had a chance, squashed like a roach. And his widow, I remember how she...

Morgan tuned out. In the next block, out of the corner of his eye, he saw a bush move, but that was non-determinative. Enough bushes.

In the event, no shots were fired. Morgan escaped toward the financial district without incident other than the conductor's ongoing saga of the poor man who'd tried to leap onto a moving cable car and lost his head, a perfect urban legend. Perhaps the killer had left after the police car appeared, or had never been to his house at all.

Or perhaps the killer didn't have to bother waiting for him, because – because why? A new worry: If he wasn't being stalked, did the killer have something else in mind? Perhaps Morgan had been meant to find the body. Perhaps he was the dupe of a devious international conspiracy and he was doing, minute by minute, what the conspirators wanted him to do all along. There they were, he imagined, following him in satcam realtime, chortling gleefully as their plans unfolded and as their creature, Robert Morgan, PhD, did their obscure bidding. The improbable thought of him! just him! being the unwitting Walter-Mitty-like pawn of a vast and evil global conspiracy cheered him: consequence without responsibility.

He got off the cable car at Powell, first making sure it had come to a complete stop, and walked the last few blocks to Montgomery.

There it was in front of him, the TruPlex, all twenty-six – he counted them – floors. The building itself was much like any other Montgomery Street tower, but instead of dark financial manipulations and currency cartels and derivatives of derivates, typical Street business, the TruPlex was the home of song, and dance, and dream. Love songs and leaping dances and dreams of fame and money and sex. Morgan's dreams. He approached the front door uneasily and, with a kind of reverence, entered.

Instead of the grand, soaring, steel-and-glass entrance hall he'd been half expecting, the TruPlex lobby was businesslike and, he had to admit it, plain. Morgan had his ID checked by a guard, was frisked, wanded, poked, groped, and waved through a bank of metal detectors, full-court-press body scanners, white-powdery-envelope detectors, and several other machines that must be checking for substances so deadly the firm didn't dare say what they were checking him for.

The receptionist was another Trudite, but at the base of her jet-black hair Morgan could see the blonde roots. "Mr. Morgan," she gushed, "We're really delighted to have you this morning." That could mean several things, not all of them unpleasant. "I'll ring right up for Ms. Taylor." She did so, winking and grinning at him the while. "Always wonderful to have reps here from the network."

Before Morgan could ask her what she meant by "the network," she had turned and cast the light of her countenance on the next petitioner for admittance.

After a very short time – too short a time, he thought – a woman approached him. She was unexpectedly tall, and unexpectedly un-Truda-like: No jet black hair hanging straight down, no baggy black dress, no dark coloring around the eyes. All business, perfectly turned out for Montgomery Street; the only employee there who didn't look like a Transylvanian corpse. And with a million-dollar smile that could have come straight from the pages of Excessively Expensive Cosmetic Dentistry Journal. And strikingly beautiful, stunningly statuesque. Morgan had to keep himself from gawking. I'd buy a sexmem of her, he thought, any day, any angle, any action, any price.

"Dr. Morgan? I'm Athena Taylor," she said. She started to hold out her hand, then froze momentarily. Morgan couldn't figure out why. Was there something wrong with him? Unzipped pants? He started to blush, but she regained her composure and completed the handshake. "Dr. Morgan!" she said, a little too heartily, "wonderful of you to visit with us! We were really worried about you when you didn't meet our company car, but I'm relieved to see you here safe and sound. Sorry for the confusion; I guess I wasn't very clear about that car." Morgan had expected a touch of insincerity, but not the undertone of worry he caught in her voice.

"Please come this way," she said, ushering him toward a small elevator. He followed her, savoring the undulating view. She waved her com, and the door opened. "This goes straight to the twenty-sixth floor," she said, "for our most honored guests."

A hum, a slight lurch, and his ears felt the pressure of ascent. "Pardon the 'network' subterfuge, doctor, that's a cover story. We wanted to keep this low key."

Morgan didn't get it. Why the special treatment? Had the murdered woman been an important person here at TruVal? Where were the police? He looked at Taylor. Looked up at her, an uncomfortable sensation for a man almost six feet tall. Most women were shorter than he, could be looked down upon. Comfortably looked down on. Not this one. "Athena," indeed. He had a mental picture of a Greek goddess in full armor, waving a spear.

"Um, what do you do here at TruVal, Ms. Taylor?"

"I'm in charge of – well, my title here is Vice President. Basically, I run the business side so Tru can concentrate on music and shows and appearances. She's the majority owner and President, of course. Everyone here but Tru and her creative staff work for me."

The elevator door opened onto a severe but stylish sitting room. Giant wallscreens surrounded the room, each silently showing Truda Vallon acting, or singing, or dancing.

"Please make yourself comfortable, doctor. Would you like some coffee? Or perhaps a soda? We're about to introduce our own line, called TruCal. Caf and decaf and supercaf, high-cal and no-cal and lo-cal, carbonated and still, cola and lemon-lime, all the combinations."

Without waiting for an answer, Taylor left the room. In his head, Morgan attempted to calculate how many different kinds of TruCal would be introduced, then tried to imagine drinking a non-carbonated cola.

Ten minutes later Athena Taylor returned with four more people: a young woman whom Morgan took to be an assistant from her papers and folders and coms; two burly butchy Trudites who didn't seem very Truda-ish, and were packing not-very-small arms; and the fourth, between the butches, long black hair, blue eyes, slight build, thin, corpse-like complexion, about twenty-five years old. Smiling exactly as he had seen her smile on TV. Exactly as he had seen her in his dreams.

"Hello, Doctor Morgan," she said, offering her hand. "I'm Truda Vallon."

Chapter 9

Morgan gaped at the hand in front of him, and the woman attached to it. So this was the famous Truda Vallon! He wondered what she would make of him, Robert Morgan, outwardly modest and humble, but inwardly a brave and decisive hero, well, if the right situation would ever present itself. Maybe.

***

Tru felt Morgan staring at her. Not quite what she expected, but he looked harmless enough.

"Another Truda Vallon?" he said. "There seem to be quite a lot of you here."

"I'm the real one."

"Would you give me a swab for DNA verification?"

"Are you serious?" What a jerk! Or maybe I'm just on edge. Calm down now. I need to treat what he said as a joke, which I'm sure it was.

"No, and of course I'm sure you're not serious," she said. "You've been through a very trying experience, Dr. Morgan. I understand that you're upset. And I understand that you don't quite trust us. I'd be cautious, too, if I'd been through what you've been through."

That seemed the right thing to say, even though she wasn't at all certain what this man had been through.

"But I *am* Truda Vallon," she said.

***

Morgan tried, but failed, to stop staring at her. She looked like her lookalikes, well, naturally! But different, too. He memorized her face and voice, not so much their appearance and sound as what these features might mean to him. Was her face pretty or striking or out of proportion? Was her voice high? Too high? With time and accustoming he would not see her face, hear her voice in the same way, could not recapture his original thought of her unless he now made a point of it. Among all those imitators, this "real one" was her own self.

He coughed slightly, trying to cover up his unease. Tru continued speaking, and Morgan realized that only one or two seconds had elapsed.

"I asked Athena," she nodded toward the taller woman, "to bring you here," she paused, "because the person who was killed, or perhaps killed, wasn't just another wannabe; she was a team member here at TruVal, and a very talented one at that. Terra was her name, Terra Lewis."

"How do you know her name?" Morgan gaped ungracefully.

"The police called us this morning, shortly before you spoke with Athena. They identified the blood as Terra's, and traced her to us."

"But the body was..."

"There was no body, Dr. Morgan. If there was a body, it had been removed. But we have to assume the worst."

Morgan considered Tru. She seemed sincere, but not at all shocked at the news that the blood of an employee and friend – Tru had called her "Terra" – had been found, possibly a homicide victim. Tru had no reason to cover up her shock, had she? Or perhaps she wasn't shocked because she'd known about it before the police called. But how could that be?

***

Tru considered Morgan. How was he involved in all this? The police had mentioned him when they'd called that morning. She had alerted Athena and TruVal security, thinking he might attempt to contact them. And if he hadn't, she'd been prepared to have her security staff hunt down Morgan and bring him in. He seemed distraught, uncertain of himself. Would he be different once he settled down?

"I saw a murder." His speech stalled out.

"Of Terra Lewis?"

"I don't know! I don't know who it was."

"How did you see it?" she prompted. "This was a mem, right? The detective said something like that. Were you on the street, or what?"

"I bought it." Morgan reddened, began to babble. "I bought a mem that saw a woman – I mean Alex saw a woman who might be being killed – from a man named Alex. I bought his mem. Of the murder."

Tru gave a start. "So that's the connection," she said. "The police told me this morning that they'd identified the DNA of one of my staff on the rooftop you saw, or that you 'see/saw,' as the police call it. That was Terra."

"But I went back," said Morgan, "and the body was missing."

"There was no body," said Tru, "according to the detective I spoke with."

"Lieutenant DeLuca?"

"Yes; he was the one who phoned this morning."

"I saw the body!" Morgan said.

He appeared agitated. Yes, she thought, he saw someone fall, saw an assailant with a gun, but how could he have actually seen the body? She paused. Maybe he was imagining it.

"When?" she asked.

"When what?"

"When did you see the body?"

"On the roof. Monday morning. I went there. To see if there was a body, if the body was still there, or if I hadn't actually – you know – ah." His voice trailed off in confusion.

Now, this was interesting. It was no longer just a see/saw; this was real.

"What else did you see?"

"Nothing. Only the TruVal lanyard around her neck."

"With a badge?"

"No. If there was a badge, it had been torn off."

"OK. Well, Dr. Morgan, you've been very helpful," she said in a tone of voice that implied that he hadn't been very helpful.

The part about his seeing the body was interesting, but at this point Morgan didn't seem to know any more than the police did. But – this man could be a problem. Tru thought for a few seconds. Why did he have to buy that damned mem? What rotten luck. Or an opportunity, if he could be kept on a leash. A short leash.

"Doctor Morgan," she said, "or Bob, if I may...?"

"Robert."

"What?"

"You can call me Robert." He had a sudden flash of Helen, his ex-wife, calling him "Bob." In her mouth, the word sounded obscene. Bob, Bob, Bah. Bah, Bah, Bob.

"All right – Robert. I'd like you to work with us to find out what really happened, and how Terra fits into this puzzle. Do you think you could do that?"

"How?"

"Well, we always have a few vacant offices here in the building. You could use one until the investigation is finished, answer a few questions for us. You'd be safer than you would be at home, surely, and you'd be available to the police when they call. I have more resources, here at TruVal, than the local police do, anyway. They're at your disposal."

"*If* the police call," Morgan replied. "I think they're through with me."

"Perhaps. But just for us, then. Terra is, was, I mean, a prize catch for TruVal when we signed her up. I want to find out what happened. I want to know if any other TruVal staff are at risk. Terra had no enemies that I know of, and I believe I'd know of any. I have to think that the killer thought Terra was me."

Well, she thought, a lot of that was a lie. But she had no idea why Terra Lewis had been shot. Everything made sense but that.

***

Morgan glanced at her bodyguards. "Surely, since Terra was alone, no one would..."

"Think she was me, with no guards?" Tru said. "But you know, or the 'bloids know, anyway, that every so often I go out on my own and explore. Experience. Be. There are so many women now who make up and dress like me that I can get away with it. Having guards around would spoil the trick, wouldn't it?"

"OK, then," he said, "Terra was the killer's mistake. Who would want to...?"

"Kill me?"

"Yeah."

"I don't know. I want your help finding out."

"Why me?"

"Because I don't believe you're involved in this plot, whatever it is." She held one finger up. "And because right now I don't know whom I can trust." Another finger. "And best of all, you have a pure and compelling motive, Dr. Morgan: find the killer before he finds you!" Three, four, then five fingers.

Morgan hesitated.

"And I think," inserted Athena, "that DeLuca suspects you of something."

Morgan stared in alarm. "What?" he asked.

"I don't know; he didn't say. But Tru and I think you should be with us for a while. Is that OK?"

Athena turned to the assistant without waiting for an answer. "Renee, please find an office for Dr. Morgan. He'll be here for, ah, for a while. I believe Mary Ann's old office is available?"

"Yes, ma'am."

Tru wished Morgan a nice day, turned him over to Athena and Renee, and went back to her office. Morgan's DNA remark had caught her off balance. She hoped no one had caught her startle-reaction.

Growing up poor, mother drunk half the time and crazy the other half, two horrible, vicious older brothers. How she had longed to get out of Spokane! And then the miracle had happened: she'd discovered her talent, her secret self; changed her name; moved to New York, then L.A. and became famous, then San Francisco to build her empire. Not that her real name was anything bad, just ordinary. But if the 'bloids got hold of it they'd dig into her past, dredge up all that awful stuff. At least she hadn't done anything criminal back then, even though she'd dearly wanted to a few times. Nothing that could put her in jail, but it would royally screw up her career.

The 'bloids hadn't found out about her past yet, and since they'd been digging frantically for the past five years, they probably never would. But now there was a problem: One of her employees had possibly been murdered, and under highly curious circumstances. And Morgan! A middle-aged sad-sack professor, he had got into this by his bad luck and mine. Too many curious types will be snooping, have already started. What to do? She thought.

Yes – perhaps.

Chapter 10

Renee escorted Morgan down a long corridor toward the staff elevators. TruVal staffers were scurrying here and there excitedly. Renee got several brief texts on her com, sent others.

"Is it always this busy here?" he asked.

"Gee, it's always really busy here, with the TV show, and guest appearances, and interviews, and all that, but on Sunday there's going to be another TruVal TV special instead of the usual weekly show. Really big! We're all really wild with curiosity here!"

"What kind of special?"

"Don't know! Staff aren't being told. Rug Row's keeping it under wraps – 'Rug Row' is what we call the twenty-sixth floor exec offices. But gee, I've heard" She glanced side to side dramatically, lowered her voice, "that there will be a big, wonderful new song from Tru, brand new, premiering with a real live hube orchestra and dancers and conductor and all, not simmed, none of it!" They got on an elevator.

***

Renee pushed the button for the twelfth floor. She thought about how exciting this all was. Not only the special, which was thrilling enough, wasn't it! But the secrecy, too. Golly, how could she hold still for another – how many days was it? She'd been running from floor to floor on errands for Ms. Taylor or Ms. Vallon for just days, now, hadn't it been? Talking to anyone she could buttonhole and trying to find out exactly what the big news was going to be. Not the new song, because there were new songs all the time. Not seeing a live conductor conducting live musicians, even though she'd never had that experience before. Her mom and dad used to talk about those things, and then sigh. But the big news must be something else. She hadn't found out, yet, what that might be. She needed to.

Needed to find out a hint at least, of what Ms. Vallon would be announcing and what she wouldn't. Before the special.

The elevator arrived at the twelfth floor. "You'll really like it here, Dr. Morgan, with us here at TruVal. We're one big happy family here! And it's always nice to have a male in the vicinity. Keeps us on our toes, doesn't it?" Renee laughed. "Lots less bad language with a guy around! You can't imagine how us girls just go on and on with all those dirty words when we're by ourselves!" Too much information, Morgan thought, although the concept did arouse him slightly.

The twelfth floor was a surprising change: quiet, cold, almost deserted. It had apparently been used for a series of stage sets long ago, then allowed to become every other floor's attic. They progressed down one silent corridor after another, finally entered a small office.

"Here it is!" beamed Renee.

"This?" Morgan asked. He had initially expected a dreary cube like any other cube, but the long journey of many corridors had fed in him a fantasy of quite a grand office, certainly larger and more impressive than Professor O'Neill's, the man who'd fired him the week before. But this office was no larger than his old one at the university!

Renee saw his face. "Oh Dr. Morgan!" she cried, "this is your admin's office. Your own is right through here." She opened a connecting door onto a truly magnificent office: very large desk, very large credenza and conference table, very large computerized coffee / tea / cocoa / spring water service, and a television receiver with a very very large 3.5D HD wallscreen. Take that and shove it, Department Head and holder of the Gravelstein Endowed Chair in Physics James Whistler O'Neill!

Renee held out her hand and her com snuggled itself into it. She wiggled a finger. "Madelyn? Renee. We're ready for you. Yes, that's 12A105. Right away, please."

They made small talk while waiting for Madelyn, whoever Madelyn was. Morgan was expecting another Tru lookalike, and he wasn't disappointed. But this one appeared older than most of the others, perhaps mid-forties. Morgan detected intelligence and a hint of iron.

"Well, guys, I guess I'll take my adieu!" Renee said sprightly. "Madelyn Lopez will be your admin. Madelyn, Robert. Robert, Madelyn. Anything you want, she'll get it for you!" With that, Renee wafted out and away.

Madelyn was all business. She showed Morgan how the TruVal coms worked, not too differently from his own, as it turned out. She told him the quickest way to get to the building's cafeteria, and where the men's room was ("probably dusty; we don't have many males here in the TruPlex!"). She handed him a pad and pen and asked him to make a note of anything he might be needing, at the end of the day, please. She escorted him to the Protect and Serve Department where he was photographed, fingerprinted, and badged. Then she brought him back and sat him down at his desk. By this time, he was mentally referring to Madelyn Lopez as Nurse Ratched.

"I'll be right outside your door, doctor," she said in a stern voice. With that, she walked into the outer office and shut the door. Nervously, Morgan sat down at his very large desk. His MegaRon chair adjusted itself for his maximum comfort, reminded him politely to sit up straight and don't slouch, and would he like to see a short video on correct posture, certified by the ASfSUS, Inc. itself? Morgan pressed no, located the TruVal com, synched it with his own, pointed a few fingers, and found himself on the Internet, but couldn't get into any of his email services. His own com wouldn't pick up anything outside the building, either.

He knocked gingerly on Madelyn's door. "Yes, doctor?"

"I can't seem to read my email."

"Outside mail services are blocked, doctor. The whole building. You'll need a TruVal email ID. You'll need Technical to set it up."

"About how long...?"

"Put it on your list, doctor. End of the day, remember?"

Morgan explored on the company's com. Email wasn't the only service blocked. The only website he could access was TruVal.TV. After half an hour, however, thanks to sponsored links, he had web-crawled his way to a local TV station's site. He searched for news about a mysterious death on a Turk Street rooftop, but found nothing.

At five o'clock he opened the door to the outer office, handed Madelyn his request sheet. "I'll be going now," he said. He had an awful feeling that he'd be stopped if he tried to leave the building.

"Dr. Morgan? We've assigned you a flat in a building the company owns."

"What?"

"Just temporary. Detective DeLuca is concerned about your safety, so he asked us to look after you. You've been shot at once, you know, well, of course you know! And it doesn't take much sleuthing to find out where you live. I did it myself."

"And this flat is...?"

"On Telegraph Hill, doctor, not far from here. It's small, but cozy and has a wonderful view! Jimmy will take you there in one of the company cars, show you how to use the security system and all that."

Then she added "Jimmy can pick you up in the morning, too, if you like. He doesn't have enough to do around here." Morgan's momentary thrill regarding the privileges of rank was damped by the thought that for Jimmy, Morgan was only busywork. "No thanks, I'll be OK."

"Suit yourself," she shrugged.

"And if I'm in the flat and want to go out in the evening?"

"Well, be careful. And don't go near your house."

"You mean I won't be locked up in the flat 'for my own protection'?"

Madelyn regarded him quizzically. "Of course not, doctor; this is a free country, after all! For now it is, anyway."

A few minutes later, A stout man walked in, his belly swaying from side to side, and introduced himself as Jimmy, no last name. Madelyn waved a dismissive hand toward Morgan, said "Have a nice evening, doctor," went back to shuffling papers. Morgan left the building with Jimmy, the exit turnstile flashing green in response to Morgan's new badge, and got into a TruVal company car. They arrived a few minutes later at the Telegraph Hill building, without incident other than raised fingers from seven peds on the street. "Four floors, doctor, four flats" said Jimmy, "TruVal leases the top three. Each has its own street entrance, which is why they're called flats, not apartments, y'know. The second floor unit is Ms. Vallon's own, but she's hardly ever there. She has a residence suite right inside the TruPlex, all the comforts of home and no commute! And the fourth floor is where we put most of our temporary guests, like you."

Morgan wasn't pleased to walk up three flights, but the view made it all worthwhile: the Bay Bridge, Yerba Buena, the Campanile in Berkeley, and when he went to the bedroom and craned his neck far enough to the left he caught a glimpse of Sausalito, and Tiburon where he'd had several uneasy drinking bouts with colleagues from Physics and (more appropriately) from Toxicology.

He stared wistfully across the Golden Gate Bridge. There would never be a Starfleet Academy there, on the bare brown hills of Marin, nor anywhere else. No manned spaceflight again, ever. Billions of people were competing for the last of the planet's resources, demanding, fighting. Nothing was left over for grand adventures. And then there was all that space junk in orbit: the last outbound ship had collided with a piece. Not more than a foot across, NBC News said, but traveling at 30,000 mph, and that was more than enough to... He sighed, turned from the window and explored the rest of his new home.

The flat was fitted out with high-tech appliances, the purpose of some of which Morgan found mystifying. Furnishings were severe and angular but expensive, in the style that was still called "contemporary" even though it hadn't actually been contemporary for fifty years and more.

Jimmy caught Morgan staring at one particular appliance. It might have been a com, but it was attached to the wall. "That's a landline phone," said Jimmy. "Connects direct to TruVal."

"What on earth for?" Morgan hadn't seen a landline phone in years, barely remembered them, didn't know any still existed.

"Security. Y'know all them coms are insecure."

So am I right now, Morgan thought.

"They can pick up voices, y'know, right out of the air, don't need to tap into a wire or anything!"

Morgan didn't encourage Jimmy to elaborate on who "they" were. "Sure can," he responded, with an air of what he hoped was finality. He was tired and wanted to collapse into sleep.

Jimmy didn't catch the hint. He went on to point out the security system control panel, showed Morgan how to arm and disarm the system, how the duress code worked, what not to do so he wouldn't accidentally have the police at his door. Opening any windows or making scratching sounds, he told Morgan, was sure to set off the alarm. According to Jimmy, there were quite a few things Morgan might accidentally do or touch that would bring the police.

"And you don't want that to happen," said Jimmy, "unless you need 'em. Alarms get them fellows juiced up, y'know? And they're itchin' to kick ass or waste somebody, y'know? If the first thing they see is you, you'd better have a shit-eating grin on your face and your hands up in the air. Way up."

"OK, I get it," said Morgan, sidling toward the door, hoping Jimmy would get the idea that it was time for him to leave now, please?

"It's them SoCalls," Jimmy continued, warming to his topic. "Y'know they're death on smut and druggies and fags and liberals, and that's all to the good!"

Morgan wondered why Jimmy was working for TruVal, at least considering his attitude toward "druggies."

"But that's why we got all this security," Jimmy concluded. "Word could get around that this place here" (he waved his arms broadly, barely missing Morgan's nose) "is owned by TruVal. Then them SoCalls 'd be here in a minute, paradin' and threatenin' and picketin', maybe worse."

Jimmy finally left, ostentatiously setting the security panel to ON as he left. The panel beeped twice and flashed an angry red light three times, then retreated into quietly armed suspicion.

Morgan explored the flat in more detail. In the bathroom, he found a selection of male-oriented toiletries that seemed to have been selected by a woman. In the only closet, he found an assortment of clothing, and a note. "We bought you stuff to wear, doctor! and bathroom stuff too! Hope our selection is really cool and everything fits!" He wasn't surprised when he saw Renee's scrawled signature at the bottom. He examined the selection. A few items that might not fit him, but not bad; it would do for a week or so. He hoped that would be enough time to solve the mystery, apprehend the killer, and then this mess would be over. But he felt a twinge of regret at the thought that it might be over that soon. Was he enjoying all this skullduggery? It was kind of fun, wasn't it, being in the middle of a complicated murder plot with a lurking killer, a missing body, flying bullets, astonishing technology, beautiful women, hiding from a ruthless killer in an elegant Telegraph Hill flat, mysterious powerful forces at play, famous showbiz types depending on him, police acting like they did on television...

His dreams of glory were interrupted by a noise; the landline phone was ringing. Someone from TruVal making sure he was settled in, or perhaps they had news about the investigation. That must be it. He picked up the receiver.

"Hello?"

"Dr. Morgan?"

"Yes, that's me."

"Dr. Robert Morgan?"

"Yes, yes."

A click. More clicks. Then the dial tone began humming a tuneless sonata into his ear. Morgan began to sweat.

Chapter 11

The next morning, Morgan walked into his outer office. Madelyn looked up. Morgan spoke hesitantly and with a worried expression, glanced over his shoulder. "Madelyn," he said, "Ah, about that landline at the flat."

Madelyn had a moment of secret amusement. No, I'm not going to volunteer any information. Let him dig for it. "Yes?" she asked.

"Someone called, then hung up."

"Did you recognize the voice?"

"No."

Good! "Well, doctor," she said in what she pretended was a lulling tone, "I'm sure one of our staff was only making sure you had arrived all safe and sound and snug and..." Don't overdo it!

"But there were clicking sounds."

"That's the recording system, doctor. All our phone conversations are recorded. Didn't you know that?"

She made herself smile broadly, was amused at his look of discomfort. The angle of her body and the set of her teeth dared him to object to such a rational institution as corporate voice capture and monitoring. "Like they are at all large organizations these days." An excellent thought occurred to her, one she couldn't resist. "Or don't they do that at the university?" She silently counted: one, two, three. "Or perhaps they do record everything but they didn't tell you about it?"

She made her smile even broader. More teeth showed. Morgan, head tilted downward, retreated to his very large office and closed the door quietly behind him.

Madelyn pulled her upper lip back over her teeth, closed one eye, and made a "two thumbs up" gesture. Too late, it occurred to her to wonder if the events in her own office, not just his, were being secretly videoed.

Toward ten o'clock, Athena Taylor popped into Morgan's new office. "Good morning, Dr. Morgan. How are things going?"

Morgan regarded her sourly. "I'm not really doing anything here. I appreciate the hospitality, but I might as well be home for all the progress I'm making."

"I really think it's better for you here, Dr. Morgan. Safer." He picked up an ominous tone in her voice.

"It would be better if I had email and web access." Madelyn had taken his wish list, but nothing had been delivered, and Technical had not come to call.

Athena appeared thoughtful. "Yes, I can see how those could help. I'll have them set up right away." After a few minutes of chit-chat, she left Morgan alone. Within the hour, the TruVal, Inc. Technical Department called to inform him that he was now **morganr@truval**.tv, temporary password **DK54i!i!i3gpPq!G7854**, and please change it to something equally obscure the first time you use it. And don't write it down, you idiot.

Morgan signed on, searched for news bulletins about the murder, found nothing. He caught up on his email, including numerous Burkina Faso Lost-Fund Spam Scams and the equally numerous "You can grow your penis three inches longer today!" solicitations. Unfortunately, Athena took that moment to re-enter his office, this time without knocking, just as Nine-Inch Penis, formerly known as Six-Inch Penis, was displaying in 3.5D HD all over one wall. She pretended to ignore it.

"I came by to see if you're set up all right down here, welcome you to the company. Are we OK here?" She nodded toward the computer's unblinking eye.

"Yes, thank you."

"Fine. I also came to tell you that Detective DeLuca is here at TruVal, in my office upstairs. He'd like to speak with you."

"Good! How's the investigation coming?"

"I think you should ask him yourself."

Morgan followed Athena down the A corridor, up the E corridor, to an elevator that lifted them, floor by floor, to twenty six. Her office, Morgan noted, was only a few steps from Tru's.

Inside, Detective DeLuca was pacing, a determined expression on his face, brows wrinkled, mouth a straight line. He nodded at Morgan, then at a chair, then at Athena, then at the door. Morgan sat. Athena left the room.

"How's the investigation coming?" asked Morgan.

"Doctor, I need you to fill in a few blanks for me."

"What blanks?"

"First, I now believe that you did see a body."

"Well, thanks a lot!"

DeLuca ignored the sarcasm. "Second, as I have informed Ms. Taylor, I believe that the body was Terra Lewis's. It wasn't the case that her blood somehow just happened to get up on that roof."

Morgan digested that information.

"Here," said DeLuca, pulling his com out of his pocket, "here's a picture of Lewis that Ms. Taylor routed to me from TruVal corporate records. Tell me if you recognize her."

Morgan stared at the photo once, then again. "Ah, she's heavily made-up – and the corpse's face was made-up – and I all I got was a glimpse." He looked again, harder. "Could be. Could very well be. I couldn't rule it out."

"But no positive ID?"

"Sorry."

The detective circled the room impatiently. "Well," he finally said, "I'm going to assume it was Lewis, or I'm out of leads."

Morgan waited. DeLuca circled the room a few more times, fixed his eyes on a wall without focusing on it, scratched his head. "Who would come back to steal a corpse? Only one reason: he didn't want us to know it was Lewis who'd been killed. That must have been very important. So important that the killer would take the awful risk of returning to the scene. There was evidence that the site had been scrubbed down, as you know. We took samples of the chemicals the killer apparently was using. They're at the lab now, may give us a lead."

Morgan wondered why he'd been invited to sit in on this monologue.

"But the killer missed a few drops of her blood. The FBI had Lewis's DNA on file because she'd held a government security clearance a few years ago. We ID'd her from that."

The detective paused. "Dr. Morgan, I need your help. My captain wants to pull me off this case unless I make real progress in the next few days, mostly because there's still no solid evidence of a crime. Never will be, I think. This might be a pro job, and professional hit men are very good at putting bodies where they won't be found. But you're 'in' with TruVal now. Office here in the TruPlex, your own admin. All these women waiting on you. I suppose they might even be sexy when they're not dressed up like ghouls. I need you to help me here on this. And I know you will, because the killer is still out there and he's proved that he'd rather see you dead than alive."

"But," said Morgan, remembering Athena's words, "don't you suspect me of involvement in the crime?"

DeLuca regarded him with surprise. "Why in hell should I suspect somebody like *you*?" he asked, peering at Morgan as if he were an annoying but harmless mutapet.

Morgan absorbed that. "OK, OK, what do you want me to do?"

"Find out anything I could use, anything at all."

"Like?"

"Like I don't know! If I knew, I wouldn't need you! Whatever. A TruVal person has got to be involved, or at least knows a few things we don't."

"We could start with..."

"With what?"

"Well, have you considered the possibility that someone other than the killer might have removed the body?"

DeLuca took that in. "Well, that's possible. But it doesn't make a lot of sense to me."

"Or," Morgan persisted, "consider this: Who was the lookalike hooker Alex shared the couch with? Have you found her? Wouldn't she be in danger from the killer, exactly as Alex was? Wouldn't she be eager to have some protection from the police, in exchange for information?"

"We're not trying to find her, doctor. Didn't I tell you that last time?" He fixed Morgan with a stern eye. "I figure we could probably pick her up any time we wanted to, unless she's fled the city. These whores all have rap sheets, at least for illegal drugs, so they've been printed and DNA'd time after time. But here's the picture: we're short-handed and the Goddamn City Council and its niggardly Goddamn budget for the Department. So we're not searching for her. Not very hard. Not unless there's a better reason than I've heard so far." He sighed. "Without a compelling reason, if a witness won't come forward there's not a lot we want to do."

Morgan took that in, wondered if the detective's refusal to recognize the importance of the hooker was the right approach.

DeLuca paused, pointed his finger at Morgan's nose. "Leave the theorizing to me, doctor. You find out what you can; facts." He picked up his coat. "Snoop!" he snapped, and stalked out, closing the door firmly. For the first time, Morgan considered the possibility that this detective might occupy the bottom floor of the police department's metaphorical outhouse, and all the shit was running downhill.

But what could he do to help out? What kind of snooping? Data without a theory? In science, you don't collect data without first having a hypothesis, a theory that the data might confirm or refute. If he agreed to help the police, he'd need to develop a theory of the crime. But then it occurred to him that he hadn't been offered the opportunity to agree or disagree.

Chapter 12

The door didn't stay closed long before Athena entered. "Well, doctor, did you have an interesting time with the detective?"

"He's getting nowhere."

"And you will."

"Will what?" he asked.

"Get somewhere. Investigate. Solve the crime. If there was a crime!"

"Were you listening to us?"

"Of course. This company has a great deal to lose if the police keep thinking that a TruVal employee has been involved in a murder."

"And so...?"

"I want to help you investigate, doctor. If there's anything to be found out, I don't want to be blind-sided by the police. I'll give you free access to all our HR, contracts, and security files. We have hundreds of employees and freelancers, and CCTVs with sound sensors. You'll have plenty of investigating to keep you busy. Madelyn is available to help you, full time. And whenever you need me, let me know right away!" She smiled so innocently that it gave Morgan the willies.

Athena stepped back and stood inside the door, her body language more than hinting that Morgan should leave now. He did, and went back to the twelfth floor.

Madelyn greeted him cheerily. "Hi again, doctor! Ms. Taylor's office called. I've loaded all the links and passwords to all that stuff she promised you, on your computer. Happy hunting!" She turned away and resumed whatever she'd been doing.

So he was in it now, willy nilly.

Morgan entered his office, closed the door, and sat down in his expensive desk chair, which expressed a burst of level-one electronic gratitude. A subconscious imp was whispering "whiskey tango foxtrot" in Morgan's head, over and over. Athena and Madelyn knew he wouldn't find anything useful in the files they'd given him access to; they must want him to spin his wheels. But perhaps – perhaps what he couldn't find, what he wouldn't be allowed to find, might be, in itself, revealing. Data.

So here's theory one: TruVal was concealing information, one or more facts, that they considered important, at least embarrassing, perhaps incriminating.

First, he scanned the CCTV files. TruVal was very thorough. Every corridor, every office, every restroom except the toilet stalls themselves, was monitored; there were no other uncovered locations. He concluded that there would be no visual clues in the building as to whatever had happened to make Terra Lewis a candidate for murder.

Second, he called up Lewis's HR data. Nothing. Why? He checked the Security data. There she was: badge info, a photo identical to the one DeLuca had shown him. A few annotations: Terra had previously worked for the National Geographic, had once held a temporary but sensitive government appointment, was brought into TruVal as an independent contractor. That explained why HR had nothing on her: she was an indie, not an employee.

Morgan checked Terra Lewis's contract records, found a generic contract / non-compete / non-disclosure, timesheets, invoices for time and expenses. She had worked sporadically for TruVal, not routine forty-hour weeks, and had done quite a bit of traveling for the company. Some weeks she billed eighty, a hundred or more hours; other weeks, little or nothing. He wondered why. Her hourly rate was higher than he'd expected, even for an indie who had to fund her own benefits.

He went through the contract records over and over, trying to find a hint of what Terra had been doing for the company. Undercover work? Spying on the competition? But there was really no competition for TruVal, Inc.

Theory two: TruVal, at least the top managers, knew very well what Terra had been doing for the company, but wouldn't tell him. There must be a reason why they wouldn't.

Theory three: Terra had been doing a kind of work for TruVal, Inc. that would cause at least a scandal if anyone outside were to find out what it was. But what could that be? Hiding secrets in Tru's life? But celebrities thrived on that kind of thing. Whatever Tru was up to, unless it was actually criminal, could be a plus, not kept secret and covered up. Certainly not worth the risk of a discovered murder.

He flipped through Terra's recent travel records. A month ago, Singapore. And planned for next month, Singapore again. Now that was interesting. He dug deeper.

TruVal's travel department had numerous records pertaining to Lewis's two Singapore trips, one she had made, the other planned, but of course she wouldn't be on the plane this time. The records were complete and legitimate. Even a visa request in her own handwriting. Air tickets paid. And there was a work assignment for her there, a meeting at a Belgian-owned establishment on the river, right downtown, and a meeting with a Singapore-based TV production company. What kind of meeting? The records didn't indicate a purpose. TruVal business, clearly. The company had paid a non-trivial amount of money for those flights. First class, at that. And with the price of jet fuel these days, the cost of a trip to the far side of the world and back could have paid his university salary for a year.

Morgan got on the Internet. There was indeed a Belgian-owned firm operating at that location, a club; had been there many years. And the local production company existed and appeared legitimate, too.

His thoughts wandered on as the day aged. Shadows lengthened across his window. The hum of business quieted. Well-dressed people scurried out of tall buildings and headed for buses or the BART, or the nearest bar: evening lay upon the Bay. Morgan put his head down on the desk, harbored musings dark and dim. He'd never find out anything the way Madelyn and Athena were "helping" him. He'd eventually give up, go home, and die at the hand of some sinister conspiracy he'd never understood. He had a fantasy of poison gas seeping through the TruVal landline in his flat.

In despair, he slammed his fist down on the desk. What was that? He heard a faint tinkling sound from inside the desk. Examining the lower drawers that he hadn't bothered opening before, he found that one of them held a glass and a bottle of liquor. Whose office did this used to be? "Mary Ann's" was it? Wonder what she did for the company. Wonder why she'd left. Mary Ann had certainly left something behind that Morgan could use right then. Or perhaps it was a gift meant for him, a nice touch from Tru or Madelyn or Renee or Athena.

"I'll call this a clue," he told himself, "and study it extremely thoroughly!" He smiled as he pulled the glass out of the drawer, then the bottle, and twisted off the cork. About to pour, he froze in astonishment. It was Glenlivet. His own favorite brand. Who could know that?

Someone who'd been in his home, that's who.

The hand holding the bottle began to shake. Then he started to think. The bottle must be a message, a threat: stop snooping. Who would want that? The killer. But how could the killer get through TruVal's security? Unless – he didn't want to go there.

He finished pouring the drink, gulped it down. Shame not to sip good scotch, but he needed a courage-fix for the confrontation he was planning. He went back to the TruVal flat on Telegraph Hill and had an uneasy night's sleep.

Chapter 13

Harold put down his glass and leaned forward. "What if you got your own mem back," he asked, "one you dumped all those years ago, y'know, the desperate thing you should maybe never have done – if you did – and then you dumped it on some unsuspecting – but he was a mem-head, wasn't he? So it wasn't really wrong to do that, right? But last week I heard about this great mem, y'know, paid a lot for it. One of those gays getting pounded. Who knows how many heads that mem had gone through, one by one? Like a rumor, like that 'telephone' game the kids play. Ended up all wrong, y'know, not the way it was at all. No, I didn't do it, not to him, anyways at least, not that I remember. It wasn't that way at all … was it?"

The bartender nodded sympathetically. "Wanna nother beer?" he asked.

***

Robert Morgan, PhD, in the still-strange Telegraph Hill flat, stretched but not too vigorously, looked out his window across the bay. First sunlight was barely touching the graceful Campanile. While he ground coffee and heated water he made a resolution. "Never resolve" had been a good motto for him, fear disguised as principle. But now things had begun to be different. Shaved, dressed, coffeed, and coiffed, he walked with a longer stride than usual down the hill, to the TruPlex, into his borrowed office.

After reading his email, most of which was sexspam in a very loose approximation to English ("Enlarge your male dignity: Help it stay as tree!!") Morgan acted on his resolve. He slipped out of his office, waved a smile at Madelyn and was gone before she could say anything. He took the elevator to twenty-six. He'd corner Athena Taylor first. The security staff worked for her; she'd need to be involved in any case. He walked into Athena's reception area.

"Hi, Dr. Morgan!" It was Renee. "Gee it's just great to see our famous investigator again!"

"Investigator"? Morgan wondered. "Famous"? What kind of rumors had been circulating about him?

"Ms. Taylor isn't here right now," Renee continued, "but I'm sure she'd really want to see you if she were! Were here right now, I mean!"

Renee's cheeriness overwhelmed a Morgan still practicing his newly found determination. "Ah," he said slowly, attempting with a severe look to damp her incessant enthusiasm, "when do you expect her back?"

"Oh, she's down on the B-1 level, overseeing the prep for our big special! There's a studio there, a real one, you know, down there with the power plant and the IT servers and all that. I guess it's not a secret any more, the special that is, since the network's been running ads at all hours, but we still don't know exactly what's going to happen. Really exciting!" She beamed even more brightly at him. "Ms. Taylor knows, of course, but she won't tell!" Renee put on a mock-pout and winked at him.

He tried again. "When do you expect her back?"

Renee glanced at her com. "Oh, she's been down there for just ages, could be back any time!"

"OK if I wait?"

"Sure, that's great! Right through there," she gestured toward a glass-paneled door and wiggled several fingers. "That's the Executive Suite Waiting Suite. I'll tell Ms. Taylor you're here as soon as she returns!"

True to Renee's word, the glass door was elaborately inscribed "Executive Suite Waiting Suite." A freelance glass-etcher, three years before, had thought so highly of his rendition of "Suite" that he'd taken it into his head to repeat it. At least that was one rumor. A competing rumor had it that he was being paid by the letter and needed the cash for his ex-wife.

Morgan looked dubiously at the glass. What corporate jughead had made up a clumsy name like that?

Renee misunderstood his hesitation. "It's OK! And I'm sure Ms. Taylor will be here in a jiffy before you know it! And she'll just *love* to speak with you!" Renee's next smile was one of affectionate dismissal.

Morgan opened the door and entered the suite, not quite knowing what to expect. He was pleasantly surprised, however, at how "suite" it was. At airports, he'd occasionally caught glimpses of first-class airline club rooms through doors that had been firmly shutting in his face. The TruVal, Inc. waiting suite, done up in the company's decorator color "TruBlu," outclassed them all. He was greeted by a hushed receptionist and shown to a squishy leather chair in a quiet corner. She hung over him briefly, her breasts reminding him of two of the more notable Alps. She briefly and efficiently pointed out the soundproof areas for com use, choice of couches and chairs, private massage and shower area, men's room with all the tingling, smell-creating and smell-destroying chemicals he could ever want, a buffet table with a vast spread of delicacies. Music of massed digital violins pervaded the room without seeming to come from any one place, or play any particular tune.

Last, but what Morgan was hoping for at the moment, there was a magnificently accoutered bar, complete with smiling bartender, towel draped over one arm. Ex-assistant professor Robert Morgan, who'd never been on a flight in any class other than coach, and who had absolutely never been in an airline club room of any class or with any class, was awe-struck. Maybe Athena would forget about him and he could spend the rest of his life here being fed, massaged, clothed, liquored, and happy. The receptionist returned to her station, wriggling her slim ass at him. He turned to the bartender, caught himself about to apologize for the early hour, and asked for a Glenlivet, neat.

Morgan needed something to read while he waited, to keep his mind from going in circles thinking about his mind. There: in racks, and carefully-carelessly arranged around the room, were all the showbiz zines he could ever want. A coffee table held an assortment of coffee table photography books. All this hard copy, he thought, must have cost a fortune to pull off the web and print on such beautiful, thick, rich, creamy paper. Morgan flipped through a few of the books, caressing each page with his fingertips. The photos did have a depth and richness of color, he had to admit, a sensuality that wallscreens couldn't match. One book caught his eye: fashion shots, including several of Truda Vallon, in exotic parts of the world: Macau, Estoril, Niamey, Bequia, Jumeirah Beach. Interested, he turned back to the cover. "Photography," it read, "by Terra Lewis." Morgan jumped in his seat. So Lewis had been a photographer! That could explain a lot. But what?

The bartender approached with his drink. "Here you are, sir. Glenlivet. Excellent choice, sir. That's Miss Vallon's own favorite liquor, ah, in a Rob Roy, of course." He sniffed slightly, as if to clear the odor of sweet vermouth from his mind.

Now that Morgan realized that Lewis had left a significant record, it occurred to him to look her up on the web. He googled her on his com and studied the first few pages. Yes, she was a respected photographer, even risking her life to shoot in war zones. A lengthy profile recorded her personal and professional life, and mentioned her zealousness to get the shot at whatever cost to the bruised feelings of friends, lovers, models, subjects, politicians, and other photographers.

Morgan found two more books of Lewis's photos. The first was of live concerts, bands of young people who apparently hadn't struck it rich yet and probably never would: hubes in a world of sims. Their music hummed at him as he flipped each page, triggering the book's micro-recordings. The groups weren't much, and certainly weren't well staged or lighted, but the photography was excellent, especially considering the conditions Lewis had been forced to work in. Page after page, Morgan become more fascinated by her mastery of light and shape, the contest between harmony and invention.

Her next book was darker: raw photojournalistic shots of generals, authorities, talking heads, world leaders, famous people Lewis had caught in compromising situations, or speaking with the wrong people at the wrong time. A Hollywood Babylon of faces and bodies, except these weren't entertainers, but real people conducting their dirty business away from the world stage. "Power," Lewis had written in the introduction, "is their sex, and conspiracy is their foreplay."

Morgan sipped his drink and sank back into leather that gave a sensuous gentle wheeze of murmuring surrender whenever he shifted his weight. He pondered long and hard about what he'd discovered about Terra Lewis. He asked for another drink, and another. After a time he'd been too comfortable to measure, he felt a touch on his shoulder. "Dr. Morgan?" Renee was standing over him, looking worried. "Are you all right?"

A very attractive young woman, he realized. Even prettier when she wasn't bubbling over with joy. A lazy grin spread over his face. He opened his mouth to say a few words he knew he shouldn't utter, thought better of it at the last second. Finally, "I don't think I care" was all he said.

"Well," she smiled, "just perk up!" In spite of his distaste for her jauntiness, her continual "just"-ing, Morgan smiled back. "Now," she said, "I just have to let you know that Ms. Taylor's back in her office, and she'd just *love!* to see you now, so you can just get out of this awful place, the 'Sour Suite' we call it around here!" Renee stepped back, entirely too happy with herself.

***

At least that was the impression Renee was careful to give: simple and happy. But that would not have satisfied her longing for – how did that old movie put it? – "a life of significance." Not much longer now, another few weeks then no more need to pretend. Renee's face slipped into hardness for an instant, recovered before Morgan could notice.

People were depending on her, Renee knew. She was pleased at the thought.

***

In another place, another time zone, one man was thinking, just then, how much he was depending on Renee. Perhaps too much. Perhaps that was a problem. He frowned. A problem that was keeping him awake. He did not like that feeling. He did not like problems.

***

As Morgan stood up, Renee noticed a look in his eye she hadn't seen in their brief prior meetings. What's got into him? Not too many of those awful drinks that Antonio serves, I hope!

I'll just take him in to the Goddess. Gosh, I'd better watch that. I might call Ms. Taylor "The Goddess" right out loud one day, and then wouldn't that be just awfully embarrassing?

"Just go right on in to Ms. Taylor's office, Dr. Morgan." She stepped out of his way.

Maybe, she thought, everything was working out OK after all; certainly Morgan seemed harmless enough, and that detective DeLuca: smart and nosy, but he was about to be moved on to another case, she'd heard, or even pushed off to another city's PD. She hung back as Morgan left. She winked at Antonio, who gave her a thumbs-up.

But Morgan didn't go right on in. Drink had raised his sense of determination as it lowered his level of prudence. "Give Athena my apologies, please," he said to Renee as he strode past her door, went another thirty paces, opened the door of Truda Vallon's office suite, and pushed past two startled young Trudites. He walked up to Tru's desk and stood in front of her, legs spread in what he hoped was the kind of he-manly pose that might intimidate her.

She looked up at him and laughed.

Chapter 14

"Well, doctor, you seem to be thoroughly annoyed," said Tru.

"What's going on?"

"What's going on about what?"

"Everything."

"Robert, I do believe you've been drinking on duty, and in the morning, too." She frowned, but not unkindly. Morgan looked down at his hand, realized it was still clutching a glass engraved "Glenlivet" in fancy cursive lettering.

"Well, I'm not the one here who does drugs," he retorted, not quite accurately.

"You mean drugs other than my expensive single-malt? Wait a minute. All this hype about my being a druggie? 'Her Highness'? Not true."

"Not 'Tru'?"

"To clear the air between us, Robert: Once in a while, yes, I take a few pills, smoke a little dope. But not much, and not very often. My PR department said I'd seem more dangerous, whatever that means, if they put out a few misleading stories." She glanced up with a frown, as if not sure that turning her PR department loose had been a good idea.

"Now sit down," she continued. "This is the busiest week we've ever had here, but I'll always have time for you." She waved him to a chair beside her desk as he caught her glancing at her desk clock.

"Now, Robert, I shouldn't be teasing you," she said, "because Terra's death – if she is dead – is very serious and I know you've been doing your best to help us out here. That's really important because that detective seems to have given up. It's up to us, now." Morgan got a slight but not unpleasant mental jolt when Tru said "us." "It's only, well, this Sunday

I'm having another 'TV' TruVal special instead of the usual weekly show, our fourth special and the biggest one yet. I'm sure you've picked up on all the buzz here in the office."

"There's a lot of frenzy, and a lot of secrecy."

"We're building suspense, Robert, and I don't want those newsies reporting what I do before I do it. They'd build it up too big, and then there'd be disappointment. Inevitably. But it's very big."

"Premiering a new song? I heard about that."

Tru beamed. "Yes, Robert, a wonderful new song that Si and his team wrote for me, and a new dance to go with it. We've been rehearsing all week on the fourteenth floor practice stage, and down on the B-1 level as well. That's where the network crew will be broadcasting from." The smile vanished. "Now I wouldn't want any news about Terra to get out and distract my fans' attention from the big event, would I?" Tru looked at her nails, placed one under another and flicked out a piece of dust.

"Of course, if you've solved the crime, then call Detective DeLuca immediately. But if not, well, then, I'd appreciate..." She spread her hands, tilted her head, and shrugged one shoulder. "Are you OK with that?"

That sounded too easy, too slick. "There's more investigating to be done," Morgan said. "Too many loose ends. For one thing, no one has seen the woman who was with Alex, or made any attempt even to contact her. For another, I just now found out that Terra was a professional photographer. Was she taking pictures from that rooftop? Of what? Of Alex and the woman? Was it a shoot, or did she have blackmail in mind? Or another reason to be up there? And how could anyone blackmail a junkie like Alex, or blackmail a hooker? Why was Lewis's being on that roof so threatening to someone that she'd be killed because of it? And why was she there in the first place? I imagine you've got quite a few talented photogs around. A chance victim? But there's all this cover-up, or at least a diversion, about two trips to Singapore. It doesn't make sense." He stopped, realized he'd worked himself into a state.

Tru reached out a hand and touched his, very briefly. "Too many questions, Robert, but no action. In all you've said, I don't hear a plan. I think we're through. Nothing will bring Terra back, if she's really been murdered. Let's drop it. It's a matter for the authorities, anyway, not for us amateurs. As long as things can be kept quiet until after the special."

"OK, OK. A plan. Well. Now. Hmm. I want to find the woman who was with Alex. The lookalike."

"Why? Her mem wouldn't be much different from Alex's, which is in your head now."

"Not the mem, but what she knows."

"Nothing, I'd guess! Just a hooker, wasn't she?"

"Don't know," he said. "We've all been assuming that, and Alex certainly thought so, but maybe she wasn't. Maybe she was there because she'd arranged for Terra's murder and wanted to see it happen."

"That's ghoulish!" Tru exclaimed.

"Not necessarily. Perhaps she wanted to assure herself that the job was done right."

Tru pursed her lips. "Well, in your mem, Alex's mem I mean, did the woman on the couch – the hooker – seem startled? Or did she react to the gunshot like she'd been expecting it?"

Morgan recalled the mem, the smells of bad dope and dirty clothes, the writhing figure in front of him, himself seeing the window over a pale, glistening shoulder. "I think," he said, "she was just as surprised as Alex was."

Tru nodded.

Morgan put on a grim face and said the first thing that came into his mind. He was being pushed by Tru, and he didn't like it. "Well, the plan. OK, we need a theory, a plan. Then here it is: I'm going to call DeLuca and ask him to dust Alex's apt for fingerprints. We'll find your lookalike." So there!

Tru gave a small, startled jump in her chair. "Now Robert, what on earth good would locating that woman do? Haven't we disposed of anything she could bring to the investigation?"

"I don't know, and you don't know. But it's a plan, and you wanted a plan. Better than sitting here in the TruPlex and doing nothing!"

"But you said she seemed surprised. That means she had nothing to do with Terra, didn't know in advance there'd be a shooting."

"You wanted a plan!"

Tru seemed about to object, then shrugged. "OK, OK. But would DeLuca arrange for fingerprinting? Crime scenes don't always get dusted, and Alex's apt isn't a crime scene at all."

"He'd dust it if I told him the murderer had been in Alex's apt. We're pretty sure the killer saw the note on Alex's door. Perhaps he went inside to find Alex, and left a fingerprint."

"Do you think he did?"

"No, I doubt it very much. I'll lie."

Morgan left Tru's office and descended to the twelfth floor, intending to call DeLuca right away. But as soon as he entered his outer office, Madelyn held the com out to him. "It's Tru!" she mouthed. He took the com from her.

"Yes?"

"Robert, I'm glad I could catch you before you went back to the flat. I've been thinking about our plan."

Suddenly it's *our* plan? "What about 'our' plan?" he asked.

"You and I should go to Alex's apt. Ask him how he hooked up with the hooker, or whatever she was. Ask him if she acted suspiciously or anything like that."

"How do you know he'll be home?"

"Maybe he won't be. But in that case we can look around his place, can't we? Maybe we could find something interesting."

Morgan hesitated. "The police..."

"We'll make a quick visit. In and out. If Alex is there and objects, then of course we won't."

"Ah, I guess, OK."

"How's tomorrow morning first thing?"

"Well, OK."

"Fine!" she said. "I'll swing by the flat at eight sharp and we'll go from there."

"OK."

"OK."

"Thank you, Robert! You're wonderful!"

Morgan had a pleasant buzz at being called wonderful by a star like Tru, and by such an attractive, world-famous, rich one at that. Coming out of his reverie, he called DeLuca. He wasn't at the station, or wasn't picking up. Morgan left him a long obscure voicemail about having discovered important info, really big, about the lookalike and needing Alex's apt dusted for her fingerprints and the murderer's right away, so they could ID them both. And DNA while you're at it, please. Then he took Mary Ann's bottle of Glenlivet to the TruVal flat. Tru's phrase "Thank you, Robert! You're wonderful!" kept echoing in his mind. Now that was too good to be true. But he pushed any doubts out of his mind as he fondly and slowly contemplated a possible future erotic encounter with Tru. The real one, this time, not a wannabe. He undressed, uncorked the bottle, and had a wonderful, sick, awful Highland wipeout.

Chapter 15

While Morgan was slipping into a delighted stupor, many small things were happening in America, and one big thing. For example, a God's eye view of the country could have revealed the following events, among many others:

• Ed Beacham of Conway, South Carolina, sat down to write a letter to his local newspaper. "If you want to stop all the building here, then you better get used to paying more taxes," he began. He went on at length until his wife reminded him, forcefully, that he'd promised to fix a broken window latch that evening.

• As the last item on the monthly agenda of the Zoning Commission of Waxahachie, Texas, one Evelyn Hocutt requested a Specific Use Permit to operate a restaurant at 5328 South Rogers Street, being Block 30 of Bullard's Addition. After minimal discussion, and after each Commission member silently remembered his or her desire to go home to dinner, Ms. Hocutt's request was approved unanimously.

• The President of the United States decided to send a littoral assault ship group and an additional 75,000 troops to Baluchistan, despite impeachment threats from the majority party in Congress. "Screw those weak-kneed bastards," he said to his private secretary, "we have to do this. Get General Russell on the com for me. And Senator Gooding, too."

• In the B-1 level of a building in San Francisco, a scientist reviewed data from the latest test of a new technology. The scientist nodded to himself and smiled. That was the one big thing that happened that day.

***

Exactly at eight the next morning, a long black TruVal company limo appeared in front of the building on Telegraph

Hill and sounded its horn three times, briefly enough not to seem peremptory. Morgan left his flat, walked downstairs, got in. Tru was with the same two bulky butchy Trudites he'd seen on his first visit to TruVal, the ones with the not-so-small firearms. Tru introduced them as Serena and Melody, waved Morgan onto the fold-down jump seat.

"Security guards," she said. "They're from Athena's Protect and Serve Department. And if we have any problems getting into Alex's apt, well, they'll make it easy for us."

They reached Alex's building, commandeered a "no parking any time" space. The Trudites exited the car first, acting like Secret Service agents escorting at least a Presidential cousin. A few peds on the street stopped and stared. As Tru got out of the car and walked to the apt house entrance, several pointed at her and whispered, snapped photos with their coms.

"Do you enjoy being stared at like this?" Morgan asked, as they ascended in the creaky elevator and arrived at the fifth floor.

"Once in a while I do. But sometimes it's too much."

"Like now."

"I'd rather be anonymous right now."

"If you didn't have Serena and Melody along, no one would..."

"Suspect that I'm the real Tru? I thought of that. But I didn't know what we might find here. There are people, dangerous types, a threat once in a while."

At that moment the four arrived at Alex's door, Tru in the lead. She knocked. No answer. Knocked again. Then she nodded at Serena – or was that Melody? Morgan wasn't sure which was which – who did something with her hands and two small pieces of metal. Whatever it was, the door opened quickly and quietly.

Tru smiled. "We're in!" and entered with the Trudites, trailing Morgan behind. One of the guards did a quick scan for danger, then stood back. The other remained just inside the door, in a heightened state of alert.

Morgan poked around the apt. Someone had been there since Morgan had visited. Probably Alex. Who else would want the place? The closet had clothes in it now, although no cleaner than before, and another layer of dirty dishes had appeared in the kitchen sink. The broken part of the large window had been covered with a large flattened cardboard box, held in place by masking tape that was slowly peeling away.

There was the couch, in the same place as in the mem. Morgan looked out the window to the rooftop across Turk Street. A yellow police-line ribbon fluttered near where he had seen Terra fall.

Tru, meanwhile, had been examining the apt. She opened the cover of a songchip player. "Robert, didn't you say your mem had music? Do you remember the song?"

"No, not really. Didn't much like it." Too late, Morgan recalled that he'd thought, in his / Alex's mem, that it might be one of Tru's songs, and now he was putting it down. He couldn't figure out how to apologize, so he said nothing. "Why?" he asked.

"Well, the player's empty now."

"Yeah, I saw it was empty when I was here before."

Morgan surveyed the apt again, trying to concentrate. Outside in the hallway, where he couldn't see them, two people had raised their voices.

***

Harold was staring at Hazel. Unlike their previous scene in this hallway, the location of their private hell, this time Harold's tone was one of pleading. Hazel, for a change, sounded exasperated, but in control of the situation.

"Well, Harold, are you happy now?" Of course Harold wasn't happy right then. He was, in fact, twitching.

"Jesus God, Hazel! Why didn't you tell me?"

Hazel gazed at him sadly, about to utter the most damaging lie she could think of. "I'd hoped that wouldn't make a real difference between us. That you'd be sensitive enough to realize, emotionally, what really matters, is..."

"Hell with 'emotionally'! Don't you know what you – did to me? I feel – dirty!" The twitching grew more pronounced.

Hazel seemed to be enjoying turning the – shall we say "screw"? She put on a deeply disappointed look, shook her head sadly. "Is that the way you really feel, Harold, about us? About what we did? Or are you just picking up on what you heard in that bar you hang out in, or what that awful commentator keeps saying on TV, or..."

Her words were lost in a stamping of angry feet that gradually faded. Hazel remained in the hallway. Gradually, she brightened, gave a small sigh, and opened the door of her apartment.

***

Morgan heard a hallway door close. Idly, he wondered what the confrontation had been about, shrugged, and returned to the business at hand.

The mem had been a single point of view: past the lookalike's shoulder, out the window, to the rooftop. Morgan hadn't had a good view of the rest of the apt from Alex's mem, or even of the couch. He'd had only the feeling of padding under his knees and the outline, against the setting sun, of a piece of furniture he and the lookalike had been kneeling on, he behind her. He went to the window again, and stared out.

Tru joined Morgan at the window. "Sorry, Robert. I don't see anything useful here. I think I've wasted your time."

"What were you expecting to find?" he asked.

"I don't know. Nothing, perhaps."

"Well, we found it."

"What?"

"Nothing."

"Are you still going to call DeLuca?" she asked.

"To have the place dusted?"

"Yes."

"I already called him. Late yesterday; left a message. I wanted him to find out who the hooker was. Don't know if he'll do it or not."

They returned to the street, now thronged by dozens of fans breathlessly waiting for their favorite superstar to emerge. Melody and Serena pushed them back as gently as feasible, and Tru waved to them as she and Morgan got into the car. They drove toward the TruPlex.

On the way, Morgan asked "I've been curious, and I hope it's OK to ask, is 'Truda Vallon' your real name?"

"Why?"

"The tabloids, webloids I should say. None of them seem to have found any record that you exist. There's apparently no birth certificate, for example."

Tru laughed. "Maybe I don't exist! But now I know an interesting fact about you: you read the 'bloids, and you believe what they say, too!"

"In this case..."

"Well, Robert, I'll admit that 'Truda Vallon' isn't my birth name. Quite a few people know that small fact, actually."

"What *is* your birth name?"

"Top secret. Have to kill you etc. etc. But nothing exotic; a very ordinary American name."

"Which is one reason no one's been able to trace..."

"Exactly."

Melody and Serena let Tru and Morgan out at the executive entrance and drove off into the building's garage.

Tru turned to Morgan. "Robert, about the big special we're doing this Sunday. The network's coming to us this time. We're broadcasting from our studio on the B-1 level, as I mentioned before. The audience is of course always hand-picked, and I'd be very pleased if you'd be part of it. And the party afterwards. The party will be in the studio, too."

"Certainly," Morgan said. "I'll even hide in back so the TV audience won't know that one of your fans is middle-aged and going bald!"

"Don't worry about hiding your face, Robert." Morgan glowed at the compliment. "The network cameramen are really careful about who they show on camera." His glow dimmed rapidly.

Morgan took his leave of Tru and got on the elevator, headed for his office to see if there was anything for him to do. Perhaps DeLuca was there with a new clue. Or perhaps Madelyn's shell had cracked and she'd discovered a human being inside. Neither was likely. He sighed, then on the spur of the moment pressed floor B-1 instead of 12. He wanted to see how the prep for the special was coming, catch more of whatever excitement was happening in the building, get a whiff of the greasepaint.

Chapter 16

At just that moment, Senator Gooding was clicking off from his call with the President. He had been deferential, of course, especially as he and the President were members of the same party. But – 75,000 more troops! That would certainly cause reverberations around the world, and all this President could think of was victory in one more dirt-poor piss-ant ex-colony. The Senator resolved to pick up the pace of his own plans. He looked at the ornamental clock on his office wall. It wasn't polite to call North Korea at this hour, but considering the importance of what he had to say, he'd be pardoned. He whispered a number into his highly secured com.

***

Morgan stepped off the elevator on the B-1 level and into the middle of a heated discussion. The network staff, it seemed, were at odds with Tru's staff about some arcana of gels and bounce boards and scrims and half-scrims and cetera cetera. Three uniformed TruVal guards were trying to keep peace between the two factions.

No one noticed Morgan as he walked past the small but agitated group, and moved off into a dark corridor, hoping to see a real stage set. He turned a corner, walked down another corridor, saw an open door.

And walked right into what had to be a memlab: Cots, probes, bottles of head-gel, computer displays of brains sectioned off and labeled like sides of beef. He was alone in the room. He examined the setup more closely, followed wires to walls, peered behind LC3D displays and IT eyes. This was no stage set; it was real. A real memlab, in the TruPlex! But far more complex than any of the three memlabs Morgan had been in at various times in his life. There were more computers, more displays, and four or five machines whose function he couldn't imagine. And more scrims and gels and boards. This was indeed a stage set – but one that really worked. The show must be going to feature a fully operational memlab! He envisioned Tru jumping and dancing from machine to machine, singing about happy memories she'd bought. Or perhaps she'd have a mournful song for the occasion, like "You didn't just send my ring back, you dumped our sexmem, too, you jerk." Could be clever, could be funny, could be sad.

***

So silently that Morgan didn't hear him, another man slipped into the room, observed him poking around the machines. The man was, as it will turn out, distantly connected to the murder of Terra Lewis, but related by such an obscure chain of causal and organizational links that no one would ever, as the Americans say, "'connect the dots." Karl-Heinz Stirner had never heard that particular saying in the months since he had arrived from the old country to take charge of – a particular research project. Research and development, actually.

This must be that Morgan I've been hearing about, Stirner thought. Rather unimpressive, isn't he? Doesn't seem to consider well-pressed clothing a priority. Or well-combed hair, what there is of it. He knew people like that at the *Universität* Freiburg. A few of them had first-rate minds. Most didn't. Or very bright but always disorderly, undisciplined, unable to concentrate on the single thing, the goal, the solution. Morgan was like a child in a toyshop right then, Stirner considered. He's about to connect that red wire to that blue wire for no more reason than to see what would happen. Stirner knew what would happen, because he had designed that machine. Morgan must be stopped before he could do something – regrettable.

***

Hearing a cough, Morgan wheeled around so suddenly that he almost pulled the red and blue wires out of the machine. "Ah," he said. "Ah. Uh."

Stirner had a mental image of Morgan as a loin-cloth'd primitive, randomly tearing things apart to find out what made them work and muttering prayers to the tribal god.

"Dr. Morgan!" he said, "Very glad to meet you at last." Smile, hand out. Morgan aimed his own hand for it, missed slightly, reddened. "Ah," again.

Morgan considered the figure before him. An interesting man, he concluded: tall, slim, very well groomed, quite attractive in a stern, unbending sort of way. Carried himself easily, but precisely. Long, thin nose. And a slight German accent. But he couldn't imagine him at a party. Not a party-party. Maybe a Party party, though, something from the late nineteen-thirties. All he lacked was a monocle.

"My name is Karl-Heinz Stirner," the man said, "and this," waving a newly freed and graceful right hand, "is the device we have been developing here. For Ms. Vallon's television special."

Morgan recovered his composure. "What does it do? Over and above being a standard memlab memory transplant machine, I mean."

"I'm not at liberty to tell you that now, doctor. All will be revealed during Miss Vallon's television show this Sunday. But believe me, you will be interested. Professionally interested in my work, that is, as a fellow scientist."

"And your field is...?"

"I have doctorates in neurology and psychology. Experimental psychology. I hasten to add 'experimental,' that is, not 'clinical,'" he smiled, "because when meeting people, if I merely say 'psychology,' they will worry that I'm reading their minds."

Well, Morgan thought, if he knows they think he's reading their minds, then he must be reading their minds. "Yes," he answered carefully, "'clinical' can be off-putting. Now when I say 'I'm a physicist,' I don't arouse fear, just a roomful of glassy..."

***

This bit of academic chit-chat could have continued on, since both men were enjoying it. But Morgan was cut off in mid-sentence when a handful of men and women burst into the memlab room, stopped talking abruptly, and stared at him. The newcomers were dressed in that worn, shabby fashion that, in mid-nineteenth century America, would have been associated with the utterly destitute. But in the twenty-first century the look was high fashion among TV technicians, gaffers, best boys, and others whose jobs paid them, per hour, about five times as much as Morgan had ever earned as an assistant professor of physics. Stirner gave Morgan a slight nod, turned and left the room.

Guards were called. Morgan was asked who he was, where he belonged, and what the hell he was doing there, sir, was pushed and shoved, had his badge examined, stared at, shaken in disbelief that anyone like him, a middle-aged male, could actually be an Authorized Person here.

A large woman who appeared to be the guard in charge stared at him three separate times, as if she expected to see something different each time. "OK, Dr. Morgan. OK, you don't remember anything you saw here, OK? Not until after Ms. Vallon's Sunday special, OK?" She "assisted" Morgan onto an elevator, selected the twelfth floor for him, gave him one last grim "OK?"

"OK," he replied weakly.

On his way back to his office, Morgan mused about the possibility of dumping a mem of seeing the TruVal memlab, and then dumping the mem of having dumped that mem. Then what kind of mem would be left?

Chapter 17

Robert and Helen Morgan married in 2012. In later years they blamed each other for proposing, for accepting, for not backing out, for letting their marriage suffer its gradual silent corruption. Helen had married a promising young physicist; Robert had married the only woman who seemed satisfied with his love-making skills.

But then Robert fell behind in his profession, and Helen began tolerating sex with him less often. Each blamed the other for both. About the year 2015 she started calling him "Bob," a nickname she knew he hated. This was about the time that Physics Chair James Whistler O'Neill also began calling him "Bob." Morgan suspected the worst, although he was mistaken. About O'Neill, anyway.

Morgan grew bald; Helen grew pudgy. In 2019 they went through a "no-fault" divorce, which should in their case have been called "both-fault." Fortunately there had been no children, nor more than a handful of stored embryos, nor much property to divide.

By 2030, Morgan had long since lost track of Helen, assumed he'd never hear from her. But today they will meet again, and not for the last time.

***

Morgan got off the elevator, strolled down the empty corridors, came past a corner and into his outer office, intending to ask Madelyn if she knew anything about the memlab on the B-1 level of the building.

And stopped cold. Seated next to Madelyn was a woman in deep conversation with her. It was Helen! He hadn't seen since their last harrowing confrontation had left him shaken and sweating.

Helen turned in her chair. "Bob!" she said, with too much enthusiasm, "How wonderful to see you again, and after all this time!" She observed him, Morgan thought, like a shark watching a skin diver and looking for the softest part. "You poor dear!" she continued, never one to spare a cliché when one was handy. "I heard all about what happened to you. Finding a body! I'd just die!"

Morgan warmed at the prospect, but didn't let his expression change.

"And being shot at! And having that awful memory transplant!"

What had Madelyn been telling her?

"What are you doing here?" he asked.

"Oh, killing time, or maybe 'killing''s not such a great thing to say right now!"

"How did you get in the building?"

"My friend Madelyn, here, signed me in as her visitor."

Madelyn smirked. Make that two sharks. "And now," Helen said, "Madelyn's twisted a few arms and got me a ticket to be in the studio audience at Sunday's big special, and the party afterward. Isn't that excellent?"

"Ah, sure! Wonderful!" exclaimed Morgan, retreating to his office and closing the door. Behind him, he heard an occasional cackle of triumphant laughter, and a blurred sound that might have been his name, repeated over and over.

Later, far too late to stem his impatience, Morgan thought he heard sounds of Helen's taking her leave. A few minutes later, Madelyn stuck her head inside the door. "It's that Detective DeLuca," she said, clicking her com.

Morgan clicked on his own com, closed the door. "Yes? Did you get my message about fingerprinting Alex's apt?"

"Yeah," DeLuca answered. "Your dumb idea. Big waste of time."

Morgan breathed annoyance.

"We did that, doctor, we printed the place. Anything useful there, you and your girlfriend and her thugs seem to have obliterated it."

"Girlfriend?"

"I checked with TruVal security. That was after I'd gone to all the trouble of getting a warrant and sending out a tech to dust that apt. The lab reported back just now. Why did we find prints of Truda Vallon and two of her security crew, and you?"

"We were investigating."

"Screw that. I wanted you to snoop inside the TruPlex, not fart around in my crime scene. Not to mention private property."

"Well, it isn't officially a crime scene. Is it?"

"It's close."

"OK!"

"OK, but it's still private property."

"If I were a detective," Morgan said, "I'd be worried about warrants and all that. But I'm not."

"Not what? Not worried, or...?"

"Not a detective."

"That's for damn sure!"

"Well, I'm sorry. But you printed the place? What did you find?"

"Piss little, like I said. You and the TruVals. And Alex, of course, and old prints from half the junkies in the Tenderloin."

"But no women?"

"Couple of hookers, but they checked out; hadn't been with Alex in weeks."

"And DNA? Did you test for DNA on the couch?"

"There was no DNA on the couch; we scanned for it. No sign that couch had ever been in intimate contact with leaky human plumbing. From what you told us, there didn't seem to be much reason to look anywhere but the couch."

"Not even Alex's DNA?"

"Nope. We don't have Alex's DNA on file, doctor. He doesn't have an arrest record, although if I were the beat cop there I'd have run him in several times myself. And he's never applied for a security clearance, thank God for saving America from dreck like him!"

Morgan's 'com screen went blank, but DeLuca's voice carried on. What's he doing that for? Morgan wondered, missing DeLuca's next several words, and losing the thread of the conversation.

"… no DNA on the couch," the detective continued. "None. And because of that, there was no point typing Alex's. Couldn't have got a court order for that, even if we'd bothered trying."

"Ah..."

"Now will you either butt out, Doctor, or dig up some useful info there at TruVal?"

"Useful information," Morgan said. "Hmmm. Well, I found out that Terra Lewis was a professional photographer."

"I knew that."

"And didn't tell me?"

"Not important. That's why she went to Singapore, it turns out: to do a fashion shoot at a nightclub."

"So?"

"So the trip she took was TruVal business. And legit."

"But why did she plan to go again, that soon after the last time? And why did she end up on that rooftop instead?"

"Looking into that, Doctor, is how you might make yourself useful."

Chapter 18

Morgan left the TruPlex and trudged toward the corporate guest suites, puffing up the steep incline. The Telegraph Hill building came into sight.

Morgan climbed the stairs to the fourth floor, settled down in his flat, and called the nearest Rollin'InDough Pizza. Pineapple and jalapeños. No, that's correct, should I repeat it? He poured himself a double scotch and sat down to think. DeLuca was ignoring the lookalike for a good reason: what info could she add to what they already knew? And yet, Morgan felt that the hooker was the key to the mystery. "Item," he said to himself, "No DNA on the couch." That meant no bodily fluids. Why not? Perhaps he, Alex rather, didn't – ah – emit any fluids, and neither did she. Wasn't that unlikely? Or maybe there was a slip cover on the couch that someone had been thoughtful enough to remove. What did he remember? What did Alex / Morgan remember?

He sat back, closed his eyes, and called up the mem once more. He told himself it was to search for clues, but the idea of a sexual turn-on was in his mind, too. Well hell, he'd paid for a sexmem, not a murder mystery. Couldn't he just enjoy himself?

BEGIN MEM (RERUN)

A soft knock at the door. Alex / Morgan reaches out a hand, unlocks, opens. A woman enters, wearing the Truda Vallon "uniform." She glances up, gives him / him an uneasy smile, hands him a songchip, asks him to put it in his player. She walks past him toward the couch.

Morgan recognizes the corner of Turk and Hyde five stories below. Across the street, he / he sees a rooftop. It is late afternoon, sunlight coming straight in. "Tru" kneels wrong-way forward on the couch, smiles back at him / him. It strikes him as odd that she doesn't ask what kind of action he wants. Oh, well, he thinks, I'm not paying, so it's her call. He undresses.

INTERRUPT MEM (RERUN)

Wait a minute: Why didn't Alex have to pay the woman? Was this a real date, not prostitution at all? He searched back through the mem. There was no indication in Alex's mem that he had ever seen or touched the woman before. Therefore she probably was a hooker. That meant that someone else had paid her to fuck Alex. Why? So there would be one, even two, witnesses to a murder? It didn't make sense.

The pizza person took that moment to knock at the door, and not softly. Morgan opened it, and saw – Truda Vallon?

"That's thirty-five even," the Tru lookalike said. "And ten more for those fracking stairs. That's plus tip. For the pizza and for the stairs too." She stared hard at Morgan, as if daring him to dispute the bill. She held the pizza just out of reach, waving it so the sinful odors of pineapple and jalapeño were sure to reach his nose.

Morgan gave her a fifty and brought the pizza inside. He finished half, put the rest aside for later, sat down to think. Something else bothered him about Alex's mem. About Terra Lewis, now that he knew she was a photographer. He settled back on the couch and called up the mem again.

BEGIN MEM (RERUN TWO)

A soft knock at the door. Alex / Morgan reaches out a hand. Morgan lets his mind wander until he reaches the part he wants to remember this time.

Morgan / Alex remembers the heat, the feeling, the humming of a disordered electric heater, the "pop" of – what was that? He / he stares out over the woman's shoulder, through the window, to the roof of the building across the street, where – what was that?

He / he notices motion on the rooftop. Sunlight glares into his eyes. He squints. A figure, apparently a woman, barely seen, is falling, a man pointing at her. Pointing with a gun. The woman is falling slowly onto the roof.

Now he remembers it for the first time: the lanyard around her neck. A badge at the end of the lanyard is drifting upward as the woman falls backwards, her arms flinging apart, hands splaying open.

INTERRUPT MEM (RERUN TWO)

But something was missing. Terra didn't have a camera. Terra Lewis, the photographer, didn't have a camera with her. That's what Morgan had been looking for this time, what he needed to confirm. If this was a shoot, where was her camera? It was clear now that the killer didn't leave with her camera, because she didn't have one in the first place.

Morgan's own wristcom, small and simple as it was, could still capture almost a full-length 3.5D movie. But Terra was a pro. She needed full control over exposure, aperture, color balance, fill light, images per second, perspective, amount of motion-correction if any. All these required size, especially the high-quality glass-composite lens. Morgan now remembered what Alex hadn't seen and hadn't known enough to miss: A camera.

Why didn't Terra Lewis have a camera with her? Because she wasn't there to take pictures? Yes, she must have gone there for a different reason. What? Or she could have been lured there. A rooftop wasn't a bad place for a meeting, even if it was in the open. None of those ever-present CCTVs, no passing patrol cars or pedestrians. If two people didn't know each other, meeting on a rooftop meant not needing elaborate recognition symbols, or catching innocents in the line of fire.

What did the lack of a camera tell us? Morgan, confused and exasperated, went back to his drink. He tried putting his feet on a coffee table. When that felt too uncomfortable he put them back on the floor. Eventually he fell asleep.

And dreamed. He was standing in front of TruVal's Telegraph Hill condo building. Afternoon was already old. Lights were being turned on one by one. Effortlessly, Morgan's dream floated him uphill and into one flat after another.

On the second floor, Truda Vallon was changing her clothes, had taken off her worklife attire. Morgan reached for her, but his hands passed through her like the hands of a ghost. He called out to her, but he had no voice. The wallscreen behind her came to life, and Morgan was there, in the screen, on the network news. He was a soldier, firing silent deadly weapons. He was also the turban-headed man who was suddenly engorged in flame, whose last thought, irrationally, was that his turban was on fire. And Morgan was the network's newsreader, too, gloating over one more American kill, one more tally on the whiteboard of war.

He looked out from the wallscreen. Truda Vallon had her back to him, and was now completely naked. He stared at her ravenously: the slim body, the light freckles on her shoulders. He approached her, wanting her desperately, but she was real, while he was only image.

The scene faded from his dream. Morgan now found himself on the third floor, where Professor and Department Chair James Whistler O'Neill was speaking in his well-rounded tones to an abashed Robert Follansbee Morgan, PhD.

"Bob, I'm sorry to have to tell you this, but the Chancellor, and the budget, and, well, the tenure committee, and a secret vote of your colleagues."

"Secret from each other?"

"No, Bob, only secret from you. That's what I meant. It was unanimous."

"Even Roseanne Gross?"

"Especially Dr. Gross. She accused you of trying to, ah, make advances to her."

"Surely it's all right to ask a colleague out to dinner!"

"It depends, Bob, on where your hands were at the time, or at least where your eyes were, or your thoughts. Not to mention that everyone but you, apparently, knows that Roseanne Gross has been, for quite a while now, ah, occupied, with or by, Sarah Cassidy of the Women's Triumphalism Department. Although 'in' might be the better preposition here, or perhaps 'on.'"

"And so I'm being 'resignation regretfully accepted'ed?"

"No, Bob, we don't want your resignation; you're fired. We've already packed your cardboard box. Please use the back stairs on your way out. And, oh yes, now that you're no longer on the faculty, there's nothing stopping us from seeing each other, er, socially, is there? For dinner and drinks, a little wine? candles? a little relaxation? Are you free tonight?" He reached out toward Morgan, spread his fingers.

Morgan fled. The ghosts of his latest firing vanished. He was now on the fourth floor, his TruVal refuge. A slim and smiling Helen was handing him a glass of wine.

"Here you are, dear, your favorite *Chateau Latour Pauillac*. I'm very happy for you, my handsome, successful, well-muscled, stunningly-ab'd, and very masculine husband, happy that you've been awarded the highly coveted Weltbau Prize and been promoted to Associate Department Head in place of that awful Roseanne Gross, PhD. I'll bet that old fuddy James Whistler O'Neill must be consumed with rage and envy right now. Oh how he must fear for his crown!"

"Yes, Helen," said Morgan suavely, clutching his wine glass with just the approved grip, "I have an understanding with the Chancellor that they'll fire Jim O'Neill as early as –" He consulted his Breguet 3330 classique automatic mechanical wristwatch in eighteen-carat yellow gold showing the day, the date, and the phases of the moon. "Five o'clock this afternoon."

"And then we'll celebrate!" she said swooningly, circling his lithe upper body with her arms.

"No, Helen, since Jim will no longer be on the faculty, there's nothing standing in my way now of seeing him. Socially, that is. Jim and I have a date this evening. Candles, soft lights. Relaxation."

"I understand," said Helen in a disappointed voice. "I always knew, actually."

Morgan woke suddenly, couldn't get back to sleep.

Chapter 19

The next day, a messenger handed Morgan an envelope. It contained an invitation for Tru's big Sunday special, an admission card suitable for attaching to one's front, and two pages of instructions on how to behave on camera. He studied the instructions, decided that it would never have occurred to him to do any of the forbidden acts if they hadn't been forbidden; especially the rule about the nose. Besides, the network cameramen would never focus on him, a member of an undesirable demographic.

He did a few minutes of housework in the flat, mostly picking clothes off the floor and stuffing them into the nearest drawer. Then he walked down to the Marina Green and back remembering the times he'd lain in the grass there and watched the Fourth of July fireworks, those innocent days before boom and blast meant war, and sparkle meant a new kind of insidious drug. He finished the rest of his pizza for dinner, accompanied by a generous dose of whiskey.

Morgan settled back, pleasantly groggy from the scotch. Time for the evening news. He needed a drink before watching this stuff; too scary for sober. The news-hour logo appeared on the wallscreen, to the tune of "I read the news today oh boy," in a Truda Vallon cover arrangement.

"Tonight's headlines," it began. He wondered, idly, if the newsreader were hube or sim, flesh and blood or electrons. If it didn't use too many "ah"s, or stumble on the pronunciation of a foreign word or two, it was probably a sim. Oh for the good old days of hubes on the news? Not really. Better this way. Nothing could go wrong now. Besides, most flesh and blood hubes looked black or white or yellow or brown, male or female, young or old, while a sim could be anything and nothing, any ethnic group and age and gender or none, any sexual proclivity.

It helped, the experts claimed, to foster the inclusiveness of aggrieved, insulted, offended, and outraged minorities, of which there were more every year, and of more specialized kinds.

Yes, as Morgan studied the figure whose mouth was opening and closing like a hooked fish, it must be a sim. Its eye-blinks gave it away: too regular, too programmed, as did its neutered voice, its generic pinko-greyish-brownish skin, its comfortable opinions that all Americans of good will could heartily endorse.

Morgan had missed the first few headlines. Now he forced himself to watch the wallscreen and listen to the voiceover.

" ...Baluchistan today, and this footage from our hidden realtime newscams shows Muslim troops stepping on U.S. land mines and being blown up, as body parts rain down on the surviving terrorists. An American force is reported to have routed the defenders, although taking heavy casualties themselves. But on the Afghan front, the push to re-capture Kabul has been indefinitely postponed, according to the Secretary of Defense, owing to the problems with..."

Was today's news a re-run? Morgan was sure he'd heard the same stories the day before, and the month before that, and the year before that.

" ...administration received more bad news yesterday, with President Stockwell's approval rating slipping to another low, as every day seems to herald a new climate crisis or resource crunch. The opposition in Congress, however, didn't capitalize on this news, their own approval rating sinking even lower than it was back in the 'tens. According to our network pundits, only the public's patriotic support for our vitally important oil wars, including the new campaign in Ras al-Khaimah, has kept the ratings from slipping even further."

Morgan tuned out. He was uneasy about all these wars. There hadn't been that many, surely, when he was growing up? Not so many at the same time, at least? He remembered a time of peace, or perhaps he misremembered. Or perhaps there had been wars, but he hadn't been told about them.

"On the home front, the Governor of Texas has declared a state of emergency as San Antonio is now completely out of water. Fleets of tanker trucks from Austin and Houston are rushing to provide supplies, but with a population of five million in the city, the outlook, according to the Governor's office, is grim. This tragedy is still not expected to compare with the massive death toll experienced in India when this year's monsoons failed.

"And now for this word." Morgan had programmed his wallscreen to go dark at the words "this word," and brighten again after this word, and that word, and all those other words, had been spoken. It was traditional, he knew, for dinner-hour ads to feature remedies for the stomach cramps, runs, farts, and heartaches of a real home-cooked meal. That's how he remembered life at home with Helen, anyway.

After a few minutes, the screen brightened.

"In national news today, the SoCalls movement won a victory when the Ninth Circuit Court of Appeals ruled that the group cannot be outlawed simply because it has repeatedly threatened violence, without a showing of actual harm done. The Justice Department is expected to appeal the ruling to the Supreme Court.

"In related news, Senator Gooding of Virginia announced that his subcommittee will soon hold hearings on the SoCalls. 'Many SoCalls are fine upstanding Americans, as we all know. But questions remain,' he was quoted as saying. The senator hinted that he had received evidence that the SoCalls were being financially supported by what he called 'sinister forces.' Buck Baker, head of the SoCalls, denounced Gooding's move, but told reporters he would grudgingly cooperate if hearings were held.

"And in local news, climate migrants from Los Angeles today continued to flood north, contingents reaching as far as Hollister, where the San Benito County sheriff's office hastily deputized citizens and formed a human barricade."

Morgan didn't turn off the wallscreen, because he was sound asleep in his chair. Sensing this, the wallscreen dimmed, then shut itself off after a few minutes. Darkness covered the earth, and gross darkness the people.

Chapter 20

On Saturday, USA RightNow, the last surviving e-paper, posted an opinion piece on "mem abuse." As customary, several forgettable people were quoted and no particular conclusions were reached, although at the subtext level a tone of stern disapproval vied with hints of illicit thrills.

The story's hook involved "snuff-memming," as recently alleged by the public prosecutor of Chelan County, Washington. A variation on having sex in order to sell the resulting mem, snuff-memmers were, it was accused, killing people and then selling their mems of the event for many thousands of dollars.

Had a crime been committed, over and above murder? But more important, had there been a moral lapse here? And if so, whose? Ethicists were uncrated, wound up, had their buttons pushed. Predictable opinions rolled out, adorned with hemming and hawing.

After ten minutes, the story had racked up more than seventeen thousand online comments, a number disappointing to the paper; but then it went viral. Programmed ad rates responded, soaring. An ad offering to buy snuff-mems appeared on the same webpage. After twenty-three seconds it was pulled by the appalled editors, but too late to stop a wave of killings over the next few days.

After its fifteen minutes of fame, the *USA RightNow* story evaporated into electrons, replaced by the latest news from the dog-show world. The network's market share fell rapidly as a hand-puppet was awarded "best of show."

But in spite of snuff-mems, the great majority of murders would still be committed for the usual reasons: love; hate;

silence; money. Tomorrow's murder at the TruPlex would conform to this tradition.

***

Sunday evening arrived. Morgan dressed and walked to the TruPlex for the special, being sure to bring his admission card. From three blocks away he could hear chaotic sounds of yelling, chanting, bull horns, sirens. He turned the corner of Clay Street and saw a crowd of SoCalls, "Father" Buck Baker on a platform in their midst, shouting slogans at his followers and punching his fist in the air. The SoCalls waved posters and placards, marching in circles like union picketers, turning toward one and then the other of two TV news crews, strophe and antistrophe. The placards bore slogans such as

"Don't Support So-called Mental Health!"

"Intimacy is Hate!"

"Leave Your Mind Alone!"

"Back off, Senator Gooding!"

Then Baker called out to the crowd, and got a shouted response:

"Mental Health is a Fraud!"

"Don't Shrink Your Mind!"

"Empathy is Complicity!"

"Insight is Blind!"

"Your Mind is Your Fortress!"

"Daddy Let Your Mind Roll On!"

Police were observing, but taking no action since the SoCalls had been, to this point at least, peaceful. Morgan looked for a TruVal guard, found one at the edge of the crowd, and showed his admission card. The guard escorted him into the building amid the shouts, cries, and misaimed spittle of the surrounding SoCalls.

Morgan and the other guests gathered in the main lobby and were escorted into elevators programmed, today, to serve only the B-1 level. Since this was an office building and not a theatre, space was limited and it seemed to Morgan that by the time the room was full, only about two hundred guests were present, tightly packed. Most were Trudites, a few with men who seemed to be their spouses or dates. He found himself side by side with Madelyn, not by his choice. Madelyn had apparently not taken to heart instruction number twenty-seven, the one about smiling at all times.

"I know what you're thinking, doctor."

"You do?"

"I read the rules, too, y'know. I'm smiling inside."

"Ah, OK. – Think the cameras will pick that up, what's happening inside?"

"Can it, Morgan. I need to speak with you."

Morgan was miffed that a mere admin would call him by unadorned surname. "I do have a private office, *Madelyn*. You could make an appointment. See my *secretary* first thing in the morning, will you?"

"That's not funny."

"Funny, I thought it was."

"Was what?"

"Was funny."

"Funny business maybe. Nothing's funny-funny at TruVal. And nothing is private, either. Your office, for instance."

Morgan found it disturbing to recall that fact, and not very funny.

"But here in the middle of a mob..."

"Right," she said. "We can talk, if you can hear me over all this racket."

"Barely."

"OK. It's about Terra Lewis."

Morgan spread his hands, palms up. "I don't know any more about her than you do, I'm afraid."

"I know. But I know more than you do. For instance, I have a good idea why Terra was killed."

"OK, why?"

Madelyn frowned. "She found out something she shouldn't have. I think there are very malign things going on inside the TruPlex here, and they're being covered up by top management. That has to be it."

Morgan was bemused by Madelyn's use of "malign." He hadn't heard that word in years, and only on public TV at that. "Are you saying that Truda Vallon is part of – whatever it is?" he said.

Madelyn glanced around. "Tru? Yes, I think so. But I'm pretty sure that the Goddess is."

"The Goddess?"

"Haven't you heard anyone call her that? Athena Taylor. She's got her hands on all the levers in this company."

Morgan was getting impatient. "Well, what did Terra Lewis find out that was so damned important that TruVal would have her killed?"

"I don't know," said Madelyn. "But there's too much hush-hush about what's been going on in the TruVal memlab. – Yes, the one you stumbled into the other day. I've heard that Tru is going to make an announcement tonight, but I'm sure there's more. Lots more. All that equipment you saw? Up to no good! Very malign!"

Morgan took a moment to take in what Madelyn had said. "Uh, why are you telling me this?"

"You connect with that detective, Lieutenant DeLuca. If I went to him, the wrong people could find out. But since you speak with him every day or so, you can tell him one more thing without any suspicion. Just don't say where you heard it!"

Morgan was definitely intrigued, although he thought that Madelyn's conspiracy theory was all shuck and no corn, as they say in Nebraska. "OK, but I'll need details. Now how did you find out about this..."

The show began, interrupting their talk. After that, they couldn't hear each other over the show's din. Morgan made a "later" gesture and Madelyn nodded. He resolved to find her at the post-special party.

Morgan had expected a very elaborate beginning to the show, an event worthy of its hype, but the special began very much like Tru's weekly TV show: A warm-up, then Tru singing and dancing. Several numbers, judging by audience reaction her old favorites, then a prolonged fanfare.

On stage, an announcer was intro-ing the world premiere of a new song by Tru "that's sure to be another chart-buster for her, the biggest one yet." Then Tru: "...all been waiting for, our wonderful new song, the one we've worked on and toiled on for oh so long, and here it is for the first time anywhere! Presenting" (drum roll) "Strangers"!

The conductor gave the downbeat and the song began. Tru struck a wide-legged pose, thrust one arm upward, and sang. A video appeared on the back wallscreen. It was Alex's apt, the window overlooking a rooftop across the street. Why had Tru sent a crew to video that? And on the rooftop, a woman dressed like Truda Vallon. And a man with a gun. This was getting really creepy, Morgan thought, a reenactment that shouldn't have been made of an event that shouldn't have happened. The picture had been doctored and edited and treated with all the techniques of CG-ers, but it was still recognizable. The woman on the rooftop was Terra Lewis. She began to fall. A puff of smoke appeared at the end of the gun. The gunman turned right, then left. Looked into the camera, looked into Alex's apt, raised his gun. His face was blurred out by the suggestion of a mask.

Two figures pulled themselves down and to the left as the window shattered. Suddenly there was screaming. His own, Morgan realized. He pulled his mind away from the spectacle, saw that his hands were shaking. This was no reenactment, it must have been his mem! Of Terra's murder! The one he'd bought from Alex! The mem didn't seem quite right, but what else could it be? How on earth did they get it from him? He didn't remember being drugged and hauled into a memlab, not that he would remember it if he had been! But he still had the mem in his own head. That was crucial. Otherwise, how could he have recognized it? Since he still had the mem, he knew it hadn't been memplanted in someone else. But how could it have been stored and gussied up for broadcast, even if he'd voluntarily given it up? As far as he knew, that was impossible.

As Tru sang and danced and the band played on, Morgan had the odd feeling that he'd heard the new song before. Passing by the fourteenth floor practice stage down the hall from the cafeteria? Or absently hummed by one of the band members passing by?

As the song ended in a long drawn-out fade and the show halted for a commercial break, Morgan suddenly realized where he'd heard "Strangers." It had been playing in Alex's apt that day and was playing now in Morgan's head to the accompaniment of heaving bodies and glistening sweat. That song had been playing on Alex's songchip player when Terra had been murdered – two weeks ago. Two weeks before its world premiere.

Chapter 21

There were five minutes of commercials and then the announcer was back, speaking in that annoying, buttery voice TV announcers had, about "tonight's big news, ladies and gentlemen, revolutionary, paradigm-shifting technology that will revolutionize" (yes, twice) "the entire music, movie, video, indeed, friends, the entire entertainment business! And here to proclaim this stunning new development from TruVal's own scientific research laboratories is, ta dah! big round of applause for her folks, please," (pregnant pause, almost ready for parturition) "Miss Truda Vallon herself!" Morgan hadn't heard the title "Miss" in twenty-five years. This show was getting to be old home week. He focused more closely on the announcer, saw that he wasn't the thirty-five year old he seemed, but was perhaps, under his slathered makeup, closer to sixty five.

Tru came back on stage, this time carefully costumed as a performer who'd finished her big number and had been toweling her hair in the – what? Not "locker room," well what did they call...?

Tru began to speak, and Morgan lost his train of thought about Tru in a locker room, even though he'd begun to fantasize what might possibly go on there, if he were to – well, never mind that right now. His attention returned to the stage. Tru faced straight into the camera with the red light and spoke quietly and simply.

"I want to tell you about a new capability we've developed here at TruVal, a technology that will be a wonderful new revolution" (third time) "for us here at TruVal and in the entertainment industry as a whole." Her serious face turned into a broad smile. "And you'll really love it!"

A curtain lifted, revealing a few pieces of the TruVal memlab which had apparently been trundled the few yards to

102

the studio. Now we'll see what Karl-Heinz Stirner has been up to, Morgan thought.

"Some of you have given or received memory transplants at a memlab," Tru continued. "It's dangerous, as most of you realize, as physicians and psychiatrists have shown. A number of persons have become unbalanced, or even emotionally scarred for life because they couldn't handle someone else's memory, or couldn't get over the loss of their own. And yet our memories are what makes us 'us.' Wouldn't it be wonderful if we could share our memories, our most intimate emotional moments, safely?

"But there is a way, and that's tonight's big news! Now you can experience other people's memories safely, the way you watch movies or TV shows. On your very own 3.5D wallscreen or your own wristcom. We call it – MemCast!"

Lights dimmed, and the band's snare drummer began a roll. Tru continued.

"With TruVal, Inc.'s new MemCast technology, any memory can be transferred onto digital optical storage instead of directly into another mind. It can be edited if desired, and then broadcast to millions of coms or wallscreens, or saved on a chip. Our wonderful TruVal scientists and engineers have been working on this for more than four years, and now it's here!"

The snare drummer was still on a roll. His big moment. Carried away, perhaps, or what could he be remembering?

"You may be wondering right now," Tru continued, "when we will show you MemCasting, or is it all talk, one of those 'future features' that never arrives? Well, we've shown you, just now! The video that accompanied my new song, "Strangers," isn't a studio production, although it's been edited and enhanced. It's a real mem, captured digitally, then broadcast for your viewing pleasure.

"TruVal, Inc. is, as we speak, filing dozens of patent applications covering various aspects of MemCast. But we will, and here I solemnly pledge, make MemCast technology available to every entertainment company anywhere in the world, under license."

She smiled. "And are you thinking ahead? Yes, there will be a MindBook on the web, where you can all hang out and share your most intimate secret memories, not telling, but showing! And a MemTube! And a Natter site where you can continuously broadcast small bursts of mind-activity to your friends without having to make any effort or be conscious of what's happening. And we're at this moment also developing NetMinx, our new outlet for download rental mems."

She paused, motioned for another drum roll. "Open your mind: share it!" She said, "no one will be a stranger anymore. No More Strangers." Softly, the orchestra took up a weepy version of the "*Alle Menschen*" theme, followed by a reprise of the new "Strangers" song. Tru bowed deeply, then walked off the stage.

On the wallscreen behind her, the slogan "Open Your Mind: Share it!" appeared in large letters, and "No More Strangers!", each followed by the inevitable ®, ™, SM, and ©.

Now Morgan finally realized why Terra didn't need a camera: TruVal photographers were seeing with their minds. Their memories were being dumped into the MemCast system, probably building up a catalog of mems to be MemCast, and sold on the web by TruVal. One memory, many viewers. Many dollars. Very many dollars. No wonder Tru had developed her own memlab, no wonder the guards and the secrecy. With patents and licensing, she wouldn't even have to produce any mems herself. Every MemCast download would rake in a few micropennies for TruVal, Inc.

The show concluded with a several final bows. The orchestra struck up the Tru theme (muted horns over cellos, with snare drum brushes making a swishy percussion sound). House lights up.

The audience applauded vigorously, whistled, raised their arms in the air, and danced (instructions five, six, seven, and eight). Morgan tried to dance, but it was hopeless; he kept bumping into people he didn't mean to bump into, and the people he would have rather liked to bump into slithered away from him like the Golden Gate's outgoing tide.

Morgan searched for Madelyn, didn't find her. Camera lights off, show over. Party time!

Chapter 22

The house lights stayed up briefly as the orchestra members left and cameras and stage paraphernalia were removed, and as drink-carts were wheeled in. Then the lights dimmed again. Morgan found a cart and asked for a Glenlivet, neat, double. He shared a few friendly butt-bumps with happy people of all sexes and genders. Smells of whiskey and perfume and pot and sweat, and other smells he could only guess at, rose and mingled. Morgan gulped his drink quickly ("because it might spill"), had another.

Again he searched for Madelyn. Had to find her. Had to finish that conversation. Something about Terra, what had Madelyn said? A clue to Terra's murder, why Terra was on that roof, why anyone had been on the roof, why it had to be Terra. She'd been photo'ing, with her mind it now seemed, but couldn't any capable photog have done that? Terra was killed because she was Terra, not because she was in the wrong place at the wrong time. Is that what Madelyn had been hinting at? Morgan got up on his toes, peered left and right, didn't see her.

Then he looked for Tru, but he didn't see her, either. Probably still in her locker room, or resting from all her exertion on the show. He very much wanted to ask her how his mem had been shanghaied and used for a video. Well, the MemCast announcement had said how, hadn't it? But he still didn't remember giving up Alex's mem, and he still had it (he'd checked two or three more times, and it was still there in all its frenzied sordidness.) Was there such a thing as copyrighting a mem? He felt violated, then realized that it was Alex who'd been violated, not him. All was confused. Party noise grew along with the temperature in the room and his level of intoxication.

Turning from another trip to the drink cart he found Renee beside him. She was, of course, excited up to the gosh / heck / golly / jeepers level, bounced up and down on her toes, told him, unnecessarily, how excited she was. She gave Morgan a peck on the cheek which he found disturbing, then floated effortlessly away through the crowd.

He spotted Athena across the room, easily enough because she was almost the tallest person there. But swimming through the crowd to reach her was difficult: waves were high, currents were shifting, and an occasional rogue wave of happy partygoers almost knocked him over. He was making progress in her direction, however, when he saw Helen squarely between him and Athena. Fortunately, Helen hadn't noticed him yet. He was able to veer away. Later, he thought, maybe never. Is never OK for you? He searched the crowd for other faces he knew.

The announcer was in the crowd, holding forth to a small group about MemCast: "This will revolutionize the world! Millions will be made!" One man in the group, on the arm of a Trudite, was saying "...privacy. Wouldn't that let anyone...?"

"Not at all, my friend!" The announcer beamed like a light bulb. "It's entirely voluntary! You don't have to contribute any of your mems if you don't want to. You won't even have to sign up for a MindBook membership!" He raised an eyebrow at the other man. "Because membership will be automatic! And a few of us don't have mems anyone else would be interested in, so I wouldn't worry, if I were *you*." The other man swallowed hard but said nothing. The woman he was with tugged at his arm, pulled him away from the group. They began an argument Morgan could see, but not hear. The announcer smiled again. O to be his dentist. O to be his tanning consultant.

Finally, Morgan saw Tru in the crowd. He wanted to ask her how his mem had been stolen, about the song, how the lookalike could have got hold of the song on a songchip. Or had that song been leaked in advance of the premiere? Or been pirated? But Tru was surrounded by a large coterie of loyal and boisterous Trudites and hangers-on, and assorted flacks and newsies; he couldn't immediately reach her. He circled her group, wormed himself in when and as he could. It took what seemed a long time, but finally when she turned her head once, there he was.

"Robert!" she beamed.

***

Public adulation had always thrilled her, she knew, even after years of being adored by millions. It was always new, always the grand thing. It was even pleasant to have Robert here, though he always seemed something of a downer. Now he looked more down than ever. But she felt – warm – whenever he was near. Better be careful with him; he was here for a purpose. Two very different purposes: his, pretty surely, and mine. Let's deal with his first.

"Well, Robert, did you like the show?"

She knew he'd ignore that question for one of his own.

"How did you get...?"

"Your mem?"

She felt – she couldn't quite explain why – like teasing him just then.

"It wasn't your mem, it was Alex's, remember?"

"You know what I mean. How did you do it?"

He was grim, she saw. And drunk.

She pulled him aside and spoke into his ear. "Let me enjoy my big night, this glorious triumph. I'll explain it all tomorrow." She pulled back, spoke louder. "Oh come now, Robert, we all have our secrets!" Laughing, she pushed him away, gently but firmly, turned back to her adoring, so wonderful to have them here right now in her moment of apotheosis, friends, or "friends."

Morgan returned to his search for Madelyn. He thought he caught a glimpse of her near the wall furthest from the stage, but lost sight of her in the crowd. While he was craning his neck to see into the distance, he found Dennis DeLuca directly in front of him.

"What are you doing here?" Morgan asked, and immediately regretted saying something that could sound like a challenge.

"I got an invitation. Like you did, I suppose. I see we both have blue stripes on our badges. I've been noticing that the suits have orange, the wigs red, and celebs surrounded by other celebs tend to be greens. We afterthoughts have the blues. How's that for discrimination on the basis of color?"

Morgan wasn't sure if DeLuca was being serious or not. Couldn't tell by his face. Morgan had never seen it with an expression that couldn't have come straight from Sherlock Holmes' mongrel bloodhound Toby.

"Anyway," DeLuca said, "you might not see me again."

"Why?" Morgan felt uneasy about DeLuca, believed that DeLuca didn't respect him sufficiently. After all, Morgan was a citizen and taxpayer, and a (former) member of the higher education establishment. But he didn't want DeLuca off the case, and now Madelyn had given Morgan a clue he needed to tell the detective about.

"I'm supposed to be reassigned. Off the case. My captain is fighting it, but he'll lose. The chief came down with a carful of heavy suits from D.C. this morning and said they were taking over the investigation."

"What investigation? There's no evidence of a crime; you said so yourself."

"I know. But I told you I believed that you saw a body, a murder. I even convinced my captain, but then..." He shrugged, started to turn away.

"Detective DeLuca!" Morgan called. "That video, 'Strangers.'That was the murder!"

DeLuca turned back to him. "Come on, Morgan; it was a fake or a re-enactment or something. Didn't you see the green-screen work?"

"OK, it was edited and CG'd and all that. But underneath it all, that was my mem. I remember it!"

"How could you possibly remember?" DeLuca asked. "If that was your mem, you shouldn't have it any more."

"I know, I know. But it was mine – my mem – Alex's, I mean! And then there's that new 'MemCast' stuff that Tru announced. Perhaps..."

***

DeLuca peered at Morgan. Perhaps TruVal, with all their techies, had figured out a way to make memplants non-destructive. The donor would therefore keep the mem, not dump it off into another person. It could even go to a server farm somewhere in the cloud. Maybe that's what the "sharing" in all that ®, ™, ᔆᴹ, and © meant. Maybe that was a MemCast feature that Vallon hadn't mentioned. Hadn't wanted to mention. But he thought her explanation was simpler.

"No, doctor. I don't think it was your mem you saw on that screen, at all. I think it was the lookalike's mem, the hooker's. I think Vallon found her, and had her mem dumped into that new MemCast system. The point of view seemed to me like it wasn't quite Alex's. Close, but not quite."

Morgan gaped at him.

"And I'm pissed about it," DeLuca continued, "because I believe the lookalike's mem was evidence of a crime. Vallon held onto evidence instead of turning it over to me."

"But you weren't interested in the lookalike or her mem."

"Not at first, but I've been coming around to your point of view about the lookalike, even more interested now that her mem's been intentionally withheld from the police. And did you notice the killer's face in that video?"

"No, I couldn't make it out."

"That's because it had been blurred, probably using computer graphics. Made it seem like he wore a mask."

"I saw that. Couldn't get a model release?"

DeLuca decided to ignore that. Why couldn't this idiot just sober up?

The detective thought out loud. "If the video had shown the killer's face clearly, then it wouldn't have been Alex's mem. But it was blurred out so you and I would think it was his. Then we wouldn't suspect that Vallon has evidence of the murder which we can use to ID the killer. And I'm pissed because I've spent time trying to locate that damned lookalike, and Vallon had her under wraps all the time! Well, that's one person I won't need to search for any more, or wouldn't if I were still going to be on the case. But now we're on to a new angle."

"What new angle?"

"Police business, Dr. Morgan: we don't tell the public everything we're doing."

"But I'm not 'the public'! No one is 'the public'! That's a construct of your imagination so you can keep secrets from people like me."

"You have a few secrets of your own, don't you, doctor?"

"Meaning what?"

DeLuca smiled and walked away. Morgan suddenly remembered that in all his excitement about having his mem stolen and broadcast, and DeLuca's insistence that it wasn't Morgan's mem at all, he hadn't mentioned what Madelyn had said about Terra. Surely the detective would be interested in that!

He tried to find DeLuca again. He couldn't have got far, not in this mob. Morgan circled the room, waved at Renee once in the distance, kept out of sight of Helen. About ten minutes later, he caught sight of the detective, near the back wall. Morgan turned to pursue him, lost sight of him, caught him again, lost him.

And then the room exploded.

Chapter 23

Morgan fell to the floor, got to his knees, lifted himself up. Smoke filled the room. Suddenly it was in complete darkness. After a moment, feeble backup lights blinked on, painting stark yellow shadows. From a distance, Morgan heard the noisy clank of a generator starting up.

Partygoers stood still in shock, speechless from concussion. Morgan felt his face for blood. Not hurt. Maybe. He took a ginger step, didn't feel any pain. He saw that people were distraught, coughing, had started walking aimlessly through the smoke. Mouths were open, working, but Morgan couldn't hear a thing. The ceiling hadn't collapsed, he saw, and he didn't smell anything burning. Like slow motion or a dream sequence, people wandered, clutching at friends, clutching at anyone, lifting men and women off the floor, weeping. He could see mouths mouthing "Are you OK? Are you OK? Are you OK?" and not waiting for an answer.

In a daze, Morgan stared, turned around and round. He saw Athena standing still, eyes wide, and then Tru, both apparently unhurt. He turned slowly until he was facing the back wall. Where part of it had been was now a jagged hole floor to ceiling, about fifteen feet across. Near the wall stood DeLuca, bending over, not moving. Perhaps he was hurt. Morgan lunged toward him. As he approached, the detective stood up. There was blood on his shirt. Morgan saw a woman lying on the floor near him.

"Is she hurt?" Morgan asked, gesturing toward the form. "Is she hurt? Is she OK? Is she hurt?"

The detective seemed shaken, but appeared to have more of his wits available than Morgan did. "No," he said. "She's dead. The only serious casualty, looks like."

Morgan stared up at the shards of wood and wallboard hanging from the ruined wall. DeLuca held up a piece of wood. "This is what seems to have killed her," he said.

Morgan stared at the piece of broken stud, a two by four about three feet long. There was a large dent in it. The dent contained a few strands of hair. "Accident?" he asked, "or not?"

"Damned if I know!" said DeLuca.

DeLuca motioned for Morgan to help him, and together they angled the woman's body up, turned it on its back. It was Madelyn Lopez.

**

Morgan woke the next day with a lighter hangover than he'd feared he'd have, but it was bad enough. He didn't remember how he'd got back to the flat. Stumbled out of the TruPlex, he vaguely recalled, spoke to no one, went through police lines, struggled up Telegraph Hill. DeLuca had been busy working with the arriving officers, talking to witnesses. Morgan had wanted to tell him what Madelyn had said before she died and why it was important, but he didn't have the will or the energy to wait until the detective was free to speak with him.

Morgan turned on the TV news. There were pictures of smoke pouring out of the TruPlex, illuminated by the light of fire trucks. The reporter said that an explosion "of suspicious origin" had destroyed the building's power plant. Bad luck that a party had been taking place on the other side of the wall, in the TruVal broadcast studio. Injuries were slight, the newsreader added, except for one unfortunate fatality.

"Popular suspicion for the bombing has focused on the SoCalls, who were holding a protest outside the TruPlex at the time. Police have downplayed this possibility, calling any conclusion 'premature.' However, they have refused to deny or verify the rumor that 'Buck' Baker and a number of his followers have been taken in for questioning."

"Meanwhile, the war in Aden has taken a turn for..."

Morgan clicked off the TV, dressed, drank a glass of orange juice, and walked downhill to the TruPlex. There was still a residue of pandemonium on Montgomery Street, but more order than he'd expected. TruVal security guards were stationed outside, explaining that power would not be restored for several days, and that the generators were able to power only a few parts of the building and a single elevator.

He observed who the guards were letting into the building: security staff, executives, and the creative staff. The show must go on, of course. Other employees were being told to go home for a few days.

Morgan rumpled his thinning hair, flashed his TruVal security badge, told the guard he was a writer for the regular weekly show and was expected. The guard, without a roster or other guidance at hand, had to take Morgan at his word.

Morgan figured that there would be no power on the twelfth floor, or anywhere else mid-building. His goal this time wasn't his office, though. He waited in line for the only functioning elevator, went directly up to the twenty-sixth floor. Tru was already there. Athena Taylor was organizing, ordering, bustling, managing, seemed to be thoroughly enjoying her crisis management duties. Tru was assessing how many of her creative staff had arrived, and what they could do without power to most of the building. Their own departments (the ones on the twenty-third and twenty-fourth floors) were powered by the generator, but the company's servers were on the B-1 level. Most had been damaged, a few destroyed, and all of that floor was without power in any case. The temperature outside was mild that morning, but the total lack of heating or air conditioning, or any windows that could be opened, would mean strained working conditions.

***

Tru saw Morgan approaching. Shit, she thought, why did I tell Robert I'd speak with him today? Today of all days. Of course I didn't know then that we'd be in crisis mode this morning. Couldn't he figure that out and leave me alone for a while? I could tell him to come back in a day, or two or three. But, since the show prep seems to be coming along OK right now, I do have a minute to speak with him. And I should. It's overdue, because I've been afraid and putting it off. I do want to understand what happened to Terra, and Robert is part of that understanding. "Good morning!" she smiled at Morgan. "Go on in to my office. I'll be with you in a minute."

Morgan entered Tru's office, this time without needing to brush back any stray Trudites, sat down and waited. "A minute" turned into thirty minutes, but then there she was, settling down at her desk, saying "Well, then" and "Here we are" and pushing papers from front to back and from back to front. That's exactly what he used to do to put off the moment, Morgan thought, back when he had to speak with a student who'd flunked a course.

Finally Tru was ready. "Robert, this is all unraveling very fast," she said. "About the special and all."

"What about the special? Seemed pretty successful to me."

"But not nearly what it could have been, if Terra hadn't – hadn't been killed."

"What do you mean?"

"Robert, we announced MemCast on the show. I'm happy to say it's aroused an enormous amount of publicity for us, and we've already taken orders for more than fifty thousand MemCasts of 'Strangers' accompanied by the mem. Can't fill the orders right now, of course, because all our servers are down, some ruined, and our backup in the cloud can't handle the volume. We're spinning up the off-site disks, though; none of the creative work has been permanently lost."

"My mem. How did you get my mem?" Morgan asked.

"*Your* mem?"

"It was edited and augmented and CG'd and all that, but I could tell." He didn't mention that DeLuca suspected it was the lookalike's mem. He wanted to see if Tru would volunteer that information, and if DeLuca's hunch had been right.

"Well," said Tru, rather breezily, "we do have our own memlab here. You stumbled across it yourself the other day."

"You heard about that?"

"Oh, yes. I could just picture a couple of beefy women stuffing you into an elevator and pushing 'close door.'" She laughed.

"But still..."

"How did we get your mem without your knowing? I'm afraid I can't tell you that right now."

"That's an awful power you have, 'mem-snatching' is what the SoCalls seem to be calling it. And that Stirner, is he your snatcher-in-chief?"

"Oh, you mean Karl? He's our principal scientist. He insisted on that title when we brought him in, but he's earned it. He was doing German government work, very hush hush, but couldn't get funding to do the kind of research he wanted to do. So he sought us out with a proposition that was – very interesting."

"What does he actually do down there?"

"Free inquiry, Robert; untrammeled research. But we did insist that he give us a few products we could commercialize."

"He seemed to be developing some super-memplant thing down there on the B-1 level. Was that your new 'MemCast,' or is there more?"

"Well, it's an improved kind of memplanting, that's all I'll say right now." She paused. "'Mem-snatching'? That isn't quite it. MemCast isn't really a 'mem-snatching' system, as you said. It broadcasts only what's fed to it. In any case, our scientists tell me that 'mem-snatching' is impossible: there has to be an aware, willing mem-donor to call up a memory, consciously remember the events and the thoughts and feelings that went to make it up, be aware of where in the continuum of the mind a particular sequence we call 'a memory' begins and ends. I can't tell you more now. Later, perhaps, it will all be clear."

"Perhaps," mocked Morgan. "Look: Are you going to level with me or not? I came here because of your invitation. You must have had something in mind, but nothing's made sense since the day I met you. And now my mem? I still have it. How could you have it too? That's impossible. Not to mention that I don't remember any of your Doctor Mengeles holding down my desperately struggling form and prying it out of my mind."

Chapter 24

Tru thought what to do with this annoyed man. Guess he wouldn't be much use to me if he were kept in the dark much longer. Now we've had a bomb attack and he could be useful. In several ways. And I like him and I think I can trust him.

"There's another explanation, Robert."

"DeLuca thinks it was the lookalike's mem that you broadcast; the hooker's mem."

"Well, he was right."

Morgan sat back in his chair. "How do you know."

"We found her, paid her to be with Alex, got her permission and pulled her mem. It's much like your mem, of course. Alex's, I should say."

"DeLuca's pissed at you for concealing evidence, but if the two mems are alike, I guess it doesn't matter."

"I didn't say 'alike,' I said 'much like.' There are a few differences, and one of those differences is very interesting."

"What?"

Tru swallowed, eyes in her lap. "She saw the murderer's face."

"All of it?"

"Most of it, as he was turning his face into the sunset. All but the part Alex saw, I believe, based on your description of the mem you bought."

"If we put the two mems together, we could ID the killer. Can MemCast do that?"

"Not really. We could find a police artist and ask him to draw a likeness of the killer based on combining Alex's mem in your mind, with a digital image of the mem the lookalike dumped onto a computer. But the accuracy wouldn't seem too promising if we did that. In spite of what they say on TV crime shows, police sketches based on oral descriptions are only

116

suggestive, not definitive. Still, we could do that. There's an off-chance we might get something interesting."

The two were silent for a minute. Then Morgan had a thought. "Tell me, Tru: how did you keep the lookalike hidden when the entire SFPD couldn't find her?"

"DeLuca pretty much worked alone on this. I think he told you that, so it wasn't 'the entire SFPD.' And – and this has to be very secret, Robert, but we have to solve this murder, and now Madelyn's death. One murder or possibly two with no apparent motive, both based on inside information: Where Terra would be and when, and where Madelyn would be and how to create a diversion at the right time. I guess – I'll have to tell you, Robert."

"Tell me what?"

"Terra was on a shoot for us. Her assignment was to photo Alex having sex with a woman who looked like me. For the special, for the 'strangers' theme. We intended to use Terra's mem of the event, not Alex's or the lookalike's. And since this was also going to be the launch of MemCast, we asked Terra not to use a camera, but to look at the scene as if she were the camera herself. Then we'd dump her mem into the MemCast computer."

Morgan attempted to take this all in. "Terra was on the roof to voyeur a sex act between a druggie and a hooker to be canned digitally and MemCasted to millions," he said, "as a video to go along with your new song. But then Alex must have been part of the conspiracy."

"Don't call it a conspiracy, Robert, it was a business arrangement. And yes, Alex knew something about what we were doing, but only a little. He signed a contract that he wouldn't transplant his mem of that sex scene to anyone, ever. We were to pay him quite a bit of money for that promise, doled out over a long period of time. The first payment wasn't to be made until after the special, to keep him honest."

"But..."

"When he saw Terra's murder he must have realized he'd have to get rid of his memory of it, TruVal money or not, or he'd be a target."

"And he sold it to me."

"Exactly. Or he would have sold it to someone else, if you hadn't volunteered so promptly. The hooker brought 'Strangers' in on a songchip, as you know. The idea was that she and Alex would develop the same rhythm in their bodies that the music has. The woman knew about it, knew to be conscious of the rhythm of the song and to respond to it, guide Alex to do the same if he didn't feel the rhythm himself."

"And Terra would record the whole thing in her mind."

"That's right. Her skills as a photographer would allow her to see in the right way, get the right exposures and angles and zooms and fades; the way she would with a camera, but she'd do it with her eyes and mind instead."

"And the woman retrieved her songchip on the way out. In the circumstances, that's not very..."

"Likely?" Tru asked. Morgan was getting annoyed at Tru's finishing his sentences for him. She'd done that from the beginning, but he'd held his tongue. Someday, he vowed, he'd really have to say something to her.

"But it was a very valuable songchip," Tru continued, "since the song was secret and under wraps until the special. That's why we didn't dare trust a download; it could have been hacked. The woman was under a great deal of pressure from us to come back with the songchip in her possession, or else."

"Then you didn't use my mem, mine and Alex's mem. You pulled the lookalike into the TruVal memlab and got hers."

"That's all that was left for us to do, so soon before the special. Since we'd set up the entire shoot, we knew who the hooker was and how to find her. Her mem wasn't as wonderful as Terra's would have been: not professional, and not the point of view I wanted." Tru stretched, suddenly appeared wiped out from the disaster of the night before. "Not as daring, either. Not as 'up yours' to the SoCalls."

"Then you're political, not just out for publicity and money?"

"I despise 'Father' Baker and all he stands for. Always have. My video is already outraging the SoCalls, but it would have been so much more delicious if Terra...." She looked down. There was a moment of silence.

"The SoCalls have been out to get me for a long time," she continued. "At first, they were peaceful. More recently, they've started associating me with the memlabs, attacking, even bombing one or two, at least they've been accused of bombings but nothing's been proved, except harassing people who visit the labs. Since the murder, I've had the feeling that they're behind Terra's death, as a way to get to me."

"Why? They couldn't stand the thought of a hundred million viewers watching 'you' have sex on television?"

"Not that there was anything to see, of course, with that couch in the way. But what was happening would have been obvious to the viewers. Not a fake Hollywood sex scene, but the real thing."

"Well," Morgan said. "Promising or not, I guess about all we can do is go ahead and get the unedited 'Strangers' video to DeLuca. I'll study it, too, and between it and me we'll see if we can piece together a picture of the killer's face." He stood up, pleased that he would have something to do that might help solve the case.

Tru sat still. "Well," she said, "let's try it. No harm in trying." She turned away, frowning. Morgan left the building. He made sure that DeLuca was on duty at police HQ, paid him a visit, outlined the mug shot plan to the scowling detective.

"I know," DeLuca said. "TruVal emailed me the unedited video before you got here. OK, I viewed it. Not enough face to go on. Oh, I have a couple of ideas on four or five professional killers who could be the ones, but if I roped them in and showed them, or their lawyers, the video, they'd just tell me to piss off. You can bet the killer will have a perfect alibi. The ones who can't account for their time the day of the murder, well, those guys wouldn't be guilty. Not guilty of our crime, anyway."

"But if we add the video to my mem? Enough to scare them into talking?"

"Not likely, but we could give it a try."

DeLuca found Morgan a room with a wallscreen, set the video to repeat that face from Tru's video turning into the sunset over and over. On the desk display he loaded a file of digitized mug shots, with display options set to "turning right, facing into the sun, then left, warm color balance."

Morgan flipped from face to face, went backwards, forwards, stared, repeated repeated until they all began to look alike to him. But finally, he ID'd three "likelies" and fourteen "possibles." DeLuca observed the process from over his shoulder. "What we need is to combine these two mems, not in your mind, but on a wallscreen," he said. "Paint a vivid picture. That might be enough to scare info out of our killer, even if not enough for an arrest. As it is, the video doesn't show enough, with you matching it mentally to what you remember."

"TruVal could use their new MemCast gadget to dump my mem to the computer, and match the two sets of images."

"How many image generations is that? Alex to you to a computer to match with another image on the computer, and then hooker to computer to match with your what's now a fourth-generation mem. I think the result would be laughed out of court."

The detective sighed, extracted a bottle from a desk drawer, took a swig, then another, wiped his mouth with the back of his hand, offered the bottle to Morgan.

"Hey, couldn't that get you fired?" Morgan held up his hand in a "no, thanks" gesture.

"Don't care. They pulled this case away from me last night after I spoke with you, even transferred my captain for sticking up for me. I shouldn't even be talking to you now. They 'suggested' I might like to resign, said they'd try to line me up with a job with the Sausalito PD, maybe better than traffic division if I went quietly. So now you see it's all theory. Even if you picked the mug shot perfectly, no one would do anything."

"Why? Because there isn't a body?"

That's what they're saying. But I think that's a cover-up. Madelyn Lopez had a body – is a body – was killed, I mean, intentionally or otherwise. But they're saying the two deaths aren't related. And I know that none of what they're saying is the real reason, whether it's true or not. A bunch of government suits – I think I told you before – took this over and aren't telling me anything." He took another swig. "Tough to connect the dots here. Not my department anymore, though." He raised the bottle again, waved it in the air in what might have been the direction of Washington, D.C. "But hey," he said, "good news: since we know we can't ID the killer for sure, anything close to supporting an arrest, I put the word out on the street about that, so you're safe to go home now. No suspect, no witness. My little farewell gift to you."

"Thank you!" Morgan smiled for the first time that day. He tried to think of something pleasant to say to the policeman by way of goodbye. "You'll like Sausalito, I'm sure."

"Don't rub it in. I can't afford to live there, y'know, except maybe to rent a half-sunk houseboat. That means two expensive bus rides a day if I keep my apt in the city."

The two men looked gloomily at each other. DeLuca offered the bottle again. Morgan felt like taking it this time, but shook his head.

"That's it?" Morgan finally asked.

"That's it."

They shook hands. "Thank you for all you've done," Morgan said.

"Thank you for screwing up my career," replied DeLuca, more in regret than in anger.

Morgan called Tru on his com, told her the discouraging news.

"That's it?" she asked.

"That's it," he said. "Nice knowing you."

Chapter 25
Two Weeks Previously

A FASHIONABLE PART OF TOWN

A thirty-something man, well dressed in conservative gray, is sitting down when his com lights up. It is good that he is sitting down, because he will find the call quite disturbing.

"Do you know who this is?"

"I can guess."

"Was the job completed?"

"Yes. Mostly. But I couldn't get the body away. There were witnesses in a building across the street. I thought you'd taken care of that. They were making a call. I saw them. Calling the police, for sure."

The thirty-something man has lied. Not about killing Terra Lewis, which he had, but about seeing Alex call the police. Alex has a great aversion to calling the police.

"Shit."

"Those people were watching me. It was a setup."

"You think!"

"I know. I know these things. And I couldn't get away if I were carrying a body. Not from four floors up in a hotel on a busy street with the cops coming any minute."

He waits for his employer to say something. The employer says nothing. The thirty-something man speaks again. "But I tore off the woman's badge, the TruVal badge, and destroyed it."

"Not good enough. Go back and collect the body like we paid you to do."

"No way."

"Do you know who we are?"

"Not specifically, a code name. But..."

"Then you might not realize what we can do to you. Any time we want. You need to have a clear and distinct impression of that in your mind."

"I suppose. Yes, sir."

"Now go back there and get that body!"

"And do what with the body, then?"

"Anything you want as long as it's never found. And com me on this number when it's done!"

***

A DIFFERENT PART OF TOWN

"We'll have to call the police!" Her voice conveyed desperation, fright, and resignation. Mostly fright.

"Unless Alex called them already."

"I doubt he'd call the police for any reason. My God, what a mess this is!"

"We can't have you implicated in this," the taller woman said. "Not right now. Not for the next two weeks, for sure."

"What are you suggesting?"

"That I dispose of the body. I'll get Jimmy to help me."

"Isn't that something or other after the fact? A crime?"

"We'll work it out, a deal with the authorities. They all know me; they might go along. In the meantime, we can't let anyone find that body, or any blood, either."

"Why? Why would the police have her DNA?"

"Terra had a Top Secret security clearance once. She got a purchase order from the Defense Department to shoot a platoon of Marines in a Muslim pacification zone. She told me once. She was very proud of those photos."

"They would have collected a DNA sample, I guess."

"Terra never mentioned it, but it's routine for clearances at that level."

"Well then, clean it up, please, Athena. Right away."

***

THE TENDERLOIN

A thirty-something man enters the aging hotel, notices an old man behind the desk. He stands carefully, his eyes taking in everything of interest without shifting. He takes special care to notice doors, corridors, and the corner of the main lobby around which, an arrow promises, are the elevators.

See/Saw

At the same time that the thirty-something man is examining the hotel lobby, Jimmy parks the rental van in front of the hotel, pulls a lumpy black wardrobe bag out of the van and wads as much of it under his arm as he can. He and a tall woman enter the hotel lobby, notice with evident relief that there are only two other people there, a thirty-something man studying a picture on a wall, and an old man behind the desk. The door to the street opens behind them. Jimmy and the woman turn their backs as another man walks in and then out of sight around a corner. Blatantly casual, Jimmy and the woman get on one of the two elevators and push the button for the top floor.

Once there, they search for the exit to the roof, find it unlocked, walk the few steps upward and out into the air, briefly disturbing a few birds. Jimmy glances ahead to make sure they are alone, and hurries the woman over to where the body is lying. They are about to put the body in the wardrobe bag when they hear a noise behind them. The rooftop door is slowly opening, accompanied by a disturbance of pigeons. They hide behind a heat exchange unit. The woman extends her body as much as she dares past the edge of the machine, peeks carefully. She sees a balding man whom she doesn't know. He is staring down at the body.

There is a sharp clatter: The woman's com has accidentally fallen from her pocket as she was stretching, and had hit the rooftop tiles. She and Jimmy freeze. They hear the sound of footsteps rapidly going away from the body, and the rooftop door opening and closing. Carefully, they peek out from their hiding place. They have evidently frightened the stranger away. Jimmy mutters something about a Goddamn lucky break and watch it next time will you or we won't be so lucky, y'know.

Hurriedly, they pull rags and bottles of household cleaners out of the black bag, and place the body inside it, tugging at its arms and legs until it fits. They move the bag to one side, then quickly and with short nervous breaths wipe up the blood that has oozed from the body, and its urine and spittle. They uncap and upend bottles of cleansers over the remains of the dead person's bodily fluids, wipe vigorously, then stuff the rags into the bag along with the corpse, and zip it shut.

Panting with the effort, they carry the bag across the roof, through the door, and into the top floor elevator lobby. One of them pushes the "down" button. They take sharp, frequent breaths as both elevators ascend. One of the elevators arrives and they rush into it, pushing and dragging the bag as best they can. As will become relevant within the next twenty-five seconds, it is of note that the hotel's management refers to this elevator as "Elevator A." Jimmy practices, aloud, the cover story they will use if anyone sees a man and a woman carrying a large and heavy wardrobe bag and becomes curious. The woman tells Jimmy to shut the hell up. She pushes the button for the basement of the building. She is still annoyed at herself for letting her com fall and make a noise, even though as it turned out that was a wonderfully fortunate thing to have happened. But it did allow Jimmy to snap at her, an event that she won't soon forget, and won't let Jimmy forget, either.

Just as Elevator A's door closes, the second elevator arrives at the top floor. The old man at the desk is dimly aware that his boss calls this "Elevator B." Its door opens and the thirty-something man steps out. He does not notice that the door of Elevator A is closing, is almost shut. There would have been barely time, if he had thought to do it, to push the "down" button which would open Elevator A's door. We can believe that Jimmy and the woman would have been caught holding the bag. They would have died, right there, if the thirty-something man had pushed the button in time. That is because he would have killed them, taken their black bag, and delivered it to his friend at the crematorium for an unscheduled off-the-books procedure. But he has other concerns on his mind right now.

The thirty-something man walks very purposely the few feet to the rooftop door, opens it, steps out into the sunlight. A few pigeons take flight.

Jimmy and the woman descend to the basement in Elevator A, find a garage ramp. The door of Elevator B, having courteously waited the programmed amount of time, assumes that all occupants must by now have departed, closes.

The balding man who was scared away by the sound of the woman's dropped com has completed walking down four flights of stairs.

Jimmy and the woman carry the lumpy black wardrobe bag up to street level. They are very cautious. Their van is nearby.

Morgan, the man who has descended four flights of stairs, is dawdling in the hotel lobby, trying to be casual, cranking up the courage to walk out onto Turk Street. He has just seen a dead body and he is shaken, not knowing what might happen next. He now sees that only one other person is in the lobby, the old man behind the desk. He is relieved that the three others are no longer in the room. He doesn't wonder where they have gone while he was on a higher floor.

Jimmy and the woman begin loading the body bag into the back of the van.

While the couple is loading the body, Morgan, who has no idea of what is happening on the street outside, says a few words to the man at the desk, perhaps unadvisedly. He is trying to calm himself before leaving the hotel, but he does go out when the old man, making conversation of a mumbling sort, mentions that there were others going up. He heard both elevators quite clearly, he says, in spite of his advanced age and questionable auditory capability. Quite busy today, in fact, yes sir indeed he says. And that couple with the big black bag! This information spooks Morgan.

Back on the roof, the thirty-something man strides over to where the body had been after he had killed the woman, the original woman, that is, not the tall woman who, with Jimmy, has now left with the body. He walks from one side of the roof to another. He glances over at the apt across the street, where the witnesses to the murder had been when they watched him kill Terra Lewis. There is no one in that apt now. He idly wonders who the victim was. Not an odd feeling, anymore, to kill someone and not even know his name. The first few times he did that, he had indeed experienced a kind of odd feeling. But this time he simply tries to figure out what has happened, and what his options are. There is no yellow tape or other evidence that the police have been here. He then remembers seeing a stout male, and a tall female, in the lobby, then not seeing them. And he remembers, too late, that another elevator door had closed just as his own elevator door was opening.

Morgan looks out onto the street through the hotel door's glass front windows. He waits until the sidewalk is almost empty. He leaves the hotel. He walks east on the sidewalk, passing directly by a large dark van.

The man and woman working in the rear of the van duck down so the balding man won't see their faces. They have no idea who he is, but they don't want any witnesses.

The thirty-something man walks to the edge of the roof and looks over the parapet, down onto Turk Street. He sees a nervous-looking balding male but pays no attention to him. What he is really interested in is the stout male and the tall woman. They have almost finished loading a large black bag into the back of a dark van. The stout man is completing this task while the woman is walking around the van on the street side, evidently heading for the driver's-side door. The nervous-looking man is walking beside the van.

The thirty-something man curses. One shot should stop the van cold. Perhaps in the confusion he can then secure the body, or perhaps destroy it. He is disturbed by the thought of what his employer could do to him if he fails.

Carefully, the thirty-something man raises his pistol and fires, aiming (he hopes; he is not familiar with this model of van) at the fuel tank. Either the van will explode in flames, totally consuming the body and solving his problem, or the van will be disabled. In case the latter occurs, he plans then to rush downstairs and, in the guise of providing emergency assistance, Good Samaritan that he is, steal the large black bag which, he surmises, contains the body he desperately wants. Then he can tell his employer anything he feels like telling him.

The man on the hotel roof raises his pistol, aims carefully, and squeezes the trigger. This has the following consequences:

-A shot from the rooftop misses Morgan by inches. Morgan feels the air go by his head, and witnesses the impact of a bullet on the van, then hears a "ping" of tearing metal. In his current state of extreme nervousness, he believes that someone has shot at him.

-The thirty-something man has no interest in Morgan, because he doesn't know about Morgan. He is glad that the balding man has not got in the way of his bullet, because then the van might not have been hit and he'd have to risk another shot. As far as the thirty-something man is concerned, that is the only reason why is he glad that the balding man has not been shot dead in his tracks.

-The van experiences a hole in one of its panels. Inside the van there is damage to a few systems, but not enough to immediately disable it. The thirty-something man is not aware that his shot has not hit one of the van's vital organs.

-Realizing that he is likely to be trapped in the hotel if anyone is thoughtful enough to call the police, the thirty-something man doesn't get off a second shot, but runs down the stairs.

***

OUTSIDE THE HOTEL

"Jesus, what was that?" The shock of the jolted van reaches the front seat about the same time as the sounds of the shot and newly punctured metal.

The stout man slams the cargo door closed and runs around the driver's side, yells "Get over!" to the woman, slides behind the wheel beside the woman who has just said "Jesus, what was that?"

"A shot," he says, turning on the motor and slamming the van into drive. Resisting the urge to peel out, he slides the heavy van into traffic and drives as fast as he dares without, he figures, risking a stop for speeding or reckless driving. His hands are shaking and the van jostles a few inches left, then right, in its lane.

"What?" The woman is confused, shaken up.

"He came back," Jimmy says. "That son of a bitch came back and tried to kill us, y'know! Now what do we do now?"

The woman steels herself. She is in charge here, after all. Jimmy is just a grunt. "TruPlex," she says. "Underground garage, bottom level. We'll come back tonight and get rid of the body."

The thirty-something man reaches street level, but the van is half a block west. He sees that it is a rental, catches two digits of the license number.

***

AT THE TRUPLEX

That night, the man and the tall woman descend to the B-2 garage level separately, meet at the agreed time. The man has brought a wooden crate balanced on a large hand truck.

Jimmy opens the rear of the van. Together, they push and tug the body, in its nondescript black bag, into the wooden crate. Then they padlock the crate, wrestle it onto the hand truck, and secure it there with two thick straps.

"This is the tough part," says Jimmy, "because the cleaning crew is on duty this time of night. They'll be curious."

"I took care of that," the woman says.

"And the CCTVs? Off?"

"No, too suspicious; the time gap would be noticed. But the daily recordings recycle every thirty days."

"That's a long time."

"That's what it is."

The two maneuver the hand-truck and its crate into a freight elevator, get off at the fourteenth floor. The woman unlocks the cafeteria door. The man pushes the truck into the cafeteria, into the freezer room, and up against a wall.

The woman inspects the hand truck carefully.

"OK, take it back, then wipe it down."

"OK," Jimmy says. "But we can't leave that crate here forever, y'know, with a body in it."

"I know, I know" says the woman, annoyed because she has been worrying about the same thing.

The two leave the cafeteria and re-lock the door. There is now a large padlocked crate in the freezer room. Occasionally in the next few days, the head chef will curse it. Once, a cook will stumble into it and skin his knee. But both will very carefully observe the official admonition pasted on the side of the crate, the one that reads "Do Not Disturb. This Means You," considering the important name that immediately follows '"You": the name "Athena Taylor, VP."

***

POWELL STREET, NEAR UNION SQUARE

Having no option, the thirty-something man reports to his contact that he has secured the body. He feels bad about lying again: it's unprofessional.

"And did what with it?"

"Burned it."

"Evidence?"

"None. It was cremated under an alias by a friend in the business."

"Very good! I guess you'll live."

"Thank you. And I won't ever call this number again."

"Doesn't matter. There won't be a com on the other end of this line five seconds from now." Click.

The thirty-something man walks three blocks, ducks into a all-day-breakfast cafeteria, has scrambled eggs and coffee, whole wheat toast, no butter. Bitch of a mess, he says to himself. He doesn't know what the stout man and the tall woman intend to do with the body. Not turn it over to the police, for sure; one com call could have accomplished that. Could he ident that van and trace who rented it? If the man and the woman were pros, it would be a dead end. But they sure hadn't seemed like pros to him.

***

IN THE WEBCLOUD

Dispersed in the webcloud, one particular transient system of sensor feeds, databases, and software agents becomes aware, if "aware" can be applied to a distributed architecture composed of dynamically allocated and deallocated components of a causal probabilistic network, that the image of a person of interest has been captured by a satcam on a rooftop, has changed her orientation from vertical to horizontal, and has begun to cool rapidly from the nominal 98.6 ± 1.3 degrees Fahrenheit.

A system functional unit designated "HUG1NN" forms a dot, connects that dot to other dots, and sets its subroutines to finding still more dots. An associated functional unit, "MUN1NN," files an interim report with its user, a group code-named "Odin." This group is more benignly known in classified government budgets by the intentionally drowse-inducing name "Intergovernmental Memorial Commission."

The system sends a deeply encrypted message to Odin informing this user, with a high degree of certainty, as to how and when Terra Lewis has met her death, by whom, and on whose orders. It observes that Odin had not previously been aware of these data.

The next day, it also collects and forwards satcam data about the comings and goings of various people on that same rooftop: a thirty-something man named Charles Barnes; a stout man named James (Jimmy) Wotton; a tall woman named Athena Taylor; and a balding, middle-aged man named Robert Morgan.

***

1536 WASHINGTON STREET, SAN FRANCISCO

The 30-ish man is well aware of his obligations to his client. But he is also subject to the typical human prejudice for self-preservation. He is therefore relieved to receive a com call, some days later, telling him exactly where one of the two witnesses to the murder he has committed lives; that this witness is at home now; and that he is scheduled to be picked up by a TruVal, Inc., company car in 25 minutes. The man looks at his wristcom, determines that he might, if he were to hurry, arrive at the Washington Street address in time to see a man stepping out of a row house toward a large, dark car. In time to take aim carefully and shoot, two to the head and one to the heart, and escape before being apprehended. He does, in fact, hurry, and arrives on foot as a cable car is passing by, and just before the dark car arrives. He waits, partially concealing himself behind a hedge. The car waits. The car sounds its horn, twice. The intended victim does not appear. After ten minutes, a large female dressed in a typical Truda Vallon outfit exits the car, walks to the front door, knocks. Pounds. No answer. Five minutes later, the dark car drives off. The 30-ish man is disappointed that he has not managed to kill the witness, a man whose name he knows, a name that was written on a hastily scrawled sign on an apt door on Turk Street, as "<u>ROBERT MORGAN, ROBERT MORGAN</u>."

Chapter 26

Robert Morgan, PhD, clicked on the message from his bank. There it was, the record of his final paycheck. Too many damn deductions and not enough to live on. He took another sip from his glass, made a bad face. In the days since he'd returned home he'd tried to economize, had with much regret given up his beloved Glenlivet and bought the cheapest whiskey he could find, a Tennessee brand called Old Sourpuss. It fit his current mood.

He'd now taken up watching Tru's weekly television show. The first time, she had devoted a solemn minute and a half for a weepy and heart-felt tribute to the late Madelyn Lopez, victim of a senseless, terrible industrial accident in her own TruPlex. Tru did the obligatory "thoughts and prayers" shuck and jive, and sang a sad song. Then Madelyn Lopez was over, all over. Gone. Not even history.

He'd re-memmed Alex's mem a few times, too, had imagined having sex with the real Truda Vallon instead of the lookalike hooker. It was excellent, in his imagination: wonderful, exciting, draining. He was sure he could have done a better job of it than that drugsodden sod of an Alex. Yes! His fantasies zoomed, climbed, exploded in ecstasy.

But there was more. He realized that he missed Tru, missed her combination of assurance and need, even missed the way she finished his sentences for him. Until after they said goodbye that last time, Morgan hadn't realized that he wanted her, not for what she could do for him in bed or otherwise, but for herself. It didn't hurt that she was worth quite a few million dollars, but that wasn't the point. Even if she were penniless – well, not quite.

His dreams came back down to earth as his com displayed his TIAA-CREF retirement balance. Have to pull it out early, take a terrific beating. But what else could he do to economize? His diet had already been reduced to peanut butter and waffles most days. He'd even asked the butcher about the price of horse meat, but had turned away after the butcher asked him what kind of dogs did he have, sir, and how many, and had they been wormed?

Morgan had worked, those first few days, on shining up his resume, posting it on the web like a note in a bottle: whoever finds this, I love you. Hire me, just hire me. Anybody want a failed physicist with experience in the entertainment business? No, not that kind of experience; mostly ducking, running, and keeping away from windows. A few companies had sent him employment questionnaires. He'd got into the habit of turning to the last question first. If it read "reason for leaving last or current position," he DELETEd the email. Current position? Well, he had his choice between prone and supine, now didn't he? Screw it.

He had received one real job offer, but there was a catch. Ed Clarty, Clinical Advisor, had seen his resume, in which, perhaps too wishfully, Morgan had cited TruVal, Inc. as job experience. "Consultant to TruVal, Inc." Clarty had offered Morgan a job as his memlab assistant, since his previous assistant had been terrorized and run off by the SoCalls. It paid minimum wage.

Only minimum wage. Clarty was certain that would be enough to get Morgan on board. Clarty didn't make much himself, so he couldn't afford more. Not like he could have made, if his father hadn't ruined his potential singing career. Well, why Morgan? Morgan was a legitimate doctor, wasn't he? And the clientele weren't likely to ask him "degree in what?" They'd assume it was med or psych. All that might be OK with Morgan, he uneasily supposed; he'd caught the scent of desperation in the man's resume. But it didn't matter what Morgan did at the memlab, after all. That wasn't the point of hiring him; not the point at all.

***

At his interview the next day, Clarty told Morgan that he'd been searching on "TruVal" in the various resume databases, which was how he'd found Morgan's resume. Tit for tat and pro for quo for quid, the short of it was that Clarty was demanding an audition at TruVal, Inc., for Tru's weekly show. Or Morgan could just shove that memlab assistant's job and go back to waffles and horse-meat dreams.

To himself, Clarty planned what he would do at that audition. Not smile and stick probes to peoples' heads, for damned sure, even though TruVal had their own memlab. No, he had no interest in that: He wanted to sing. Sing what? Sing whatever. Natural voice, utterly enchanting, any style from opera to ole' opry and everything in between. Everybody had told him that in high school: enchanted with his voice, the amazing things he could do with it. And he could even read music, after a fashion. Taught himself, very proud of that. Let me sing you a few bars right now over the com, Dr. Morgan, so you can hear for yourself how great I'd be on The Truda Vallon Show!

No, thanks. The gist of Morgan's improv response to Clarty went something like this: You don't have to sing anything to me over the com. Yes, I believe you, but you know, the sound quality of an older model of com – Certainly. Of course I'll set it up with the TruVal producers. Discovering your talent? Why, they'll be overwhelmed, always searching for new faces, never can have too many. Ah, it can't happen for two or three weeks, of course. That's the cycle, you know. You didn't know? But as soon as they're open for auditions, I'm sure that blah blah blah.

Morgan got the job and agreed to start work at the O'Farrell Street memlab the following day.

Chapter 27

Morgan had been afraid that Helen would appear in his life again, at least to gloat, now that he was down and out. She was good at gloating, nationally ranked. Her specialty was gloating about things he didn't know about and she wouldn't tell him about, except to point out with unsubtle hints that there was a reason for her to gloat and that he'd never ever find out what that might have been. Was still being. Might be, again and again. Might never have stopped.

But he'd had no contact from her, hadn't laid eyes on her since that fatal party at the TruPlex. He hadn't heard from DeLuca recently, either, or from anyone at TruVal.

He raised his glass again, drank. Got to stop drinking this moose pee; can't take it anymore. He had to believe that the police or the FBI or TruVal security was continuing the investigation of Terra's presumed murder, or Madelyn Lopez's possible murder. Maybe. But maybe it was all over: two unsolved deaths. Was there anything he could do here on Washington Street, broke and about to lose his home?

Well, where the hell were we in this convoluted caper? Morgan thought through all the loose plot threads, things that had never made sense to him, or that he'd never followed up, and now never would.

First, was Terra Lewis the killer's actual target? Or would any TruVal photog on that roof at that time been shot?

Who was the killer? A principal, or a hired gun?

Where had Lewis's body gone? Who'd taken it? Why? And why had someone tried to obliterate all traces of her blood? Presumably, so no one would know it was Lewis who'd been killed. But after a few days or weeks, at most, her absence would surely have been noticed, reported in the papers. She was, after all, a notable person in her circle.

And did Terra's Singapore trips have anything to do with her death, the one trip she made and the other trip she didn't live to make? The dates of that planned trip were coming up soon, now. What had been going on in Singapore, if anything, that could be related to her death?

Morgan had heard Baker hint that the SoCalls had a spy inside TruVal, a spy who "knew something." Then, he thought Baker was blowing wind, but as it turned out there was something to know about, after all: MemCast. A technology that the SoCalls would love to hate. Perhaps the last chance we'd all have, not one at a time in a memlab, to know each others' minds, to understand, to see the wonders. But no, that was the kind of psychogarble he'd never been comfortable with.

Morgan sighed. Not my problem, he concluded. Rest of my life I'll work in the O'Farrell Street memlab, helping the horny get off on other people's sex lives. Hell with it.

Morgan had started dreading bedtime, putting it off, going to sleep later and later. Every night he would go to bed, have bad dreams about his married life with Helen, or "marred" life as he usually thought of it, complete with quotation marks. This particular night he woke up at three a.m., the last dreadful dream still in his mind. Helen had been laughing at him, flaunting her unfaithfulness, forcing him to scent the other men who'd been with her.

Could he go to a memlab and dump that dream? After all, he was about to start working in one; he could plug himself in any time. But dreams were different from memories. Not stored the same way in the mind; chancy to dump or memplant. Of course if you remembered a dream, then the memlab could dump that mem for you. Well, then: Morgan could try to re-enact his entire stupid and ill-fated marriage night after night in his dreams, and then remember the dream and dump the mem of the dream each day, not the dream itself. But that might not do the trick. A few people, he'd heard, could dream to order. Morgan had never been able to do that. Oh, well. What crap we come up with at three a.m.! He turned over and tried to get back to sleep. Tried not to dream.

***

Morgan had told Clarty that TruVal auditions were every two or three weeks. How long could Morgan stretch that out before Clarty got wise? Already, on Morgan's third day on the job, Clarty was becoming impatient. Morgan could tell that he was beginning to doubt Morgan's ability to arrange an interview. And in fact, such doubt was justified: Morgan had done nothing about a potential audition. Who could he call at TruVal? It would have to be someone he knew. Athena? She wasn't on the right side of the business. Tru herself? What could he say that would interest her in a singer who'd apparently never sung in public since high school? Call in a favor? What favor? He sighed. Well, he could hang onto this job at the memlab a few more days, probably, before he'd be fired. Earn a few more bucks, if Clarty actually paid him.

The work was getting to him already, being the memlab assistant. Greet clients at the door, get them to sign all those forms, make sure they had enough money and were willing to part with it, turn them over to "clinical advisor" Ed Clarty. Easy, right?

But now there were complications. Not only were the SoCalls coming by more frequently, acting more hostile, finding more garbage to throw at the building, but the lab clientele had changed, too, and all because of Truda Vallon and her MemCast announcement. On this day, for instance, he had shooed two young men out the door who might have been, in less complicated times, simple horny memlab customers. But not anymore.

"That's five hundred like you said, right?

"Well, I've been thinking. This mem I'm selling you, it's MemCast quality, y'know. You could turn right around and sell it to one of those new porncast outfits for a lot more than five hundred. And maybe residuals, too."

"What are you saying?"

"I'm saying that at five hundred you've got yourself one hell of a deal. Too much of a deal for me to go along with right now. Look at it this way: that mem, the one in my head now – and yes, I'm playing it back right now and let me tell you it's the best fuck you've always wanted to have in your whole Goddamn life, three, four, five people at a time, couples and singles both, AC/DC, mix 'n' match – that's worth ten, twenty thousand in MemCast royalties. Or more."

"But then why..."

"My friend," he patted the other man on the shoulder and then pulled his hand back quickly, "I don't have time to market this mem. I'll let you have all that profit. Thousands! Not to mention playing it to yourself and getting off on it until you decide to sell. But I need five thousand from you right now; then you get rich from it instead of me."

"But you said five hundred!"

"Not any more, buddy. It's worth a lot more than..."

"Screw you!"

"Just you try it, asshole."

The two men glared at each other. Pushing and shoving, Morgan figured, were about to break out. He escorted the pair out the door with soothing words, explaining that when they'd agreed between themselves on a deal, any deal at all! they could come back.

Outside the door, over the din of the SoCalls' chanting, he could hear the would-be seller saying "And copyright. You could copyright that sucker real easy, sell copy after copy after copy."

Chapter 28

During the mid-afternoon lull the next day at the memlab, Clarty opened up a new topic. "Ah, Dr. Morgan?" Here it comes, thought Morgan. No audition, no job. But that wasn't what Clarty had in mind.

"What would it take for me to turn my memlab here into a real MemCast business?"

"Hmm. Equipment, I guess, a license from TruVal, a few training sessions."

"What do you think of the idea?"

Anything to distract him from an audition that will never happen. "Ah, wonderful idea, chief! And there are plenty of interested parties in this neighborhood who'd be happy to sell their mems to you for..."

"*Sell* wasn't quite the business model I had in mind, doctor. Suppose we tell them their mems will earn them a fortune on MemCast, and they can even retain copyright. But we charge them, oh, a few hundred, maybe more, for putting their mems into MemCast format, professional packaging and all that."

A light was beginning to dawn in Morgan's head. "We get the money up front, and then we wouldn't..."

"We wouldn't have to market, or distribute, or anything like that. That would be a client responsibility."

"Which they wouldn't know how to do."

"Most of them, no. Even if they did, I think their returns would be zero to slight. Most of their mems would be garbage, of course. If they were any good, they'd have been snapped up by one of the new commercial MemCast publishers."

"That sounds like a win-win!"

"A win for you and me. Too bad about the suckers."

"That's great!" Morgan was secretly appalled, but he didn't want to dampen Clarty's enthusiasm for something that promised to divert his attention from TruVal.

"Now," said Clarty, pulling himself up to his full height, "the clincher: For only a few hundred more we dub in a musical accompaniment, more interesting than moaning and groaning and yelling over and over 'O God O God O God do it to me!' And that would be," he concluded triumphantly, "our exclusive: A song by the one and only Ed Clarty, famous new guest star of TruVal's weekly TV show, singing in any style they want, any style at all!"

Clarty returned to his office, whistling off-key. So much for making him forget that stupid obsession.

The next morning, Morgan had barely arrived at the memlab when his com played a few bars from "Strangers": Call coming in.

"Hello?" He couldn't help himself. It always sounded like a question, put him immediately on the defensive. But the caller, sounding hesitant and agitated, didn't pick up on that.

"Dr. Morgan! Thank God you're there, thank God!" Morgan was reminded of Clarty's "O God O God!", but this was Athena's voice, the Goddess herself. Considering the situation, Morgan hesitated over whether to respond by calling her "Athena" or "Ms. Taylor," punted.

"Yes, I recognized your voice. What's up?"

"I'm in trouble, doctor! I've been avoiding getting Tru involved in this business but now she insists! Ten o'clock tonight, right after her show rehearsals, I've got to confess!"

Morgan was mystified. "Ah..."

"I want you here, doctor. For moral support. And Tru trusts you; she'll listen to what you have to say. But mostly because you're friends with that policeman and he may be our only hope now. My only hope for staying out of jail!"

"But you said he suspected me. And then he said he didn't."

"I'm sorry about that. I think I intentionally misheard what he said. Wanted to keep you away from the investigation, I'm sorry, but now..."

"I'll be glad to help. Sure, I'll be there at ten. But what..."

"It's about Terra Lewis's body. I hid it. Jimmy and I hid it. To protect Tru, so her big special, the biggest one of all, wouldn't be completely overshadowed by that awful, sordid murder. But we can't keep it secret forever, hidden, the body that is, where it is, and now Tru insists on knowing, and I can't find Jimmy anywhere!" Her voice had risen to a shriek.

"OK, OK. I'll be there. At the TruPlex?"

"Yes. Right. Tru's office. Please be there!" She hung up abruptly.

Athena had a confession to make. Why involve Morgan? She'd given him one or two reasons, but they didn't sound very convincing. But this was his chance. He could get back into TruVal, maybe find a way to make a little money, at least enough to keep him in peanut butter and waffles.

***

The sun shown brilliantly and twitterpated birds circled Technicolor flowers. That was the image that struck and stuck in his mind, when his com rang a few minutes later and he saw Truda Vallon's face on the screen.

"Robert, I need you. It's important."

The birds sang even louder, and the sun nearly burst its equator.

"Why?" he asked. That was a dumb thing to say, he thought. It might occur to her to change her mind. He should have said "I'll be right there." However, in the event, no harm had been done.

"We found Terra's body."

"Did the police..."

"The police know nothing about this. Terra's body has been here in the TruPlex since she was shot. All this time."

"Are you going to..."

"Call the police? I'll do that later. Right now, I want you here to help us figure out what to tell them, and to control the damage."

"Why me?"

"I trust you, Robert, and your wise counsel. And I miss having you here. And you know the background, so I won't have to do any explaining."

"Athena called me about the same thing a minute ago."

"Oh? Well no damn wonder. She's in it up to her long pretty white neck. Are you going to be here after my rehearsal?"

"Yes."

"Great! See you then."

So, he thought, the pot boils. Tonight should be interesting.

But first, he wanted to speak with Alex again, if he could catch him before that night's meeting. There were loose ends that Alex, possibly, could tie up, that would put Morgan in a stronger position on Rug Row, maybe give him critical background on what Athena had been up to.

He knocked on Clarty's office door, explained that he had to leave right then and take care of matters related to Clarty's forthcoming audition at TruVal. Clarty was delighted to give him the rest of the day off. Morgan waved goodbye and left through the alley door.

Chapter 29

He walked the few blocks to Turk Street and up to Alex's fifth-floor apt. Since it was still morning, he figured Alex might not have bestirred himself for the day, or could still be awake from whatever misdeeds he'd been up to the previous night.

He knocked on the door. Again, louder. No response. Self-consciously, he tried to speak through the keyhole loud enough so Alex could hear him, but not loud enough that everyone else on the floor could hear, too. Hazel or Harold, for instance. But why bother whispering? Last time he'd been afraid of a killer, but that was over. There was no reason why he couldn't ...

At that moment, Alex opened the door. He was dressed in a dirty T-shirt and even dirtier undershorts.

"Uh, hi. Do I know you? Don't I know you?"

"I'm Robert Morgan, as in '<u>ROBERT MORGAN</u>, <u>ROBERT MORGAN</u>' that you wrote on your door. Remember?"

"Uh, the mem. Right?"

"Right."

"Well, man, I'm really sorry about – I guess that was a shitty thing to – but, well, preservation, go with the flow, had to stick it to somebody else, whoever was handy." Alex took a step back, assumed a defensive stance which struck Morgan as pathetic.

"Forget it," said Morgan. "No harm done. And the gunman isn't after me anymore. Today, I just wanted to ask you a few questions about that hooker."

Alex brightened with relief. "Oh yeah! I remember. Actually, I don't remember, but I've got this mem of thinking about the mem, you know how that goes, before I gave it to you, that it was really cool – or hot – or something." He spread his hands and shrugged one shoulder. "I don't think I can help you."

"You've called hookers before, haven't you?"

"Well, yeah. I guess."

"Have any of them ever brought their own songchip?"

Alex seemed puzzled. "Why would they do that?"

"Maybe to heighten the moment. Or it could be their 'trademark.' Or perhaps for some other reason."

"Could be, now that you mention it, but that's never happened to me. Sounds cool, though! Wow, man! Could be some high-class piece of ass that I never could..."

"OK, OK," Morgan interrupted. "The hooker brought a song to your place on a songchip. Wanted me, ah, you, to play it while we – you and she, I mean, were fucking."

"Brought it on a chip? Why not download it online?"

"Yeah, I thought that was odd, too. Look, Alex, had you heard that song before?"

"Ah, I don't remember. The memlab, y'know."

"OK. Right. But maybe you still have that songchip here in your apt. I wondered if you might have..."

"The songchip?"

"Right. I noticed it wasn't in your player."

"When you 'visited' me."

"Yeah."

"Yeah. Well, if there was a songchip, the hooker must have grabbed it on her way out the door. I sure didn't find one here in my place. Damn!" He shook his head in disappointment. "Could have sold it."

Morgan peered around him. There could be a chip underneath one of those dirty plates, or socks, or in all the other trash that was littering the apt. It would be hopeless trying to find a piece of electronics the size of a fingernail. Retrieving that chip had been pretty good presence of mind for someone who'd been shot at not five minutes before. But that chip had been valuable: an unreleased Truda Vallon song. Now that "Strangers" had been released, though, the chip's value wouldn't be more than a few bucks.

"Got it!" Alex said, "I just remembered: she didn't mention any chip to me."

"When was that? You dumped the mem, remember? How could you remember what she said?"

"She called me a couple days before we met, I mean, to set up the date. Said I didn't have to pay anything, a friend had paid. She said it was one of my buddies. Who'd paid, I mean."

"Which buddy?"

"Didn't say. Actually, I don't have a lot of buddies." He stared blankly off into the distance, as if his life could have been different. A friend. Someone to blow pot with, for instance, or shoot up with.

"Did you believe that?"

"Believe what?

"That a buddy paid her."

"Not really. Any buddy of mine with enough money for a whore would buy her for himself, not for me."

"Nice to have buddies like that, I guess. Anyway, this woman called you, said she wanted to come by in two days and have sex with you."

Alex put a hand to his forehead. "Ah, right."

"And it wouldn't cost you anything."

"Right. And she'd pay me not to go to a memlab and sell it. Pay me a lot. That was real odd."

"Anything else?"

Alex paused and thought, a task that did not, apparently, come easily to him. "Well," he finally added, "she wanted to make sure we could do it on my couch facing the big window, not in the bedroom."

"Why?"

"Dunno. My bedroom is a mess, y'know, and she mentioned that. Maybe she's fussy about where she fucks? Who knows? Maybe just a quirk."

Finally, Morgan thought, I'm getting somewhere. "Alex, how did she know you had a couch facing the window? And how would she know your bedroom was such a mess?"

"Ah – dunno." He was quiet for a moment. "Must've been here before! That's it! She'd been to my place before."

"Well then, had she been here before?"

"Ah, not that I remember, since I don't remember anymore, what she looked like, that is, but..."

"But you sell sexmems once in a while."

"Yeah, when I get laid, then I pick up a few bucks, you know. Nothing wrong with that."

Morgan bore in. "She could have been here before, then, maybe even more than once, and you wouldn't remember."

"Yeah. That's right."

"Alex, you don't remember ever having had sex with anyone, do you."

"Ah, no. Guess I've done that, but I got laid off, see, a long time ago, and if I can get a little money for a sexmem, well, then..."

There was a pause.

Morgan didn't think he'd be getting anything more of value out of Alex at that point. "OK, Alex, thanks. And remember the good news: we're both off the hit list for witnessing a murder."

"Yeah, man, I figured. I really owe you for that, letting me set you up like that." Nervously, he reached into his pocket and pulled out a joint. "But I don't appreciate all the attention."

"Our look-see in your apt?"

"Yeah. I saw where you'd moved the furniture around. I guessed it was you. AND I didn't appreciate the police tech spreading black dust all over the place, AND those goons escorting me out of here and holding me for a couple of hours."

"What goons?"

"Your guys. TruVal security. Oh, they were nice enough, and even gave me a thousand bucks so I wouldn't tell the cops I'd been kidnapped, like I'd tell the cops anything! But I still didn't like it much."

"What did they do to you? Did they hurt you?"

"No, no, hustled me out, put me in a car, big fancy car with a permit flag, y'know? Drove me around Golden Gate Park, around and around."

"For two hours?"

"For two hours, like I said. Felt like six. Always clockwise. Told them I was getting dizzy but they told me to shut up. Had to piss but they wouldn't let me out of the damned car. Then they got a call from somebody and brought me home."

"When was that?"

"Oh, I guess it was about a month ago. Ah, I remember. It was the day before the cops dusted my apt."

Morgan was stunned. That was the same day he and Tru and Melody and Serena had searched Alex's apt. No wonder they hadn't worried about finding him at home! Well, add another big question for Tru and Athena!

"Got a new couch out of it, though," Alex said.

"What?"

"Got back from the park and my old couch was gone and there was a new one. Not 'new' new, but a lot newer than the old one."

"Did TruVal do that?"

"Damned if I know! I was riding around in a big car getting dizzy and trying to keep from pissing my pants!"

"Very generous," said Morgan with a touch of irony.

"Liked the old color better, though," said Alex.

"What?"

"A darker shade of brown. Went better with my décor."

Morgan turned and opened the door to leave. He heard two familiar voices in the corridor, but this time he didn't care if they saw him or not. All that risk, all that sneaking, was over. He walked straight toward the elevator and brushed past them.

"Hazel, I'm sorry for what I said. Can we get back together?"

"Your new girlfriend dumped you already?"

"Oh, no, that's not..."

"I heard about it. Don't deny it."

"OK, she dumped me because I preferred you. She found out."

"Bullshit!"

"Women are OK, but I..."

"Bullshit!"

If there was any more to this enlightening conversation Morgan missed it, because his elevator had arrived, opened its door, engorged him, assimilated him.

Chapter 30

Morgan went home and toasted a frozen waffle, celebrated by covering it with store-brand strawberry jam. Could he get a few dollars of consulting money out of TruVal for his time that night? Then maybe he could afford that real natural organic save-the-world jam he'd been wanting for so long. He pulled out his bottle of Old Sourpuss, sniffed it, put it away. Stay straight; had to keep his wits. His job at the memlab couldn't last more than another week or two. Thoughts of blackmailing Athena Taylor for whatever she'd done crossed his mind. No, not that. His situation wasn't that desperate. Yet.

Allowing plenty of time for transit connections, he arrived at the TruPlex early. A guard on duty scanned his badge, called him "Dr. Morgan," smiled at him. Seemed like old times again, even though he hadn't been gone that long. A sense of entitlement, an elevated level of gravitas, coursed through him. He quickened his pace, then glanced at his wristcom. Too early. Wouldn't look good to go up to the twenty-sixth floor and wait. Wouldn't be cool.

He elevated to twelve, curious about his old office. There it was, but the inner office was empty. Everything had been removed. Madelyn's outer office still had its furnishings, but showed signs of having been disturbed, by police judging by the yellow tape draped mournfully over the desk. All the desk drawers were open and empty. Black dust that hadn't been cleaned up very well lay on the desktop. Morgan wondered if they'd picked up Helen's prints, not just Madelyn's. Or if Helen had carefully wiped down that part of the desk, because she knew the police would...

But that was all surmise. Helen had never shown signs of being murderous during their marriage. Even the items she'd thrown at him had been mostly symbolic, even though one had struck him and ruined his good suit. He laid the blame for that, charitably, on poor aim and her highly agitated state.

He looked at the time again. 9:35 p.m. Oh, well. Time for coffee. The cafeteria, he knew, closed at three p.m., but outside the door were several vending machines, including one with coffee. He walked up the two flights to fourteen. The corridor lights had dimmed to the 'night' setting. Morgan was almost at the cafeteria door before he saw that it was ajar. Anyone there? Still serving, perhaps? But it was dark inside. He retreated to the vending machines, flashed his badge at the Jumpin' Java™ machine, pressed a series of twelve buttons that, he had learned, would eventually dispense ordinary black coffee, waited while the machine took time to compile and execute the appropriate source code modules.

While the cup was making its perilous descent from the Cup Stack Object inside the machine, programmed to meet up with the spurt of hot liquid beginning to descend at the same time from the Brew Object, Morgan noticed that the cafeteria door had swung open. A thirty-something man in a brown UPS uniform and a cap pulled low over his eyes was emerging, pushing a dolly with a crate on it. Morgan turned back to the coffee machine, which was flashing "please complete your customized customer satisfaction survey by pressing 'yes.'" Morgan pressed "no," and a plastic door reluctantly swung out of the way. Morgan turned, reached inside the machine, and pulled the cup toward him just as the UPS man passed by his left shoulder. Odd, where he had seen that man before? And then he remembered: wasn't that "UPS man" the killer? The one in Alex's mem?

Although he wasn't quite sure he was right about the ID, Morgan turned back and did something he would never have anticipated doing: he yelled "Hey you, stop!" The man turned toward him and reached into a pocket, came toward him with purpose in his eyes. Morgan, by now deeply regretting having said "Hey you, stop!" even though that had occurred only three seconds before, did the only thing he could: he threw the hot coffee in the intruder's face and ran down a corridor, turned quickly into a sub-corridor and then one of several sub-sub-corridors, and hid. The intruder ran past him, ran in other directions briefly and then toward the elevators, his footsteps thudding down the main corridor until they were lost. Morgan heard a door open and close; the stairs, he surmised. He looked around desperately for something he could use to spread the alarm: an intercom, a fire alarm, whatever. But he didn't see anything likely. He pulled his com from his pocket, called TruVal, received a recording. "If you would like to – press or say –" Punching zero repeatedly did nothing. Finally he managed to connect with the guard on duty, stumbled through a confused set of instructions on what had to be done. After several questions that took precious time, the guard promised to alert guards at all building exits to a man in a UPS uniform.

That, for now, was all Morgan could do. And now it was almost ten o'clock.

Morgan ascended to the twenty-sixth floor in a high state of agitation, entered the luxurious confines of Rug Row. He found Athena tearful and cowering, quite different from her usual confident self. He was about to relate his disturbing confrontation on the fourteenth floor when Tru walked in, frowning. She nodded absently at Morgan and walked up to Athena, took up the same kind of wide-legged stance that she had laughed at Morgan for using. It reminded Morgan of the akimbo-wrestler pose from one of her dance routines.

"Look, Athena," she said, "I know I let you take Terra's body off that roof. I know it's partly my fault." Morgan stared mouth-open at this news. Both women ignored him. "But we need to stop putting this off. Tell me what you did with the body, all the details. And then we're going to speak with Hersch and ask him to call the police. I'll protect you all I can."

Morgan surmised that Hersch was the company's lawyer.

Athena appeared a little calmer, now that there was something to be done. "Jimmy and I took the body," she said. "That much you knew already. We had identified an industrial dump site south of town, had all these elaborate plans. Jimmy rented us a van so we wouldn't be using a TruVal company vehicle. But then, when we got the body into a bag and were loading it in the van, someone shot at us, right there on Turk Street!"

"He was shooting at me!" Morgan interrupted. Again, the women ignored him. "Wasn't he?" he insisted, to a continued absence of response.

Athena continued explaining to Tru. "OK, yeah, Morgan was there, on the street. I hadn't met him then, remember? So I didn't know who he was. But it was Jimmy and me the shooter was aiming at, pretty surely because we had Terra's body. We finished loading the van as fast as we could and took off. But I looked back and saw a man – it must have been the one, the shooter – trying to make out our rear license plate. I knew we couldn't take that long drive south in this van, not with a man with a gun who might be able to track us. We knew we'd have to get rid of the body as soon as possible, and the only place I could think of was the TruPlex!"

Tru was outraged. "Right here *my* building?"

"Sorry, ma'am. Yes, right here in the building. In a crate in the cafeteria freezer room, so it wouldn't..."

"Stink," said Tru.

"Right," Athena continued. "We used my master key to unlock the cafeteria, and we hauled it in. That's where it is now."

Tru and Athena were silent long enough for Morgan to realize the implications of what they had just said. "Wrong!" he blurted. "That crate is sitting in the middle of the main corridor on the fourteenth floor, next to a puddle of coffee!"

They looked at him in astonishment, finally listening to him. Morgan told them how he had blundered into someone whom he surmised was the killer, how the killer had run off and Morgan had called the guard on duty. Conveniently, Morgan didn't mention his display of prudence, running away and hiding. But after all, the killer might have had a gun. Probably had a gun. At least a knife, maybe.

"Were the guards in time to stop him?" Tru asked.

"I doubt it, or they would have called up here to tell you they'd detained an intruder. But there's CCTV, and I believe we need to secure those video files immediately, and by that I mean right now!"

"Now?"

"If Terra's killer could get past all your fancy security and into the building, posing as a deliveryman long after business hours, why wouldn't he be able to delete CCTV data?"

"Right!" The three ran to the express elevator, descended to the lobby level, and looked for the guard in charge of the night shift.

Athena knew where the CCTV data files were kept. As soon as she had located the guard, she ordered him to go with them to the B-1 level and unlock the doors to the server room.

As Athena com'd the on-call tech manager, Tru saw Morgan examining the ruins of dark machines. "There was quite a bit of damage from the explosion," she said, "but as you see we've cleaned up most of it. The power and security systems are OK now, and our basic memlab equipment, at least, was saved, although several components were destroyed."

Athena connected with the tech manager, and between the two they identified the three CCTV servers that monitored the fourteenth floor, the elevators, the stairwells, the entrances, and the building exterior. Following his instructions step by step, she copied the server contents for the past three hours onto DAT media, removed them from the machines.

The process took until after midnight, but when it was finished Athena let out a long breath, put the tapes in her purse, smiled for the first time in two hours, and said "There!"

Chapter 31

They went to the fourteenth floor and wheeled the crate back into the cafeteria freezer room, arranged it where it had been before, and shut the outer cafeteria door.

"OK," said Tru. We're back to square one. But we can't leave that body in the freezer very much longer. We'll have to involve the police."

"Square zero," said Athena, "because there's someone on the loose who knows where Terra's body is."

"Minus one," added Morgan, "because the killer sure didn't figure it out by himself. How did he find out about the body? How did he get into the building?"

Athena looked saddened. "I think I know. I haven't been able to reach Jimmy all day." She tried again on her com. "Still no answer. The killer saw our license plate as we drove away, or at least part of it. Even one or two numbers or letters, and seeing the rental company's name on the back, plus the time of day, and he'd eventually be able to figure out who'd rented it."

"That must have taken him several days," said Tru.

"Evidently. But finally he must have got to Jimmy, forced him to reveal where the body was, took his TruVal security badge. I hope all that happened to Jimmy was getting tied up, not..."

There was a moment of shared silence.

"Well," said Morgan finally, "between DeLuca and me we've narrowed the suspects down to four or five likelies, and a dozen or so possibles: guns for hire. I didn't see more of the man's face tonight in the corridor than I saw in Alex's mem, probably less. If we could ID the exact person, we might be able to pressure useful information out of him – like a hint as to who hired him to kill Terra – even if we might not have enough to lock him up.

"I think it's time to involve that lookalike, the hooker you hired to have sex with Alex. You admitted you did that," he added, looking at Tru. "I'm sure you can find her, with all your corporate resources, even if she's left town. We can get her mem of the event, hopefully with the killer's face. We'll bring her to the TruVal memlab, have her memplant the mem in – me!"

Athena and Tru looked at him, startled, then traded glances.

"You know," Morgan continued, "Or actually you don't know, of course, but I spoke with Alex again today. There's something fishy about this whole lookalike hooker thing. He was rushed out of his apt before we," he nodded at Tru, "arrived that morning. I'm sure you know about that, because it was TruVal security that kept him busy driving around Golden Gate park for two hours before they let him go home."

"You're right, Robert," Tru said. "I wanted to search his apt without his getting in the way and giving us a hard time."

"And the couch," Morgan continued. "Alex got a new couch out of the deal. Not really new, but different. Clean. No stains. Now I don't know about you, but in my experience having sex on a couch is very likely to leave stains that can be DNA'd."

He stared hard at Tru. She looked at him calmly and said "So what?"

"So," he said, "Whose DNA is on record these days?" He ticked off the answer. "Anyone who's had a security clearance higher than Secret. That's one. Anyone who's paid to have a lab type his DNA. That isn't public information, but it could be subpoenaed. That's two. And anyone with an arrest record. That's three. Now, our hooker has very probably been arrested, and numerous times at that. Even though prostitution isn't strictly speaking a crime any more, the police have ways of keeping the traffic down. On Ellis Street they call it 'harassment.'"

Athena looked at him. "Dr. Morgan, where is all this going?"

"Where it's going is that the couch was switched because the guilty party, and by 'party' I mean both of you, didn't want anyone to find the hooker who had sex with Alex, even though her mem, combined with mine, might be able to ID Terra's killer. You didn't want the police to be able to DNA her from, ah, 'substances' they might find on that couch.

"If I had both mems in my head, each one with half a view of the killer's face, I could – I hope! – ID him. Then we could go to the police, tell them about Terra, run the mug-shot app again. A positive ID and a body might be enough to persuade the police to bring the killer in, grill him, make him an offer, threaten him, whatever it takes, to find out who hired him to kill Terra Lewis.

"Therefore," he struck a dramatic pose but immediately realized he'd overdone it, "I conclude that you don't want anyone to find the killer. Meaning that you two were behind the whole thing.

"And so, I am now prepared to go to the police and tell them the whole story. You'll have time to hide Terra's body again, and I can't stop you from doing that. But my testimony, and Alex's, should be enough to get you both in a whole lot of shit!"

Tru's and Athena's faces were pictures of, at the same time, astonishment, amusement, and distress. Not the faces of murder conspirators, Morgan realized, not that he'd observed such faces except on television. Now, if they were really guilty, at least on TV one of them would be sure to say "I don't know what you're talking about!" Wait for it.

"Robert," said Tru, gently touching Morgan's arm, "you're wonderful, but not much of a detective. Why would we need to have a man dress up in a UPS outfit and come here at night and sneak into the TruVal cafeteria? We could have had that crate hauled out in the middle of the day calm as could be, and no one would have suspected anything."

Morgan had no answer for that.

"And why would we ruin our wonderful, outrageous photo shoot by killing the
photographer anywhere, not to mention right there where it happened? If I'd wanted to kill Terra, I could have had the murder done anywhere, with less risk to me personally, and less disruption to my business and artistic goals. And why would I have the killer go away, and then come back to get the body? And take a shot at Athena, here, while he's at it?"

"He was shooting at me!" Morgan interjected.

Tru ignored his remark. "Look, we didn't do it. And I think you know that."

Morgan felt deflated. "But what is it? What's so damned secret about that hooker, unless she's down there on the fourteenth floor, in a crate in the TruVal cafeteria next to Terra? Is that it? No, I don't think so. I think you're covering for her when I need her mem. And I don't know why you're covering up."

Athena and Tru were silent. Then Athena looked at Tru again. Tru cleared her throat, and said "Robert, it was me."

"*What* was you?"

"I had sex with Alex that day. There was no hooker." She laughed uneasily. "No one paid me; I paid him! Now will you stop grandstanding and help us figure out what the hell we're going to do next?"

Chapter 32

Morgan's head was spinning with the implications of what Tru had said. He had had sex with the real Truda Vallon! Well, no, not he, but Alex. But Alex didn't have the mem any more, Morgan did. Therefore it was Morgan who had had sex with her. Hadn't he? Isn't memory the only way to tell what happened from what didn't happen? And to whom? He felt the mem coming back. He felt the tingling of anticipation, the scent of sex, the quickened breaths, the touching, the arousal, the release, and now to these he added the thrill of gaining the unobtainable woman, being part of her fame.

"All right," Morgan said, his head still wheeling, his feet floating off the floor as if seated on a gigantic invisible balloon. "Will you do it? Will you memplant me with your mem of having sex with Alex?" He felt a sudden rush of resentment that she, his cherished goddess, would let Alex, that ultimate loser, that drugsodden, scrawny...

"Yes," Tru said. "Yes I will. That's the only way."

***

Actually, she thought, that wasn't the only way. There was another way, more interesting. Slightly risky, but then she wondered why it had occurred to her at all. Yes, it would be interesting, even exciting, if Morgan's / Alex's mem were copied into her mind, on top of her own, which she need not give up. Need not, that is, if she were to use one of Stirner's developments that TruVal hadn't yet announced, that the firm was keeping secret until the right time to announce it as a MemCast mid-life kicker. We'll do it, she decided, copy her mem into Morgan's head and his into hers.

She'd tell the TruVal memlab crew not to give Morgan a hint that anything was happening other than an ordinary memplant, the kind he'd had, the kind he was helping perform, these days, in that seedy commercial memlab. And then she'd have Alex's and Morgan's mem in her mind as well as her own, all playing in parallel. It would be interesting, she mused, to feel how Morgan's mind had re-shaped Alex's experience with her. Who was the real Morgan inside that head? In that body? She became warm at the thought, felt warmth creep up along her legs, settle into her belly. Yes. This will happen.

She breathed deeply and smiled at Morgan. "I'll need to set it up with the lab team. Can you come by at, oh, two o'clock tomorrow?"

"Certainly."

"Come directly down to the B-1 level, then. Ask for me." Tru could see that Morgan was hesitating. "What is it?"

"I – ah – have a job now."

"I've heard. Should I write an excuse note for your boss?" she teased.

"This is serious," Morgan said. "I get paid at that lab."

Tru realized that she'd been thoughtless. "Well then," she said, "how can we make this right with – the O'Farrell Street memlab, isn't it?"

"That's the one. I work for Ed Clarty. He's the franchisee. And – and yes, you could make it right with him, if you would."

"How?"

"He desperately wants an audition. For your show. He's a singer, at least according to him, but I've never heard..."

Tru laughed. "Is that all there is to it? How vain people can be! You know – or probably you didn't know – that we don't have auditions at all. We work through talent agents, monitor other TV shows, send our reps to concerts to scout out new faces." She laughed again. "*Of course* we'll stage an audition for this Ed Clarty, the friendly memlab man! We'll invite him in and let him sing a few 'memorable' songs for Jayne Chang, my Creative Director. Then we'll shine him on as long as we need to." She paused, laughed again. "Sounds like fun!"

The three wished each other a good night. Morgan went home and contemplated the mems in his head, eagerly anticipated the new mem to come. His mind-thrills soon enough became body-thrills as well. Then he slept and had pleasant dreams the memories of which, upon reflection, he had no desire to dump.

***

Athena wanted to go home, too; she was very tired. But she had to view those CCTV files of the UPS impostor, and her home wasn't set up for that. She let herself into the TruVal security office, turned on a viewing machine, and mounted first one tape and then another. It was a long process, but by the time she had finished she had had several detailed views of the man. Yes, she thought, she had no idea who he was, but he was definitely a professional by his bearing and his lack of indecision, at least until he ran into Morgan. Who would guess that the doctor would actually challenge a killer? But perhaps he had just blurted it out before he thought of his own safety. And then it was funny to watch Morgan running and hiding, the killer frantically trying to find him like in an old-time movie, and then Morgan looking for a lever to pull that would alert the security people and finding no levers, become more and more frantic as the deliveryman slipped out a door and drove away.

But this was serious business. The "UPS man" was pretty likely to be Terra Lewis's killer, and he must have been ordered to retrieve the body. Why? This wasn't in the plan, was it? She com'd an 804 number. Ring ring ring, "Do you know what time it is?" She guessed she could pardon a cliché from a man who'd been awakened at – what was it? 12:38 a.m., that's 3:38 a.m. Eastern.

Athena apologized, and then explained what she'd seen on the tapes. "Was he one of ours, sir?"

"No. We wouldn't do that. Why would we?"

"Then who?"

"Do I have to spell it out?"

"I guess not."

"Well, if that UPS man didn't manage to get away with that body, I don't care. Doesn't matter to us either way. Right?"

(silence)

"Right?"

"Certainly, sir, certainly not, I mean. Right."

"OK, I know what you're thinking. It's that loose cannon again who's behind all this. I think you're right. Do you think we can do something about him?"

"A little late for that, sir."

Sounds of annoyed breathing crossed three time zones at the speed of light. "I guess you're right. Well, goodnight, Athena."

"Good night, senator."

Chapter 33

The next day, a happy and relieved Robert Morgan showed up for work at the O'Farrell Street memlab, only to be greeted by a sign on the door that read "CLOSED!" Having his own key, Morgan had no need to call or knock. He entered and found a deliriously happy Ed Clarty.

"You did it!" Clarty yelled. "TruVal called me this morning! They've scheduled me for a audition! Oh I love you, Morgan!" He actually tried to hug Morgan, an attempt that Morgan dodged.

Morgan realized that his scheme had turned, disastrously, in the wrong direction. Clarty was supposed to give Morgan enough time off to pursue the murder investigation, while still paying him in return for arranging the audition. Clearly, that wasn't Clarty's response.

"You're giving up the business?"

"Yes, yes! No need to run this crappy outfit now, deal with all those shitty jerk-offs looking for their next hard-on. No, indeed!" Morgan had never before heard Clarty utter any word more colorful than "shucks." "I'm going to be rich, Morgan! Rich! Famous! And all the ass I'll ever want, all of it Real! Real! Not a mem, not a sim!" He went on in this vein for several minutes. Morgan heard the waffles and peanut butter calling his name.

"Ah, Mr. Clarty." Morgan tried to get Clarty's attention, failed, tried again, finally succeeded. "I got you that audition. I did that for you. You owe me."

"So? You can have the whole Goddamned business!" Clarty roared, spreading his arms and swinging them in an arc. "I'll trust you for the franchise fee, pay me any time you want, any time!" Clarty turned, tossed Morgan a ring of keys, and marched out the front door, blowing kisses at the assembled

SoCalls and parting their amazed multitudes like Moses at the Red Sea.

Morgan went into the memlab office and sat down to think. Given that CLOSED sign, he doubted that the SoCalls would be bothering him the next day; that was a plus. He called up the memlab's bank balance on line. There wasn't much in the bank, but it would pay the next month's rent at home, buy waffles and the occasional pound of soyburger. He sighed. Would he have to re-open the place and run a memlab the rest of his life?

He found a bag of potato chips in Clarty's bottom desk drawer, opened it. There was a fine patina on the chips, as if from the hand of a rare and undiscovered artist of the past. The chips were, in other words, very stale. He ate them anyway.

***

At one o'clock, Morgan entered the TruPlex. He showed his badge and was greeted respectfully and allowed to enter forthwith. He went to his office on the twelfth floor for lack of anything better to do. He had been there only a few minutes when there was a knock on his door, followed without pause by the entrance of Athena's tall form. She glanced at his wallscreen, seemed relieved not to be facing the giant penis once again.

"Good afternoon, doctor," she said. "Did you get enough sleep after last night's adventures?"

"Not quite, no."

"Well, I stayed up, myself, viewed all those CCTV recordings. Nothing."

"Nothing?"

"I didn't get a look at his face. He seemed to have a good idea where all the cams were, and he was wearing that UPS cap you mentioned."

Morgan was disappointed. "Ah, he's a professional. I guess it's his job to know where companies are likely to put their cams."

"And at what height and at what angles," she added helpfully.

"Yes, that too. But did you see him outside? In a vehicle of some kind?"

"A UPS van. I called UPS and they confirmed that one of theirs had been stolen, found abandoned later."

"We could have the police check for fingerprints."

"The killer's a pro, remember?"

"OK. Oh, well." Morgan sat glumly. "But now I'm due in the TruPlex memlab."

"Certainly, doctor. Sorry I couldn't help." Morgan and Athena left his office together, then went their separate ways.

At two o'clock, Morgan was ushered into a small waiting room on the B-1 level, much cleaner and more expensively furnished than the memlab he'd started to think of as "his." After only a brief wait, Tru entered the room in a simple robe.

"Good afternoon, Robert. Are you up for this?" She blushed as she realized what she'd said. Gallantly, Morgan ignored her gaffe, said he was ready for the machine. They went into the lab itself and positioned themselves on adjoining cots. A woman who introduced herself to Morgan as Clinical Advisor Leila started the anesthetic drips and pressed the cool gel-covered probes against Morgan's temples, behind both ears, and at the back of his head. Morgan was attentive to their exact placement, having a new-found professional interest in the process, and in Leila's soothing cotside manner.

***

Tru was apprehensive, never having gone through a simple memplant, much less the procedure for which she was about to become the first human guinea pig, the first one aware of exactly what was happening, anyway. Perhaps she shouldn't have involved Robert in this. What if something were to go wrong? But the procedure required two people, and one of them, she had determined long ago when the research first began, would be herself. She wouldn't allow anyone else from TruVal, Inc. to be experimented on until she'd subjected herself to it.

Poor Robert, she thought, with all your trust I'm abusing you again. You think you're getting my mem added on top of Alex's, and that I won't have the mem anymore because the readout is destructive. But I'm getting Alex's mem, and your mem, too, at the same time you're getting mine. Because this was the feature of MemCast that hadn't yet been announced:

163

Two-way non-destructive memplants. Each person would receive a mem, just as if the other person had been drained of it. But both would have the same memory. Both will have had the same experience. The two would be one. Memory sharing; the ultimate intimacy. The SoCalls' ultimate nightmare.

I should trust Robert with this secret. But not yet. It's too dangerous. Too many groups would want this technology too badly.

The anesthetic hit Tru's system and she dozed peacefully off.

Tru and Morgan came back to consciousness at about the same time. They looked at each other.

"Well, Robert, I suppose we should get together tomorrow, after that mem has had a chance to sort itself out in your mind, and see if you have a better picture of Terra's killer, one good enough to visit the police with, to speak with their artist. Or of course you could go to SFPD yourself. You don't need me, now that I haven't seen the murder anymore!"

I'm getting a clearer picture of the killer, she thought. The same picture Robert must be getting. The killer's face is becoming clear, three-dimensional. We'll have him!

Morgan was beginning to see a face in his own mind, too, like a 3D photograph. It was – yes – one of those hit men DeLuca had shown him. Not one of the principal suspects, one of the possibles. Not sure, though; let the mem jell a while.

"Sure," he responded to Tru's question. "Nine o'clock? And I do need you for this, Tru. Now that DeLuca's been kicked off the case, I don't know anyone there anymore. Your name should get us attention pretty quickly."

Morgan returned to the O'Farrell Street memlab at what would have been closing time if it were still open, made sure all was secure, and went home. Better start thinking about hiring staff, he thought.

Truda Vallon returned to her office, asked not to be disturbed. The sun drifted down into the Pacific. She envisioned great clouds of steam rising from the point of impact. Her office lights dutifully turned themselves on, but she flipped a reluctant "off" switch. Shouldn't interfere with the auto-processes, an annoyed red light reminded her. Well, if being rich and famous didn't permit you to overrule some damned computer, what would? Darkness ascended from Montgomery Street up the sides of the city's towers. Ten floors, twenty. The top of the tallest building was finally enveloped in a moonless blackness. Tru leaned back in her chair and remembered Alex / Morgan's memory of having sex with her.

Chapter 34

Back at 1536 Washington Street, Morgan had a quick dinner, settled down in his favorite chair. No booze. Not now. He didn't bother turning on the room lights as the last sunlight speared across the city and touched the far wall, then disappeared. Morgan remembered.

BEGIN MEMS

A soft knock at the door. Alex / Morgan reaches out a hand, unlocks, opens. Tru, nervous, wonders about this man she's never met. A druggie, Athena had said, not much of a specimen and probably not very clean, but he's the right one for the shoot, and we needed that rooftop right across the street. Perfect. She's hesitant, Morgan realizes, about having sex with Alex, a little disgusted. She enters, wearing the Truda Vallon "uniform." She looks up, gives him / him an uneasy smile. Through Alex's face, Morgan smiles back. I need him to play "Strangers" for me, I can't forget that. She hands him the songchip, asks him to put it in his player. Alex / Morgan takes the chip from her hand. A warm hand, he / he notices. Soft. There's the couch, where Athena said it would be. I walk past this frail, scrawny man toward the couch. God what a filthy apt. Getting fucked by him won't be much fun, Tru / Morgan thinks, but he's probably too strung out to do much damage. He's fussing with the player now, and he can't see my face. Why did I agree to this? It sounded so cool, so daring, so in-your-face. But it's too late to back out now. OK, I'm putting this chip in the player. Whatever she wants to hear. Am I supposed to move to this music? Hope it's slow. Too much coke for me to want to move very fast. I think I should touch him now. I'm supposed to lead him to the couch; he won't know to do that. I guess I should touch her now. Looks like she wants us to use the couch, not the bed. Well, whatever, she's paying. I guess I should take

166

off enough clothes to do this. Why isn't she taking off all her clothes?

Alex / Morgan / Tru blink in the glare of sunlight. I need to face the window, right? This is a little awkward for my knees, balancing this way. She's facing the window. That's OK, won't have to kiss her. Never liked to do that. Most hookers don't let you kiss them. Why? Afraid of germs? What a joke.

OK, here we go. I'm the guy but she's paying. I guess today that makes me the hooker. Why would she want me? I'm cute, everybody says so, but I'm a mess. Too far gone on this shit. Tried to stop once, twice. OK, here we go. This whole scene would be funny if it weren't so completely gross. He's doing something down there. I need to help him. I've got to remember to move with the music. What's that music? Sounds like a Truda Vallon song, but don't think I've heard it before. Maybe I'll beg that chip off her when we're done. Or steal it. Maybe she'll forget to take it with her.

Morgan is suddenly overwhelmed by a sensation he should have anticipated, but hadn't: As Tru, Morgan is being fucked by a man. And fucking a woman. At the same time. Sensations from both flood Morgan's mind: each shove and thrust from both Tru and Alex, not two mems at the same time, but one, a composite. A synthesis of two minds and two bodies, now three bodies. Suddenly, Morgan feels like an intruder. Let it be: there is no Morgan here, there is only Tru and Alex. It's all in my mind. There is no Morgan here. Back off. Turn off your mind.

Tru is sensing Morgan's presence. He's here, he's part of all of this. He's changing things, so slightly I didn't notice right away. Making the event more intellectual, isn't that just like him! But more sensitive, too. Tru is suddenly overwhelmed by the knowledge that Morgan has no idea that he's part of the – he must think he's some kind of sick voyeur. But it isn't that way. Not at all.

It's rather nice.

They remember the heat, the sounds of street noise and colliding flesh, the humming of a disordered electric heater, the 'pop' of – what was that? Alex / Morgan raises his head from the neck he's been nuzzling, stares out over the woman's shoulder, through the window, to the roof of the building across the street, where – what was that?

Something's happening. Why is his grip stiffening like this? I should open my eyes. Maybe there's someone at the door, or – what? Across the street, there on that rooftop. I'm not supposed to look directly over there. Terra said it would spoil the effect. But there she is. That's Terra. What's she doing, falling over? Did she trip?

She's falling backwards. Over to the right, there's a man pointing at her. Pointing. The woman is falling slowly onto her back. The gun, he's pointing a gun! A puffy cloud is gathering around its muzzle. My God! He's killing her! He's killing Terra!

The man with the gun turns to his right and then to his left, stops, looks again. His face – I can see all of his face as he turns, as he looks. The nose, unusual but not unattractive, the eyes, their slightly uneven sizes, the hairline, the way the hair is parted. He's pointing the gun at me, now. Is he pointing that thing at me? Duck! He / he / she hear a crash of breaking glass, feel a shower of fragments, then a rush of cool air.

The silence feels like it lasts forever. Then a jerking of muscles, can't take a breath. The beginning of panic.

END OF MEMS

Chapter 35

Early the next morning, Morgan showed up at the TruPlex. He didn't feel like eating anything from the cafeteria, considering what he knew was in the freezer. He bought a bag of pretzels from one of the vending machines.

When he appeared shortly thereafter on Rug Row, pretzels in hand, Morgan noticed that Tru seemed uneasy.

***

Renee had noticed it too. Was there a problem with Tru? Had something gone wrong with the memplant? Renee was running from place to place, making an extra effort to be very nice to Tru, very pert, offering to run errands, offering coffee, whatever you want, shoot just let me know! Athena arrived and the three went into Tru's office and shut the door, leaving Renee behind and wondering what it was all about this time.

***

"How are we going to work this?" Morgan asked.

"As chief security officer," Athena said, "I suppose I'm the most appropriate one to make the call. The police know me, at least my name."

Tru nodded.

"Are we all OK with this?" Morgan asked, trying to figure out what was bothering Tru without asking her directly.

Tru nodded again. Athena simply said "Yes."

Athena pulled her com from her purse, linked it to Tru's and Morgan's coms with a flick of her finger, and said "Police HQ, special line" into it.

To Morgan's astonishment and envy, it took less than six seconds for a voice and face to appear, put on the guarded smile of a veteran civil servant, and say "Ms. Taylor! How are you this morning, ma'am? Anything we can do for you?"

"Good morning, Sergeant King."

***

Sergeant King beamed: A prominent member of the security establishment had recognized his face, and his name, too! Now if the Chief could do that, life would be sweet.

"Sergeant, we have a real problem here at TruVal. It's about Terra Lewis, you remember the case, our missing photog. Lieutenant DeLuca was handling it, but I understand he's no longer with SFPD. I'd like to speak with whoever has taken on his workload, that case in particular."

The Sergeant frowned, turned his eyes away. Morgan could see his hands busily poking at a screen. Less than a minute later, he turned back.

"Ms. Taylor, that case has been closed. No one is working it now. I'm sorry." His face put on a look of real sorrow.

"Well, Sergeant, based on how the department is organized, if the Lewis case hadn't been closed, who would have been the logical person to handle it?"

After a few minutes at his screen, he said "Ah, that would be Lieutenant Marcus or Lieutenant Graves."

"And who do they report to?"

"That would be Captain O'Brien."

"Thank you, sergeant. Now would you please transfer us to Captain O'Brien?"

"Sure thing, ma'am."

Their com screens blanked. Soothing music played for a few seconds, then the picture returned, this time showing a scowling middle-aged man with gold-colored accents on his uniform.

"Captain O'Brien?"

"Yes. What can I do for you, Ms. Taylor?"

Athena hoped she wouldn't have to tell O'Brien about the body in the freezer. That would be very embarrassing, not to say incriminating. But a deal could be worked out. Maybe. Right now, all she wanted was to have the case re-opened and the killer ID'd.

"This is about the Terra Lewis case that Lieutenant DeLuca was working on before he left."

The scowl deepened. "That's closed."

"Yes, I know. Sergeant King told me."

***

So that's the creep who transferred this woman to me, the Captain thought. Can't say no when he needs to, eh? Not very good performance for a representative of the San Francisco Police Department. He'd have to have a word with the Sergeant's supervisor. Maybe time on the beat would straighten that Sergeant King out.

***

Athena took a deep breath. She glanced at Tru and Morgan, and plunged in. "We can now positively identify the gunman, Captain. Lieutenant DeLuca and a witness had narrowed the field to four or five likelies and a few more possibles. I'd like to meet with one of your officers, and our witness, and go through the mug-shot book. We can pick out one specific perp. I'm sure you want to wrap this up, Captain, add to your arrest statis..."

"The mug-book's on line now. It's an app."

"But it's not accessible outside the sworn service. I tried."

"That's too bad. I can't spare any officers to work with you. We're very busy here. And the Goddamned City Council and their Goddamned budget cuts." A series of indistinct but definitely unhappy sounds radiated from the Captain. "Look," he continued. "The case is closed, that's that. And even if your witness can ID this supposed killer and his hypothetical murder –and why couldn't he do it before if he can do it now? Memory doesn't get better with time! We're not going to reopen it. Orders from Chief Ramsey himself, and even above that. Don't try to go over my head on this and don't ever tell him I mentioned his name!"

***

Athena felt like saying "We found the body!" but couldn't bring herself to do it. There had to be another way. A way that might keep her out of jail.

"Thank you, Captain, for all you've done," said Athena in a voice that measured twenty below zero. She clicked off before O'Brien could add his own cheerful good-bye. She turned to Tru and Morgan.

"Well, gang, do we tell him there's a body?"

"I thought you were going to do that," said Tru, crossly.

"Not the best play here, I think." Athena paused. "Doctor, did you say that Dennis DeLuca had been transferred to the Sausalito PD?"

"Not transferred," said Morgan, "more like banished. SFPD apparently made a deal with Sausalito that SFPD would let Dennis go, and SPD would pick him up the next day."

"Whatever," said Athena, "he's there. I think we should have a talk with him. Before we tell SFPD about the body, that is."

Tru looked worried. "The longer the body is where it is, the more it's a time bomb. The killer would suspect that we'd have put it back where it came from, to keep it from rotting. He could..."

"OK, OK," Athena answered, "we'll hurry this along. Today, if we can get hold of DeLuca, we'll lay it all out, see what he has to say." Athena had the kind of firm set to her mouth that said "this had better work." "But he'd be obliged to tell SFPD about the body, and immediately, too, regardless of his own feelings about his ex-employer. And they'd take the case away from him and bury it again, like they did before."

Tru and Morgan nodded and were silent, realizing the truth of what Athena had said.

"Look," Morgan finally said, "we do need to dispose of the body, before the killer tries for it again or gets someone else to snatch it. Let's move the body to a place inside the Sausalito city limits and tip DeLuca on where it is. Anonymously, of course."

Tru was distraught. "Dump Terra? Dump her like much garbage?"

"We can be gentle," Morgan answered. "Rent a room for her maybe. And in any case," he said, looking at Athena, "would being dumped be worse than being crated up and left in a freezer like so much hamburger?"

"There's a problem, doctor," said Athena. "We'd be giving the detective nothing to go on. Do we call him the next day and say 'Lieutenant, we heard you found Terra's body. Oh, and by coincidence, we can now ID her killer.'"

"Ah, right. But I want him to have the body. That way he'll have proof that Terra was murdered, didn't just disappear into one of those foreign countries she goes to. Well, let's put the body in Sausalito as we've been discussing, then I'll call Dennis and tell him what we did and why. Level with him. Ask him to call up the mug-book for me."

"That's a big risk!"

"Any better ideas?"

An absence of sound indicated that no better ideas would be forthcoming. The group searched the web, made calls, found a boutique hotel in Sausalito with multiple separate entrances, agreed that would be a suitably upscale near-final resting place for Ms. Terra Lewis, photographer to the stars and almost-stars.

"Too bad that Jimmy–" Athena stopped, saddened. "He could have orchestrated all this."

"Have you found Jimmy yet?" asked Morgan.

"No," said Athena. "And I don't think we ever will."

"Jimmy wouldn't have aroused suspicion wheeling a crate inside the building and down the elevators," Morgan added. "None of us could do that without getting the kind of attention we don't want."

"I hate to involve anyone else in this," said Tru, "but we're going to need help in any case. I'm going to sound out Melody and Serena, tell them just enough, swear them to silence. If they won't help us – and after all, we're talking here about indictments, jail time – I won't insist."

"How soon can that happen?"

"Today. Let's try for today, anyway. Athena, they work for you. Will you ask them to see me ASAP?"

"Certainly."

"Then I'll let you know if they're in or out. If they're with us, we can go tonight."

The three exited Tru's office. Renee was still fluttering around the office being helpful, as cheery and ebullient and effervescent as ever.

What the heck had been going on in there? she wondered. Those three looked really grim. Not TruVal business, I think, or Morgan wouldn't be involved. I'd heard something about a guard being hustled down to the B-1 level, CCTV files being pulled. I really should tell my contact about this, but he'd just ask what it was all about and I don't know that yet and jeepers I'd just look dumb. Maybe later.

"Hi, guys!" said Renee. "Cheer up. It's a great day to be alive!"

Chapter 36

At eight that evening "the conspirators," as Morgan thought of them, met in the practice studio on the fourteenth floor. He was excited at being a conspirator. Athena looked stern and determined. Tru looked scared. Melody and Serena had blank, controlled expressions. Melody had brought a hand-truck.

***

Serena was thinking "just following orders" and trying to remember the various successes and failures of that defense. Who was that? Some German? Didn't do him any good, did it? But security officers are supposed to follow orders. Yes, your honor, I was following the orders of my superior. I was afraid of losing my life if I disobeyed. Well, I was afraid of being fired. Well, I wanted a superior performance review the next time. I've never had one of those. Oh? But moral decisions are made at the supervisor level, your honor, not at mine. That's above my pay grade.

***

Tru, Athena, and Morgan descended separately to the garage on the B-2 level. Melody and Serena went to the cafeteria, placed Terra's crate on the hand-truck, pushed it to an elevator, and also descended to B-2. They met in front of the black corporate stretch limo that Athena had reserved.

Melody and Serena carefully lifted the crate into the limo, and the five took seats inside, Serena driving. They drove out of the Montgomery Street building, careful not to speed or run any red lights. The city was very quiet, with only a few buses still on the streets. Serena drove up Columbus Avenue, around the north end of Russian Hill, circled back toward 101. Just as she turned right onto Lombard Street, however, she saw blinking red lights behind her, and the brief whirr of a siren. She pulled over.

"Jesus, Serena!" Athena shouted, "did you run that red light?"

"No, ma'am! Not at all!"

"Then what – Oh, shit! The special-permit flag."

Serena suddenly realized that she hadn't put up the small flag that permitted private vehicles to be on the streets. "Ma'am, I forgot."

"Well that's too damn bad, isn't it!"

***

Serena was saying to herself "following orders, following orders" over and over. Yes, your honor, but I was ordered. No, your honor, I had no choice, none at all. Threatened me, they did. But I decided to do the right thing in spite of all their threats. I was just about to report this heinous scheme to the police, or at least to other people I know who could maybe do something about it, I have friends, you know, one or two who are really powerful and very secretive, but at that moment, as I was picking up the phone...

***

Officer Gaillardia saw that it was a stretch limo, an expensive member of the breed at that, and was being driven carefully. With five people inside, most of them women. Likely they had a flag, just forgot to fly it. Anybody with a ride like that would have a flag. That's how the system worked. A warning, not a ticket? But he had a quota to fill. Not really a quota, as his superiors kept pointing out at every review he'd ever had, "but if you're out there on the street doing your job, you'll naturally pick up, oh, twenty a month, wouldn't you say that was a reasonable, ah, not a quota, but a reasonable number to report each month? Now here we have your record" (http://'s flipping by) "and you had only twelve. Now what do you suppose could explain that?"

Officer Gaillardia stepped out of his cruiser and approached the limo, cautious out of habit. The driver's window rolled down, and a hand extended, holding papers. He ignored the hand. One of those damn Trudites, he thought as he looked inside, and a big ugly one at that. Where do they all come from? What do they think they're proving? And another one beside her, and a smaller one in back. And a tall woman, yes, looking very elegant here, a nice piece, I would expect! She must be the owner, looking like that, like she's in charge. And a man, inconsequential fellow, balding, nervous. What's his bit? Not the tall woman's squeeze, I hope! How would a jerk like that rate a...

The patrolman came back to the moment. Should he address the driver as Ms. or Ma'am? With all that makeup on, who could tell? Could even be a Mr.

"Ah, I'm sure you know you can't be out here without a permit flag."

Serena smiled at the officer. She was very much tempted to blurt "I was following orders!" but restrained herself. "Yes, sir" was all she said.

Officer Gaillardia took the papers from the woman's hand. Registration, license, special permit for a flag. Everything seemed to be in order, but no flag. He peered into the limo. "Look, he said, I'm sure you just forgot. But every patrolman in the city could stop you tonight and have the same conversation we're having."

Serena forced herself to smile. "Yes, officer, but we're not going far, only to..." and stopped herself before she could say "over to Marin."

"Well, in any case I know of several officers who are out here, tonight, buddies of mine. And they might not be as lenient as I'm willing to be."

Serena pulled her hand back into the car.

"Well, I'm going to let you go this time, and give you a temp flag you can fly. It's only good through tomorrow noon, remember that. Now, let me see those papers one last time." Serena handed them over. Gaillardia looked through them, gave them back along with a temp flag. "OK, he said, "have a good evening and drive safely."

He went back to his cruiser, fondling his two new five hundred dollar bills. Well, I won't make my quota this month, he thought, but that's how the system works.

Chapter 37

Serena affixed the temporary flag to the limo's multiwave antenna. They continued west, through the Presidio and over the bridge, exited right and down into Sausalito. Morgan's thoughts went back to when he'd lived there, many years before, fresh out of the military. Not much different even now. The former Glad Hand restaurant had changed hands again, he observed, and the Nameless Barber Shop had long ago been christened. But the Casa Madrona was still there. It had metastasized from a middling-sized building on the hill flanked by small cabins into a large, by Sausalito standards, maze of additions on additions.

"I called," Athena said to the group. "There are several units at the Madrona vacant right now. I picked one from their on-line diagram that should be secluded enough. We'll have to keep a careful watch, though."

Serena maneuvered the limo as close as she could to the unit Athena had selected, not easy and not very close owing to the narrow lanes and steep hillside. "Well, this will have to do," she said. They were barely uphill from Bridgeway.

Looking as casual as possible, Melody walked up to the unit Athena had selected, used her burglar tools to get inside. Melody examined the room, satisfied herself that it was vacant, carefully left the door slightly ajar and returned to the limo. "OK," she whispered.

Morgan was elected most innocent looking and went ahead of the rest, alert for anyone who might notice. Melody and Serena followed with the hand-truck, pushing, tugging, and puffing their way up the hill. Tru and Athena hung back as a rear guard.

As they had all hoped and expected, no one was on foot in the area. They pushed the crate into the room, placed it gently on the floor.

"Leave the hand-truck," said Athena, "in case we run into anyone on the way back. Wipe it down." Melody wiped it down. They surveyed the unit carefully, including the door, for any evidence they might inadvertently be leaving, found none, walked separately back to the limo.

No one spoke a word on the way back to the city, but in their minds they were busy processing relief, worry, triumph.

***

That was a close one! Serena thought. Lucky I knew about the payoff, how much to donate, double for a limo, extra because it's a Benz, and Ms. Taylor and Ms. Vallon understood, finally understood my frantically waving open hand, five fingers twice, over and over, just in time to find the money and push into my fist to give to that nice officer. Did you attempt to bribe me, miss? She was afraid that she'd hear that, but what's a girl to do? Don't you know that's a felony? I'm going to have to take you in. This is a serious offense, a second-class felony. One more word out of you and it'll be first class. Hold out your hands, wrists together. Oh, you were following orders? Tough shit. Tell it to the judge. No, I'm not going to give you back your money, it's mine now. You have the right to an attorney. If you're stupid enough to hire any of those crooks who hang around City Hall, well then you deserve to be fleeced as well as locked up for two to three. I see that look. Kiss my ass!

***

Tru was confused. What am I getting myself into? Deeper and deeper. I should never have set up that shoot, that's what started the whole thing. Imagine, real sex on prime time TV. Not wrong, no, I'll never believe that. But imprudent. Stupid. Deserve to lose my show, my career. All because I wanted to show him, show him up, get him mad, make him faint with rage. He was too good a target for me not to try. Not like Morgan. Not like my dear Robert.

***

Well, it's done, Athena thought. Terra's body will be found. The police will wonder how it got there, why it hadn't rotted. Guess an M.E. will be able to figure out it had been frozen all this time. That will hit the headlines: "Found: Frozen Stiff!" Then the cafeteria employees will remember that there used to be a crate in the freezer. Is it still there? No, disappeared. I saw it yesterday when we were closing up at three o'clock, officer. Wonder what happened to it? And now a body in Sausalito. Do you suppose...? And remember whose name was on that crate! Yeah, Athena Taylor's name. You don't suppose she had anything to do with this horrifying crime, do you? Oh no, not Ms. Taylor! But she did seem a little on edge, preoccupied. Perhaps....

***

Serena handled that scene with the cop pretty well, Melody thought, at least finally, though I was sure she'd blow it before it was over. I don't think that woman is cut out for security work. She's too cautious, thinks too much. Not like me. I've heard a rumor that she's going to be promoted. And she was always telling me how bad her performance reviews were! That's the end of us, of "Melody and Serena," I guess. But I deserve that promotion, not her. Wonder how she maneuvered herself into getting it? Following orders, she was always going on and on about that. But she didn't seem to be following orders all the time. Not TruVal's orders, anyway. She gets calls once in a while and won't tell me where from or anything about them. Not from her non-existent boyfriends, that's for sure! Stinking luck for me that she'd handled that cop OK instead of being hauled off for attempted bribery. Wouldn't that have been a hoot, though! Woo hoo!

***

Morgan worried how he'd ever explain this to DeLuca. Sure to get him in trouble again. He barely arrives here in Sausalito and this body follows him across the bridge, like a George Romero zombie. Morgan felt bad about that, because he thought of – to his surprise he suddenly realized it – thought of DeLuca as his friend, a kind of brother. He wondered what DeLuca thought of him. Not a lot, probably; few people ever had.

Morgan stammered a few incoherent syllables. DeLuca was silent, finally said "Look. I'll pretend to be surprised when the hotel calls us about the body. It will take SPD a day or two to get around to ID-ing her from her DNA, because most Americans haven't been typed. First they'll go through the routine of checking missing persons and fingerprints and all that kind of thing. You'd better come over here to my place right away so we can go through the mug-book app. The killer may disappear, or "be disappeared," as soon as it's known that Lewis's body has come to light. We need to rope him in before that can happen. What time is it now?"

"Ten-twenty."

"OK, how soon can you get here?"

"Where's here?"

"I moved into a houseboat at Gate 5. That's in the north end of Sausalito. Waldo Point."

"How'd you get rich enough to do that?"

"Nowhow. Wait 'til you see the place; it's one iceberg short of a Titanic. I'm sub-renting, anyway."

"Thanks, Dennis." Morgan hung up and turned to Tru. "I need a car."

"OK, I'll call down and clear you. They'll have a car ready, no limo this time."

"For sure! I'll be exposed enough as it is."

"And remember to fly the damn flag!"

Chapter 38

Lieutenant Dennis DeLuca began brewing a pot of coffee, looked at his wristcom, swore. Almost eleven. He really liked to be in bed by ten and, here in the ultimate rich-hippy 'burb, he was getting used to doing that, at least during the week. Once in a while he'd be rousted out of bed if a man had offed his wife, or vice versa. But normally, everything was cool in Sausalito. Not like in the city. Not like in the "Feemo" district. But all that was over. Here he was, informed politely to ignore pot and coke users, even heroin or sparkle users if they looked reasonably wealthy, not bust them as he might have done in the city just to get the body count up. A different place, indeed.

After his disappointment, anger, rage at being fired from the SFPD, he'd begun to settle in, was getting used to the slower pace. But now here was Morgan again, like a bad dream from the past, and Terra Lewis whose body Morgan had apparently donated to him. How old was that corpse? Where had it been all this time? Was there anything left? What did it – smell like?

The last thing he needed was Terra Lewis. But she had been killed. If Morgan really had a body to show him, that proved it, just as DeLuca had suspected. And he might have a chance to show those suits in the city – whoever they were who'd closed down his investigation – that there was something real here. A case. A capital case. DeLuca smiled, a thin, tight smile. "Bastards," he muttered, "bastards."

***

Morgan maneuvered out of the TruPlex garage, fumbled to locate the headlight switch on the unfamiliar model, barely found it in time to avoid a taxi coming in from a side street. He retraced the limo's route from earlier that night, but didn't exit the 101 until Marin City. He doubled back a mile, found a place to park near Gate 5, found the pier Dennis had mentioned. The first six houseboats were monuments of over the top marine architecture, and very large. The eighth was only slightly smaller. He almost overlooked the small ark (as they were called in Marin) between numbers six and eight. What a dump! Leaning to one side, needing a coat of paint very badly. There was one light on, and light was leaking from all four sides of the front door and half the siding on the pierwise side. This must be the place. A rental an honest cop might be able to afford. Somehow, he felt comforted.

Morgan stepped on board, edged past a few decrepit chairs, knocked on the door.

**

"Coffee, doctor? This might take a while."

"Sure. Black, no sugar."

"Just as God made it." Dennis smiled. In spite of this new headache, he realized that he liked Morgan, was glad to see him again.

"Praise God from whom all coffee flows," replied Morgan, echoing the second half of a TV comedy catch-phrase. "Starbucks?"

"Are you kidding? It's Freed's. I make a pilgrimage there once a week."

"Great!" Morgan responded, with the first positive emotion he'd felt all night.

Dennis deployed the coffee maker while Morgan, too nervous to sit, walked in eight-foot circles around the small room.

"Leftovers?" DeLuca asked. "I've got stuff in the fridge from KaBob's Mid-Eastern."

"No, thanks," said Morgan. "Just coffee."

Finally the coffee was ready. Dennis served Morgan a mug, poured one for himself, settled down in front of the display screen.

"The logon's not stored on my com," he said. "Security precaution, you know, have to key it in." He opened a drawer and pulled out a keyboard, blew dust off the top, plugged it in to a port on the side of the screen, typed in his name and three separate passwords.

"No riddles you need to solve to get online?" Morgan teased.

"Yeah. The riddle of the stinky corpse!" DeLuca replied.

"She's not stinky. Not yet."

"How's that?"

"She's been hanging out in the TruPlex cafeteria's freezer."

"Jesus! It's enough to make me a vegetarian."

The screen lit up, displaying a stylized logo of a tall ship passing under the Golden Gate Bridge.

"Now," he said, "I just got here and I'm still a little clumsy with this system." A few false starts later, he had bridged his way from the SPD site over to the State of California mug-shot subsystem. "Now all that stuff we did in the city, those faces we looked at, I can't access the results of what we did then, because they're gone; we'll have to start over. I remember the general description, so let's reconstruct those results. You say this fellow was one of the ones we'd tagged as possibles and not one of the likelies?"

"That's right."

"OK." DeLuca frowned, concentrated. He flicked through face after face, keying in bits of description.

Morgan wandered off, not being able to assist at the moment. He went outside, looked out over the water. It was low tide. An odor of mud and dead things penetrated the air. Got used to it, he guessed, if you lived here. He edged sideways around the boat's narrow walkway, not trusting the railing to keep him from falling into the muck. There was no one in boat number eight, he saw. At least no lights were showing inside. By the faint pier lights he made out a sign on its side: "National Historical Landmark." Now what was that about? Right then he heard Dennis yelling "Morgan! Get your ass back in here!"

He finished his circuit of the listing houseboat and came back inside.

"Got twenty-four faces here," Dennis said. "I hope your memory's better than it was before, like you said."

One by one, they flicked through the 3.5D-displayed faces. Morgan picked out four for a closer look, although he was pretty sure that number two was his man. They went back through the four, and Dennis displayed full-length shots, put the faces in motion: as if talking, as if chewing, in alarm, in repose, a threatening face, a grim face, a questioning face. "Pretty good sims, aren't they?" Dennis asked, with a hint of pride in his voice. "Dynamic musculo-skeletal structure analysis. 'DMMSA''s what they call it in the Department. Now: who's our bad guy?"

"That one." Morgan pointed at number two.

"That is—" Dennis pulled up a file. "That's Charles Llewellyn 'Charlie' Barnes. Gun for hire." He pulled up more text. "Ex-military. Suspected of an assortment of contract killings over the past ten years."

"No convictions?"

"No convictions, and damned few arrests. I see here Santa Rosa tried to get him on a WMD conspiracy charge when they couldn't nail him for murder, but he beat that. Very suspicious, anyone's getting out from under a WMD charge these days."

"Rich customers buying prosecutors or judges?"

"Not that overt. I think it'd be more like influence, power, a few hints dropped here and there in the right places. Flagrant outright bribery? Not very often, at least this side of Chicago. Not at the higher levels, anyway. Suppose," he said, turning off the screen and standing up, "I have this Charlie Barnes brought in. Then what?"

"You're the cop, you tell me!"

"He'll have an alibi. And your dead evidence, Robert, stinks in more ways than one. It would never be admitted in court. Charlie's got to be smart to have survived this long. He'll know exactly where he stands with me."

Dennis sat down again, tried to concentrate. It was after midnight, and he was tired.

"Look," Morgan offered, "Barnes tried very hard to retrieve that body, at great risk to himself. Twice. He's just a hired gun; why should he care if the body is found or not? There's not likely to be anything in or on the body that could point to him as the killer."

"So?"

"So the client must have paid Charlie to get the body, or perhaps to make sure it was never found. And Charlie failed. Failed twice, in fact: once on the rooftop and once at the

TruPlex. Now perhaps the client doesn't know that he failed. Charlie could be in deep shit to some very powerful forces, if it were made public that Terra's body had turned up."

"OK, I'll buy that."

"Bring Charlie in. Threaten to tell the news media that Terra's body has been found, if Charlie won't tell us who the client is."

"Won't work. As soon as that body turns up the media will know. SPD wouldn't keep that from the press. No reason to, and the department couldn't keep it secret very long, in any case."

"Well," Morgan thought out loud, "then we bring him in ASAP, before his client can off him. We might learn a few things."

"Not likely that he'd tell us anything of interest. But I agree that he's in danger, and we should have a talk with him right away." Dennis made a few calls, entered data into two or three PD apps. "There. If he's in one of the places where he usually is, we'll have him by morning."

"If he's not in hiding."

"No reason for him to be hiding yet, not until he hears that the body's been found. And hiding now would look suspicious to his client, wouldn't it? " Dennis leaned back. "I need to sleep now."

"Wait a minute," Morgan said. "What about the autopsy?"

"What autopsy?"

"Of Terra Lewis. Maybe she was killed for something in her body. A secret bio weapon, or..."

Dennis laughed. "You've been reading too many bad sci-fi mystery novels, Morgan. For one thing, autopsies aren't routine unless there's a good reason to have one or required by law; they're expensive. And by your account, even if we did an autopsy the first thing the doc would find is a bullet hole in her head. End of autopsy, without compelling reason to go further. Tox screens and all that cost even more money, and our one part-time specialist is overwhelmed. And a screen wouldn't pick up what it's not looking for, you know. Secret new bio or chem agent? No way!"

Morgan was silent. After a while, DeLuca said "Tomorrow's going to be busy. Look, Morgan, I really need my sleep!"

Morgan got up to leave. "But," A new thought had struck DeLuca. "Barnes should be ashamed of himself."

"Why?"

"If he was supposed to clean up all the blood, it didn't work. There were lots of chemicals, but pretty ineffective. Household chemicals, stuff you find under the kitchen sink. Amateur hour. That's not like Charlie, he's better than that. And why clean up the blood and not remove the body at the same time?"

"Then do you suppose there was someone else involved?"

"In the hit? But you – I mean Alex – didn't see anyone else, did you?"

"Could have been concealed somewhere on that rooftop."

"Charlie works alone, or at least never with amateurs. No, I think Charlie was surprised at seeing himself being watched, and when he failed to kill Alex and the girl immediately, he knew he wouldn't have time to take the body or do the cleanup, so he left the scene."

"And then that 'someone else'"

"I think so. Someone else went to the rooftop and tried to clean up the blood, but did a lousy job of it. Amateurs."

Chapter 39

Morgan left. He was sleepy, too, but he needed to return the car to the TruVal garage before he went home. He wondered if Athena and Jimmy had been the ones using those household chemicals, and if so, why.

Morgan drove back toward the city, slowly, deep in thought. There were very few cars on the bridge, a few lonely buses, a truck or two. One car had left Gate 5 about the time he did, but it was well back of him. He swung off the bridge, followed what little traffic there was onto Lombard Street. He didn't notice that the car behind him had come up close until it flashed its brights. Morgan was in the middle lane. Why didn't the other car just pass? Morgan pulled over to the curb lane anyway. The car behind him moved over, too. Morgan slowed down. The car slowed down. Morgan speeded up. The car speeded up. A chase? Morgan had always admitted to himself that his driving skills were no better than average. He was aware that those who knew him believed that was far too positive an evaluation. Morgan gripped the wheel tighter, slowed to twenty-five. The car behind slowed again, also. Morgan checked to make sure his doors had auto-locked. Where was Officer Gaillardia or his buddies when he needed them? Or was this Officer Gaillardia himself, angling for another thousand? Morgan didn't have that kind of money on him, had never had, actually.

He drove faster. He was almost to Van Ness now. He'd have to make a decision very soon. Was he going to try a Steve McQueen down the twisty part of Lombard? Yes, everyone in the city had driven down that hill, most at no more than seven miles an hour, if that. And everyone in the city had imagined himself flying down that street, yelling at the top of his lungs, thirty, forty, fifty mph, miraculously missing traffic barriers, flying over bushes and gardens, watching the evildoers behind him losing control of their muscle car and dying in a fiery crash.

No, not for him. Morgan turned right on Van Ness, then left on Broadway toward Montgomery. Too late, he realized that once in the Broadway tunnel he'd be fair game for anyone who wanted to shove his car into the wall, sparks flying, pin him in, open their doors, draw slouch hats down over their eyes, pull very large pistols from under their suit jackets, grunt toughguy words from the corners of their mouths.

Who could he call? DeLuca was miles behind him now. He com'd Tru's office, even though he doubted she'd be there. The com blinked and buzzed. Finally, he heard Renee's voice. What was she doing there at one in the morning?

"Hi, Dr. Morgan! Wow, isn't it pretty late for..."

Morgan interrupted her and uttered a confused series of frantic incomplete sentences, the gist of which was: "I'm in a TruVal car and being tailed. I'm on Broadway now and will be at the TruPlex in five minutes, if I step on it and run every light between here and there, which I fully intend to do. I want you to make sure the garage entrance is open for me, and then close it as soon as I pull in, before whoever is following me can get in the garage too."

Renee seemed deeply concerned for his fate, without losing any of her cheerfulness. "Sure, Dr. Morgan, no problem! See ya!"

The tunnel was dead ahead. Idly, Morgan wondered if he would have a momentary realization of what had happened before the pain set in, or if it would all be over instantly, a muzzle flash and then oblivion. In a welter of worries he barely missed a cab, almost collided with a truck. Zooming across Columbus Avenue at sixty-five miles an hour he missed again, another truck this time, winning the day's "up yours, you honky dick-head" award from the driver. The car behind followed him through the tunnel, but made no move to cut him off. Turning right on Montgomery he saw the TruPlex a block ahead. But the other car was accelerating, making its move. Abreast of the TruPlex, Morgan suddenly hit the brakes and the second car went squealing ahead of him, cut to the right to block him off.

But there was the TruPlex garage, its metal barricade slowly rising. Morgan drove in, scraping the car's roof in the process, sparks flying. To his relief, the barricade lowered behind him.

More slowly, he descended to the B-2 level, parked, got out of the car, knees and hands shaking. He leaned his head and arms on top of the car and tried to breathe. Safe at last. He wouldn't bother going home, or even to the TruVal flat. Rug Row sounded a lot safer right then.

He stood up straight, looked for the nearest elevator. The garage was wreathed in shadows. One shadow moved, and Morgan's muscles jolted in fear. Where could he hide? But then the shadow spoke.

"Are you OK, Dr. Morgan? Golly, that must have been some kinda ride!" Never had Renee's mindless smile been more welcome. "I guess that was just some kind of warning," she added in a cooler voice.

Chapter 40

Renee escorted Morgan to Rug Row and left him alone. He called DeLuca, told him what had happened, warned him that the suspect car had been waiting at Gate 5. Could they have mistaken Morgan for DeLuca? DeLuca wasn't happy about being awakened, but thanked him for the alert.

Morgan curled up in the Sour Suite, dozed off in a leather recliner. It enfolded him, measured his temperature needs for a quiet sleep, warmed itself to that delicious level, hummed tunes appropriate for Morgan's approximate age, estimated gender, and state of muscular tension. Morgan fell asleep.

At nine a.m., he awoke alone in the Suite, poked around in the cooler for something to eat. He waited for Tru and Athena to arrive, then related his adventures and told them what DeLuca had said. They agreed that DeLuca would have to be the center of action. They'd wait for word from him before doing anything else.

As they separated, Tru hung behind. "You must be a wonderful driver!" she said.

Morgan was about the accept the compliment, but then decided to be honest. "No," he said, "only average."

"Then they could have killed you."

"Any time," he admitted. "Any time they wanted to. Guess they didn't want to."

"I wouldn't like to see you killed, Robert," said Tru, touching him lightly on a sleeve. "I'd miss you a lot."

***

At that very moment, Sausalito Police Detective Lieutenant Dennis DeLuca was the center, if not of action, at least of attention. As soon as he'd heard that the SFPD police had put Charlie Barnes in a car and were hustling him to Sausalito at his request, DeLuca put an anonymous tip into the system about a body in a crate in a particular room at the Casa Madrona. It wasn't long thereafter that word spread through the department of a sensational find, followed quickly by rumors of who had tipped off the police, and why, and who the corpse might be, and why she'd been killed.

It took less than an hour, more quickly than DeLuca had anticipated, before the Chief called him in to his office.

"Lieutenant DeLuca, it seems that an old case of yours has followed you here from SFPD."

"Oh? How's that?"

"C'mon, DeLuca, this can't be a coincidence. The body's been identified as belonging to – or having formerly belonged to – one Ms. Terra Lewis, a stellar and occasionally notorious photographer who was reported missing more than a month ago."

"You're not serious!"

"I am, and I don't think this is any surprise to you. What's happening?"

Since DeLuca hadn't expected the body to be ID'd this soon, he wasn't quite ready with a foolproof line of bullshit, but he gamely made the attempt. "Yes, I heard about the body, last night, from a – source."

"What source?"

"Don't know," said DeLuca. I'm trying to ID the source but no luck yet. But the source told me, very convincingly, who killed Lewis and dumped her body at the Casa Madrona. It was Charlie Barnes."

***

The Chief thought he might have heard the name "Charlie Barnes" before, or maybe not. Should he confess his ignorance? He hated to do that in front of a subordinate. But it would be far worse in front of a superior. If he just nodded sagely at the detective he wouldn't find out, at least here in real time, about who Charlie Barnes was, what threats that name could conjure. He might need that info right now. His superiors might this very moment be fingering his name on their coms, about to ask him "Who the hell is Charlie Barnes?" That could happen really soon. "You're the Chief of Police and you don't know who Charlie Barnes is?" A decision was made.

"Who's that? Who's Charlie Barnes?" the Chief said, his face reddening slightly.

"A long time hit man," replied DeLuca. "The database shows he's done two or three hits a year for at least a decade. Suspected. He's very clever, never been touched or even put on trial. For murder, anyway. But I think we can get him this time."

The Chief was silent. DeLuca continued. "This would be great for the Department, sir. SFPD spends years trying to nail a ruthless, cold-blooded killer, fails miserably – think how that would play on TV news! – and little SPD gets him." DeLuca waited in anticipation, wondering if he should add yet another layer of fragrant narrative.

The Chief sighed, finally spoke. "They shut you down on this very case, DeLuca. SFPD backed down pretty quickly, I hear, after one word from Washington, and we're about twenty times smaller than SFPD. I don't want any trouble over here."

DeLuca swallowed. "SFPD is bringing Barnes over right now. He'll be here within an hour."

"For what?"

"For questioning in the death of Terra Lewis."

"What? Why? You must realize that if Barnes is here at ten, a carload of lawyers will be here by eleven, writs in hand."

"I don't think they can do that in an hour, but that's OK, I only need an hour."

"You won't get anything out of him. Drop it. Send him back to San Francisco."

"After his victim's body turns up here in Marin? How would that look?"

"His alleged victim."

"OK, OK. Look. I just want to ask him a few questions. I know we'll have to let him go, probably won't even manage an arrest. But I need that hour! And don't forget, we have to quiz him or the Department will look damned foolish, having him sent over and then turning him away."

"Thanks to you!"

"You're welcome!" DeLuca walked out into the hall, took a deep breath, reserved a holding room. Yuba City, here we come.

***

Half an hour later, Charles Llewellyn Barnes was facing Dennis DeLuca across the traditional battered steel table.

"I want my lawyer."

"He's on his way."

"I have an alibi."

"I'm sure."

"Then why am I here? You know you're going to have to let me go, and soon." He looked at his wristcom. "I'll be out of here by noon. Maybe I'll have a really nice lunch at a place you can't afford. How about the terrace at the Casa Madrona? Yes, I think I'll go there right after you admit defeat." He showed his teeth in what wasn't, quite, a grin.

"The press knows you've been detained."

"Not to my liking, but if you've already called them, there's not much I can do, except complain to them about being hassled and victimized, waste of taxpayer money. They eat that victim shit up, don't they, those fuzzy-ass liberals. They like to beat up on the Department, too, or so I've heard."

"Well, victim, even if that's what going to happen we've got a few minutes here. Let's play a game."

Barnes was caught off guard. "What are you up to? What kind of game?"

"A pretend game, the O.J. game, remember? Let's call it 'If I had killed her.'"

Barnes thought for a moment. "OK, OK, I remember who O.J. was. Killed a couple of people the cops said, got off, wrote a book about it, made everybody else look like an idiot. Way to go! But why would I do that? I couldn't have killed – ah, who was it? Because I was in a hot game of billiards at the time. At the time, that is, I heard from someplace else that the shooting occurred. I was over in Emeryville, and I've got four buddies who'll swear to that."

"Buddies with felony arrest records."

"Doesn't matter. That's reasonable doubt."

DeLuca leaned forward. "That's just it, Charlie. We can't pin this one on you, so why not help us out here?"

"Again, why should I? What's in it for me?"

"Protection."

Charlie guffawed. "My friends – I got lots of friends, lots of protection. No one lays a finger."

"Until this one, Charlie. Some very powerful people were behind this killing. You're sharp. I think you realize that, whether or not you know who they are. This goes way beyond the typical hit, disgruntled capo or betrayed husband. Right now they're probably telling each other 'ol' Charlie's been picked up. But talk to the cops? No way!' But maybe then they have second thoughts, like 'Don't want to take any chances, now do we? We'd better make sure.' And they make a call. – I think you need that protection."

Charlie kept the superior look on his face, but DeLuca could see fear creeping into his eyes.

"What kind of protection?"

"Nothing fancy, no witness protection program. I'm afraid I don't have the authority to do that."

Charlie looked startled. "Then you're fishing, aren't you? Nobody's backing this investigation."

DeLuca paused, then decided to lay it all out. "That's right. That's one of the reasons, in addition to your four good buddies who always tell the truth, that you won't get tagged – for this one, anyway. But that's another reason why you should play the O.J. game with me. I can get you out of town, get your stuff together for you, since you can never set foot in your home again over there in the city, get you into a safe house out of town, maybe Fresno, until the local cops ask me what the hell I'm doing and on whose authority. Then you just disappear."

"Or?"

"Or you walk. Right now, before your lawyers get here. Right out the front door into the daylight with me, my arm around my good ol' buddy Charlie's shoulder, with plenty of fuss and fanfare, shaking your hand and telling you how the earth moved for me and all that shit. I won't be standing beside you, shouting 'Guess who's been here at the station spilling his guts. It's good ol' Charlie!' because I won't have to. Whoever's waiting for you outside the station, standing around and looking innocent, it won't be your four buddies or your lawyers. In fact, it might be one of your esteemed colleagues." It was DeLuca's turn to show his teeth.

Charlie pondered that. "OK, we'll pretend. But no recording."

"OK." DeLuca flipped a switch.

"And in case there's a hidden backup still recording this, I want to hear you say, in a nice loud distinct voice, 'I haven't read Charles Barnes his rights, because he's not a suspect for anything.' Can you say that?"

DeLuca scowled, said "I didn't read Charles Barnes his rights. He's not a suspect – in the Terra Lewis case. That will have to do, Charlie."

"All right," he shrugged. Let's do this."

Chapter 41

Meanwhile, at the TruPlex, Jayne Chang, TruVal, Inc.'s Creative Director, has burst into Truda Vallon's inner office unannounced. She is now stopping directly in front of Tru's desk and, having suddenly realized that in her enthusiasm she has infracted one of the major unwritten rules of the firm, is beginning to stutter and stammer an apology, and to wave her arms inconsolably.

Truda Vallon is now looking up from her comp screen and contemplating the transformation of what she had known, until that moment, as the cool, reserved beauty of Jayne Chang. Tru tries to put on a severe and disapproving face, but can't quite bring it off.

"Jayne, what is it?" The tone and tenor of Tru's voice anticipates one or more of these responses:

-The building is on fire.

-All the show's stagehands have gone out on strike.

-Somewhere unpronounceable, a nuclear device has exploded.

-TruVal's music director has gone Christian and is changing the words to all the songs.

-A great *folie furieuse* has infected the Creative staff, causing them all to stutter and stammer and wave their arms.

Jayne Chang is blushing. The word "spastic" occurs to her as an adequate characterization of how she must look to her CEO right now. Nevertheless, she delivers the words she is here to emit:

-"Ms. Vallon! He's wonderful! Terrific! What a voice! Better than Sinatra! Even better than La Rosa! I'd like to put him on the next show, right up front!"

It dawns on Tru what must have happened. The *folie* option becomes more plausible by the second.

"Ed Clarty has had his audition, then?"

"Yes! O God O God O God he's wonderful!"

***

"OK, Charlie," DeLuca said forty-five minutes later, "we've got possibly useful info out of you so far. To remind you, we're pretending here, you know, no admission of guilt. So to continue: why did your client want you to clean up Lewis's blood from that rooftop?"

"What?"

"Her blood. And other precious bodily fluids."

"I didn't do that."

"We're pretending here, remember?"

"I didn't do that, pretend or otherwise. It wasn't a requirement of the job."

DeLuca sat back and went "hmmm," like a toaster about to pop. He tried not to reveal surprise, but he was surprised.

"OK, what about removing the body."

"That was a requirement."

"But you didn't remove the body."

"Just suppose, lieutenant, that the – client had assured the ah, contractor that there would be no witnesses, but there were. Two of them."

"So you didn't think you had time to remove the body before the police would arrive."

"Sounds about right. At least, if I had done it that would have sounded about right."

"And then you – the contractor, rather – felt the need to delete the witnesses."

"Could be."

"So he – the contractor – went to the place where the witnesses were, but found no one home. But there was a sign on the door, something about a memplant."

"That's plausible."

"And the contractor tried to find and delete the person who'd acquired the mem."

"That's reasonable to assume."

"And failed."

"Yeah. Hung around his house for a while, never could get a shot off."

200

"And the other witness?"

"Couldn't find her. I think none of the contractor's friends could find her, either, or even ID her. Like she never was."

"Now, more about that body. The contractor, one might suppose, found out where the body had been hidden by asking a polite question of the man who'd rented a particular black van and had put the body in the back."

Charlie's eyes darkened. "You might say."

"Now, that man – let's call him 'Jimmy,' – was a friendly sort, and was happy to tell the contractor exactly where the body was, and lend him his ID badge as well, allowing the contractor to enter the building."

"Sounds logical."

"So tell me, Charlie, here you were in the building, stolen UPS uniform and all. You knew the body was in the cafeteria on the fourteenth floor. Now, how did you get into that cafeteria, considering it was after hours and locked up?"

"Ah – the friendly guy who'd rented the van. He might have had a key to the cafeteria."

DeLuca stopped being nice. "No, he didn't! I know that. No reason ever for Jimmy to have a key to the cafeteria. And the one time he needed to get in after hours, he used someone else's key. So tell me!" He sat back, continued in a slightly softer voice. "You could have said 'stole it from the cleaning crew,' which I might have believed. But you didn't have to steal it, did you. *So where did you get the key to the cafeteria door?"*

Charlie Barnes became very uncomfortable. "Stole it from the cleaning crew, maybe?" he said warily.

"Too late for that answer."

"OK, OK, it was left in a particular place inside the building. On a ledge on the fourteenth floor, outside the cafeteria. Up where it could be reached but not seen from below."

"And you don't know who put the key there."

"No. Someone called – she called the contractor, I mean, told him where the key would be waiting."

"She?"

"Yeah, a 'she'."

***

An hour later, a squad car left the Sausalito Police Department garage, a man hunched down in the back seat. The man was delivered to an intercity bus station in San Francisco, where a friend who happened to be a police officer handed him a ticket and told him where the express to Fresno was currently boarding. "Don't come back," the friend said. "Up your ass," Charlie Barnes said.

At the same time that Barnes was mounting the three metal steps into the bus and then scurrying to the back head down, Detective Lieutenant Dennis DeLuca was on the com with Robert Morgan, Failed Physicist. We join the conversation now in progress, as recorded in four separate top-secret databases, operated by four top-secret agencies each of whose existence was unknown to the other three.

"...and after all that good info, Robert, a surprise: Barnes had been ordered to remove the body as soon as he'd shot Terra, but he got spooked when he saw Alex and the woman watching him, so he ran away. Came back for the body, he said, after his client threatened him."

"But what about the TruVal lanyard?"

"That was Barnes' idea, spur of the moment, after he realized he wouldn't be taking the body with him. Something to prove he'd earned his pay."

"And used it to get into the TruPlex later?"

"No, it wasn't keyed for after-hours access. Lewis, remember, was a contract free-lancer, an indie, not a TruVal employee. It was Jimmy's badge he used."

"I guess we'll never see Jimmy again, then."

"'Fraid not."

Well, so much for Terra's body. How about the blood?"

"Not in his instructions to clean it up. I asked him about it, he didn't know. 'Not in my orders' was all he said. I believed him."

"Therefore," Morgan said, "if whoever hired Barnes didn't want anyone to know that it was Terra Lewis who'd been killed, and hence he ordered the body taken away, well, that person didn't know that Terra had ever been DNA'd. Didn't even suspect it, apparently."

"Yeah. We typed her from a Defense database. She'd had a Top Secret clearance at one time."

"That means the military wasn't in on the murder plot, or if they were, they were pretty stupid."

"Not the U.S. military, at least," said DeLuca.

There was a pause. "So," Morgan said, "no clues at all about who paid Barnes and gave him his instructions?"

"Nothing solid. Barnes, of course, preferred not to know, didn't know, and certainly never asked. He did say that the voice on the com sounded American, but he suspected that the money transfer originated, as far as he could tell, outside the country."

"But it was in U.S. dollars?"

"Right."

"Then how could he tell it didn't come from a New York bank, or from right here in the city?"

"Time of day. The transfer occurred at exactly two and a half seconds after half-past five in the afternoon, San Francisco time. Not the normal time of day for a programmed transfer, which is what it looked like, given that two and a half second lag. But what really caught Charlie's eye was that the transfer occurred the day after he'd received the funds."

"How...?"

"East Asia, my friend. Across the date line."

"There's money there," Morgan said, "Trillions. Criminal syndicates have accounts everywhere these days, don't they? Even in China. An interesting detail, but it only shows that Terra's murder was ordered by an organization with tentacles in at least one foreign country."

"I suppose."

"OK. Now, did Barnes have any idea as to why anyone would want Terra killed?"

"Not a clue. One of those things he preferred never to know."

"Too bad you couldn't record you and Barnes. There might be one or two clues."

"What do you mean 'too bad'? Of course I recorded it! I'm shipping it to your com as we speak."

Chapter 42

Dispersed in the webcloud, a secure subsubroutine had received a command to issue, anonymously, a customized death threat to one Robert Follansbee Morgan, PhD, based on parameters uploaded from a trusted system. There was a chargeback of several thousand monetary units. Exactly which currency was used for chargebacks such as this fluctuated based on currency futures predicted to obtain for the next few milliseconds. The specific nature of the threat was, in each case, customized to induce a condition in the subject known, in the appropriate professional terminology, as "becoming unglued" (DSM-VI code 294.85).

Based on highly secret standing orders, the subsubroutine informed the entity known to it as Odin that the threat had been issued. The subsubroutine was aware that it was not Odin itself that had ordered the threat to be issued.

***

Morgan began to sweat. Jesus! Yes, they could have run him off the road at any point in that long drive from Gate 5. Better go back to the memlab and live a quiet life helping those who can't get enough tail in person get off on others' sex lives. Why risk his neck? He'd never claimed to be brave. Well, he could take physical pain, he'd found that out once or twice, but not bullying, not an angry mind versus his. Never had been able to do that. His marriage – it could have been different if he'd shown a little backbone.

The more he ran through his memories of life with his ex-wife, the more pissed off he became. Damn it! This time, he was not going to cave. He could be ornery. He could be stubborn. Especially with people he didn't have to see face to face, like that message on his com. He stopped sweating, now determined to see it through. He com'd Renee, asked her to set up a meeting with Tru and Athena for three o'clock. He gulped the rest of his tea and walked out of the Sour Suite.

Heidi noticed his new demeanor. What did Antonio put in that tea? she wondered.

***

At three o'clock, Morgan entered Tru's inner office. Athena was already there. "First of all," Tru said, ignoring the fact that Morgan had called the meeting, "let's slip that hint that we're in the process of recovering Terra Lewis's memories, as we discussed this morning. Anonymous emails to the right blogs, not too blatant."

"On it," said Athena.

Tru turned to Morgan. "What next?" she asked. "Your meeting, Robert."

"Suppose," he said, "Suppose Terra discovered something, on that first Singapore trip, that she wasn't supposed to. An important secret."

"Like what?"

"I don't know. But we do know that Terra had a reputation, at least among her fellow photogs, of being ruthless; anything to get the shot. Suppose she got a shot she shouldn't have. Or overheard the wrong conversation, or someone thought she might have overheard something she shouldn't have. What would Terra have done? She might well have used that information for leverage, even pretend she'd heard more than she really had."

"Blackmail? Money?"

"Don't know. I have the impression that Terra would want something more important than money, like access to influential rain-makers. And she was making enough money from her work, you know, to make her wealthy. She'd have preferred influence, introductions, connections."

He looked into Tru's face, then Athena's.

"Perhaps money," Morgan continued, "would have been safer for her to demand. Important people are used to paying unimportant people to shut up and go away. But if Terra had made other demands, demands that could pose a danger, however unlikely, of exposing a VIP or some top secret enterprise, well then...."

Tru pointed at him and did an imitation pistol with her thumb and forefinger. "Right," said Morgan. "And then the second trip might have been to reconnect, to get, perhaps, an important introduction or to meet whatever demands she'd made."

"But the second trip didn't happen, because she was killed first, on that rooftop."

"Right. I believe she was killed so she wouldn't go back to Singapore and cause trouble, probably more serious trouble than she knew she'd stumbled into."

The three were thoughtful for a moment. Then Athena spoke up. "Why the rooftop? That's a pretty exposed place. And how did the killer know she'd be there?"

"On your second question, Athena, I have no idea," said Morgan. "But as to the first, I've thought about that. Very few rooftops have security cams, pointed inward, that is, not pointed down at the street. There would be little chance of collateral damage, if an assassin really cared about that. And probably most important, the killer wouldn't have to know who he was supposed to shoot, wouldn't need a picture or even a description: his instructions would be to go to this specific place at a specific time and kill the only other person there."

"And I have an idea how the killer knew Terra would be right there at that time," said Tru, "one we can easily check. The where and when of TruVal's photog assignments have never been confidential. Anyone in the company could find out Terra's basic itinerary. And she herself might have twittered or blogged or RSS'd about it beforehand."

"About photographing with her mind? Wasn't that highly confidential?"

"Yes, it was. But Terra was briefed on that aspect only immediately before she was sent out, the day she died. She walked in with three cameras that day and was told to leave them in the office."

The three were silent. Then Morgan said "OK, I guess that's as far as we can go on that topic. Now, how about Terra's body?"

"What about Terra's body?"

"I believe that Barnes was ordered to get rid of it so no one would know, for sure, that it was Terra who'd been killed."

"Why?"

"The Singapore connection, for sure. A missing person doesn't generate the kind of questions that a body does. At least, not having a body lying around would delay serious investigation as long as needed."

"As long as needed for what?"

"Don't know. As long as – until something could happen – but I'm floundering here."

Athena said "We've said that Terra might have been going back to collect on a blackmail scheme."

"Collect from whom?"

"Well, who knows? Singapore is a big city, its own country. A great deal of money and commerce. Where do we start?"

"And why?" Tru asked. "Robert, have you got anything more solid than suspicion? We really don't know that Singapore had anything to do with it."

Morgan sprang his surprise. "Yes, I do. The money that was paid to Charlie Barnes was transferred from a bank in Singapore."

"How do you know that?"

"The time and date stamp. Charlie Barnes told DeLuca that the transfer appeared to be programmed, and had been initiated at two and a half seconds after five thirty p.m., San Francisco time, but dated the next day."

"East Asia, then, I suppose," said Athena. "But that's a big place."

"Five thirty p.m. here is nine thirty a.m. in Singapore," he replied. "Singapore banks open at nine thirty."

"And surely elsewhere, too."

"Of course. But in the other two logical places, Shanghai and Hong Kong, banks open at nine."

Morgan paused while the two women took that in.

"What about Tokyo?" Athena asked. "When I was there I think I remember the banks opening at nine thirty."

"Yes, I checked that out," said Morgan, "but Tokyo's not in the same time zone; it's an hour off."

Tru's thoughts had been leading her down a different path. "Why wouldn't Terra's second meeting have been scheduled for here, in San Francisco? Or at least in New York instead of a second Singapore trip? She seemed to be calling the shots on this."

"The other parties might all be Singaporean," Morgan said, "although I think that's unlikely. No, we're talking about one individual, or more than one, who does business in East Asia, and whose presence in Singapore for a routine, recurring meeting wouldn't arouse any special interest, but whose absence on those same days might. I think we need to find out who of importance was in Singapore on the dates of Terra's first trip, and who are also scheduled to be there on the dates of her second trip, the trip she won't be making."

"That could be quite a few people," Tru offered.

"And we can't get hold of every important person's schedules," Athena added, "even if there's nothing very secret about them. And these people seldom travel alone. Two or three from each company or country's government agencies. That's thousands of itineraries to sort through."

"But," said Morgan, "we wouldn't be looking for two or more people from the same organization; they could meet at home. We need one," he held up a finger, "from organization or country A, and," another finger, "one or more from B. Two people who aren't normally seen together."

"For instance?" Tru challenged.

"Well, hypothetically," he said, "how about an African strongman and a European banker? Or a Russian – any Russian – and the head of a radical Islamic group? Or..."

"Got the point," said Tru. "Athena, how can we get that information?"

Athena frowned and concentrated for a moment, then said "Ah, news clippings, for a start, local press web sites. And I can try to get into airline passenger lists, Singapore government visa records. Neither would be easy, maybe not even possible, not for us. Of course, if I call in a few favors from my friends in government...."

"I wouldn't, Athena," said Morgan. "Too dangerous, for them and for us. Let's go with the clippings for now." Tru nodded assent.

"That means we're running two initiatives now," Tru summarized. "The Terra's mems rumor, and the guest list of the most prosperous city-state in East Asia."

With that, the meeting broke up.

***

Outside Tru's office, Renee had been wondering what the three had been up to. She received a call. "Drat," she said, disappearing around a corner to take it. Tru stepped out of her office to ask Renee a question, didn't immediately see her.

Chapter 43

Athena subdivided the two tasks among her own staff in such fine detail, and added so many more irrelevant and misleading subtasks, that none of the staff had any idea what their boss was up to.

Two days later, early results were in.

"First," Athena said when she had called Tru and Morgan together in her office, "I don't think our 'recovered memories of the dead' rumor is going anywhere. We picked up the usual jokiness, of course, opportunists, even web sites advertising that "memories of your past lives can now be recovered!" although you have to die before you can remember them, and then it would be too late. More important, none of the usual players, that is, government spy agencies, large corporations, terrorist propaganda machines, are moving on this. No one believes that memories of the dead can be recovered."

Tru shrugged. "Well, that's a dead loss."

"Not quite," Athena responded. "If I were one of those parties I'd at least investigate, just to make sure. But no one is doing that, as far as we can determine from the chatter. That means that..."

"They know!" Morgan broke in. "The 'secret' capabilities of MemCast must not be very secret, after all. The players must have an idea what MemCast can do, and so they know it can't get the dead to talk."

"That was my conclusion, too," said Athena. "Not only governments, but the other handful of major forces in the world; they all know. That means we've been penetrated. Badly."

"By the SoCalls?"

"Possibly, but I doubt it. Their blog chatter is way off base in – critical ways."

210

"These forces," Tru said, "if not the SoCalls then other groups, they know what MemCast can do, but I don't think they have the technology yet to replicate its functions. If they did, they wouldn't have been interested in us, wouldn't have been causing us so much grief. Perhaps we should go public with MemCast? About everything it can do? And open-source the code."

"Why?"

"Before we're shut down, or raided, or blown up. As a measure of protection."

"That's fine," said Morgan, "but not yet. We're still in the dark here. We need to understand what was behind Terra's killing before we do anything that might have unintended consequences for us or for the country."

"All right," said Tru. "I guess I agree, at least for now. We'll drop the Terra's memories angle. Now, what about the Singapore trips?" She turned to Athena, "Any progress?"

"Actually," said Athena, "I've come up with perhaps too many leads. There's an important global economic conference coming up, on the dates Terra was supposed to be there the second time, and also several other conferences, not even counting visits by one group with another group without a formal conference's being involved at all. We're cross checking with the dates of Terra's first visit right now. We'll have preliminary results by tomorrow, but there's no way to guarantee that we'll ever be able to identify most of the possibilities. People come and go, use private jets, false names not necessarily for illicit purposes, and so on. Many are flying in and out of Singapore every day on business, or to sight-see. Some of them happen by the Belgian bar, or one of the other clubs on the Boat Quay, or wander from one club to another, or hang out on the riverfront just people-watching. I don't see how we can pare down that list to a manageable number of suspects."

"Well," Tru said, "I think we need eyes on the ground there."

"Where?" Athena asked.

"In Singapore. On the same dates Terra would have been there."

"Who?"

"I was thinking of Morgan. And that policeman, Detective DeLuca, if he can be persuaded to go."

That evening, Morgan visited DeLuca again, on houseboat number seven. The lieutenant was downcast. "Your stunt really did a job on me," he said. "The chief doesn't believe it was just coincidence that I happened to get an anonymous, untraceable tip about Terra Lewis's body. 'Why you?' he keeps asking me, and I tell him 'It was my case in the city. Who else is a tipster likely to call?' Then he wants to know why it took so long for the body to show up, and by the way where was it all that time? And I answer, how the hell should I know? And he asks me if I have any theories as to why it wasn't in an advanced state of decomposition and I give him the same answer and he suspends me."

"What?" Morgan jumped in his chair, almost spilling the coffee DeLuca had offered him. "You were fired?"

"Suspended. Would have fired me outright but the union, department regs, all that procedure stuff. And with pay, at least for now. But in a week or two the chief will make nice to the union and I'll be canned."

"You can come with me."

"Where?"

"Singapore."

"Where Terra went, where she was supposed to go? What for?"

"We believe that on her trip there, Terra saw something she shouldn't have. Or at least, a powerful person or faction believed she'd seen too much. And then, based on what I read about Terra's drive and ruthlessness, she'd tried to capitalize on what she saw."

"Playing with fire."

"Playing with a group whose power and reach and ruthlessness she didn't fully appreciate."

"What's the plan?"

"Our flight leaves tomorrow night. It's the same flight that Terra was supposed to be on, and first class thanks to one of TruVal, Inc.'s subsidiaries. Load a few books on your com; it's more than eight thousand miles. We'll be staying at the Raffles, because that's the hotel Terra had reservations for – for the trip she'll never make."

"Sounds ominous."

"But they – whoever 'they' are – won't be expecting us."

"Want to bet?"

Chapter 44

Their wide-body left only twenty minutes late. Morgan and DeLuca settled back. DeLuca had a bourbon, Morgan shook his head. Needed to be clear about what they would be doing. As he anticipated, in the day since he'd told the detective about the flight, the policeman had developed quite a few questions and objections.

"Well," DeLuca began, "Why shouldn't all these bigwigs meet and mingle? Are we supposed to bug them? It's hard enough to hear anyone in a club, even across the table."

"That's just it. Terra Lewis probably wouldn't have overheard anything. I'm guessing she noticed two people who weren't likely to have their heads together, or one well-known person at least. She took a photo. They noticed."

"In a nightclub crowded with hundreds of other people?"

"Maybe. Or outside, or in a boat moored along the quay."

"And the person she'd shot demanded she delete the image from her cam?"

"Could be. And maybe she did. But that must not have been enough for them. Terra had a critical piece of knowledge, the bare conjunction of two faces. And I think she tried to sell her silence about that knowledge."

"These would have to be two people Terra knew?" DeLuca asked. "So it would occur to her to wonder what they were doing together?"

"Not necessarily. Not if at least one were famous, photographable, frequently photographed, in fact."

"Like a head of state."

"Any famous person. An actor or a sports hero for instance."

"But actors and sports heroes don't normally pay to have anyone killed."

214

"They might off their enemies themselves, but I agree that they don't tend to hire hit-men."

"Maybe," DeLuca put his hand on his chin. "Maybe a politician with his girl friend, or with a whore, or with another guy. From a country where that would be a big scandal."

"Hold on," Morgan said. "Look, we're guessing here. You and I will have to hang out, investigate. You're the detective. I'm an ex-assistant professor of physics and newly anointed proprietor of a grungy San Francisco memlab. TruVal's media team loaded my com with a copy of their facebase: photos of everyone who's appeared in the media in the past several years, anywhere in the world. The FBI has a facebase too, of course, and a lot larger than ours, but we couldn't get into that."

"That could be a million faces."

"It is. A million plus on TruVal's version, even excluding sports and entertainment figures. That's not including anyone who put their own faces on the web, only people actually written about, or holding an important or highly visible position."

"OK."

"TruVal gave me a copy of FaceMatch software, which you can copy from my com onto yours. Any faces you or I could catch on our coms, we can check against the TruVal facebase."

"It's accurate?"

"They demo'd it for me at TruVal. FaceMatch is pretty accurate if you're working with clear facial shots. It narrows down the field, at least."

"That means we've got facebase," DeLuca said, "and the software to use it."

"And a list of VIPs who are supposed to be here for meetings of one kind or another. Government, trade, NGOs, that sort of thing. Officials who might have been here at the same time as Terra's visit before, or at least people we don't know were *not* there at that time. Athena's team pulled up the lists, and tagged the facebase photos."

"That means we're ready."

"Guess we are."

"Not," DeLuca said. "Do you have any ideas more specific than 'hang out and investigate'"?

"Not really. You're the detective, as I said. I was hoping you'd figure out where we should start."

DeLuca sighed. "Well then OK, I guess I'm in charge. Now then, here's what we'll do. Not very exciting, but police work isn't exciting until a bad guy pulls a gun on you, or tries to make you his hood ornament. It's mostly plodding and poking and snooping and squeezing informants and listening to rumors on the street and getting tough with people and guessing. Mostly guessing.

"But here it is: We know Terra stayed at the Raffles. That's why we're staying there, as you said. And we know that the club where she was doing her shoot at was on Boat Quay. That's three or four blocks from the hotel. She could have gone to other places, but she was in Singapore for only two-three days, so let's concentrate on the hotel and the quay. We split up, keep a sharp eye out, watch out for anyone who might be wheels, who might attract a suspicious mind like Terra's. You know the scene: flunkies paying attention to them when they talk, holding umbrellas over them, kissing their butts, saying "Yes, Chief," crap like that. Take as many com pix as we can get away with of anyone who fits that description, and who they're with. You go to Boat Quay, I'll be here at the hotel."

"You get the easy job?"

"I get the job where it's hardest to be unobserved. On the quay where you'll be, visitors, tourists, businesspeople will be taking pictures. Start at that Belgian club, both inside and out, but prowl the quay, that's several blocks. Don't stay long in one spot, but don't hurry. Don't try to look like what you think a detective should look like! Better play the tourist. Anyone asks, you're here for a convention. Read the hotel's meeting board and pick one out, any one. Eye Patch Dealers. Pheasant Pluckers Anonymous. Whatever. Pick something dull. We don't want you to have to field questions you can't answer. A few hours during the day, but mostly this will be evening work."

Morgan digested that as the plane settled into a holding pattern, then descended gracefully into Changji through pink and purple afternoon clouds.

Morgan and DeLuca checked into the Raffles, got adjoining rooms. DeLuca had dinner sent up for them. "We don't want anyone seeing us together unless we can't help it," he explained.

After dinner, Morgan and the detective went their separate ways. Morgan had noticed that the Southeast Asia Society for Physical Research was meeting that week in the hotel. A wonderful cover, since he could talk physics if he needed to, if he met a beautiful mysterious female physicist whose eyes were black pools and whose breasts could stop traffic cold in the middle of Orchard Road. Oh, I'm here speaking at the conference, he could say, casually but importantly, about my research. Keynoting, in fact. Yes, I'm being very modest about my research, but it's quite crucial. Quantum events generating alternative time tracks, you know. Oh, you didn't know? Well, it's a pretty obscure field of research, although it's vitally important to the future of the world and the entire universe, and may I buy you a Singapore Sling, Miss? I'm the department chair at my university, and a Weltbau Prize winner. Black belt and fencing master, too. Your eyes are like black pools. Yes, I was examining your pools and not what you thought I was examining. For now, at least. Catch breath, say it: I'm in room 523 at the Raffles. Yes, that is impressive. You've never been there? Oh, you've never been in room 523, you mean. Well, we could buy a bottle and go to up my room, 523 that is. You could look out the window at the lights of the city with your black pools of eyes while I stand behind you and see their reflection in the glass. I could draw closer. You could feel my breath on your neck. We could then...

Morgan's Pheasant Plucker fantasy was interrupted by a stream of long black official cars that almost ran him down. Better watch where I'm going, he thought. He arrived at Boat Quay, pulled out his com, and tried to appear casual. He floated in and out of bars limiting himself to one drink in each, but after several bars he was well-greased. He snapped shot after shot of the glamorous of the world.

One man took a picture of Morgan. Morgan didn't notice.

Chapter 45

At two the next morning, DeLuca and Morgan regrouped in the policeman's hotel room. DeLuca made a cutting remark about knowing, now, what physicists really looked like. Morgan instructed his com to run FaceMatch, comparing the photos he'd snapped with Athena's facebase. DeLuca did the same. There were no immediately suspicious results.

"Well, we're getting to know the terrain," said DeLuca. "How about you?"

"I can eliminate clubs where only the locals go," said Morgan, "or only tourists from Iowa. Seemed like Iowans, could be from lots of places. Three clubs looked especially promising. I'll go back there tomorrow."

"That's today, now."

"Right."

"And you can broaden your search. Look in the hotels near the Quay, at least at lunch time and again at happy hour, or whatever they call it here. People going in and out, limos stopping. Remember, we're looking for a notable or important person, but especially we're looking for two or more together."

"Is this a needle in a haystack?"

"Maybe. But we believe Terra was supposed to meet one or more VIPs here, on her trip that never happened, and we think it was to collect whatever she'd extorted from them. This date wouldn't have been chosen randomly. It would have been a time when the men – or women – would be here anyway. Then their mere presence wouldn't arouse suspicion, or would at least be convenient for them. And Terra had seen them together on her first trip, in public very probably. They had caught her interest. Why? If Terra was interested, there should be something about them that should catch our interest, too, especially considering that we're actively looking, and she wasn't." He paused. "Now, I need my sleep!"

Morgan returned to 523, undressed and pondered black pools.

By noontime, Morgan was wandering the Quay and into one hotel after another. DeLuca said he'd be staying at the Raffles and making a few excursions in the area nearby.

The next two a.m. they regrouped, this time in room 523 which had played such a prominent supporting role in Morgan's fantasies, said things like Any luck? Not much. How about you? A few Arab princes. Did they meet anyone? Well, tomorrow's our last day here. Maybe we'll get lucky. What do we do if we come back empty-handed? Remember, we're looking for the interesting. The unusual and interesting: a face out of place. I'm sleepy.

***

Day dawned to sheets of rain. Morgan bought a raincoat in the hotel shop, a very expensive raincoat because that was the only kind they condescended to stock. He hoped TruVal would reimburse him for it. They had given him a generous expense advance, but he needed more than reimbursement; he needed money to live on once he got back to the U.S. And the water was soaking through his old shoes. Here he was, walking in the rain, and DeLuca must still be lounging in that five-star hotel and not drinking Singapore Slings in the Long Bar because only tourists from Iowa or Yuba City did that, according to him. Oh, well.

Morgan's peregrinations took him to the InterContinental. He walked in, door obsequiously swung open by a uniformed lackey who seemed to be impressed by Morgan's raincoat but not his shoes.

Morgan strolled the lobby, poked his head into three dining rooms, had lunch in the least formal of them, waited out the rain. On his way out of the hotel, he saw a face out of place. Where had he...? Morgan had seen that face before, but not in person. American, likely. On television? Deeply lined face, wagging jowls, weary looking, about fifty years old. Where? A TV producer? A superstar banker? Then he remembered the face from a newscast: it was V. Nelson Gooding, the junior senator from Virginia.

Morgan didn't remember exactly what the senator was noted for except hostility to the SoCalls, but surely he was worth keeping an eye on. Morgan followed Gooding out of the hotel and around a corner. Suddenly and apparently by accident, the senator ran into another man who also seemed to be about fifty years old, another American or perhaps European. Literally ran into a man wearing a white shirt. "Mr. White," Morgan decided to call him. Mr. White stretched out a hand to keep Gooding from falling. Gooding said something to Mr. White that Morgan couldn't hear. Was it "Watch where you're going, dickhead!"? But the senator didn't seem angry. Morgan held his com at his side, snapped as many photos as he could. The two said no more than another ten words to each other, then each went a different way.

Morgan studied Mr. White as closely as he dared. Quite well dressed. His encounter with Gooding had almost looked intentional. Morgan was reminded of a few thriller movies. Had these two exchanged passwords? Slips of paper bearing the deadly formula? The coded name of a traitor, or of the man, their pawn, whom they plotted to install as the next President? Morgan's fantasies threatened to run away with him, as they often did.

But now, Morgan had to decide whom to follow, Senator Gooding or Mr. White. Each was moving away at right angles to the other. Had they noticed him? He had a sudden quiver of feeling that he, himself, was being followed. Nerves. Shake it off. Got a job to do. But there he was standing still while both Gooding and White were moving rapidly out of sight. Which to follow? Well, he had started with the senator, and should probably stick with him. Right or wrong, he had to choose one or the other, right now! Morgan hurried after the senator, ran across a busy street. Too obvious! he thought, as taxi horns sounded. But Gooding didn't turn around.

Four blocks later, Senator Gooding turned into a small bistro. Morgan waited five minutes, then walked in, quickly located the man he was following. He was seated at a table, alone. Morgan took a table halfway across the room.

Gooding ordered. A coffee was brought. Morgan ordered sushi. Gooding sipped his coffee. Morgan's sushi arrived. Morgan stared at it, being used to Americanized sushi rolls that didn't wave their tiny tentacles at the customers. Gooding ordered another coffee. Morgan made a stab at his sushi with a chopstick. The sushi ducked. A man entered, sat down at the table next to Gooding, ordered coffee. Serious eye contact ensued. Gooding and the other man gave each other tight little smiles. Gooding paid for his coffee and left the restaurant. After less than a minute, the other man did the same. Intrigue! Skullduggery! Morgan was sure that this was the pair Terra had photographed, and it was he, Robert Morgan, PhD, who had spotted them, not that smug Dennis DeLuca!

Morgan left too many Singapore dollars on the table and hurriedly followed, snapping photos as he went. Outside, Gooding was holding hands with the other man. They were making interesting motions with their mouths.

Morgan was suddenly deflated. Not an international plot, a pickup!

He went back to the Raffles and had a headache.

At six p.m., DeLuca knocked on the door of 523. Morgan reported his adventures of the day in detail. "Probably futile. I think I followed the wrong man. Got the feeling I was being watched, too, a case of nerves. Well, I guess I'll search for Mr. White on facebase now, and get more info on Senator Gooding."

DeLuca held out his com. "You mean these two?" DeLuca's com screen displayed a photo of Gooding and Mr. White, with Morgan's raincoated back in the foreground.

"Where the hell did you get that?"

"I took it."

"Were you following me?"

"Absolutely. Think of it this way: An individual or group arranged for Terra Lewis to be killed. Terra was supposed to be in Singapore today, but was shot instead. But they are here, these perps, because they were scheduled to be here. Had business to transact, legitimate or otherwise. And it might seem noticeably odd if one or both cancelled, or perhaps they have a tight deadline. They're alert, aren't they, at their meeting.

Perhaps a little nervous. A photog got them once, became a nuisance, had to be dealt with at risk of their own exposure. Could it happen again? Had to be very careful. Had to be looking out for anyone who might be too interested."

"So what?"

"I've been following you for three days, Robert, staying alert for anyone showing alarm at being followed by you, or being photographed by you, or being sleuthed by you."

"Was I that easy to spot?" cried Morgan the great sleuth, in despair.

"Yeah. More than 'easy to spot.' You were, I would say, 'intrusive.'"

"Shit!"

"Good shit, Robert. When Senator Gooding and 'Mr. White' split up so hastily, possibly as a result of your observation, I saw that you were following the senator. Since that angle was covered, I followed Mr. White. White, I believe, seeing you going after the Senator in the other direction, relaxed. After that, he was easy to follow."

"And?"

"And he met briefly with a man, East Asian by appearance and gesture. Let's call him 'Mr. Gray.' Mr. White gave Mr. Gray a small object that very much appeared to be a memchip. Now, why do you suppose they would use chips?"

"Because they knew that wireless transmission could be compromised. Because they knew, or suspected, that any transmission they might attempt to make would be monitored."

"Exactly."

Morgan took a deep breath. "Intrusive," indeed! "Well," he said to DeLuca, "let's see who this coterie is!"

"OK, I'll start with our senator. DeLuca flicked a few virtual knobs on his com. "He's a member of the Senate commerce, science, and transportation committee."

"Commerce. That makes sense if he were here as part of a trade delegation."

"And," continued DeLuca, "he's the ranking member of the subcommittee on communications, technology, and the Internet."

"We're getting closer!" Morgan said. "Ah – what's a ranking member?"

DeLuca re-read the information. "Seems to mean that he's a member of the minority political party. But we knew that, didn't we? Virginians usually are."

"I saw Gooding on TV," Morgan said. "He's the one who's investigating the SoCalls."

"OK," DeLuca said. "And he met another man, apparently quite innocently, over coffee, while you were going *mano a mano* with your sushi. And," he looked at his com screen, "he's here on Athena's database of notables known to be in Singapore. In fact," he touched the screen, "he's part of a Congressional trade delegation meeting here this week, on the subject of Internet commerce across national borders. No secret there, it's routine government business and right up his alley, it seems."

"*Apparently* innocent?"

"As you described it, Robert, the conjunction of Gooding and the other man seemed like an ordinary pickup. Discreet because this is Singapore, after all, not San Francisco. But for all we know, those two might have been play-acting, pretending it was all about sex."

"Watching, like me. 'Intrusive.'" The word still stung.

"Yes, like you. Now let's see who this Mr. White is, the man you abandoned and I followed." The com zipped by picture after picture. Faces streamed by in a blur. End of file. Repeat. Repeat. Finally, DeLuca pressed escape. He turned to Morgan. "He's not in facebase."

"Meaning?"

"Could be he's not prominent enough. There are a million-plus faces in facebase, but out of ten billion human beings in the world..." he shrugged. "Or, he could have disguised his face in any number of ways, although his features didn't appear altered to me." DeLuca paused, frowned. "Or," he said, "or he could have been deleted from facebase."

"How could that happen?"

"Washington could do it. Witness protection does it all the time. But any agency, any local law enforcement or even a private security operation, with a good enough reason, can request the FBI to not actually delete the face, but make it inaccessible to a search. And then," DeLuca developed a worried expression, "when a search is initiated on that face, the requesting agency would automatically be notified."

"So they'll know someone's seen their man, is interested in him for some reason?"

"That's it. Right now, if my guess is correct, a bell is ringing in some heavily shielded office, and a voice is telling a person with several different aliases that a Lieutenant Dennis DeLuca of the Sausalito PD has taken a picture of the man we've been calling Mr. White, in Singapore."

"Is there cause for alarm here?" asked Morgan, his voice a little high.

"You bet your sweet ass there's cause for alarm," said DeLuca.

"Well," said Morgan, "we're flying back to San Francisco in a few hours. If we lie low we'll be out of here soon."

"Yeah, I guess that's all we can do. We've made good progress, though; we'll have lots to move on when we get back. But first, let's see if we can find out who the senator's pickup and Mr. Gray are."

Chapter 46

Dispersed in the webcloud, a computationally efficient expert system of Bayesian belief universes detects that a particular face has been searched in a facebase. Accessing the most recent setting of its parameters, the agent messages several different subscribers (who may themselves be software agents) who have indicated an interest in the person whose face that is. The agent knows one of these subscribers as "Odin." The agent remains receptive to any return message that a subscriber may respond with. Appropriately commanded, the agent's repertoire includes arranging for elements of an appropriate clandestine organization to

-Inform the owner of the face that he or she has been the subject of a facebase search, or

-Create a new identity for the person corresponding to the face, or

-DELETE the owner of the face, or

-Do nothing.

No return messages have been forthcoming. Yet.

***

The investigation of the man Senator Gooding picked up was very brief: no match was found in facebase, no near miss. "This man could be anyone or no one," said DeLuca. "But I think the action we want to follow here is Mr. White and his meeting with Mr. Gray."

"Describe Mr. Gray for me," Morgan said, "since you saw him and I didn't."

DeLuca closed his eyes and concentrated. "Tall, slim, thin face, prominent eyes. Forties perhaps. Slight smile I would call ironic or sardonic, not sure there's a difference. Bearing reserved and formal but graceful, not rigid. Very self-assured. Born to money or authority, but didn't seem military. Looked to me more likely Korean than anything else, but I could be wrong about that."

More faces streamed by. Finally, the blur slowed. This time, twelve faces were displayed on DeLuca's com. "Most of these are blurry in the facebase database," he said." That's why the software is having trouble figuring out which of these is the best match."

DeLuca displayed his own photo of the man. He and Morgan eyeballed the twelve, one by one, comparing them with DeLuca's photo. They were able to eliminate or seriously question eight. "Not really out, DeLuca said, "but we now have a working assumption that one of the remaining four is Mr. Gray, who was handed a small item by our Mr. White today."

"Who are these four?"

"This com has limited info." DeLuca flipped a few screens forward, then back. "All four are Korean. Three North, one South. A-list types. I'm going to have to pass these names back to Washington to check who was where today. With luck, all but one of these four will turn out to have been at home, or enjoying the gross or subtle pleasures of Bangkok. Odd man out is our man."

"Are you going to transmit...?

"No way; too sensitive. This will have to wait until we get home."

***

Morgan stayed awake most of the way back to SFO. DeLuca curled up against an arm rest and slept soundly. As first class passengers, there seemed to be a kind of moral obligation to consume alcohol, certainly an expectation, but Morgan resisted. Not great to be in the middle of a blurry haze, not great to be numb. He couldn't get the taste of bad whiskey out of his mind. Wretched stuff, should be called Sourpiss instead of Sourpuss. The flight stopped over in Seoul for refueling.

So Mr. Gray was Korean. South or North? Must be North, he reasoned, because a U.S. senator's meeting with a South Korean would surely pass unremarked. But – meeting with a North Korean? If Gooding were on the appropriate Senate committee, it might make sense for him to meet a North Korean diplomat clandestinely, to work, for instance, on a deal that couldn't yet be announced publicly. But he wasn't on Foreign Relations. Or there could be a darker connection between the two. Much darker. The plane took off again, making a tight turn off the runway to avoid North Korean airspace. Morgan had visions of the plane's straying a micro-inch over the line, Northern missile crews aiming their missiles, firing. Would he see them out the window, those missiles, half a second before he became a scattering of body parts and molecules? He signaled to the flight attendant and asked for a Glenlivet, double.

***

The Truda Vallon Show that week featured its usual fare, a mix of Tru singing and dancing, guest acts, an interview with an aspiring film director best known for his astonishing haircut, and then, premiering for the first time tonight on television, folks, please give him a big round of applause and welcome ta dah! The one and only sensational songster Ed Clarty!

The customary backstage snickers didn't last long, as Clarty launched into a song (sad), and then another (manic), and finished with a reprise (very sad). When he began the first (sad), the ViewerTron display read 17, a number that could only mean that millions of toilets all across the land were about to flush. With (manic) the number climbed into and through the 30s and 40s, and when (very sad) poured lugubriously forth the number rose and rose, and at Clarty's final bow a glorious 89 was touched, and caressed, and bloviated upon without end.

Clinical Advisor Ed Clarty had become, in other words, and perhaps those other words were, well, a little trendy, a little illiterate and pseudo-folksy but it did fit the country's mood, right now when the vast lumpenproletariat needed cheering up from their battles with the economy, and their politicians, and those wars, all those wars. Well, the words most otherly spoken, by now surely an anticlimax to reveal them I'm afraid, were "sensational meta-incredible phenom."

***

"OK," said DeLuca on the com to Morgan late the next day. "I got the scoop from Washington on Mr. Gray, or at least all the scoop I'm likely to get for a while. Come on over after work."

"What work?"

"Aren't you back at TruVal?"

"Yeah, but they're not paying me."

"How do you live?"

"At the moment, by cheating on my expense report."

"You too? Glad to hear you're a true Norman Rockwell American!"

"Don't joke about it."

DeLuca realized that Morgan was serious. "OK, I won't, he said. I'm sorry. Hey, come on over and we'll sort out our Grays and Whites while I treat you to dinner."

"Out?"

"Call-in. You can pick the cuisine when you get here."

"Sounds good."

***

Earlier that day, legs stiff from hours of motionlessness and groggy from not enough sleep, Morgan had briefed Tru on what he and DeLuca had found in Singapore.

"Senator Gooding? V. Nelson Gooding?" Tru asked.

"That's right. Do you know him?"

"Not personally. That stiff-necked SOB has gone out of his way to avoid being seen with me or mentioned in the same breath!"

"How come?"

"Well, for one thing, he's planning to hold hearings not only on the SoCalls, as we know, but also on MemCast, although that hasn't been announced yet. He thinks it's a threat to the moral fiber of America."

"Like TV, the Internet, and the printing press?"

"Apparently."

"Have you been asked to testify, or subpoenaed about what TruVal is up to?"

"Not yet. I actually called his office and volunteered to testify, got put off."

"Your being there would attract quite a bit of publicity for him."

"That's what I thought, too."

"Well, that's interesting," said Morgan, "but not quite to the point. Gooding's being in Singapore wouldn't arouse any suspicions."

"Was he there when Terra visited before?"

"Yes; and he's been there several times."

"To meet his lover?"

"Always official business, regardless of where he might have been putting his business unofficially."

"Do you suppose Terra noticed Gooding with his lover, and she was blackmailing him?" Tru asked.

"Doubt it. There might be a brief flap, but Gooding's unmarried and popular. He'd survive. It would be a much greater risk if he were caught paying blackmail. Don't forget: it's always the cover-up that gets you, not what you did."

"Nixon."

"Right. Like Nixon and all those congressmen and governors."

"Who's left?"

Morgan paused. "DeLuca's playing his contacts in the FBI and other places in Washington. I hope he'll have news for us soon."

Tru leaned back in her chair, smiled, held out her hand to him. "So, Robert Morgan, international sleuth! You've come a long way from that day in the Hall of Wallscreens, when you asked me that dumb question about DNA'ing me!"

"And," he said, "an ex-professor who's had to cash in his retirement account, and a proprietor of a debt-ridden memlab that's currently shut down for lack of anyone who knows how to perform memplants."

Morgan was hoping that Tru would say something like "Dear Robert, you must be totally impoverished. Here's a check for a million dollars. You've earned it, and I'll never miss it." But Morgan was disappointed in his quest to become solvent once again. All she said was "Let me know what DeLuca finds out. And you can use your old office on the twelfth floor whenever you need a place to sit, any time. You're always welcome here."

Morgan exited Rug Row, mindful of the fact that, the last time he'd seen his TruPlex office, it was bereft of anywhere to sit.

Not wanting to bother arranging for a TruVal company car, Morgan took a bus to Sausalito. Now that most private cars were outlawed, bus service had become plentiful, and offered three classes of service. But not even third class was cheap, owing to the price of gasoline and natural gas. Morgan counted his cash, thinking that he might have to ask DeLuca for a loan. He had enough to get back to the city, but that was about it. He'd better have a filling dinner that would last him a day or two. Or he would have to keep scarfing free food in the Sour Suite.

Chapter 47

He reached DeLuca's houseboat as the sun was setting behind the hills of Marin. To the northwest, the top of Mount Tam was covered with a light dusting of snow. Morgan had seen snow there only three or four times in his life, and he couldn't remember when the last time was.

DeLuca was in the shower. "Make yourself comfortable," he yelled through a foggy crack in the bathroom door. Morgan went outside, circled the houseboat, inched along the narrow railing. The ark in slip six appeared to be pleasantly occupied. He saw the outlines of a man and a woman, backlit through light curtains. One silhouette hoisted a glass, then the other did the same. Morgan sighed. That had been his vision of life with Helen, but it hadn't worked out. Never good enough for her, even though she seemed never good enough for herself, either. He raised a glass, she threw a fit. Maybe it was his fault, a little bit, all that drinking, not paying enough attention to her, treating her as "the whore on the pedestal," as she'd once put it, throwing the expression in his face along with the contents of a cup of cold coffee, dishes to follow, headlines at eleven. Life with a stranger.

He walked a few feet along the railing and looked over at ark eight. There was the plaque he had noticed before. This time, he read it.

National Historical Monument
On This Houseboat Lived
THE KINGSTON TRIO
1959-1962

In spite of himself, he was impressed. THE KINGSTON TRIO? The name sounded familiar. Famous, weren't they? Singers. Now, what were their names? He thought hard, then remembered. It was Peter, Paul, and Mary. Wasn't that it? No, it was Tom, not Peter. Tom Dooley, that was it. Satisfied with himself, he went back inside DeLuca's boat and sat down.

Morgan idly wondered if DeLuca would emerge from his tiny bathroom naked, but when he entered the living area he was wearing a shirt and pants. "What'll it be?" he asked.

Dinner, Morgan remembered. He was being asked about dinner. "What are the choices?" he said.

"Well," DeLuca concentrated. "We've got the Moo-Moo Hawaiian Dairy Bar down on Bridgeway, and a branch of Hibachi You Betcha! in Mill Valley."

"Pizza."

"Pizza?"

"Pizza, if that's OK with you."

"OK, sure. There's a Rollin'InDough's right down the street." DeLuca called and ordered pizza for them with a side of garlic bread, plus two liters of whatever new concoction PepsiCo had dreamed up that week to maximize its food store display space.

***

On his third slice, Morgan, mouth full of crust, couldn't wait any longer to ask. "Well, Dennis," he mumbled his tongue around the bready mass, "who were Mr. White and Mr. Gray?"

DeLuca reached for his notebook, flipped it open. Morgan took a swig of Pepsi Seventeen. "Well, let's see," said DeLuca. "Let's back up a minute. Of course we already knew about Senator Gooding. I think we've got to consider him a suspect in Lewis's death, if only because he was in Singapore when she was there last month and then again now, on the dates of the trip she never made. The downside to his being a suspect is that Gooding's presence in Singapore was no secret, and his position made it logical for him to meet with many people, including perhaps a few who might be considered representatives of an enemy state."

"In secret."

"Yes, but that could be explained away if it ever came to light. Back-door diplomacy. Nothing awful enough to inspire murder. But..."

"'But?'"

"But there's a complication. I need to tell you my thinking about Mr. White now."

"Which is?"

"None of my contacts can match a name to Mr. White's face. He's a true mystery man."

"Too bad."

"But we might know a little about him."

"What's that?" Morgan asked.

"That he took something from the senator, probably that memchip that we were guessing about, and a few minutes later passed it on to Mr. Gray, the Korean."

"How do you know that?"

"I said we *might* know about Mr. White. We both saw him collide with Senator Gooding in the street. Neither of us saw anything change hands. But you, as I recall, said the whole scene looked staged, because Gooding didn't seem to be annoyed by another man's physically running into him."

"I thought it might have been staged, but it could have been an accident, one of those things."

DeLuca ignored that and continued his line of thought. "Then the question is this: I saw Mr. White give Mr. Gray a memchip. Now, did Mr. White bring it to the show himself, or did he get it from Gooding and pass it on."

"A go-between."

"Precisely," concluded DeLuca. "If the senator was afraid to be seen in public with this particular Korean, then he would have every reason to use an intermediary, a man he could trust, to hand off the memchip."

"But just a minute ago you said that his position allowed him to contact people from various countries without necessarily arousing any suspicion."

"Yes, I did, but I meant government representatives. Therefore, if my theory is correct, then this Korean, Mr. Gray, is outside the official government chain of command, someone the senator couldn't afford to be seen with or questions would be raised. Therefore, not a representative of a foreign leader. Not a senior diplomat. And perhaps the North Korean government would be very unhappy if it knew that Mr. Gray was meeting with a member of the U.S. Senate."

"Then the need for secrecy might not have been on the American side at all!"

"That's what I'm thinking," said DeLuca.

"The two of them must have been suspicious, afraid of being observed this time," Morgan added. "But before, on Terra's first trip, perhaps they weren't that worried, didn't take precautions."

"Back then," DeLuca said, "the senator might have passed something on to Mr. Gray directly, without bothering with a go-between. Handed the memchip over a table in a club, the Belgian club on Boat Quay, for instance."

"And was photographed."

"Right. Photographed because Lewis recognized the senator. Perhaps just because it was interesting, a United States senator in an exotic setting, dancing girls in the background and all. Perhaps she wasn't suspicious of the Korean. Perhaps she never even noticed him. But in any case, she was observed and it didn't matter if she suspected anything amiss or not. She was a witness to a highly secret transaction, and would have to be taken care of."

"Do you think she was contacted?" Morgan asked.

"I think so. Subtly. To see if she knew anything, whether she was a real danger or not. But Lewis was sharp. She smelled deceit, smelled importance, decided to cash in."

"And scheduled a second trip."

"Suppose they asked her to come back to Singapore," DeLuca said. "To get that payoff or introduction or whatever it was she'd demanded. Wouldn't she be lulled by being asked back? She'd be on high alert only after she reached Singapore again, no need to be careful before the trip, nothing to fear until then, surely? She probably thought she could let her guard down for the time being."

Morgan digested these hypotheses along with the last slice of pizza.

DeLuca reached into a cabinet and pulled out a bottle. "Dessert wine," he said, pouring a small amount into two glasses, "to settle the stomach. To offer it our apologies for insulting it with pizza. It's a black muscat, Central Valley."

Morgan took a sip, didn't like it.

"Now," DeLuca continued, "let's talk about Mr. Gray, my big surprise of the evening aside from the black muscat."

"What's that?"

"What kind of position were we assuming he had in North Korea?"

"Well, I was thinking Army, although you said 'not government,' and the military is a big part of the government there. The North Korean Army is very powerful. Or perhaps he's an aide to the Likable Leader, but with no official position."

"Close, doctor. My contacts in the FBI identified him as a Jeong Ja-yu. He's a science administrator, head of a lab complex in Namp'o. That's not very far from the capital. He's not military or diplomatic at all, just as I suspected. High-ranking, but hadn't previously been of interest to our side, mostly because his lab didn't seem to be working on WMDs, or any kind of weapons system, for that matter."

"Previously? Meaning he's of interest now?"

"I had to tell my contact why I wanted to ID him, before she'd tell me whose picture she'd matched him with, and who he was. And now yes, there is interest in Washington, at least at the backgrounder level."

"What kind of science does this Jeong do?"

"His research complex is quite large, conducts studies across the scientific spectrum: biology, physics, neurology, geology, and a few more-applied areas like computer science, space, and medicine. The man himself is a biochemist but that may not be significant, considering the range of activities he's responsible for."

"What's the connection between Senator Gooding and Jeong? Why was Gooding giving him a memchip?"

"Damned if I know. But I think we've ID'd a motive for murder, and a perp."

"The senator!"

"Not clear. Gooding may never have known about the scheme to murder Terra Lewis. The senator is hiding a secret involving North Korea, for sure, but that may be on behalf of the Administration, not any more nefarious than anything else our government does. It's possible that Jeong, the North

Korean, was the one who decided that leaving Terra alive was too risky. If so, he would have every reason *not* to let Gooding in on his intentions."

"Then what's our next move?" Morgan asked.

"Nothing. The FBI knows what we know. Of course they aren't directly concerned with Terra's murder; that's a local matter. But I think they'll make a few inquiries at Homeland, the White House, CIA, NSA. If they find anything amiss, I'm sure it will be settled quietly, and our scientist Dr. Jeong will find himself disinvited to any further meetings with American officials."

"That's all the punishment he's going to get?"

"That's how it's done."

"Unless we tell the press."

DeLuca regarded him sternly. "I wouldn't do that, Robert. I wouldn't do that."

By this time it was ten p.m., and DeLuca was already yawning. Morgan took the hint.

"I guess I'll tell Tru we've gone about as far as we can on Terra's murder," Morgan said. "She won't be happy, but she may be relieved that the violence will very likely end there."

"Assuming Madelyn Lopez's death was an accident. We still don't know that."

Morgan waited for his bus in the night chill. He realized he hadn't dressed warmly enough, stamped on the sidewalk to keep warm. "On the war path," he muttered, then realized that his war path had now come to a dead end.

Back at home, Morgan made a haptic gesture at his wallscreen.

"North Korea fired another test missile today, this one, with a dummy nuclear warhead, splashing down in the South Pacific off the coast of southern Chile. Experts noted that this distance is equivalent to that from Pyongyang to New York City. The U.S. Secretary of State issued a bulletin denouncing this 'irresponsible warlike threat.' The North responded that the flight was entirely over international waters, and the Secretary of State could just, as their official translation put it, 'cram it.'

"Refugee boats are washing up in many parts of the world now, with thousands reported dead. Scientists laid the blame on ocean-current dynamics. These currents have been slowing worldwide for several months, a number including our own Gulf Stream occasionally shutting down entirely.

"President Stockwell, during his address to the annual conference of the American Exceptionalism Association, took to the mikes to plead for calm, referring to both the Korean situation and the ocean currents. 'Remember,' he said, 'you love your country.'

"And on the lighter side of the news, celebrations were held across the globe yesterday to mark the birth that brought estimated world population above the ten billion level. Several countries vigorously disputed the honor of bringing hube number ten billion into the world.

"When we return, a special report on Why Our Schools Are Failing. And now for this word."

Click.

Chapter 48

The next morning, Morgan decided to walk from his home to the TruPlex. He needed the exercise after all that pizza. And he didn't have enough money stored in his com to pay for a cable car or bus.

A few minutes later he regretted having to walk, because he found his way blocked by a large and boisterous demonstration. By the SoCalls, as he quickly discovered. Should he try to make his way through them, or back up a block and go around? Go right on through, he decided. Free country, a public thoroughfare. Damned if he'd go out of his way because of a bunch of damned paranoid rabble with nutty ideas!

He started through the crowd, tried to get past the thickest pack of them, but was surged and nudged toward the middle. There was Buck Baker, he saw, but not speaking this time. He was standing quietly, smiling fondly at the makeshift podium where a remarkably dull speaker was going on and on about the SoCalls' favorite topics: mental health, memplants, and government mind control. In the speaker's opinion, the three were more or less identical.

"Do you know, friends, that according to psychiatry's own diagnostic manual, what's included as a so-called 'mental illness'? How about sadness, sorrow, grief, boredom, shyness, anger, forgetfulness, even bed-wetting. They're not signs of a living, breathing, free human being. No, they're all signs of – guess what?"

"Mental illness!" a few replied on queue.

The speaker continued. "We don't have problems any more, problems we can grapple with and solve together with our loved ones. No, no, my friends, we have 'illnesses' that only professionals are qualified to deal with! And those professionals make millions off you and your taxes. Doesn't it make you 'sick'?" He chuckled into his bull horn. No one laughed.

Morgan surveyed the crowd. People were cleaning their nails, fiddling with their coms. They seemed to be waiting for something, perhaps for Father Buck to speak. Morgan turned his attention back to the young man on the podium.

"Power relations, the old game. Daddy government will tell you what to think. Tell you if you're so-called 'mentally ill' or not, and 'not' doesn't come up very often! And with memlabs, now the government could, if they wanted to, delete any inconvenient memories you might have, memplant more uplifting memories into your head, memories more expressive of the dog-like devotion they expect from loyal citizens. TruVal, Inc., you know, has their own memlab, right here in San Francisco. Well, we heard from a good source that what they're doing there is a lot more than innocent MemCast entertainment. What could that be? Something the government doesn't want to be caught doing in their own labs?"

Morgan decided he'd heard enough, although he was disappointed that he hadn't had the opportunity to hear from Father Buck in person again. Then, as he was edging his way through the crowd, he saw a familiar face on the opposite side of the group. Was that Helen he glimpsed in the distance? He turned away too quickly to be sure.

Finally arriving at the TruPlex, Morgan showed his badge at the door, nodded to two Trudite guards, and elevated to the twenty-sixth floor. Renee, of course, spotted him immediately.

"Oh Dr. Morgan!" she gushed, giving him a toothpaste-ad smile, "are you back already from wherever it was?"

"Singapore," said Morgan.

"I suppose you'll just love to see Ms. Vallon right away! And I just know she'd just love to see you right away, too!" All this love was overdoing it, Morgan thought, even for Renee. "I'll just buzz her right now!"

"Wait a minute," said Morgan. "I've had a long trip and I need to organize myself a little, first before I see Tru, that is. I mean. A little bit, a few minutes."

***

Renee wrinkled her brow slightly at Morgan's apparent confusion. Poor thing, she thought, something's got to him. Just that long trip? Or what he saw there. Yes, I heard about that, doctor. And not from you or from that detective, either. Too bad the two of you have been meddling.

"No problem," she beamed at him, glanced at a schedule on her com, and then at another. "It seems Ms. Vallon will be free in, oh, half an hour. How does that sound?"

"Sounds fine," Morgan said. He'd already turned and was walking toward the Sour Suite. He hadn't had any breakfast, and couldn't wait to sample the morning's buffet offerings. He swung the door open and went inside.

***

Renee thought what to do. I guess he's going to tell Ms. Vallon all about it, about our friends and all that. Then Tru will decide to do something that might not be too smart, all things considered. Wow, I'd better get an alert off right away!

Her fingers waved gracefully above her com. In another part of the building, a coded message flashed briefly on a screen.

Chapter 49

"Oh Robert, it's good to see you again!" Truda Vallon smiled broadly. Morgan felt a rush of warmth from her, took a deep breath. "What did you and Lieutenant DeLuca find out?"

Morgan launched into what he had a feeling would turn out to be a long, convoluted, and utterly confused narrative. At that moment there was a knock on Tru's office door, and a head appeared around its edge.

"Hi, Dr. Morgan! Tru, the guards let me know that Robert was here. Mind if I sit in?"

"Come on in, Athena," Tru said. "You're right in time for the debriefing."

Debriefing? They were expecting something formal? With Power Points, maybe, and laser pointers? Red, blue, or green? He wished that Dennis had come along. Dennis would know what to say, how to say it. There they were, the two most important executives of TruVal, Inc., waiting for him to speak, beaming at him expectantly. There! Tru was looking at her wristcom. This was like freshman physics, except he didn't have to please those kids, satisfy their curiosity, give a damn if they looked at their wrist watches back when there were such things, shook them in anger and disbelief. He'd read from his last year's lecture notes which were from the year before, and the year before that, with a few adjustments because physical research had, in spite of Morgan's intense desire for stability, progressed, by the proverbial leaps and bounds, actually, out of all bounds, in spite of his wish that everyone would stop doing research for a few years and catch up with what it all *meant*, for Christ's sake!

Morgan came back to the present. "We were just starting, actually," he said, and smiled at Athena, who smiled back, walked into the room, and took a chair.

Morgan rehashed the saga of Senator Gooding and Mr. White and Mr. Gray. When he got to the part where DeLuca's friends in Washington had ID'd the North Korean as the man in charge of the Namp'o research establishment, Tru let out a cry of "So that's it!" She and Athena glanced at each other with meaningfulness thick enough to grill and serve to hungry predators.

"We should tell him," said Tru.

"I agree," said Athena.

"Tell me what?" asked Morgan, pointerless hand poised in mid-air.

"We believe," said Tru, "that our researchers developed MemCast beyond the functionality we had specified."

"Karl-Heinz Stirner?" said Morgan.

"Yes. Stirner and his team. When we were cleaning up after that explosion on the B-1 level we discovered, well, more equipment than I, for one, had ever authorized – at least twelve million dollars worth. And evidence that Stirner had been paying the salaries of at least ten high-priced science and technology consultants."

"But surely, his budget?"

"It was all off the books. Off TruVal, Inc.'s books, I mean. Stirner was getting money from an outside source, using it to buy equipment and pay experts to set it up, perform research tasks for him, and run tests."

"Where was he getting...?"

"His money? It took us a while to discover that. Our accountants couldn't figure it out, for some reason." Tru glared at Athena. "So I bypassed them, hired an outside auditing firm." Athena looked grim.

"And?"

"The auditors discovered that the extra money was coming from the government, part of the federal budget that's not itemized. For many years, Defense and the intel agencies have used pots of money like that to fund projects they don't want known to the world at large, usually for good reason. Oddly enough, and probably not coincidentally, this kind of government tie-in is what the SoCalls have been accusing us of."

"Who…"

"Pulled that 'secret' money out and gave it to Stirner? We don't know. Very few members of Congress, even, would know. We asked our own Congressman to find out, and he came up blank. Athena, you should have been more attentive. You should have known about all this."

Athena looked down at her knees. "Yes," she said, "my control systems failed."

"Whatever you call it," said Tru, "it didn't work."

There was a long silence. Finally, Morgan looked up at the two women. "But what had Stirner been up to," he asked, "and when I mentioned the senator and the Korean, how did that…?

"The easy question first," Tru said. "MemCast, as we announced during the TV special, allows mems to be captured digitally. Like a memlab, actually, but a donor's mem goes into a computer, not into another person's head. Once in the computer, the mem can be edited, shaped creatively if we want to, and then sent out via cable, satellite, broadcast TV, the Internet, social web sites: millions of identical copies. It becomes, in essence, a movie or TV show. That's the technology we paid Stirner to invent and develop, and he did. And he developed a few more features for us that we haven't announced yet, nothing very startling. But now we're finding out what else he did, without telling me."

"Without your money," Athena remarked.

"Well hell yes, and that makes it even worse!" Tru exploded. "Right here in the TruPlex, out of my control. I'm responsible for a project I had no say over, because it was withheld from me! A secret government operation. God only knows why they couldn't do their research in Langley or Greenbelt or Belvoir or some other secure place!"

"I guess I'll have to tell you," said Athena.

"What? Do you know what's going on?"

"Ah, yes. It happened this way, Tru: A government official came to me about two years ago. TruVal was in the lead in the race to develop various kinds of advanced memplant technology, thanks to the investments you'd made. That was common knowledge. The government, they wanted to 'juice it up' as they put it; speed our research a little. Shorten time to market. Add a few capabilities."

"A little! And I can imagine the kind of capabilities a government would be interested in."

Morgan, who'd been feeling left out of the discussion, asked "Well, what capabilities did Stirner add, or what has he been trying to add?"

Tru looked at Athena, who took a deep breath, and said "Nothing very threatening: multi-way, non-destructive memplants. That's two new features: you can donate a mem to another person, and still keep it in your own head. And, you can donate your mem to multiple recipients, not just one."

"That's implicit in the 'non-destructive' feature," Tru said. "If you still have the mem, you can donate it over and over."

"Yes, but there's more. Stirner developed a technique for donating a mem to multiple recipients at the same time."

"And the U.S. government gave this capability to the North Koreans?"

"It seems they did. Possibly in exchange for their scrapping a some of their nuclear missiles, or pulling back a few kilometers from the South Korean border; a tit for tat of some kind. But I'm guessing here. A secret deal we'll all probably be told about twenty or thirty years from now."

"Well, OK," Morgan said, "developing that 'see / saw / saw / saw' feature might soak up a few million dollars, but it doesn't sound like it would have a big payoff for the government. Commercially, maybe, but the government wouldn't be interested in that. Certainly the North Koreans wouldn't care about commercial potential. And it doesn't sound like anything that should be kept top secret." He pointed a finger at Athena. "Then why was it? Kept so secret, that is. Secret enough that it had to be done outside a government lab, secret enough that you couldn't even tell the president of TruVal, Inc.?"

Athena spread her hands in a gesture of ignorant innocence. "That's the way they wanted it," she said. "They paid us – not me personally! – and swore me to silence."

"And corrupted Stirner? And killed Terra Lewis?"

Athena laughed. "Stirner had been corrupted long before this, I'm afraid. And, well, before you have to ask, I need to tell you that I fired him yesterday. He and all his off the books staff. The specialists left in our memlab now are continuing to commercialize the original MemCast concept: broadcasting mems digitally for entertainment. And as for Terra, I suppose that the North Koreans, paranoid as usual, had her killed so that someone, perhaps the Likable Leader himself, wouldn't find out that the new technology hadn't come from their own lab in Namp'o but had been invented by foreigners, mostly by the hated Americans. A matter of face."

She looked apologetically at Tru. "It's all over. Now you can fire me if you want to."

Tru put on a very serious expression. "No, Athena, you can stay. You run the business side of TruVal very capably. Or did, until this mis-step. Just swear that there'll be no more secrets from me."

"No more secrets," said Athena.

"All right," said Tru. "I guess Terra's killer will never be brought to justice, but at least this Charles Barnes or whoever it is doesn't seem to be a threat any more. And the rest of it is out of our hands. Get back to work."

Athena left, but Morgan hung back.

"Ah..." He didn't know whether to dare call her 'Tru' or not right then. "I have a problem."

"Your office?"

"No, the office is OK. It's – money."

"What about money?"

"I'm broke. I need a job. I know we're through here, most of the angles resolved. But I'm not at the university anymore, and the memlab isn't back in operation yet, and the retirement I cashed in is gone, and..."

Tru laughed. "Is that all, Robert? Certainly we can find money for you. I'll create a position here, Special Assistant to the President. Is that OK? I'll put you on the payroll for a year at a very nice salary, and you won't even have to show up! Relax. You've earned it. Spend a month or two on the Big Island; the South Kona Coast is wonderful. I'll have a check cut for you today, for the first three months."

Morgan, flushed and stuttering with gratitude, thanked her and backed out the door of her office doing little bows. He retreated to the Sour Suite and asked Antonio for a Glenlivet, neat. He stared at the glass for a long time, took one sip. And then another. And then he put it down and walked out of the suite, keeping an eye out for Alps. Renee was, thankfully, nowhere to be seen.

Chapter 50

Somewhere in the TruPlex, a woman picked up a landline telephone, one of the few still in operation. She dialed clumsily, the motion awkward and unpracticed. Three buzzes, then a cautious "Yes?"

"It's all been smoothed over now and no one suspects a thing. Vallon has been fed enough of the answer to keep her happy, but not the important stuff. And don't worry about Stirner; his work is done. You can get rid of him. In fact, you should do that right away. And tell that clumsy Korean he needs to clear everything with us before he gets any more stupid ideas. I know we need his lab for proof of concept, but he's a risk. Who's his second in command? Any good?"

There was an answer, and a brief discussion. Then she hung up. Thank God for the shielded landline. Golly, she just wouldn't dare say this stuff over a com!

***

Morgan was home, relaxing and contemplating his good fortune. He was now well off, could almost pretend to be rich. For the next year, anyway. After that – don't think about it. What a luxurious feeling! He swore he'd never eat peanut butter or waffles again, never hanker hungrily for horse. Happily, he went to bed and contemplated his new title. Special Assistant to the President! Although "special" no longer had the clout it used to have. Morgan remembered that, in his youth, special meant especially good, outstanding. Buick even made a car called the Special. But then the corruptors came, and "special" came, ever so gradually, to mean inferior. No manufacturer would name a car the Special these days. Was Tru conscious of that when she picked out his title? Oh well, good wages for a year. Should he invest some of it in his memlab? Spruce it up?

He'd have to hire a new clinical advisor. And a new assistant. Maybe Heidi would like to – and then he was, at last, asleep.

The next morning, Morgan again contemplated his life as consultant to the stars and budding memlab mogul. But something was bothering him. Too many loose ends were hanging out. And most of them seemed to be hanging out in Athena's office.

One, he itemized to himself: What was Senator Gooding up to? Selling MemCast to the Koreans. Part of a government deal, or private greed? The result could be equally disastrous.

Two: What was on that memchip? Presumably, the enhanced MemCast technology that Stirner had developed, or "MemCast Plus" as it was called now. Too bad. America will have lost the lead in one more high-tech industry.

How could One and Two have added up to murder?

And who had known about all these events? Who had been in charge of TruVal security and all the other activities? Who had been able to ensure that Barnes could get into the TruPlex at night, as heavily guarded as it was. Even with stolen ID, that wasn't supposed to be possible. Who had hidden the cafeteria key where Barnes could find it, if the story Dennis had pried out of Barnes was really true? Who else but Athena Taylor? Athena would have had no trouble neutralizing or bypassing the security system, getting Barnes into the building, letting him into the cafeteria.

But then why did Athena and Jimmy take such laborious pains to hide the body in the first place? So it wouldn't be found. And...

I need Dennis, he thought, to help me sort this out. He com'd the houseboat. No answer. He com'd the Sausalito Police Department. When he asked for Dennis DeLuca, he was put permanently, it seemed, on hold. He com'd the houseboat again, left a message. And then another one.

Finally in mid-afternoon, Morgan received a brief text: "Dr. Morgan: Please refer all further inquiries to the Chief, SPD, regarding this matter. /signed/ D. DeLuca."

Dennis must have been told off or scared off. Judging by the prose style, his messages were being monitored, too. The Sausalito police department, never very happy with him, had caved. That must have been it. Now a second PD, after San Francisco's, had been bullied, probably also by the Feds. Why? Well, to keep Terra's death a mystery. Why? So a meeting between a U.S. senator and a North Korean scientist would remain secret? Why? To give MemCast Plus technology to the North Koreans? But they could have asked TruVal, and with export control approval could simply be licensed, or could have obtained it via some friendly intermediary. No, it must have been because Gooding and Jeong were up to something highly unauthorized, something the Congressional leadership didn't know about, something the West Wing itself didn't know about. If the senator had been on official business, no matter how secret, murder wouldn't have been the solution.

Morgan wrote a brief note, stuffed it in his pocket. He entered the TruPlex as casually as possible. As he badged himself in, he knew that Athena would, if she wanted to, know that he had entered the building. As he walked across the lobby and into the elevator, he knew that three separate CCTV lenses had caught his image. Athena could know exactly where Morgan was at all times in the building, know who he was speaking with, knew what they were saying, thanks to the sound-sensors in each camera. Perhaps TruVal Security was executing programs, even now, that would recognize, and report instantly, the use of certain words by anyone in the building: "conspiracy," "Gooding," "Singapore," and "Korea" would be good places to start.

Morgan elevated to the twenty-sixth floor. There was Renee, already geared up for another exciting, action-packed, joyous day. She bubbled over at him. "Great to see you again this soon, Doctor! Congratulations on your new position with the company! We'll just have to find you a place to sit right here on Rug Row!" and on and on.

"Do you suppose," he said, "nothing urgent, of course, but do you suppose that Tru might be available for a few minutes this afternoon? No, nothing special. Mostly wanted to thank her for..."

After a burst of "no problem"s, Renee put Morgan on Truda Vallon's calendar for three-thirty p.m. Morgan retreated to the Sour Suite to wait. The Alps were in full view. Small but interesting earthquakes seemed to be shaking the mountains, frequently in his direction.

At exactly three twenty-two p.m. Morgan walked out of the Sour Suite, crossed the floor to Tru's inner office, went inside and closed the door behind him. Tru looked up from her desk, glanced at a wall clock.

Chapter 51

It wasn't like the doctor to be early, she thought, or just walk in, even though he was due in seven, no, eight minutes. Why did he have his finger to his lips? Well, all right, I'll play along. He's pulling a crumpled slip of paper out of his shirt pocket, handing it to me. What's this about? So here's the note. What's he saying? "Don't trust Athena. Meet me in Union Square in one hour. Don't tell anyone."

The note had not been signed. Well, OK, I'll go along with this. Did the doctor have a romantic tryst in mind, or more skullduggery? A tryst could be interesting. Had he booked a room at the St. Francis? Fusty, but romantic in a missionary-position sort of way.

Morgan left Tru's office. At three twenty-nine p.m. and fifty seconds, Truda Vallon stuffed the wrinkled note into a pocket.

Exactly ten seconds later, a monitor on a lower floor turned itself on. Athena looked intently at the CCTV image, turned up the volume.

"Well," she said to herself, "the doctor's right on time."

***

Morgan entered Tru's office. "Hi, Robert, good to see you again!" she said. "What can I do for you?"

"I wanted to thank you again for my new position at TruVal. And I've decided to hire staff and re-open the O'Farrell Street memlab. I considered selling the franchise, but that sale probably wouldn't fetch any more than enough to pay off its debts."

"Well, Robert, that's real progress. I don't think Ed Clarty will be needing his memlab back for a while." She laughed. "And I can't see you swabbing gel on people's heads and sticking probes on them for a living."

"All right, then. I'll be off."

"Where to?"

"Sausalito, to see Detective DeLuca. He's been sidelined by his superiors in the PD, but he was able to get me a message this morning that he'd got new information on the case – all very hush hush – about secret federal government involvement."

That ought to set off the alarm bells, get them pointed the wrong direction. Of course he'd be nowhere near Sausalito that day.

***

Exactly at four thirty, Morgan and Truda Vallon met beside the monument in Union Square. Morgan motioned Tru over to an umbrella-topped table. "For satcams, in case..."

"Anyone's watching us from a thousand miles up? Robert, next you'll be telling me that there are sensors in the ground under the monument here, listening to us from below!"

"Ah, physically speaking that would be very difficult, Tru."

"Well, I guess you still have a little sanity left," she smiled. "Now tell me: Why do you think Athena is up to more than she's already confessed to? That was bad enough!"

"DeLuca and I believe that Senator Gooding passed a memchip along to a top North Korean scientist. I believe that chip contained technology developed here in the TruPlex that you weren't told about. If it were only the MemCast Plus capabilities, it wouldn't take a U.S. senator to deliver it to a foreign power. And it wouldn't have been cause for a murder that was, when you think about it, very risky to arrange and execute. Gooding gave something to the North Koreans he shouldn't have, and Athena knows what it is."

"Robert," Tru said, "I agree that Gooding seems to be working on a secret and possibly illegal plan, but it could be an advanced nuclear capability, or a computer program to help the Koreans watch their citizens, or one of many, many different things having nothing to do with me, or with us, with MemCast, or with Athena."

"There's one way to know for sure. We need to set up a meeting between Athena and Senator Gooding, and listen in.

Make him believe that Athena has important news that she has to tell him in person."

"News about what? The senator will want a hint, at least."

"About," Morgan thought hard. "About Jeong, the North Korean scientist. We figure that Gooding knows or suspects that Jeong's a loose cannon. Tell Gooding, as 'Athena,' that she's sniffed out even more, and more reckless, things Jeong is up to."

"Like what?" Tru asked.

"We'll say we'll tell him at the meeting."

"Are you saying that if the two of them take the bait to meet, then we'll know, not only that they know each other, but that they're involved in this Korean scheme."

"If it is a Korean scheme."

"What else...?"

"North Korea could be only part of it, Tru. We don't know."

"Then what, Robert? If Athena and Gooding are plotting, what does this do beyond confirming our suspicions? We already know that the Feds have shut down investigations in San Francisco and Sausalito. What could we do to derail this plot, whatever it is! My company is big, but not that big."

"Publicity. Tell all."

"Who would believe us? We'd need proof."

"We'll have to get them together on some pretext, confront them and record what they say. Get them to confess."

"How could we arrange that? How could we get Athena to fly all the way to D.C. for a few minutes' talk? That's not realistic. She'd be suspicious. Why would she do it?"

"Could you send her to Washington on some TruVal, Inc. errand?"

"Well," Tru thought for a minute. "She's the business side of TruVal. I could task her to meet with House staffers related to regulatory policy, something about MemCast licensing, how we pledged to let all comers license it and how we're planning to implement that policy."

"A plea for them to let business alone."

"Yes. They hear that all the time. And," Tru brightened, "we should do that in any case!"

"So if she's going to Washington, and if she's part of a dark plot with Gooding, she's sure to meet with him while she's there."

"And therefore we don't have to fake a message to Gooding that Athena needs to speak with him," Tru said. "She'll do it on her own initiative if they're really involved in a secret scheme."

"And how do we intercept communications between Athena and..."

"Gooding? Since I'm the CEO, my desktop has access to every system at TruVal, but I've never used that capability, wouldn't know where to start."

Morgan resisted the temptation to say "Just like a woman!" "I can help you do that, I think. Shouldn't be too difficult. User interfaces are pretty friendly these days. But..."

"One of Athena's security systems may be watching? How about a cover story: you're in my office for an appointment, and I mention that something's not working in Windows 10, ask you to give me a hand. You sit down at my desk and get into the security system, put a trace on Athena's outgoing, all media."

"Wouldn't she..."

"Find out we're spying on her? Not if we put the trace on right after I order her to go to D.C. If she's going to call Gooding, I think she'll do it right away. If we're lucky – and if I'm right about her – we'll pick up the call. As soon as they hang up, we'll disconnect the trace."

"Well," Morgan sounded dubious.

"I can't think of a better way," said Tru. "I know she may not be able to reach him right away, but what else can we do?

"OK, Tru, let's do it. I'll drop by your office at – how about ten o'clock tomorrow. And if we need to meet again at the TruPlex to discuss anything sensitive, it has to be in a toilet stall."

"What?"

"They're the only places in the building not covered by CCTVs and microphones. Madelyn told me so."

"Men's, or women's?" she smiled.

"Don't you have a unisex restroom in the building, for families with small children for instance? Malls do, and most large buildings."

"Now that you mention it, Robert, I've seen one or two of those. One's on fourteen near the cafeteria, I think."

"Yes, that's a logical place."

Chapter 52

The next day, Tru happened to mention to Morgan that Athena would be visiting D.C. briefly. "I made a call to the appropriate House committee. The staffers will be glad to speak with her, low key off the record and all that."

"Oh, that's interesting," said Morgan, trying to appear uninterested, "when?"

"Next Thursday, a week from today. I'm about to mention it to Athena. Oh, and by the way, Robert, I'm having a little trouble here on my computer, and I hate to call tech support for every little problem; they'll think I'm really stupid."

"I'm sure tech support has as much respect for you as they do for any other user."

"That's what I'm afraid of."

"But as long as I'm here in your office," said Morgan, "I'll be glad to help. Save you a little time, I guess, and save you from having to deal with the gear heads. What seems to be the problem?"

"Windows 10. The sleep function doesn't seem to work. The system keeps waking up."

"I can assist you with that," said Morgan. "Could I sit at your desk here?"

"Certainly," said Tru. "I have a call to make right now, so take your time."

Tru stood and crossed to the far side of her desk as Morgan sat down. She com'd Athena as Morgan pulled up the TruVal Security main screen, logged on as Tru with top-level security privileges, searched for something that might be a transmissions monitor, found it, set up a trace on Athena's com. He saw Tru's call coming in, saw Athena picking it up.

"Yes?" Athena said. Tru briefly explained that she'd booked Athena for a meeting on the Hill for the following Thursday.

"That's fine!" said Athena, "I'll be glad to speak with them about our licensing plans. Put their minds at rest about it, and perhaps pre-empt their usual awkward inquiry."

"Right," said Tru. "Good luck."

Morgan saw the call disconnect, and then wait, and wait. Seconds, minutes. Morgan was getting nervous. The longer he had a trace on Athena, the greater chance it might occur to her to see if she were being traced. But finally – and Morgan saw that it had been only four minutes – she placed a com call to area 202, was transferred to voicemail.

"Senator Gooding," Athena said to the patient computer, "This is Athena Taylor. I'll be meeting with a bunch of House staffers next Thursday. I'll be arriving in Washington the day before that, about noon. Do you or your staff have a few minutes for me late Wednesday, maybe? I should fill you in about the broadcast regulation implications of our recent MemCast announcement. Since I'm briefing the House side on this, I'd like to give your Senate subcommittee a heads-up, too."

Morgan disconnected the outbound trace. "Pardon me, Tru," he said, but your machine is working now, so I'll be running along."

"I'll walk you out," Tru said. "I'm going to the cafeteria, myself."

"Renee would..."

"Pick up something for me, I know. But I've got her on a crash project at the moment."

The two left Tru's office. Morgan rang for the express elevator to the lobby, Tru got on the local, pressed fourteen. Morgan exited the express elevator at the lobby level, immediately walked to a local and elevated to fourteen. Casually, he slipped into the family restroom, saw a black-booted toe peeking out from one of the booths. The booth door was unlatched.

Morgan entered the toilet stall, found himself in very close quarters with Truda Vallon. He'd imagined this kind of closeness many times, but never thought it would occur in a restroom booth, snuggled up beside the toilet. He waved his hand at the flush sensor for white noise.

"Very good cover in Athena's message," said Morgan.

"No one would question it," said Tru. "And now we've confirmed that Athena has a connection with Senator Gooding."

"Our outbound trace would have been detected easily," Morgan said, "if it had occurred to her to look, but she was busy on her own call. I left the inbound trace on, and the recording function. Inbound will be safer than outbound, because the senator's response could come from almost anywhere, in any medium. And we don't have to pick it up live, just record it. Whenever Gooding gets back to Athena, we'll catch it. I set up a folder called spam-2 on your desktop. Keep an eye on it."

"If they make a date to meet," said Tru, "we'll need to be on a flight, but not the same one Athena's taking."

"And not from the same airport or to the same airport, to be extra safe."

"Right. She'll be going non-stop, SFO to Dulles I'm sure. I'll get a reservation from, oh, Oakland to National."

"Can you use a pseudonym?"

"Yes. I can get special VIP treatment from the airlines and TSA as long as they know who I really am, but I wouldn't be able to swing that for you."

"OK. Well, either I need an excuse to be in D.C. at the same time as Athena, or I need to hope that no one from her side is tracking my movements."

"You could fly to Chicago or New York, then fly to D.C. on a different airline with a separate reservation. I think that's about all we can do. And hope that no one is seriously watching."

Morgan flushed the toilet again. "OK," he said. "You fly non-stop, then, and I'll catch up with you at the hotel. Do we know where Athena is staying?"

"Not yet. But when that info comes through the TruVal travel reservation system I'll get us a room nearby."

The words "us" and "a room" jolted Morgan's libido. "A room"? Not "two rooms"? Well, a room could mean two in the same hotel. Perhaps adjoining. Perhaps the door between them could accidentally be unlocked with a word and a folded bill or two at the front desk. For the first time that day, Morgan forgot about the Alps.

"We need to regroup as soon as the senator's response comes in," said Tru.

"Right here," said Morgan, pointing at the toilet by accident, which immediately flushed. "How about tomorrow morning, nine o'clock? If he's going to get back to her, he should have done it by then."

"OK."

Chapter 53

At nine the next morning, Morgan was waiting for Tru on the fourteenth floor, restroom C, toilet stall number three. He waited several minutes. Probably she couldn't break away without suspicion. Busy executive. Busy woman. At twenty-one minutes after nine, Tru slipped into his booth and pulled the latch closed. Morgan flushed the toilet.

"Got it!" said Tru. "He bit. The senator wants to meet with Athena at seven o'clock Wednesday evening."

"We're in business!"

"Almost," said Tru. "The good news is that they're not meeting in the senator's office in the Dirksen building. I thought that option was unlikely, anyway. Too many of the wrong kind of people would be observing. And they're apparently not meeting anywhere else in that building. I could have got us in there, but not easily, and not untraceably."

"Then where?"

"That's the bad news. Gooding's note just said "The usual restaurant. Dinner.""

"Didn't say to ask for Mr. Smith, or anything like that?"

"His face is too well known in Washington for him to pretend to be anyone else. But he probably made the reservation under an assumed name. At the restaurant they'll know who he is, give him privacy and top-class treatment."

"Where is this usual restaurant? How can we find out?

"We'll have to follow him."

"Or follow Athena."

"But we're not experts in tailing, and as you've heard I haven't been very expert at any kind of sleuthing lately!" Morgan said. "We've got one chance at this."

"Do you know who we need?" said Tru. "We need Dennis DeLuca right now."

"He was pretty incommunicative the last time I tried him."

"Try him again, Robert. Offer him a nice consulting fee from TruVal, Inc., and a free first-class ride to Washington. I own a few small special-purpose companies. They're production firms, graphics designers, that sort of thing, a legal convenience for my TV show. One of them will be happy to pay for DeLuca's ticket without anyone's being able to detect that it was TruVal, Inc., that's actually sending him. Not for two or three days, anyway."

That afternoon, Morgan sent an email to Dennis DeLuca: "Hi, Den. Got an extra air ticket from San Jose to D.C. (attached) and a swanky hotel and pocket money too, courtesy of a company my wife's cousin owns, it's that snooty rich cousin Sylvester. Well, I sure hope you can make it, since I've heard you're at loose ends these days! We'll have fun chewing over old times, take in a titty bar or two, hang out with the whores on Thomas Circle, get over our grief about Mom! (signed) Your Loving Brother Arty."

The next morning, the response came back: "Arty. OK, you bastard, you're on. Heard D.C. was a hot town, lots of nooky. I could use a break and some ass, too, out of uniform, of course. See you at SJC!"

***

At a quarter past five Wednesday morning, Morgan met up with DeLuca at the San Jose airport. "Where's your 'tru' love?" DeLuca asked.

"She's flying another route, direct," Morgan said. "We get the milk run: here to O'Hare, heli to Midway, fly to National. Sorry about that."

"In case someone's on the lookout?"

"Right."

"That won't fool them."

"There's something to be said for complexity," Morgan answered. "I hope any interested parties won't figure out where we're really going for about the next eighteen hours. After that, we don't care."

"That means we can fly home non-stop?"

"Sure."

"Good! I can catch up on my sleep then!"

"In the meanwhile, you can catch me up on what's happening in Sausalito."

DeLuca rolled his eyes, cleared his throat, and settled back into his tale of woe.

***

At five p.m., the three met in Tru's room at the Washington Court Hotel on Capitol Hill. "I picked this place," she said, "because it's a block from where our travel system says Athena is staying, the Liaison."

"Do you think she'll go to her hotel before her dinner meeting with the senator?"

"At least to check in and change, I would think. That's a long flight. And her plane got into Dulles at two o'clock: plenty of time to get into the District and get settled." She looked back and forth between Morgan and DeLuca. "Do we have a car?"

"Yeah," said DeLuca. "I com'd Hertz from the plane. It's parked in back of the Liaison now, probably gathering a new parking ticket every half hour."

"Or being towed?"

"Hope not. I couldn't risk letting the attendant put it in the garage. It would take too long to get it out on the street. I left a few pieces of cop paraphernalia in plain view on the seat, hope the locals might cut me a break – professional courtesy."

"Is the car a dark color?" asked Morgan, half seriously.

"Of course it's dark, Robert super-sleuth. Only by coincidence, though, since I didn't dare tell Hertz I needed to drive something dark."

"Immediate com to Homeland?"

"Something like that, these days."

Tru had been showing signs of impatience. "Let's get organized here. First, who's doing what to cover all our bases? Dennis, you're the detective."

"Yes, ma'am," said DeLuca without a hint of irony. Morgan could tell that he was impressed by Tru's determination.

"First," DeLuca said, "I've seen Ms. Taylor only once. Do you have a photo of her?" Embarrassed, Tru said that she didn't. She pulled out her com, got into the TruVal.TV web site, clicked on "Executive Officers," selected Athena's picture, synched it to DeLuca's com.

"Pretty good likeness, actually," said Tru. "And she's tall. Six feet one or two."

"Yeah, I remember the height factor."

"And a great body," added Morgan, a little too enthusiastically for Tru's taste. She scowled at him. Was that a hint of jealousy, Morgan wondered, or the standard female knee-jerk?

"Second," he said, "there's a restaurant at the Liaison."

"That's called the Art and Soul."

"I checked it out. I don't think it would be suitable for a quiet, intimate meeting. I believe they'll go to a different place. But they could be. That means we'll need one of us to keep an eye on the restaurant: street entrance and entrance from the hotel, both."

"Are we going to tail Gooding?" asked Morgan.

"I don't see how we can," said DeLuca, "He could be leaving his office in the Dirksen building from any one of several exits, or drive out of the garage, or be driven. Or he could have been in a different office building today, or the Capitol, on business. It's not easy to see who's coming out of a garage at this time of day, and you can believe there will be Capitol cops who'd take a dim view of idlers."

"Even a fellow cop?

"Especially a fellow cop. They'd have even more questions."

"We'll have to follow Athena, then."

"Right," said DeLuca. "It's five thirty now. We need to start watching for them pretty soon in case they're headed out into the countryside. So here's where we'll be stationed: Ms. Vallon, you stand across the street from the hotel restaurant's street-level entrance. If you see Gooding or Taylor, com me immediately. And try not to look like a street-walker, please. If the police hassle you, move away and let me know.

"And what about you?" Tru asked.

"I'll be inside the Liaison, in the lobby or near the desk. It will look like I'm waiting for someone, which of course I am. I'll com you as soon as I see Taylor. Hopefully, there won't be a convention of women basketball players in the hotel, and I'll be able to pick her out. If the senator comes by to get her, or if she gets into a cab, I'll jump in my car and tail them.

"Robert, you'll be outside the hotel. Don't let Taylor see you! If I com you, that means I've seen her. You get a cab ASAP and wait for her to exit the hotel, with the senator or without, and follow whatever she gets into. I'll be doing the same in my car. We won't be able to play car-tag. If the streets get too deserted, one of us will have to drop out of the chase. That will probably be you. I'll let you know if and when I need you to do that.

"Of course, if she walks down the street, our job will be easier. There are several restaurants here on New Jersey Avenue, or within a block or two. Whatever, we'll all rendezvous outside the restaurant when we know which one it is."

"Then what?"

"Then we'll go inside." DeLuca said, "and have a nice dinner!"

"No, seriously."

"Hey, I'm just here to tail a suspect. You," he nodded at Tru and Morgan, "are the ones with the plan. That is, I hope you've got a plan for what we do when we find Taylor and Gooding together!"

Uncertainly, and with a glance at Tru, Morgan said "We'll confront them. We want them to know we know."

"Oh, and then what?" DeLuca countered, "Why shouldn't a vice president of TruVal, Inc. be meeting with a member of the Senate about the economics of your very prominent and influential business? After all, you sent her here to meet with House staffers, why shouldn't she see a senator, too? Sounds like initiative to me!"

"OK," Tru said, "we've got nothing real on Athena. But we have plenty on Gooding: his secret meeting with a North Korean scientist."

"That could be explained."

"Yes," Tru acknowledged, "barely. But meanwhile the newsblogs would eat him up. You know what the American public thinks about North Korea: we're superior to those heathen pajama-wearing slants, but we're scared shitless of their nukes. Not a great combination of attitudes. Not highly conducive to world peace."

"That's our lever, the Korean Connection," Morgan said.

"It's not much," she said, "but it will have to do."

Morgan frowned. "It's that very connection that cost Terra Lewis her life, don't forget. I think we'll be able to get the senator's attention."

At six o'clock, the three left the hotel and took up their positions.

Six fifteen.

Six thirty.

Six forty five.

Chapter 54

DeLuca's normal confidence was developing stress-marks. He thought he might call up to Taylor's room on some pretense and see if she was still there. Yes, he should do that. Morgan and that walking corpse were depending on him. How did he get his ass into this particular sling, anyway? Because he liked Morgan, and didn't want to see him floundering, trying to play cop. Well, here he was, Dennis DeLuca, cop, floundering himself.

DeLuca strolled up to the desk, picked up a house phone, asked to be connected to Ms. Taylor's room, please. Just as he heard the first ring, the elevator door opened and there she was, and she was alone: Athena Taylor, all six feet one or two of her. He suddenly recalled how gorgeous she was.

He turned his face away out of habit. She'd seen him once, might or might not remember him. With his right hand still holding the receiver to his ear, he used his left to pull his com awkwardly from his pocket, signaled Morgan to grab a cab. Then he walked as fast as he could without breaking into a run, went out the door ahead of Taylor, nodded at the doorman, ducked around the corner, and got into his rental.

Morgan stepped into one of several waiting cabs – cabbies always knew where wealth gathered – as Athena was exiting the hotel. The doorman waved a cab over, she got in. Morgan was almost embarrassed to utter such a cliché, but he did: "Follow that cab!"

***

The cabbie said nothing. He'd heard it all before, all those Americans hung up on their love lives or their sex lives, and they never seemed to know the difference between the two. They had so much of everything they wouldn't know how – if the electricity stopped endlessly pouring out of a wire, if their shit didn't endlessly disappear into an underworld tomb – wouldn't know how to survive, would wander the streets helplessly looking for their mommies. Yes, his fare this time was another typical American, no beard and not much hair, middle-aged, following a sex goddess who'd probably led him on and then turned him down. Well, from her looks getting into Tamij's cab she was worth the effort, not following her, no, that is the pathetic American way, "chicken" as they say here, but not a man's way of taking, and claiming, and having, and carrying away. That's a real man's way, the way we do it in the Toba Kakar, how my father found my mother, how I was....

"Yes, sir, I am keeping up but not getting too close, as you asked. Do not worry." Now, I am going to panic this stupid American with no hair a little bit, he thought.

"Sir, please know, that as we follow my friend Tamij's cab, that we ourselves are being followed by a dark gray Nissan Altima. Do you think this may perhaps be the tall woman's husband and that he is perhaps angry?" The American doesn't seem to care about that. In fact, he smiles. What, blessed be God, is going on here?

The cabbie got on his radio and said a few words in a language Morgan thought might be Arabic but it didn't sound quite right. The cabbie signed off and turned back to him.

"Do not worry. I have spoken in broken Arabic to Tamij in the cab ahead – trusting that the tall woman does not understand a word of it – broken Arabic because I am not Arab myself, you know, and Tamij is not, either, and his language is not mine and mine is not his, but between the two of us we know a few words of Arabic and so that is how we speak with each other in the presence of Americans. It happens that the tall woman with the long beautiful legs that you very fervently desire is being driven to Seventh and Pennsylvania: the 701 Restaurant, in fact. Many best-dressed Americans go there in my taxicab and they always tip very generously. Sir? Are you listening to this extra service I am providing for you?"

Morgan didn't immediately answer. He was on his com to DeLuca, telling him Athena's destination.

"OK, said DeLuca, "drop off. I'll keep following in case she changes her mind, and I'll com Vallon to meet us there. See you shortly."

"Fine." Morgan clicked off, asked the cabbie to pull over and wait a few minutes, then continue on to the 701.

The cabbie smiled, made sure that Morgan was preoccupied at the moment. He pushed the secret button under the dash that added ten dollars to the fare. This one will pay, he thought. And when we pull up to the 701 I'll "goose" it as my friends the American cabbies say, I'll just goose that button one more time.

DeLuca was waiting for Morgan in front of the restaurant. A few minutes later, Tru arrived in a second cab.

"The menu is interesting," he said to her. "I told the maitre d' that two friends would be joining me and I'd be waiting for them outside. We have a table reserved in the name of Dennis Artzebasheff."

"Who's that." Morgan asked.

"That's me," smiled DeLuca. "I think it would be neat to have a brother named Arty Artzebasheff!"

They entered and were seated. The maitre d' raised one eyebrow at Tru's appearance. She ignored him. Tourists, he thought. I'll bet they even have one of those damned coupons. That's the problem with advertising. I'll have to be more forceful with the eyebrow next time.

DeLuca ordered a Manhattan, no bitters, easy on the vermouth please. Tru and Morgan said "water."

***

Armando the sommelier shamed them into ordering an expensive brand of bottled water without even needing to raise an eyebrow. Armando was highly pleased with himself. A great talent. He knew his water upstream and downstream and knew how to work a room. He was much more talented, much more subtle than the maitre d', that fusty old man whose eyebrows flapped like birds on a windy day.

Tru glanced around the room as unobtrusively as she could. A worried expression crossed her face. "I don't see them," she said.

"There's a small private dining room, behind you and to your left," said DeLuca. "The Curtain Room. I noticed it and asked about it when I made our reservations a few minutes ago, in the guise of setting up a business luncheon next week."

"Are we going to go in there?" Morgan asked. Tru's worried expression had migrated to his own face.

DeLuca still seemed untroubled. "As soon as I've had some of that Manhattan!" he replied.

Fifteen minutes later, Morgan, Tru, and DeLuca had separately, and casually, risen from their chairs and headed toward the restrooms. They diverted at the last second and converged on the small private dining area in back. Senator Gooding and Athena Taylor had their heads together in intense conversation. The senator had just taken a forkful from a plate of crabcakes and baby lettuces.

Athena saw them first. She gaped and stood, then resumed her composure. A flicker of worry crossed the senator's face, but he said nothing and kept his seat.

"Tru!" said Athena, "What...?"

"Am I doing here? I wondered the same thing about you. Sit down, please."

"I'm having a private dinner with a member of the U.S. Senate," she said. "I'm representing TruVal, Inc., here. I'm saving your business!"

"Not North Korea's business? Sit down. We need to speak briefly, and then we'll leave you alone."

Athena sat down slowly. Morgan and DeLuca pulled up chairs and also sat.

"Senator..." Athena began, but the senator raised his hand.

"Ms. Vallon," he said, "we weren't expecting you, but I knew that sooner or later we'd need to talk. I'm going to spell out for you what's about to happen. This is for two reasons: First, because you can't do anything about it, and second, if you're willing to cooperate, or at least go quietly, things might go well for you, or at least better than the alternative I have in mind. And well for our country too, of course."

Morgan had expected a scene, perhaps the police, at least being tossed out of this hoity restaurant and told never to come back – but not the cold, confident assurance, the senator clearly in charge.

Athena's face was a mix of feelings: Relief at avoiding a scene, at least for now; pleasure that the senator had quickly taken charge; concern that he seemed about to divulge their secret.

DeLuca was quietly enjoying the scene. He'd set this event up, choreographed it, made it happen. Detective Lieutenant and Master Plotter Dennis DeLuca! Now the senator was the lead actor. DeLuca could sit back and enjoy the ballet, the movements and attitudes, the music of confrontation.

Truda Vallon was alarmed. She'd expected vehement denials, threats of calling the police, demands that the maitre d' throw out these troublemakers. She hadn't expected what she was hearing now.

Chapter 55

The senator looked around the group. "Ms. Taylor, here, tells me she revealed a few of the secret capabilities of MemCast that Stirner and his team developed for you. Developed for us, rather, using an infusion of funds laundered from various places in the Federal budget. But she didn't tell you everything."

"How could you steer all that money to TruVal without the administration's knowing about it?" Morgan asked.

Gooding smiled. "You've answered your own question – Dr. Morgan, is it? Of course a few key players in the administration knew about it, approved, deflected questions. A small group of key people, of which I am honored to be a part, founded a very obscure agency known as the Intergovernmental Memorial Commission to receive and disburse funds to places where these funds would have a desired effect. Justice was asked to 'persuade' the San Francisco and Sausalito police departments to shut down their investigations into the death of Ms. Lewis, in the interest of national security. The intel agencies were very happy to cooperate when we – Ms. Taylor, Stirner, and I briefed them on the great benefits that would accrue. Benefits, I must stress, to none of us personally, but to the United States of America.

"Those new capabilities of MemCast that you knew about, Ms. Vallon, were really diversions. Features we could dangle in front of you while we went about our more serious work. Features you could tell the world about, to keep it content and amused."

"Bread and circuses," Morgan interjected, "like Rome."

"Yes, doctor. But there is a limit to the effectiveness of bread and circuses. Recall that the Roman Empire was subjected, time and again, to revolts, coups d'état, schisms, defections, massacres of minorities by crazed mobs."

"Well then, what does MemCast do that you haven't told us?"

The senator nodded to Athena. "I'll let Ms. Taylor explain that. She's been in closer touch with Stirner and his research team than I have." Athena swallowed, looked at Tru almost apologetically.

"Lost dogs," she said after a moment. Morgan, Tru, and DeLuca stared at her blankly. "ID chip implants to identify lost dogs. And then chips to locate them: GPS simulated with cell tower networks. And then chips embedded under our own skins, containing our entire medical history. I'll bet each of us has one of those."

"I don't," said DeLuca.

"No matter," said Athena, "enough Americans do to form a network. And the situation is similar in every other developed country and a few of the less developed ones as well. Those microchips aren't just passive data drives anymore. All current models contain microprocessors and transceivers, intended quite innocently so that physicians can help you when you need help. They're programmed to send out a signal that a medical emergency has occurred, and what kind of emergency it is, and receive data in return.

"Now liberals – I don't want to say so-called liberals! – have objected for years to these medinfo chips as a violation of privacy. But we, our government, I mean, isn't really interested in citizens' health data, except statistically. But another group, that is, a handful of far-sighted and influential officials in various agencies where the senator here is well known, well, those people saw a further use for these chips, a higher calling." She paused.

The senator spoke up. "To cut this short, and pardon me, Ms. Taylor, Stirner has met our requirement to invent a way to broadcast memories, not via television or digital datastreams as Ms. Vallon, here, announced on her TV special, but directly into minds, through the existing microchip-under-the-skin medinfo network. Occasional proximity to someone with an underskin chip is enough, if you don't have your own. If the same memory is broadcast for a long enough time, eventually the entire population will have it, believe it was their own experience. Remember," he said, and smiled at his unintentional joke, "that they will not recall going to a memlab and receiving a memplant. Thanks to Karl-Heinz Stirner, we will now be able to package donor memories and broadcast them into recipients' minds, millions of people.

"It's an oddity of our species that we may not always trust our wits, our reasoning power, or even our own opinions. But we do trust our most vivid memories, and if there are any inconsistencies between these memories and what we otherwise know, well, memories win every time. Remember the child-abuse scares of the past century? The classic East Wenatchee case?"

"And you see," Athena interjected fervently, "all this new technology still requires a willing mem donor. It's not stealing your thoughts. It's not mind-reading or 'mem-snatching.'"

"So," Morgan was confused. "So I, for instance, would remember doing something I hadn't done, or remember believing something I've never believed. That's just an improvement on the kind of memplants that are routine at memlabs like my own. Where are you going with this? What's the point, other than not having to undress and get grease all over your head?"

"The point, Doctor, will become clear when you understand why we gave this technology to the North Koreans."

"And why is that? They're our enemies, aren't they? The newsbloggers won't be happy when..."

Senator Gooding raised a hand. "The newsbloggers would be delighted if they were ever let in on the secret, and here's why: North Korea is unstable, as we all know. People are starving. Unrest is rising, not least among their military. The whole country is restless. In a nuclear-armed country, at that, with a long history of hating and fearing the outside world. They've made threats to attack America, for no possible benefit except to keep their own citizens in line! The deal I made will help the Likable Leader calm his people. We – our associate Dr. Jeong in North Korea, I mean – told him that he could give every North Korean memories of how much the regime has done for them. They will remember how much they love him. They will remember that food might arrive any day. In exchange, the North has agreed to stop its threats against the South, against Japan – and its threats against the United States."

"And scrap their nukes?"

"There's no way they would be willing to do that. But with domestic tranquility, the need to prove their military might to their citizens will be greatly diminished. Jeong Ja-yu, you see, is a man of peace, as am I. Jeong's laboratory in Namp'o has now implemented this new technology, the systems on that memchip I gave him through an intermediary in Singapore. Jeong has started calling it People's Mem, a name selected by the Likable Leader himself. Their laboratory has trained volunteers – memory donors – to imagine certain scripted and approved sequences of thought."

"And can you – can they – really do this?" Tru stared in disbelief.

"It's simple in concept," Gooding said, "but not easy to engineer. The CIA tried to develop this sort of capability years ago, but gave up."

"Not gave up, as I recall," said Morgan. "They were shut down by Congress when word leaked out about what they were trying to do."

DeLuca had been listening with growing agitation. "This whole thing is awfully dangerous," he said. "How do you know that the North Koreans won't program their people, and their military too, to 'remember' how much they hate America and Japan, how urgently they need to use those nukes right now, before larger nations can confiscate them? Senator, this isn't playing with fire, it's playing with nuclear catastrophe. Ms. Taylor, why did you do along with this insane scheme?"

Athena touched DeLuca's sleeve. "Patience, detective. There's more."

Chapter 56

The senator smiled at the group with serene benignity. "Yes, detective," he said, "that's a good point. But we anticipated that possibility and implemented effective countermeasures. Deep inside the programming of this People's Mem technology we gave them is an override for any memories the Koreans might load into it. We've pre-loaded our own memories, using loyal Korean-Americans borrowed from our armed services. The mems feature high levels of verisimilitude and cultural sensitivity."

"I'm sure glad you're sensitive about something!" Morgan blurted. "You're going to get the North Koreans to broadcast these fake mems to their own people. They think they'll be propagandizing them the way their leaders want, but we'll be propagandizing them, instead, the way your 'Intergovernmental Memorial Commission' wants."

"Exactly," Gooding said. "That's the idea. Render them harmless. They will soon remember how well protected they are by their nukes, how much good will they have toward their neighbors, and most of all toward America. So much good will that they would never use those nukes against us, nor against anyone else, either, except in the direst self-defense. That's a lesson I'm sure they won't forget. Won't be able to forget, I mean."

"That means you're lying to them. Who's next, Russia? China?"

Gooding smiled again, picked up his fork. "No, indeed," he said, and took a bite of crabcake. "North Korea is our proof of concept. No foreign adventures beyond that." He took a tiny bite of baby lettuces.

Morgan thought "proof of concept"? Then what would –? He gaped with sudden recognition. "You're going to 'People's Mem' American citizens! That's what you're really up to!"

"Yes," said Gooding, no longer smiling. "There's a great deal of unrest in America, too, as we see on the wallscreens every day, rising threats from our own people, protests against our various wars. Home-grown terrorists are becoming of more concern than the foreign ones, and not just Islamists anymore. Not to mention those water riots in the Southwest, which can only grow worse as our continent continues to dry out.

"All this is interfering with our government's ability to rule the country effectively and efficiently, not to mention finding enough money to pay for the rapidly escalating costs of intelligence, counter-terrorism, police, and all our wars. What we have is an inefficient use of resources that could be deployed in more positive ways. Similar to the situation in North Korea, actually, calling for a similar response, a similar firmness on the part of government. We're using North Korea as our guinea pig, because there's so much similarity to where we're headed here in this country. In addition to far better command and control, a People's Mem applied to Americans will save us enormous amounts of money. I've seen estimates of the first FY cost reductions alone of..."

"Enough!" Tru said. "That's enough, senator. I'll expose what you're doing. A quarter of the adult population of this country will be watching my next weekly show five days from now."

The senator didn't raise his eyes from his plate. "They'll think you're a nut," he said quietly, "if you tell them that. If your show actually airs."

"Not if I People's Mem them before you do, from my own lab. A harmless mem that will demonstrate what this technology can do, a memory I'll predict on my show, and then the next day when they all remember, they'll remember it wasn't their memory at all, but something I predicted, made happen. Perhaps a new song that they'll remember without ever having heard it."

The senator looked thoughtful, pushed back his plate. "Good crabcakes," he said, and turned to Tru. "There are only two points I need to make concerning what you've just said. First, regarding your 'quarter of the adult population.' My, ah, associates, those who know considerably more about high-tech than I do, know how to manipulate those realtime ViewerTron numbers. Perhaps they've been doing that already, to artificially boost your numbers, to promote our cover-up of Stirner's secret work? In any case, they know how to reduce your ratings considerably, and undetectably, and very quickly.

"And second, Ms. Vallon, TruVal no longer has advanced memcasting capability. The explosion at the TruPlex took care of that. Ms. Taylor here was able, owing to her position, to bring in small quantities of a high explosive over the space of several weeks. Then, a 'maintenance contractor' was requested by her office to perform a few jobs on the B-1 level. The explosion occurred that night."

Tru was red-faced and furious. "Athena, what the hell are you doing? I trusted you!"

Athena put on a look of defiance. "I respect you, Tru, and I owe you everything. But I love my country; that's trumps. We're ready to go operational now, here in America. We're just waiting to make sure the Korean experiment was a success."

"And did you cause that explosion on the B-1 level to cover up what you're doing, and to get rid of Madelyn? I'll bet she figured out this ghastly plot you're involved in."

"I thought Madelyn was getting suspicious," Athena said. "I'd heard rumors that she was an undercover plant of the SoCalls. And yes, we did stage that explosion to destroy a few rooms of memplant equipment we didn't want discovered after the equipment had served its purpose. Unfortunately, there was a slight screwup and the explosion occurred while there were people nearby, not at three in the morning as I had ordered. But we didn't kill Madelyn, at least I didn't order her to be killed. I'm pretty sure her death was an accident, because she was standing too close to that rear wall. Trying to peek in and see what our memlab was up to, I think, using the party as a diversion. In any case, her death saved us from a moral dilemma."

"What moral dilemma?"

"The morality of murder, Tru. 'It is better that one man should die for the people,' as the Bible says, 'than all perish'; or one woman, in this case. But we didn't have to kill Madelyn. No one has to die. In fact, many will be saved with this peaceful application of science and technology."

"But Terra..."

"I'm very sure that Terra Lewis was killed on orders of the North Koreans, as you suspected, even though they've never admitted it to us. I know the senator and his friends had nothing to do with it. In fact, they felt that Terra's murder was a blunder, because it would arouse interest. Too many questions would be asked. And that's exactly what happened, wasn't it? And it got worse because the killer wasn't told to mop up the blood. That was another of Jeong's mistakes. His security people had no idea that Terra had ever been DNA'd, since she was 'just' a commercial photog." Athena smiled at Morgan. "You and detective DeLuca were hot on our trail, and all because Jeong panicked. We found out what Jeong had done almost immediately after Terra was killed – our webcloud-based systems picked it up – but of course by that time it was too late to stop it.

"But that's over. Can't you see it, Tru? Dr. Morgan? Love. Harmony forever. An end to civil discontent, to riots. Peace in our time." She had a faraway look in her eyes. The eyes of a true believer, Morgan thought.

"Nice speech," said Gooding, with a hint of mockery.

"Senator," said Morgan, "You're investigating the SoCalls because they're against any kind of memory transplanting, aren't you? You'd like to shut them down."

Senator Gooding frowned. "The SoCalls, yes, they've tried to rouse the public against the sort of thing we're doing. But their protests are more of a nuisance than a threat. What really alarmed us was that we knew they had a spy in TruVal, Inc., and for a very long time we didn't know who it was. They'd found out part of what we're doing. Not much, thank God, and not very accurate! But they had got wind of our code name, 'Odin.' If they had connected that name with the Commission's name, they could have traced our financial dealings. Yes, they and their spy knew enough to be dangerous."

"Madelyn Lopez," said Morgan.

"That's right, doctor. We discovered her identity shortly before Ms. Vallon's TV special. In fact," he chuckled, "we had ordered our operative at TruVal to – quietly – 'delete' her, as we say. But in the event, there was an explosion and she was taken out by less unnatural means. An accident, as Ms. Taylor has said."

DeLuca had perked up on the word "operative." "Your operative!" he blurted. "You mean Athena Taylor!"

Athena looked down at her plate. Gooding laughed and said "Oh no, detective. Ms. Taylor, here, is more of a fellow traveler, 'enlisted as a volunteer' as the old hymn goes. Our real operative at the TruPlex is someone else entirely." He rose from the table and headed out of the restaurant. "I'll remember those crabcakes," he said. He walked out onto Pennsylvania Avenue and got into a waiting cab.

"Now," said Athena, "I guess there's no point in my meeting with those House staffers tomorrow. I'll go back to TruVal and clean out my desk. Oh, and Senator Gooding has an open tab here," she added. "You're welcome to stay and be his dinner guests."

Chapter 57

Robert Morgan and Truda Vallon huddled together on the flight back to San Francisco. DeLuca again made productive use of his time by sleeping.

"What do we do now?" Morgan asked Tru, not really expecting an answer.

"I guess I'll go back to having a weekly TV show," said Tru. "Won't have the same excitement, now, knowing that my ratings seem to have been seriously inflated by Gooding and his friends, and are about to be deflated to about the level of late-night infomercials for Japanese steak knives."

"You'd be famous in any case," Morgan said. "You have enormous talent."

"Maybe. But I think I'll retire and turn the whole thing over to Ed Clarty; he's the rising star now. I have plenty of money, enough to last us our next eight lives, at least."

"Us?"

"I'm getting used to you, Morgan. I don't want you to have to go back to that dreary memlab. Besides, living on a cable car line might be fun."

"If you want to be lulled to sleep by the click-clack of the cable." he said, "you have to get to sleep by one a.m. That's when the line shuts down at night."

"I could do that."

There was a long pause as each realized what they were getting into. For Tru, it was especially worrisome. Her agitated thoughts were interrupted by Morgan.

"Have we wrapped it up?" Morgan asked.

"What?"

"What happened, what didn't happen, who did it, why they did it. Motivation and all that. Epiphany. Arc."

"Pretty much, I guess, but not very happily."

"Except for Clarty."

"Yeah," she sighed, "except for Clarty."

"Well, we still don't know about Madelyn. Was she murdered, or was she collateral damage from the blast on the B-1 level, as the senator and Athena told us last night?"

"Do we have to know?"

"It's not idle curiosity, Tru, or a need to tidy things up in a neat bundle. If she was killed intentionally, a murderer is still out there. Who knows where he will strike next?"

"Or she."

"Yes, or she."

"And that 'real operative' within TruVal, Inc., that the senator mentioned," Tru said.

"I think he was just keeping us off balance. Athena did all that bad stuff, didn't she? There was no need for anyone else."

"Perhaps."

Tru turned away, regarded the passing clouds underneath them. That "perhaps" had caught in Morgan's mind, stuck there like a hangnail. He poked DeLuca gently in the ribs. Receiving no response, he poked harder.

DeLuca opened his eyes. "Are we there yet?" he asked.

"We're over Utah," said Morgan.

"Then why did you wake me up? I don't need a drink, I don't want any more peanuts, the oxygen masks haven't descended, and the plane doesn't seem to be crashing. I don't even *like* Utah. So please, I'm going back to sleep now."

"Something's bothering me, Dennis."

(Silence. Closed eyes.)

"Dennis, I need your detective's mind on this."

"Oh well." Deluca looked up, stretched, yawned, and scratched his head with both sets of fingernails. "I guess there's no stopping you."

"Sorry."

"Tell me what's on your mind." DeLuca closed his eyes again, but wasn't drifting off.

Morgan cleared his throat and began. "How do you suppose Jeong was able to trace Terra Lewis to TruVal, and know exactly when she would be on a particular rooftop? If Terra was trying to shake him and Gooding down, she certainly wouldn't introduce herself by saying 'Hi guys, I'm Terra Lewis from San Francisco!'"

DeLuca frowned. "Well," he said, "Terra was a well-known photog, and had business on Boat Quay. With those two factors, and having seen her face, it wouldn't have been tough for either Gooding or Jeong to ID her and trace her back to TruVal."

"OK, that answers part of my question," said Morgan, "and I'm sure you're right. But think about the rooftop. Say that Jeong called an associate in the U.S., paid him to arrange Terra's death. This person would have contacts among hit men. He picked Charlie Barnes, probably because Barnes was local. He told Barnes when and where to go for the hit. But how did Jeong, or this associate, know this where and when?"

"Athena Taylor had easy access to photog assignments," said DeLuca. "Everybody at TruVal did. They apparently weren't considered confidential."

"OK," said Morgan, "But Athena was Gooding's tool, and Gooding was opposed to the hit. According to him, he didn't even know about it until after it was done. And I believe him."

"I believe him, too," DeLuca agreed. "Not least because of that screwup about Lewis's blood. Athena would have known that Terra could be DNA'd. But then, if Athena didn't tell Jeong's associate where Terra could be conveniently snuffed, who did?"

"There must have been another spy inside TruVal," said Morgan, "not Athena. A mole. That operative that Gooding mentioned, perhaps. He – or she – must not be working for Gooding, then, but directly for Jeong. Gooding doesn't seem to realize that." He hesitated, then said "Dennis, I'm worried by what Gooding doesn't know. I think he's lost control of the situation."

The two sat in silence. The softly clouded land beneath them became, without thought or remark, Nevada.

"So who's the mole?" DeLuca finally asked. "You're the guy with the inside scoop there, office and all, and now a fancy title."

"B'soom," said Morgan, "beats the shit out of me. There are hundreds of TruPlex employees. Any one of them could have been turned." He mentally ran through the roster of people he knew at the TruPlex, realized there were many others he didn't know, had probably never even seen.

"But hold that thought a minute," DeLuca said, "because it brings up a larger question. Isn't it too damn coincidental that the exact person who threatened to shake down the evildoers in their quest for Super MemCast Plus technology, Terra Lewis that is, would be working for the company where that technology was, at that very moment, secretly being developed?

"Yeah. That never occurred to me," Morgan replied.

"Then there's only one plausible answer," DeLuca continued. "Lewis arranged for that photog assignment in Singapore as a cover. Oh, the assignment was probably real enough, but she sold TruVal and the Belgian club on the idea and scheduled it for a date when she knew that a person involved in the secret research would be there to meet the other major player.

"Gooding. And Jeong!"

"Exactly." DeLuca continued. "She didn't stumble onto those two. She must have gone there specifically to catch them together. She had blackmail on her mind from the start! She had sniffed out, perhaps only a hint, that something odd and secretive was happening in the TruPlex, with Stirner and his new team. She was around the building a lot, had the balls, so to speak, and the inquisitive mind of a photojournalist. She followed up, found things out. Instead of reporting her suspicions to Tru or Athena, she saw an opportunity for herself."

"She probably assumed that both Tru and Athena were in on it."

"OK," DeLuca agreed, "that may be right. That's another reason she wouldn't go to them."

"So when Jeong found out that Terra was part of the TruVal organization, he contacted his mole who was already there."

"And this mole could easily plan a time and place for Terra to be killed most conveniently and with the least risk. But the mole apparently didn't know about the Alex arrangement, didn't know there would be inconvenient witnesses, including Truda Vallon herself. But Taylor knew all about those arrangements. She and Tru planned the entire Alex thing themselves, in secret."

"Well then," Morgan said, "given that, Jeong's mole couldn't have been Athena Taylor. We still don't know who it was. It could be anyone at TruVal. No special clearances or access were needed. The mole could be a manager, an admin, a security guard, or even one of the cleaning crew. Someone who could be turned, subverted."

"Anyone can be turned," said DeLuca.

"Even you?"

"Right circumstances, yeah. But the right circumstances never seem to come my way," he sighed.

They arrived at SFO at ten in the morning, stumbling off the aircraft stiff and groggy, all but DeLuca, who'd had a refreshing sleep from Virginia to Utah, soothed by the engines' white noise and calmed by the plane's vibrations. They found the baggage claim, satisfied several officiously sniffing dogs, retrieved their luggage.

"I'm off," DeLuca told Tru and Morgan, "to Sausalito. To see if I have a job any more. If not – and it's probably gone – well, then, I'll settle back on my leaky houseboat for a while and make a few calls, try to pick up the pieces of my life."

"Yuba City?"

"Lord, I hope not! But I have buddies in Alturas, up in the mountains. They say the town is looking for a new chief. That's a nice, quiet, scenic place, very rural. A good place to hide out from the shit-storm you folks are headed back to. And don't forget: today is Friday the 13th. Watch your back!"

Morgan held out his hand. DeLuca grasped it, smiled broadly. "I never had a real brother," said DeLuca. "But I guess I've got one now, 'Arty'! I just had to save your bumbling civilian ass from making such a mess at sleuthing."

"I'm glad you did, Dennis," said Morgan. "I needed saving. And I never had a real brother either – until you." Morgan hugged DeLuca, and the two backed off with a touch of embarrassment. "Good luck in Alturas or wherever," he said, waving good-bye.

"Wherever, it'll be a better place than where you're going to, O victim of our dedicated public servants!" said DeLuca, waving back. He picked up his bags and walked away. Morgan looked after him until he was out of sight.

Chapter 58

Morgan and Tru took a cab straight to the TruPlex. But at the entrance they were met by armed guards, strangers. TruVal, Inc.'s own guard force was nowhere to be seen. A crowd had gathered beside the entrance, shouting and asking questions. Most of the crowd seemed to be reporters. A few SoCall protestors stood across the street. They looked confused, uncertain what to do now, what to protest against.

"What the hell is happening?" Morgan asked.

"I don't know, but I don't think it's due to the SoCalls," said Tru. "They look as mystified as everyone else."

They approached the entrance. Tru didn't attract any special notice, since most TruVal, Inc., people wore exactly the same outfit and makeup. They struggled through the crowd, finally reached the entrance. A blank-faced guard was saying, over and over, "No admittance today, no admittance today. The owner has sold this building. Go home. No admittance, no admittance."

"Tru," said Morgan, "don't you own the building?"

"No, it's a real estate investment trust, a bunch of investors. I just lease it. Very few businesses in the city own their own buildings; they don't want to tie up capital."

"Are you saying that Senator Gooding's friends could own this building through a shell corporation and you'd never know?"

"Pretty much, Robert. They could, and it seems they do."

A distraught Athena Taylor emerged from the building carrying a cardboard box. Quite a change from the armor-plated goddess of Morgan's fantasies. Athena saw Tru in the crowd, walked over to her. "My God, Tru, I never intended this to happen!" she said. "I had no idea Gooding would go so far as to shut down TruVal!"

"Making sure, perhaps," said Morgan.

"Sounds like something that Korean would do."

"Jeong?"

"Yeah."

"Well, maybe..."

"Then what do we do now?"

"I don't know!" Athena said in what was almost a shriek. "I've called the senator four times and he hasn't returned any of them!"

"No," said Morgan dryly, "I guess he wouldn't. Chicks don't seem to be his thing. Well, Athena, is it as wonderful as you thought it would be when you signed on to this red-blooded patriotic initiative? Did the earth move for you?"

She stared at him. "Don't rub it in, doctor. I'm a victim here, too. I've been lied to, misled, abused!"

"I think rubbing it in right now is really wonderful," Morgan answered, "and I'm not through rubbing yet."

"Oh!" Athena uttered, and turned away. She walked down Montgomery Street alone, tossed her cardboard carton into a trash bin halfway down the block.

At that moment, Renee appeared at the main entrance. Tru and Morgan saw her at the same time, ran to her.

"Renee! Thank God!" Tru said, "What's going on here? Did that real estate investment trust really close the building down?"

"Gee, they did!" beamed Renee. "I guess those darn owners just wanted to use the building for some other purpose."

"But we have a lease!"

"Think you can find a copy? I doubt it. Not very quickly, anyway. I went through our servers and gosh, those records just seem to be missing. And I have the feeling that your attorney, Mr. Herschenswinger, won't be able to find his copies, either, that is, if anyone can find Mr. Herschenswinger. And even if you do get hold of the lease, I think there might be a boilerplate clause in Article XVII that lets the tenant pay a penalty and just walk away."

"But the business," insisted Tru, "TruVal, Inc. We're still in business. Even though we've lost our physical space, we still have our intellectual property, the TV show..."

"Gone," said Renee. "Do you know who your majority owners are, right now? I didn't think so. Well, they met last night – I should say *we* met last night – I called the meeting. We voted to liquidate the corporation and disburse its assets, pay off and cancel all outstanding contracts. That's after we called the network and got out from under the agreement for your show. Oh, there was pissing and moaning from their side but ultimately there was nothing they could do but let us cancel. I think they've already found a replacement for your time slot.

"And, golly so help me there wasn't much money left after the corporation's indebtedness was paid off, and all those contract penalties, and I'm sure so don't ask that you weren't aware of much of TruVal's debt load – it was sure a lot! – but you'll still walk away with a few million dollars, not that that buys much anymore. Just look for a check in the mail, *Tru*!" Renee turned and started back into the building.

"Wait a minute!" called Morgan.

Renee tilted her head toward him. "Yes?"

"Did you kill Madelyn?"

"Actually, I didn't. I was going to, because she was a SoCall spy and had found out too much. I don't have any of those 'moral dilemmas' that naïve bitch Athena used to talk about," she said, glancing down the street in the direction of Athena Taylor, whose tall form could now barely be discerned. "Other than what to call my boss to her face! As far as I know, Madelyn was clobbered by a stud – ha ha, that's a joke, isn't it? – when that explosion occurred. I might even have steered her over to that side of the room, just might. Golly, I'm sure not confessing anything here but perhaps I knew just when that explosion would occur. But no, I didn't actually kill her myself." She turned back toward the building and entered it with a light step and a toss of her hair. The new guard corps did everything but genuflect as she passed by.

Sounds of cheers and applause erupted from behind Tru and Morgan. They turned and saw an ebullient Ed Clarty wading through the crowd toward them, being adored by frantic fans and giving off handshakes, kisses, and autographs.

"What happened, Tru?" he asked. "I heard the news this morning, couldn't believe it."

Tru explained what seemed to be the situation. "I'm afraid," she concluded, "that my show is gone, and so we won't be able to feature your singing anymore. But I'm sure you'll have other opportunities."

"Well, yes," he said. "In fact, last night I got a call from the network. A weekly slot had unexpectedly opened up, and they wanted me to fill it! Me! My own show! The Ed Clarty Show!" He looked upward, perhaps to contemplate his own glory, or to thank the appropriate god for his sudden good fortune.

"I'm sure you'll remember this moment," said Morgan drily. Clarty didn't get the connection, looked at him with a simple homely smile.

A few reporters had noticed their byplay and were starting toward them. "Let's get out of here!" said Morgan.

"They're probably after Clarty now, not us," said Tru.

"Then I guess it's time for our exit."

He and Tru walked rapidly out of range, through the band of SoCalls, found a coffee shop and sat down. Tru held her head in her hands.

Morgan was feeling overwhelmed. "Well," he said, "we're screwed. And our country is screwed, too."

"No one would believe us," Tru said. "No point going to the press or buying spots on television."

"As Gooding said, everyone will think we're a couple of nuts. And now, since you've been shut down, we've got a highly suspect motive: we're a couple of sore losers."

"But a couple, anyway," said Tru. "I need you with me, Morgan. At least right now, while my head is spinning and I can't think straight."

"I'm here," said Morgan, "because I want to be here."

Tru considered her options. There was only one, and it was a long shot, and painful as well. "Robert," she said, "there is something we could do."

"What's that?"

"Go to the SoCalls. Tell them everything. They hate any kind of mind control. They tend to believe it's happening even when it isn't. They'd listen."

"And sooner or later Gooding will surely use his People's Mem to suppress them," Morgan said, "another reason why they might pay attention to us before it's too late. But all that rant of Baker's against TruVal, against MemCast, against you – would he believe you've suddenly switched sides?"

"Not switched sides, found out the truth. What Gooding is up to is much more damaging than MemCasting, or memplants. That's all personal morality, not the future of the entire country."

"And the future of the world. This broadcasting of fake mems into millions of people's heads won't stop with North Korea and America, for sure. Every government in the world will want that capability and, one way or another, they'll get it. And use it."

Tru snapped her fingers. "The churches! They'd be threatened, too. Maybe we could appeal to the churches."

"I'm sure Gooding will make nice with them, won't try to have the public 'remember' that they're atheists or anything like that. He'd have no reason to interfere with the religious practices of law-abiding churches."

"But a few radical sects could threaten what he's doing," she said, hopefully.

"The public could 'remember' that these are fringe groups, wackos, child-molesters, gun-toting Kool Aid nuts who should be raided by men with guns, shot down or shut down or locked up without mercy."

Tru sighed. "Then what's left? I suppose we could give up and settle back to a comfortable life and spend my money until it runs out. How about that? Or run the O'Farrell Street memlab as a mom and pop team? I take their money and you plant the probes?"

"I guess those are our choices. But I don't want to give up yet. I'm not ready to settle back and maunder on and on about the good old days."

"Are we back to talking about joining up with the SoCalls?"

"Wouldn't get us anywhere. They'd put you on display as a penitent convert, a prize catch if they believed you at all. That is, until Gooding shuts them down."

"I could appeal to Buck Baker personally."

"What would you say to him?"

"I'd say 'Hello, father.'"

"Like his followers do?"

Tru hesitated a moment, swallowed. "No, Robert, 'father' as in 'my father.' He's my father."

Chapter 59

"*What?*"

"I ran away from home when I was fifteen because things got really bad there after my mom died. I changed my name and never contacted him again. That was before he became famous, of course, or infamous. He'd always been threatening to move to Idaho, 'where they'll appreciate me' he used to say. After I left, he finally did. I have two older brothers. After I left home I never got in touch with them, either. Last time I had them checked out, one was working back in Spokane, and the other was in Des Moines on unemployment."

"Where does he think his daughter...?"

"Where I am? He doesn't know. I have no idea if he even wonders about me anymore."

"OK, well, it's getting dark. Why don't we spend the night at my place, and then first thing in the morning find the SoCalls and ask them where Buck Baker is. The worst they could do is turn us away." Morgan held his breath. His history of successful propositions was largely a matter of late-night fantasy.

Tru looked worried, lips tight together.

"OK," she said, "my Telegraph Hill flat belongs to the company, so I don't think I'd be welcome there anymore." She said nothing else on the cable car ride up Russian Hill and halfway down the other side.

***

"A little dark, isn't it?" Tru walked around Morgan's living room, peeking into corners.

"Row house, the only windows are front and back. Yes, it's a little..."

"Dark curtains, dark furniture, dark hallway all the way back. Robert, you need to lighten up this place a little."

He laughed. "And lighten myself up, too. Isn't that what you're thinking?"

She stared at him. "You know, Robert, I've never heard you laugh before."

"Ah, sure I laugh, I guess. Once in a while. When there's..."

"Well there is, now. Something to laugh for, not laugh at or laugh about. And your laugh is very nice!"

"'Nice,'" he said. "'Nice' isn't a very..."

"Yes, it is. In all this grim world, if we can't get to 'joyful' or 'exuberant' anymore, then 'nice' will do. Will have to do." She was silent for a moment, then brightened. "What's for dinner?"

Tru and Morgan scrounged the kitchen shelves and the refrigerator. Morgan didn't have much on hand, and they settled for tomato soup and toast.

After dinner, they went back to the living room, settled down on the sofa. Gathering up a few shards of courage, Morgan approached her, held out his arms.

"Wait, Robert," she said. "First, let's go back through that mem, Alex's mem, that you bought."

Morgan was miffed at being put off, and didn't see the reason. "I could do that, Tru. It was – interesting, ah, exciting even, having your mem combined with Alex's, for me to be in your head. But you don't have your own mem of it anymore; you memplanted it to me. What are you suggesting?"

"I do have the mem, Robert. I didn't tell you, but I used one of Stirner's enhancements, one of the few, as it turned out, that he told me about to keep me happy and in the dark. Remember I mentioned that he developed a way to make memplants non-destructive? The donor still has the mem."

"And remembers donating it?"

"Yes."

"You..."

"You got my mem and I got yours at the same time, back there in the lab when we were both under sedation. I remember what you remember about Alex having sex with me, and I remember having sex with him, too. But it wasn't only Alex. You were there, Robert. Your mind had been working on that mem, consciously or not. When I got your mem I felt – you in me. And I liked it. Not the sensation, although that was part of it, but that it was you."

"What do..."

"Lie back, Robert. Hold my hand and go through the mem, slowly, in real time, in more detail than you ever have before. Talk me through it and I'll follow along. And try to ignore Alex. I've ignored him the last few times I've remembered what we did together."

"Well," said Morgan hesitantly, "I suppose..."

"There's a reason, Robert. You'll see. Are you ready?"

"OK."

BEGIN MEM

A soft knock at the door. Morgan reaches out a hand, unlocks, opens. Tru is nervous, wonders about this man she's never met. She glances out the window. The site, at least, is perfect. Morgan wonders why she's hesitant; it's like she's checking out the place. Not like the whores he's called in before. With them, it was wham bang, pay up. No, that was Alex. She glances up, gives him an uneasy smile. Through Alex's face, Morgan smiles back. No, my own face. Alex isn't needed any more; we're through with Alex now. Tru remembers "Strangers." I need him to play it. She hands him the songchip, asks him to put it in his player. Morgan takes the chip from her hand. A warm hand, he notices. Soft.

There's the couch, where Athena said it would be. God what a filthy apt. Why did I agree to this? It sounded so cool, so daring, so in-your-face. But it's too late to back out now. OK, I'm putting this chip in the player. Whatever she wants to hear, dance to the music, rock, boogie, whatever. Hope it's slow. I'm not in the shape I used to be when I was in my twenties. I think I should touch him now. I'm supposed to lead him to the couch; he won't know to do that. I guess I should touch her now. Looks like she wants us to use the couch.

I should take off enough clothes to do this. Why isn't she taking off all her clothes? I need to face the window? That's not a great idea, since I'm not very limber any more. Well, whatever – she's paying.

OK, here we go. He's doing something down there. I need to help him. No, not there, *there*. Hope he likes it that way, or this will be the world's shortest sexmem. What's that music?

Morgan is suddenly overwhelmed by the sensation he should have anticipated, but hadn't: As Tru, Morgan is being fucked by a man. A synthesis of two minds and two bodies.

Morgan reaches for a place he thinks he should be touching. Touching softly, and then more eagerly. They like it that way, he's always heard in the podcasts. Except Helen, that is, who never liked it any way. He reaches...

INTERRUPT MEM

Morgan came out of the mem with a jolt. "You're..."

"Male," she said, "at least anatomically."

"But..." Morgan was stuck in single-syllable mode.

He used to look at me that way, she thought sadly – what way? – that way, the way I liked him to, showing he wanted me. And now he never will again. But he had to know. She couldn't just walk away. Not now.

"My birth name is Linn Baker," Tru finally said. "Dad gave me his middle name as my first name. It was my grandfather's family name. I legally changed it, quietly, a few years ago, to Truda Vallon. Hersch, and a few dollars placed into the right hands, made sure no one could trace it. But even Hersch didn't know I was born a male."

"Why...?"

"A part in a musical, a touring company out of New York. I knew I could do it. My lucky break, once in a lifetime whether it really was or not and all that. But the only role they were auditioning for was female. So I did it. I dressed as a woman. I'm slim and shorter than average, of course, like my father. Luckily the role called for me to be completely dressed, and I was able to – pull it off," she smiled, "and don't you dare get any nasty ideas about that!"

Her joke broke the ice. Morgan relaxed slightly. Now his scientific curiosity took over.

"Why didn't you have...?"

"An operation? I certainly thought about it, even planned it once: Vacationing in country A, spokesperson says, highly guarded, all the time really in country B, at a hospital. But I knew that someone, some day, would tell. The 'bloids would pay millions, millions. In hard currency, too, not in dollars. My career would be in ruins. But then, over the years, I got comfortable with myself, with who I was. I could have sex of a kind, as long as I pretended to be one of those 'Trudites' who pretend to be me. It added a new level of *frisson* for me, too, that Terra was photo'ing me: Real sex for an unreal person."

"You're not unreal, Tru. You're very real. To me. Ah, do you think of yourself as a – a woman, now?"

"Twixt and tween, I suppose. I can get into frames of mind where I'm one or the other, but mostly I'm – I'm me. I'm what I am. I'm comfortable with that now. I'm comfortable enough to – want you, if you want me too."

Morgan twitched involuntarily.

Tru sighed. "Well, it's late. I'm going to bed. Your sofa? We'll tackle Baker tomorrow."

***

The next morning they took the cable car to Union Square, walked a few blocks here and there randomly until they heard distant shouting. "Bet that's them!" she said.

It was. A young man was standing on an overturned crate near an intersection, trying to rouse a few distracted followers by shouting into his bull horn. More people were trickling in from different directions. There was no sign of Baker.

Morgan approached an older woman who was eating a bagel. "Miss," he said, "do you know if Mr. Baker will be here later?"

She scowled at him with hostile suspicion. "Father Buck? Who wants to know? You a newsblogger?"

He had a sudden inspiration. "Yes," he said, "yes I am. And I'd like to ask Father Buck a few questions. For my blog. Audios two hundred thousand distinct user IDs."

The woman still looked suspicious. "Not enough hair for a blogger," she said inanely. "And they're pushy, not damn polite like you are. I don't believe you."

Tru, seeing that Morgan was making no headway, stepped in front of him.

"You're right, miss. We're not really newsbloggers. What we really want is to join your group. Volunteer our services.

Knock on doors, send out spamfliers, anything else we can do for the Cause."

"Why pick on me?" she whined.

"Well, ma'am, because you looked like you'd know all about the organization. You'd be one of the leaders, wouldn't you?"

She blushed. "Naw, a believer, no one special. You'll have to wait and talk with Father Buck himself. I'm afraid I can't help you much. Mostly I just march and chant. He should be here..." She consulted her wristcom, "about now!" She smiled at Tru, ignored Morgan. "Welcome to the group! We can always use more strong minds and willing hands. Lose that Truda Vallon outfit, though. You're no Truda Vallon and the attire wouldn't fit in with the group. He'll be here about now," she repeated.

And about then, Morgan saw the charismatic figure of William Linn "Buck" Baker making his way through his adoring followers toward the man on the overturned crate. As he came closer, Morgan saw that he was with a middle-aged, chubby, frumpy woman in an ill-fitting bright red dress.

Tru saw his interest "Is that anybody?" she asked him.

Morgan slumped inside his clothes. "That's Helen," he said. "I used to be married to her."

He remembered those red outfits – suits, dresses, casuals – that she wore when it suited a particular mood. She was wearing one when she confronted him and declared her independence, her intention to divorce him. "The red dress of grievance" he'd called it, but never to her face.

Helen hadn't noticed Morgan yet. Baker stepped up on the crate, took the bull horn from the young man. "Thank you, Ken. Are you ready?" he shouted to the crowd. The group, now considerably larger than it had been, roared back "We're ready!"

"Are you ready for some kick-ass?" he called. "Let's kick some butt!" came the response.

"Well," he lowered his voice but was still clearly audible. "Guess what? TruVal, Inc. is no more! We did it!" The crowd roared again. Baker moved his body dramatically, reminding Morgan of Tru's televised dance moves. "No more mem-snatching! No more MemCasting! No more – we can hope and pray and struggle for – no more memlabs!"

The crowd chanted fervently:

"Mental Health is a Fraud!"

"Empathy is Complicity!"

"Your Mind is Your Fortress!"

"This afternoon," Baker continued after exactly the right rhetorical interval, "this afternoon we're going to march right over there to O'Farrell Street and make sure that memlab will never open up again! That's one! There'll be more!"

More cheers.

"But now, a word from my associate Ken Larson who has an important message for you." Baker handed the bull horn back to the younger man, who quickly organized the collection baskets.

Morgan caught Baker's attention, but unfortunately attracted Helen's as well. Helen whispered to Baker, and they moved through the crowd toward Morgan and Tru like herring through a school of shad.

"Dr. Morgan!" Baker boomed, "Helen and I have to meet you, she told me."

"Yes, dear," said Helen to Baker, "you do. I'd like you to meet Robert Morgan, failed physicist, ex-assistant professor, ex-husband, and – and this seems to be his friend, the costumed corpse. Is that right, Bob?"

Morgan flushed red, then said "Ah, Tru, I'd like you to meet Helen Morgan."

"'Meany,' Bob, not 'Morgan,'" she said. "I took my maiden name back."

"Maiden," said Tru, "what a lovely image that word evokes. I really didn't place you as the maiden type."

Helen glared at her. Baker was staring at Tru. Helen noticed this unacceptable behavior. "Buck, dear, haven't you seen dozens of these – refugees from those old 'Ring' movies?"

"Not this one," said Buck. "I think this one is real."

Chapter 60

Tru studied him. "Good call. I'm Truda Vallon, and yes the TruVal operation has been closed down, seems like for good, although I wished you hadn't taken credit for that."

"*I* had a great deal to do with that, dear," purred Helen.

Morgan was very interested. "How? It's all over now, so you can tell me."

Helen turned to Baker, with one eye trained on Tru. "I've always had to be careful what I tell poor Bob here. He'd always get it wrong, put the worst possible face on it. Over and over I used to plead with him, my dearest Bob, you have deep-seated problems. Please, I kept telling him, get professional help, but..."

Helen suddenly realized she'd stepped over the line in seeming to advocate psychotherapy. Baker glared at her. She swallowed, took a literal step backwards. "That was his idea," she concluded lamely, "psychotherapy. I never wanted him to do that. Rots the mind, you know."

Ignoring her desperate back-pedaling, Baker turned to Tru. "Well, I wouldn't admit it in public, but you're right. I had nothing to do with your downfall, and I was as surprised as anyone else. Wish I had! But I didn't. Then why are you here?"

"Mr. Baker," Tru said, "I believe – I'll always believe that what we did at TruVal was harmless, even beneficial. Songs about sharing our innermost feelings, MemCasting, helping people connect with each other, even if it turned out to be sex most of the time. And yes, providing moral support to the memlabs. My – Dr. Morgan, here, owns one, in fact. The one on O'Farrell Street that you're about to shut down."

She took a breath. Helen had almost regained her composure. Tru had two minutes, Morgan estimated, before Helen's attack would begin again.

"But you've always been right, Mr. Baker," Tru said, "about the threat. I know it now. Our government is out to anesthetize our minds."

"Just call me 'Buck.'"

"There is a conspiracy – Buck," she said, "to control our minds by broadcasting memories of how much we love our government, how much we like to obey, broadcasting straight into our heads. I heard it from Senator Gooding's lips not three days ago. It's he and a few key groups in the administration who are behind it. And I'm ashamed to admit that most of the research that went into this horrid scheme was done in the TruPlex itself, using government funding I didn't know anything about, I swear!"

Baker said "Well, maybe those tinfoil-lined hats weren't such a..."

"Bad idea after all," said Tru, "although I'm not sure they'd help." She turned to Helen. "Robert told me you were at the TruPlex, visiting Madelyn. Was Madelyn one of your SoCalls spies? I heard that she was. Help me out on this."

Helen hadn't been expecting such an outright plea. "Well, yes," she said. "Well. Yes. Madelyn was working for me, for Buck here of course, feeding us information on what TruVal was up to, although we didn't know the full extent of it until now." She raised her voice. "And you killed her!"

Morgan intervened. "We had nothing to do with that, but it doesn't matter anymore because the result is the same. That explosion was intended to destroy evidence of what Gooding's group was up to, since they had already completed their R&D. Unfortunately, it killed Madelyn as well."

"'Unfortunately'? Helen sneered. "You don't know that. She could have been the target."

"They were intending to kill her, but..."

Baker intervened. "Wait a minute. We can rehash history later. The question now is what do we do? If Morgan and Truda are right, wrecking one memlab won't make a hill of..."

"Beans," Tru said. Baker stood still, mouth open. He looked at her more closely.

"Your favorite saying, wasn't it always? And I always used to interrupt you when you said it."

Baker looked stunned. Morgan knew what was coming, was relieved that Tru seemed to be handling it well. He saw Helen becoming agitated and knew exactly what that meant: something was happening that Helen didn't understand. Her finest rages had been over her failure to understand him. Occasionally he'd even goaded her into them so he could be the wounded, offended one. The victim. An awful sickness, a *folie à deux*, an agonizing pleasure. It would be very easy to slip back into that life, so easy....

"Are you in drag?" Baker blurted. Morgan's thoughts returned to the present. Helen laughed, not making the connection. "You look like my kid," he continued, "the one who ran off. But he was a boy. All Edith and me had were boys. Who are you?"

"I'm Linn Baker," said Tru. "My career is ruined now, so I don't care who knows. I have two brothers I haven't seen since the day Mom died. It's a long story how I – changed. Because of show business, mostly. But I'm here now because I hope I can help you stop this disaster that's coming. I guess you're not drunk all the time anymore, and I hope you don't beat up your – girlfriend here like you did Mom and me."

Helen glared at her. Baker cringed, then put on a defiant expression. Tru continued. "But there's no time to rehash, as you said, and tell each other how great the old times were, OK? Right now, how can we work together on this?"

Baker raised his arms as if to embrace his long-lost son, hesitated, lowered them. "OK," he said. "Tomorrow noon. I had a small rally planned for Union Square, but there's still time to make it a big rally, call the press, promise a big story. Will you stand up there with me in public? Testify and prove that you're Truda Vallon and that you were all wrong, all this mem-snatching and memplanting and empathy crap?"

"I can prove I'm Truda Vallon, and I'll stand with you," she said. "I'll apologize for hosting the government research and tell them what it is and how dangerous it is. But I won't apologize for sharing mems, linking minds. I believe in that. It's beautiful, even if it's sometimes painful. It helps us see who we are, and who others are."

Helen had been standing by, fuming. "I'll speak, too," she said.

Baker stared at her. "What about?"

"TruVal murdered my friend Madelyn, because she was about to expose their little racket."

"Honey," Baker said in a soothing voice, "that's a little too much content for tomorrow. We want the press to get a clear picture here, not muddy their waters."

Helen colored, began to breathe heavily and stand on tip-toe. Morgan knew the deadly warning signs of imminent Helenism; Baker seemed not to.

"And besides," he said, "I guess we don't know really what happened with Madelyn, and your speaking voice isn't exactly..."

"You are an asshole," Helen said to Baker firmly but quietly. "You are as much of a stupid Goddamned asshole as my dolt of an ex-husband here. He shows up with this – whatever that thing is, and you fall all over her – him. You know I've been telling you that you should put me up there with the bull horn, ever since you proposed to me. Now do it, or," she made a grand dramatic gesture with both arms, almost falling over because she was still on tip-toes, "or I'm through!"

"Aw, Helen honey."

"Aw, Buck honey," Helen mocked, doing a surprisingly good imitation of his voice, "Aw bullshit, honey." She turned and stalked off, shoved her way through the crowd and marched off down the street, waving a finger behind her.

Baker looked crushed, unsteady on his feet. Morgan tried to keep a straight face, but couldn't, and hid his smile behind his hand. Tru saw the situation and tried to save it. "Look, ah, father, I'll be there tomorrow. And don't worry; Helen will come back to you."

"Nice of you to say that, Tru. Do I call you 'Tru,' like they do on TV? But I think she's gone. I never saw that side of her before, never knew she was like that."

"Maybe you two should have shared a mem," Tru said.

"Right," added Morgan. "How about mems of her married life with me?"

Baker straightened and glared at both of them. "Now don't you start that, too! Just be at Union Square at two o'clock tomorrow! Glad to meet you, Dr. Morgan. Right now I've got to get up there and start speaking instead of that Ken Larson who's the dullest SOB to ever climb a crate. See you tomorrow – Tru." He looked at her with troubled eyes. "And I guess we've got more important things to do now than to hassle that memlab."

Morgan and Tru spent the rest of the day strolling downtown, window shopping, talking about their lives. After dinner in Chinatown they went back to Morgan's house on Washington Street.

The sun disappeared in the general direction of North Korea. Morgan and Tru undressed, looked at each other warily. Hesitantly at first, they approached, touched.

"Are you ready for this?" she asked.

"I don't know," said Morgan. "I guess I'll find out."

"I'd like to download a song for us," she said.

"One of yours?"

"I recorded a cover; it was on my TV special. It's an older song, but I made a few changes."

She said "Truval.TV" into her com. A soothing voice, in programmed overtones of regret, sighed "four oh four not found. Four oh four not found."

"They shut down my web site!" she said. "Damn! But there are mirror servers." She pressed a few virtual keys. The song started to play through Morgan's wallscreen.

I hear the music, close my eyes
feel the rhythm wrap around me
Take your passion and make it happen
Take hold of my heart
Memories come alive, you can dance right through your life
I hear the music, close my eyes
I am music now
I am rhythm now.

Half an hour later, Morgan had found out. "I guess we can love each other," he said.

Tru laughed, touched him. "That was a half-assed declaration," she said, "but I'll take it." He turned to her again.

Now I'm dancing for my life
I am music now
I am rhythm now.

Later, they were relaxing. Morgan considered having a drink, decided not to. Maybe he never really liked the stuff. No, that's not true, he had liked it. He'd liked his friend a lot. But that was before. He hadn't had enough booze to get really dizzy in – was it days, now?

He turned to Tru. "Do you think our minds are changing already? Maybe the Korean experiment worked and Senator Gooding's unleashing his memplants on us now? I wonder what it would feel like."

"To remember what you don't remember? We've both done that already."

"But I remembered it was someone else's mem, not mine. Whatever happened never really happened to me."

Tru considered. "Because you remembered going to the memlab and hooking your head up with Alex, and then with me. But if you never did that, if the memory simply came into your mind, you'd think it was a real mem, your own mem of events that really happened to you, thoughts you'd really had – wouldn't you?"

"I guess so. I hope we never have to find out."

"Maybe we'll find out without knowing we've found out."

Morgan frowned. "Do you suppose it's happening to us already? The ultimate 'see/saw' as 'think/thought'?"

"Gooding said he was going to wait until the North Koreans had tried it on their own people, make sure it worked OK, before he turned it loose on Americans," Tru said. "And maybe by now he knows that it worked OK. Jeong thinks that his People's Mem will make North Koreans love their government, trust them without question."

"But they'll really love America instead, never want to use their nuclear weapons on us."

"But do you think – Robert, if Gooding, Stirner and his team, I mean, could hack into that chip, making the Koreans love America, don't you think that Jeong's lab might be able to detect it? They're probably every bit as smart as Stirner's group."

"And delete the hack?" Morgan asked.

"Yes, or reprogram it. Repurpose it. Make it do something else."

"Do what?"

"Whatever they want it to do!" said Tru. "I'm scared."

"Oh well, you're going to expose the whole rotten conspiracy tomorrow. And do you know why Gooding and his crew were so secretive? Because if the President or the Congressional leadership found out what he was up to they'd close him down instantly, like they did that CIA project before. That means all we have to do is make a big noise tomorrow, tell the truth. Washington will hear us."

"They'll think we're nuts," Tru said. "Gooding was right about that."

"But they'll investigate. They do that instinctively. Government investigates whenever there's an allegation, whether or not they believe it, even though they're denying it up and down. To cover their butts, if for no other reason. And Gooding will be found out."

"I sure hope you're right," she said.

"Right. Let's get a few hours' sleep. We need to be fresh for tomorrow."

"In a while," she said. "I'm not finished with tonight yet!"

"I love you," they said to the other at the same time, clasping their thighs together and moving softly, then with more urgency.

I hear the music, close my eyes
feel the rhythm wrap around
Take your passion and make it happen
Take hold of my heart
I am music now
I am rhythm now
Memories come alive when I call
I am music
I am rhythm now
No more strangers.

Chapter 61

Morgan awoke as the sun was coming up, sunlight flooding the tops of the buildings on Washington Street, not yet touching the cable car tracks below.

He rummaged through his refrigerator. Two eggs, orange juice. He uncapped the juice, sniffed it. Not too far gone. He peeked into the bedroom. Tru was just waking. Morgan continued his quest for anything edible, opened and closed drawers. A packet of instant cream of wheat, half a box of pancake mix. He examined the instructions on the box, hoping it didn't require the milk he didn't have.

Tru walked into the kitchen, gave Morgan a hug. He kissed her joyfully.

"It's wonderful having you here, Tru. Short rations, though!" he pointed at the assembled food he'd arranged in straight lines on the counter top.

"They'll do fine," she said.

"Wonder what's happening in the world," he said. "There's a radio here." He looked around. Hadn't had that radio on in months. He couldn't locate it immediately. Only a few stations left, anyway, now that almost no private cars were on the roads. CNN/Fox would have headline news on his wallscreen in a few minutes.

"You know, Robert," said Tru, stretching, "I'm very happy here."

"Me, too," he said. "I feel good about things now. Even about those North Koreans. It's hard for me to believe how much we used to get worked up about all those nukes and missiles they have. They're really our friends. We almost forgot that."

"Yes," said Tru, "I remember. I remember now."